ALSO BY
EMMA SCOTT

LOST BOYS
The Girl in the Love Song
When You Come Back to Me
The Last Piece of His Heart

FULL TILT DUET
Full Tilt
All In

EMMA SCOTT

Bloom *books*

Published by Bloom Books, an imprint of Sourcebooks
P.O. Box 4410, Naperville, Illinois 60567-4410
(630) 961-3900
sourcebooks.com

Originally self-published in 2016 by Emma Scott.

Cataloging-in-Publication data is on file with the Library of Congress.

Printed and bound in the United States of America.
LSC 10 9 8 7 6 5 4 3 2 1

This book is about brothers as much as anything else. It is dedicated to my brother, Bob, who set me on this path—unwittingly—with one magical email and a suggestion. You set me on this journey telling love stories—my calling—and changed my life forever. With thanks and love, this one is for you.

AUTHOR'S NOTE

This book was not easy to write. It was not the next story I sought to tell. But it would not leave me, despite the pitfalls and difficulty. It scared the crap out of me, to be honest, but begged to be told. Because I believe love stories come in all shapes and forms. Some people meet, fall in love, tragedy strikes, and they persevere together—maybe fall apart—come back, and find peace in the love they had. But what about those who fall in love when the tragedy is already looming on the horizon, in plain sight? What is love worth to those who are at the end of their journey instead of the beginning? Love can begin at any time, at any stage of life. That is the beauty—and hope—of this human existence. I hope this love story does justice to that idea.

I firmly believe in the concept of happily ever after. For everyone. No matter how or who or *when* they fall in love. Because that love existed, they felt it, and that is worth everything.

Love always wins.

PLAYLIST

"Lightning Crashes" // Live
"Hurricane" // Halsey
"Chandelier" // Sia
"Yellow" // Coldplay
"My Heart Will Go On" // Celine Dion
"River" // Bishop Briggs
"Free Fallin'" // Tom Petty
"Chasing Cars" // Snow Patrol
"Spirits" // The Strumbellas
"Hallelujah" // Rufus Wainwright (lyrics by Leonard Cohen)

Part I

FULL TILT *(N)* *(POKER):*
playing emotionally instead of
rationally; making impassioned
rather than logical decisions

JONAH

FIFTEEN MONTHS AGO

WHITE LIGHT PIERCED MY EYES. I STRUGGLED TO KEEP THEM OPEN, then gave in and let them fall shut again. I listened to the machines instead, let their sound pull me out of unconsciousness. The beeping pulse was my heart. My new heart, pumping slowly in my chest. Yesterday, it belonged to a twenty-three-year-old basketball player who'd been in a car accident outside Henderson. Now it was mine. Grief and gratitude danced at the edges of my awareness.

Thank you. I'm sorry, and thank you…

God, my chest. It felt as if an anvil had crushed me, smashed my ribs. A great swelling agony lurked underneath my sternum, which had been cracked open like a cabinet, then stapled shut again. Somewhere within the deep, heavy ache was my new heart.

I groaned and the sound surged out of me, riding a current of pain.

"He's waking up. Are you waking up, honey?"

I forced my eyes open, and the light was merciless.

Maybe I'm dead.

The white of hospital sheets and stark fluorescents seared my eyes, then settled. Dark shapes took form. My parents hovered over me on my right. My mother's eyes were wet, and her hand reached to brush a lock of hair from my forehead. She adjusted the nasal cannula that was jammed up my nose, though it probably didn't need adjusting.

"You look wonderful, sweetheart," she told me in a tremulous voice.

I felt like I'd been run over by a freight train, and before that I'd been deathly sick for weeks. But she didn't mean I looked good. She meant I looked *alive*.

For her sake, I managed a smile.

"You did good, son," my father said. "Dr. Morrison said everything looks real good." He gave me a tight smile, then looked away, coughing into his fist to hide his emotion.

"Theo?" I croaked and winced at the deep bruise of pain in my chest. I breathed shallowly and looked for him on my left.

He was there, crouched in a chair, his forearms resting on his knees. Strong. Solid.

"Hey, bro," he said, and I heard the forced lightness in his deep voice. "Mom's pulling your leg. You look like shit."

"Theodore," she said. "He does not. He's beautiful."

I didn't have the energy to give my brother a joke. All I could manage was a smile. He smiled back, but it was tense and hard. I knew my brother better than anyone. I knew when something was eating at him. Anger burned in him like a pilot light, and now it was flaring hot.

Why...?

I cast my gaze around the room, and then I knew. "Audrey?"

The air tightened, and my mother jumped as if someone had poked her with a needle. Looks were exchanged all around me, like birds darting over my bed.

"It's late," my father said. "She's...gone home." He was a city councilman, and he'd turned on his politician's voice, the one he used when he needed to tell an unpleasant truth in a pleasant way.

My mother, a kindergarten teacher and adept at comfort, swooped in. "But you should rest now, honey. Sleep. You'll feel stronger after you've had more sleep." She kissed me on my forehead. "I love you, Jonah. You're going to be just fine."

My dad took my mom by the shoulders. "Let's let him rest, Beverly."

I rested. I fell in and out of fitful, pain-soaked sleep until a nurse tinkered with an IV in my arm, and then I slept deeply.

When I awoke, Theo was there. Audrey was not. My new heart began to thump a dull, heavy pang. All the adrenaline circuits were reconnected, or whichever hormone it was that kicked in when something you thought could last forever was over.

"Where is she?" I asked. "Tell me the truth."

Theo knew whom I meant. "She left for Paris yesterday morning."

"You talked to her? What did she say?"

He pulled his chair closer. "Some fucking sob story. How she had a plan for her life and this..." His gaze swept the room.

"This wasn't it," I said.

"She couldn't hack it." He tore his hand through his hair. "Fuck, I shouldn't have said anything."

"No," I said, shaking my head a little. "I'm glad you told me. I needed to hear it."

"I'm sorry, bro. Three years. Three years you gave her, and she just..."

"It's okay. It's better."

"Better? How the hell is it better?"

Already, my eyes felt heavy and wanted to close, to drop the curtain and let me sink back into oblivion for a little while. I didn't have the strength to tell him that I didn't hate Audrey for leaving me. I had seen it coming. Even sick with a rapidly failing heart, I could see how she twitched and jumped, eyes darting to the door, plotting an escape route from my illness and the life it would leave me.

It hurt. I felt every one of those three years we'd been together

5

like a knife driven into my new heart. But I didn't hate her. I didn't hate her because I didn't love her. Not in the way I wanted to love a woman—with everything I had.

Audrey was gone. Theo could hate her for me. My parents could marvel at her cruelty on my behalf. But I let her go, because at that moment, I didn't know she'd be the last...

Chapter 1

KACEY

JULY, A SATURDAY NIGHT

I WAS DRUNK.

Why else would I have my cell phone in my hand, my thumb hovering over my parents' home number in San Diego?

Drunk dialing, I thought. *Not just for ex-boyfriends anymore.*

I snorted a laugh. It came out more like a sob and echoed around the stairwell. I sat in the dark, narrow space, knees pulled up, trying to make myself small. Invisible. On the other side of the cement wall, I could hear the muffled shouts and whistles of three thousand people waiting for Rapid Confession to take the stage. Our manager, Jimmy Ray, had given us the ten-minute cue a good twenty minutes ago, and my bandmates were probably looking for me.

I took a sip from my Evian water bottle, three-quarters filled with vodka—because I'm clever like that—and contemplated my phone. I dared myself to call. I warned myself not to, to just put it away and join the band in the green room. We'd hit the stage, play for yet another sold-out show. I'd get hella famous, make some serious money, and continue to screw a different guy every night.

Because rock and roll.

What a joke. I wasn't rock and roll. I looked the part, especially tonight in my miniskirt, thigh-high boots, and bustier. My hair— bleached to almost white—curled around my shoulders in pinup-girl perfection. My lips were painted red, and my eyes were lined in black. Tattoos decorated my skin, adding to the impression of a grunge rock chick, but they weren't part of the costume. They were mine.

I looked the part, but I felt like a piece of glass, shattered and scattered all over. I didn't know who or what I was anymore, but I glittered prettily in the spotlight.

I took another sip of vodka and nearly dropped my phone. I fumbled to catch it, and when I lifted it up, I saw I'd hit that big green call button.

"Shit…"

Slowly, I put the phone to my ear. My mother answered on the third ring.

"Hello, Dawson residence."

My heart dropped into my stomach. My jaw worked, but I couldn't make any sound come out.

"Hello?"

"I…"

"Hello, may I help you?"

She's going to hang up!

"Hey, Mom. It's me. Kacey."

"Cassandra."

I hated that name and hadn't used it for years. But wrapped around those three syllables, I heard the relief in my mother's voice. I *heard* it.

"Yeah, hi!" I said brightly, too loudly. "How, uh…how are you guys?"

"We are fine," she said. Her voice was hushed now, as if she didn't want to be overheard. "Where are you calling from?"

"Las Vegas," I said. "Because we're on tour. Me and my band? Rapid Confession? It's a sold-out show tonight, our second night in a row. Actually, most of the shows on our tour have been sold out. It's pretty great. We're hitting the big time."

"I am very happy for you, Cassandra."

I heard my father's influence behind my mother's words, turning her into a goddamn robot spouting lines she'd been forced to memorize.

"And our latest single? 'Talk Me Down'? Well…" I bit my lip. "It's number six on the Billboard Hot 100. And I…well, I wrote it, Mom. I mean, my band and I wrote it, but the words…they're mostly mine. And 'Wanderlust'? I wrote that one too. It's number twelve on the charts."

Nothing.

I swallowed. "How is Dad?"

"He's fine," my mother replied, her voice almost a whisper now.

"Is…is he there?"

My mom sighed, a tiny exhalation. "Cassie…are you safe? Are you taken care of?"

"I'm doing good, Mom," I said. "And I'm a success. This band… we're a hit."

God, I hated this. The pathetic tone of my voice, bragging about the band's accomplishments, begging my mother to feel happy for our success when I hardly felt a thing myself except the need to be loved. It was like a hunger that was never sated. A desperate starvation twisted and twined into my guts, tangled in ravenous knots I couldn't unravel.

I could never quell that awful appetite. Only drown it in alcohol for a little while and try to puke it out the next day.

"Mom? Please, just tell Dad…"

"Cassie, I have to go."

"Wait, can you put him on? Or just…can you tell him you're on the phone with me right now? Just do that, Mom. See what he says."

Silence. "I don't think that's a good idea," she said finally. "He's been…cheerful lately. No upsets. I don't want to disturb him."

"Is he still mad at me?" I asked, my voice wavering. "It was four years ago, Mom. I'm not even with Chett anymore."

Chett ditched me in Las Vegas four years ago, leaving me broke, heartbroken, and reeling. A cross-country tour, a record deal, countless one-night stands, and two new tattoos later, and here I was, a wayward kid again, begging her parents to forgive her.

I fought back the tears. "I told you this, Mom. But did you tell *him*? Did you ever tell Dad I was homeless and sleeping at the Y when he kicked me out? *Homeless*, Mom. I was fucking seventeen years old."

I heard her swallow hard. Forcing down tears and emotions and everything she wanted to say but never would. She hadn't told Dad anything about me other than that I was still alive, that she had heard from me and I was doing well. She kept to her script, no matter how many times I begged her to try out some new material.

"You should have known better than to bring that boy home," my mother said, mustering a little firmness. "You knew how it would upset your father."

"Everything I did upset him," I cried, my voice clanging around the stairwell. "Nothing was ever good enough. Yeah, I knew bringing Chett home was a bad fucking idea, but I *wanted* to get caught. Do you know why, Mom? To force Dad to talk to me. And how goddamn sad is that? His own daughter. His own *child*."

"Cassandra, I have to go now. I'll tell your father I heard from you, and—"

"That I'm doing well?" I finished. "Not *well*, Mom," I snapped and wiped my nose on the back of my hand. "We're a fucking *sensation*. We're the *next big thing*…"

"You know I don't care for all this foul language, Cassandra," she said. Now her voice was turning to stone, walling me out. But I couldn't stop.

"You tell Dad that, okay? You tell him I made it, and that I did it without his fucking help or approval or…or his goddamn roof over my head."

"I'm going to hang up now, Cassandra."

I sucked in a breath, instantly regretting every word. I needed to hear more of her voice. "Mom, wait. I'm sorry. I'm so sorry…"

The line was quiet, and I thought she'd hung up until I heard her draw in a shaky little breath.

I eased one of my own and closed my eyes. "I'm sorry. Tell Dad…" I swallowed down the tears. "Tell him I love him. Okay? Please?"

"I will," she said, though I didn't believe it. Not for a second.

"Thanks, Mom. And I love you too. How are—"

"I have to get off now. Take care."

The line went quiet for good.

I stared at my phone a few moments more. A tear splattered onto its face, and I wiped it away with my thumb. I thought about pressing the call button again. I could call her back and tell her I was sorry for swearing. Or I could call back and say I wasn't fucking sorry at all. I was never calling again. I was as done with them as they were done with me.

Are they done with me?

The thought made my heart ache. No, not yet. My mother held on. She needed my phone calls. I knew that. But if I never called her again, she wouldn't call me. I knew that too. She was still a bystander in her own child's life.

I slumped against the concrete wall. I could hear the crowd on the other side growing restless. It sounded like a thunderstorm moving closer. If we didn't take the stage soon…

I needed a smoke.

I pulled a battered soft pack of cigarettes from the top part of my thigh-high boot and lit it from a matchbook tucked into the cellophane.

I drew in deep, exhaled, and slumped lower against the wall, weighed down by all the tears I didn't cry over the last four years. They threatened to burst out now in my own thunderstorm. I battled it all back, inhaled it hard, wrapped it in smoke, and pressed it into my gut, where it sat like a lead weight.

11

Dad won't even talk to me.

I exhaled the thought back out. *So what? Who cares what he thinks? He's never given a shit in twenty-two years, why would he start now? Fuck him.*

A brave speech, except I would've given anything to hear my dad's voice and not have it be laced with disappointment or anger. To hear him say he missed me or he loved me. To be told I could come home any time I wanted and the door would be open…

But he'd shut and locked that door, maybe forever, and the foundation on which I'd been built was crumbling to dust.

The crowd roared on the other side of the wall. They were clamoring for us. For me. They loved me.

And as Roxie Hart would say, I loved them for loving me.

I took another pull from my vodka and rose from my crouch just as Jimmy Ray busted through a door on the landing above mine, looking frantic and wound up.

Our manager was in his mid-forties with thinning hair. His suit—always Armani since a mid-size label signed us three months ago—hung a bit loose over his lanky frame. His wild eyes landed on me, and he collapsed against the wall in exaggerated relief, his hand over his heart.

"Jesus, kitten, give me a coronary why don't you? The gig was supposed to start half an hour ago."

I ground out the cigarette under the heel of my boot and plastered a smile on my face. "Sorry, Jimmy. I had an important phone call. But I'm good now. Ready to kick ass."

"Glad to hear it. This crowd is going eat us alive if we don't get out there, a-sap."

I moved past him, but he stopped me, his hand on my chin, studying my face.

"You been crying?"

I sucked in a breath. Jimmy Ray wasn't anyone's idea of a father figure, but he'd been good to us. Good to me. I felt myself start to wilt under his kindness, wanting to tell him…

"Because your makeup is smeared," he said. "Make sure you fix it before you go on, yeah?"

I nodded mutely.

"Attagirl."

He smacked my ass lightly to get me moving and followed me out of the stairwell, back to the green room, where the rest of the band was waiting.

Chapter 2

KACEY

THEY WERE ALL DRESSED IN FULL CONCERT GEAR: LEATHER, VINYL, AND lots of chunky costume jewelry. Violet, our bassist, wore her brown hair pulled tight to one side, revealing the small black raven tattooed in the shaved skin of her scalp above her ear. She gave me a nod and flashed me the peace sign.

Lola, my best friend, sat in a deep chair, spinning her drumsticks deftly around her fingers. She jumped up and came to me, peered at my face through shocks of black and electric-blue hair. Her dark eyes were sharp, observant, and full of concern.

"You okay? Where'd you take off to?"

I was spared answering by Jeannie, our lead singer. She'd been doing her vocal warm-ups but stopped in the middle of a scale.

"What the actual fuck, Kacey?" Her eyes, lined in kohl as black as her skintight leather pants, zeroed in on me. She was a pretty gal, our fearless leader, or would be if not for the perpetual constipated look on her face.

I felt the weight of the room on me, heavy and accusatory. I crossed my arms over my chest, affected a pinched, slightly Midwestern older-lady voice. "*Hello, Jeannie, who's bothering you now?*"

Lola snickered, and Violet muffled a laugh behind her hand.

"Who's bothering me? You..." Jeannie's confusion morphed to irritation. "Wait, are you quoting some stupid movie at me again?"

"Stupid?" I gaped dramatically. "*Ferris Bueller's Day Off* is nothing short of a classic. A national *treasure...*"

Jeannie flapped a hand, her bracelets jangling. "Whatever. If you devoted as much time to the band as you do to partying and watching eighties relics—"

"Come on, Jeannie," Violet said with a sigh. "Let's not start any shit right before the show. She's here. We're fashionably late. So what?"

Lola nodded. "Only newbies start a show on time. She's ready to kick ass, right, Kace?"

"Oh, stop coddling her, for chrissakes," Jeannie snapped at Lola, and then Jimmy swooped in and pulled her aside, talking soothingly to her in a low voice

Under my breath, I said, "*Mmm-mmm-mmm, what a little asshole.*"

Violet burst out laughing, but Lola's eyes flickered to my "Evian." She was a human Breathalyzer, that girl. Quickly, I tossed the bottle in the trash before she got wind of its contents and laid another of her patented lectures on me. The vodka had already started to work anyway, putting me one giant step back from reality, as if I were behind a pane of glass.

"Let's not fight, ladies," Jimmy chided, bringing Jeannie back to the center of the green room. "Three thousand paid ticket holders are waiting."

"He's right," Jeannie said and mustered what we called her "fearless leader" expression: stiff and serious as she eyed us in turn. "We need to get focused and give them the performance of our lives. Circle up."

We formed a ring in the center of the green room, holding hands, while Jeannie murmured a sort of vague invocation. Violet was a Buddhist, Lola an atheist, so the group prayer was more about channeling our energies, being grateful for our opportunities, and getting the four of us in tune with each other so we could play as one cohesive unit.

Is this what I want? I mused while Jeannie droned positive affirmations. I suspected the answer was no, but I'd come too far now. Lola was counting on me. If it hadn't been for her, I'd still be on the streets. She'd taken me in after Chett ditched me, and we'd gotten this gig together. She needed me to *not* fuck this up, and I needed to *not* be a fuck up.

"Forget every other show," Jeannie was saying, her typical closing statements. "Forget we've been on the road for months. These fans deserve our best, so let's go out there and perform as if it's the first day of the tour. Blood, sweat, and tears, ladies."

We made loud noises of agreement to get amped up, then headed out.

Lola pulled me aside. "Are you okay? For real?"

"Sure, I'm fine. Totally."

"Where were you?"

"Oh, I…I called my parents."

Lola's shoulders slumped and she covered her eyes with one hand. "Oh shit, no. No, no, no. I keep telling you to give it up. It always bites you in the ass, Kace. Every time. You get all upset, then you get even more wasted than usual."

"No, no, it was great!" I said. "I only talked to my mom, but…well, my dad said hi. I heard him in the background. That's a start, right?"

Is this where you're at? Lying to your best friend after all that she's done for you?

Lola looked shocked. "Really? He talked to you?"

"He said, 'Hi, Lola.' He really did."

Lola studied me through narrow eyes and finally relented.

"That's great, Kace," she said, hugging me. "I'm really happy for you. To be honest, I've been worried lately. You party twenty-four seven and have a different guy in your bed every night."

"Not *every* night," I said. "I have my dry spells. Like Tuesday."

Lola snorted.

"Let's go, girls," Jimmy reappeared at the door. "They're waiting."

I flashed Lola a reassuring smile. "We're going to kick ass at this show tonight. I promise."

"I wish you'd promise not to party so fucking hard afterward. Maybe you'd be able to *remember* how kick-ass the show was."

I pretended to be affronted. "That is the least rock and roll thing I've ever heard in my life. Keith Richards would roll over in his grave if he heard you talk like that."

A smile twitched Lola's lips. "Keith Richards isn't dead."

"See? Nothing to worry about."

She rolled her eyes and laughed, slinging her arm around me. Protectively, as always.

Hugo Williams, the Pony Club's head of security, appeared at the green room door to escort us to the stage. His dark eyes were warm and kind as he smiled at me, his teeth white and bright against the dark of his skin.

"Hey, Hugo," I said as we filed out.

"Hey, sweets," he said in his deep baritone.

This was only our second night at the Pony Club, but Hugo seemed extra considerate of me, going out of his way to make sure I felt safe.

Jimmy slung an arm over my bare shoulders. "Sounds like a rowdy crowd tonight, Hugo."

I smiled up at the bodyguard. "Hugo'll take care of me. He's my hero."

The big bodyguard nodded, like a soldier given an order, and led us to the stage. We took winding back hallways with pipes running along the ceiling. Our footsteps clapped and echoed on the cement.

Jimmy turned to me. "You ready?"

"Born ready, Jimmy."

"That's my girl."

I joined my bandmates at a short flight of stairs that led to the stage. A roar went up—the crowd responding to the MC taking the mic.

"Las Vegas! Are you ready for Rapid Confession?"

Another wave of sound, like an avalanche ripping apart the walls of the venue.

The door opened, a dark rectangle blazing with stage lights. We streamed up the short flight of stairs and onto the stage. My red Fender was waiting for me on a stand. I looped the strap over my shoulder and saw Jeannie throw me a nod and a nervous smile—a peace agreement. I nodded and smiled back—agreement accepted.

Lola clashed her drumsticks over her head in a four-count lead-in to "Talk Me Down."

I played my goddamn heart out. I wrote "Talk Me Down" for myself. It was an anthem to everything that scared me about where I was going and what I was doing to myself. Nobody knew it was mine. I sang backup to Jeannie's melody. But when I played, my heart came out. The music carved open my chest, flayed my ribs, and showed the world everything inside.

I shredded my solos. All the liquor I'd drunk on an empty stomach turned the stage lights into blurry orbs of white. The faces in the crowd melted together, becoming one roaring, churning electric mass. I fed off the energy, sucking in their screaming approval and spitting it back out with every chord and progression until my fingers bled, and at the end of the show, I nearly smashed my Fender on the stage.

As the last notes of the last song vibrated in the air and then vanished, the crowd lost its collective shit. I was lit up like the Fourth of July, running along the lip of the stage, slapping hands with the front-row audience. They grabbed and pulled me over the edge. I laughed and laughed, surfing on a wave of adoring hands, drunk as hell and high on being loved.

The boulder of Hugo and his team rolled into the crowd, hauled me down, and marched me out. But I didn't want it to end. I called to the crowd around me.

"I love you all so much! Come back with me…" I pointed at random strangers. "Come with me! Let's keep the party going…"

Hugo dragged me to the green room, where the band was celebrating. Champagne spewed through the air in gold and foamy arcs. I grabbed a bottle out of someone's hand and downed half of it in one pull. I shouted at security to let in the small crowd I'd invited.

"They're with me!" I cried.

About two dozen pushed their way in. My bandmates were all too high on the heady success of the show to care. Jimmy looked like he was going to fly straight off the ground.

Tossing the champagne aside, I grabbed a bottle at random from the long table of post-show food and drink. Jägermeister.

A bold choice, I thought with a laugh, and let out a scratchy whoop after the liquor burned its way down my throat. The room, filled with my new friends, cheered back. Strange faces I didn't recognize, whom I'd never remember tomorrow. People who were here for the music and the free booze and entertainment, and for me, their patron saint of Good Times. I climbed onto a table, and they cheered and raised their bottles to me.

They love me.

The room began to spin as if I were on a carousel. It was too packed in here. No air. Security was trying to squeeze in through the wall of bodies. Glass shattered. Some in the crowd cheered, while others cursed.

Lola yelled for me to get down before I broke my ass, then was lost in the crowd. The huge, hulking shape of Hugo parted the sea like Moses. I tried to lift the emerald-green bottle to my lips for one final slug, because this party was exploding, and I was going to hit bottom and shatter into a million pieces.

My father's words, four years ago, resounded in my head with just as much clarity as if it were yesterday. *Get out! Get out of my house!*

"No," I said, then louder, blearily, my mouth thick and clumsy around the words, "*You* get out. This is my house. *My* house."

19

I raised my bottle in the air. *"This is my house!"* I screamed, and a hundred million voices raised their own bottles and cheered me on until the sound tore through me like wind through tissue paper.

I laughed or maybe cried, then staggered sideways. The liquor bottle slipped from my fingers just as I slipped from the table, straight into Hugo's waiting arms. I saw the blackness of his T-shirt; then the blackness behind my eyes swallowed me whole.

Chapter 3

JONAH

THE SIGN ABOVE ME BLINKED OFF AND ON. RED AND WHITE. *PONY Club.* The edges of the metal were rusted, and three of the bulbs lining the edge were burned out. It looked cheap. Gaudy. Like a lot of Vegas. But when I squinted…

The lights blurred, and I could imagine globes of white and red glass. Glass beads, maybe. A bundle of them held together with wire to make a bouquet. My mind pulled the red beads out long, making flattened petals. A poinsettia with white baby's breath. A Christmas bouquet of glass that never needed watering. My mother would like that. Or maybe Dena. I started to pull out the battered little notepad I kept in the front pocket of my shirt to jot the idea down, then stopped.

Christmas was five months away.

A soft ache tried to take root, and I squashed it with practiced ease, like a lump of gum pressed under a table.

Keep to the routine.

I withdrew my hand and left the notepad where it was.

It was getting loud in the Pony Club. The show had supposedly ended an hour ago, but the shouts and whoops of some epic party were loud and clear—if muffled—through the cement of the venue's back wall.

I pulled my cell phone from the front pocket of my uniform slacks to check the time. It was nearly 1:00 a.m. The limo was commissioned only until two, but I could already tell this was going to be a night of enforced overtime.

But what did I care if the job ran late? I didn't sleep much these days, and I could use the money. I'd stay until the band and their manager came oozing out of the venue, wasted and reeking, and take them back to the mega mansion in Summerlin where I'd picked them up at five that evening.

The upside to driving at night was it left me time to work during the day. The downside was the *downtime.* So many empty hours spent waiting for my fare to get done with dinner or the show, or to finally emerge from the casino, stinking of booze and smoke and—more often than not—mourning their losses at the blackjack or poker tables.

Limo drivers tended to band together at events, lined up outside the venue in a train of sleek black or white vehicles. I saw the same faces at different jobs, and some were my own coworkers at A-1 Limousine. But I had to avoid smoke, and I wasn't interested in making new buddies. I kept to myself, to my routine.

I leaned against the limo and looked up. No stars could conquer the lights of Vegas. I'd have to wait until my best friend's Great Basin camping trip in a few weeks to see actual stars. But the Strip was its own kind of constellation. A riot of garish neon color and glittering lights, it was beautiful in its own way, as long as you didn't look down.

At my feet, in the gutter running between the street and sidewalk, were cigarette butts, a crushed soft drink cup from Dairy Queen, and a flier for a nudie show off the Strip. Shattered glass glittered green under a streetlamp.

One of the other limo drivers approached me. "Got a smoke?"

This guy was young. Younger than my twenty-six years, anyway. Sweat beaded his brow as he looked at me hopefully. Even in this summer heat, he was still wearing his service's livery, a maroon polyester jacket with gold piping. Newbie. My black jacket was on the front seat and had been since the band and their manager exited my limo nearly eight hours ago.

"I don't smoke, man," I told him. "Sorry."

The *sorry* was code for *conversation over*, but this guy didn't catch on.

"Shit, I ran out an hour ago," he muttered. His name tag read *Trevor*. "Hey, who you driving for? I got a bunch of sweet-sixteen richies seeing the Rapid Confession show." He barked a laugh. "Spoiled rich brats. I mean, what's worse than that?"

"I can't imagine," I muttered.

My phone vibrated with a text. Probably my brother, Theo, with the hourly check-in. I pulled the phone from my pants pocket. *Yep.*

What's up? You good?

Rolling my eyes, I took a screenshot of the midnight check-in: the exact same message and my reply that I was fine. I hit Send.

He texted back. Dick.

I smirked, typing. You make it so easy. Go to sleep, Teddy. I'll call you in the morning.

"I wonder who has the band," Trevor said, glancing down the line of limos. "If I had those bitches, it would be epic. Night *made*."

Another photo text came in, this one of Theo's middle finger. He hated when I called him Teddy. Almost as much as I hated it when guys called women bitches.

I turned to Trevor to tell him to get lost when the Pony Club's back door banged open and the sounds of raucous laughter, shouts, and shattered glass spilled onto the street. A huge bodyguard hurried out carrying the limp body of a woman, her leather skirt hiked up her thighs and her head hanging so that her blond hair spilled over the bodyguard's arm.

I gave Trevor a little shove out of the way and opened the limo's passenger door. The bodyguard never broke stride but bent his hulking form over to lay the girl inside, on the long leather seat that ran opposite the door.

Trevor sucked in a breath. "That's her! The blond…the guitar player for RC." He looked at me like I was his hero. "*You* have them?"

The bodyguard reemerged from the limo and towered over Trevor, his hands balling into fists. "Is this your business?"

Trevor cringed and backed off. "N-no, sir."

"Are you going to tell anyone what you saw here?"

"No. I sure won't."

"Good answer." He turned back to me. "Take her home. Quick. Before the paparazzi show up. It's a fucking riot in there." He jerked his head toward the venue, where the shouts were louder, punctuated by shrill cursing and more breaking glass. "I gotta get back." He jabbed a finger into my chest. "You make sure she gets home safe."

I saw the concern bright in the guy's dark eyes boring into mine; then he was loping back to the venue. Sirens wailed in the distance, getting closer.

With the huge bodyguard gone, Trevor crept forward, peering into the limo. "Dude. *Dude,* she is smokin' hot."

I had to agree with Trevor's assessment, but the girl was also passed-out drunk. Women needed to be coherent and conscious for me to entertain even fleeting sexual thoughts. Trevor's tongue was lolling out of his mouth, and I slammed the door shut, disgusted, cutting off his view.

"What are you going to do with her?" Trevor asked.

I paused at the driver's side door to stare. "I'm going to take her *home,* asshole."

Trevor held up his hands. "Jeez, chill out. I didn't mean…"

I didn't hear the rest as I climbed into the car and shut my door.

Trevor wasn't going to keep his promise to the bodyguard about the girl in the back seat. No chance. And the news of whatever happened in the Pony Club was going to hit the streets anyway—the sirens were guarantee of that.

Just get her home, finish the job, keep to your routine.

I pulled the limo away from the curb. I hit traffic on the Strip and lowered the partition to check on the girl. Her skirt was still hiked up, showing a fishnet-clad thigh and part of a tattoo. More inked patterns snaked up the pale skin of her forearms, and a larger one covered her right shoulder. The rounded tops of her breasts were pushing out of the bustier thing she wore. But I was looking for her chest to move, to show me she was breathing.

I wondered if I should veer to Sunrise Hospital—my home away from home—when the girl gave a groan and rolled to her side. I watched the streets in front of me while listening to her heave what sounded like a barrel's worth of booze onto the limo floor. The smell of regurgitated liquor filled the confined space.

"Awesome," I muttered. "This is why they pay me the big bucks."

When she was done retching, the girl—the guitar player, according to Trevor—slumped back on the seat to moan softly, her eyes still closed, her white-blond hair sticking to her cheek.

I turned off the Strip, found a dark empty side street, and pulled over. I climbed in the back where my fare lay sprawled on the long seat, stepping around the mess on the floor to sit near her head to brush the hair from her face.

I hated to agree with Trevor about anything, but this girl was beautiful. Even passed-out drunk and reeking of booze, puke, and cigarette smoke, she was stunning. Large eyes fringed with long dark lashes, broad mouth with full lips painted a deep red, and shaped dark brows that contrasted with her white-blond hair.

I reminded myself I was there to make sure she wasn't going to die on me, not waste time ogling her. I'd had a lot of pretty girls in my limos over the last few months. Lots of *drunk* pretty girls. This one was no different.

This girl—I wished I'd thought to get her name from the bodyguard—was breathing better, and some color had returned to her face. Upchucking a fifth of liquor probably helped. Satisfied that she didn't need a hospital—though I didn't envy the epic hangover she was going to wake up to—I concentrated on getting her home so I could call it a night.

I drove northwest to the Summerlin neighborhood. The big house was a pale peach-pink color with white columns and a circular drive, and it was totally dark.

"Shit."

I got out of the limo and rang the front bell, hoping someone's personal assistant or maybe another security guard was around. Nothing. I tried the front door on the off chance it had been left unlocked. It wasn't.

I went back to the limo and fished out my cell phone from my pocket and called A-1's dispatch. Tony Politino was working the lines.

"Tony? It's Jonah. I need the contact number for the Rapid Confession job."

"You got *that* job?" Tony let out a wolf whistle. "Lucky bastard."

"Not as lucky as the cleaning crew," I muttered. "You got the number or not?"

"Hold up…"

I rubbed my eyes and waited until Tony came back on.

"Jimmy Ray. He's their manager," he said. He droned the phone number. "And hey, sneak a few pics for me, right? The blond? She's fucking smoking."

I glanced at the girl sprawled on the back seat. An insidious thought crept in. I *could* take a few pics of her, sell them to a gossip rag, and make a killing. I'd lose my job, of course, but with the money from the photos, I wouldn't need it. I could spend all day, every day at the hot shop and never have to worry if my installation would be finished on time for the gallery opening in October.

It was a nice fantasy, except for the small fact that I'd never forgive myself for being such a low-life scumbag. That I'd even entertained the idea was repulsive. I chalked it up to tiredness, along with the heavy pang of dread that lurked behind every waking thought, ready to ooze out if I let it. The fear that told me I was running out of time and the installation would be left forever unfinished.

"Keep to the routine," I muttered.

"What's that, bro?" Tony asked.

"Nothing; thanks for the number."

I hung up on Tony and called Jimmy Ray, the band manager. I remembered him—he stuck out like a flashy used car salesman in my memory. A skinny middle-aged guy who dressed and acted like he was a decade younger, trying to be slick. He talked to the women in the band as if they were his meal ticket instead of human beings.

Jimmy Ray answered the phone on the fifth ring, but talking was impossible. Loud music blasted from behind him, and the chaotic sounds of a hundred voices shouting and screaming almost drowned him out.

"Hello, what? *What?*"

"Mr. Ray," I had to shout. "I'm your driver."

"What? I can't hear a fucking thing."

"I'm from A-1 Limousine—"

"Who the fuck *is* this?"

I rubbed my eyes. "Elvis. Elvis Presley. Rumors of my death have been greatly exaggerated…"

"Look, whoever this is, I've got a damn catastrophe on my hands. Call me back."

More shouting, and then it all turned muffled. The guy had probably put the phone in his pocket without hanging up.

I ended the call on my end and checked the time. Just after 2:00 a.m. On the darkened street, no lights heading my way, no one coming home. I glanced inside at the nameless girl.

"What am I going to do with you?"

The urge to take her back to the Pony Club and hand her back to the bodyguard was a strong one, but that poor bastard probably had his hands full.

I shut the passenger door to the limo and got back behind the wheel. This whole scene felt seedy and wrong. I wanted to get her someplace safe, and while taking her to my apartment wasn't exactly kosher, it was better than seeing her splayed out drunk in the back of a puke-splattered limo.

"I hope you realize this is highly irregular," I told her as I navigated out of the Summerlin estates. "Totally *not* in the employee handbook. In fact, I seem to recall watching an educational video about this sort of thing, 'How Not to Get Sued into Oblivion.' Step one, don't take your fares home with you, especially if they are of the *blackout drunk and female* persuasion."

At two in the morning, Vegas showed its dark underbelly. The streets were filled with the most desperate: gamblers hoping to salvage some of their losses, hopeless drunks, drug dealers, and prostitutes. This was the Vegas I hated, but as I crossed the Strip heading east, I passed the Bellagio. My smile returned. There was real beauty in Las Vegas. You just had to know where to look.

The Bellagio's lobby ceiling was one place. In my rearview was another.

The girl passed out on the long seat threw one tattooed arm over her eyes and gave a little moan.

"We're almost there," I told her gently. "You're going to be okay."

Chapter 4

JONAH

I PULLED THE LIMO TO THE FRONT OF MY APARTMENT COMPLEX. I lived in a cement box of a building, with pale-gray stucco and crooked railings peeling lime-green paint.

"I know it's not the luxury villa you're used to," I told her, "but beggars can't be choosers, am I right?"

The girl, still deep in her booze-soaked nap, wasn't in a position to choose anything.

I parked the limo along the side of the building as close to my first-floor apartment as I could get. Illegally parked but hidden from the street.

I jogged to my front door, unlocked and opened it, and flipped on the light near the door. Back at the limo, I climbed in and sat beside the girl.

"Hey," I said, nudging her arm gently. "Hey. Can you wake up for me?"

She didn't stir.

"Shit." I heaved a breath. "All right, here we go."

She was a slight thing, maybe five feet five inches, and couldn't have weighed more than a buck ten, but the alcohol had turned her to deadweight. Her limbs were limp, and her head lolled. I struggled to get her out of the damn limo without banging her head on the door. I hoped to half carry, half walk her inside, but she was like jelly oozing out of my arms.

I sucked in a deep breath and lifted her under her knees and back, cradling her, so that her head rested against my chest.

Dr. Morrison would have a conniption if he saw me lifting an entire human being. Theo would lose his shit. But neither of them was there now. Another perk about the night shift: aside from a text or ten from Theo, I was free of the scrutiny that only reminded me of my predicament when I was trying to put it aside and keep to my schedule.

I carried the girl through the open door of my place and kicked it shut behind me with my heel. I laid her out on the couch and sat beside her to catch my breath. I was winded, but it wasn't bad. A few deep breaths, and I was back in business.

"That wasn't so tough, now, was it?"

The girl's full lips were parted, and she was breathing easy, a thin sheen of sweat over her forehead and across her chest. I couldn't imagine she could be very comfortable in those boots and bustier. Not that was I about to do anything about it. It was bad enough I had her in my apartment. Even taking her shoes off might add fuel to whatever PR nightmare was awaiting me tomorrow. I wondered if I could lose my job over this. Over her.

Now that she was safe, I spared a thought for my situation. I needed my job. I had the perfect routine going, and I couldn't let one goddamn thing throw it. I was supposed to go back to the Pony Club to pick up the band like I'd been hired to do, but then what? Bring them all back here to get their guitarist? And was it a good idea to leave her alone in the first place?

I looked at the girl. Young woman. I guessed maybe twenty-two.

She was out cold, but her beautiful face was at peace, her brows unfurrowed for the first time all night.

I sighed. *It's late. Let her sleep.*

I called A-1 back and told Tony I had the stretch and would have it back at the garage by 7:00 a.m. Tony warned me that our boss, Harry, would lose his shit to know one of his cars was out. Not to mention I'd left the band stranded at the Pony Club.

"But then again, Harry fucking loves you," Tony said. "You're his favorite driver."

That was true, which was why I was entrusted with the Rapid Confession job in the first place. Still, I was taking a huge fucking risk with my job—a job I desperately needed.

With a frustrated groan, I chucked the phone onto my old junker of a coffee table in front of the couch. It clanked against one of three blown-glass pieces sitting on its scratched wooden surface.

From the hall closet, I retrieved an afghan and draped it over my houseguest, then set a glass of water and two aspirin from my personal miniature pharmacy on the table beside her. A peace offering should the girl wake up and wonder if she'd been kidnapped by a crazed, knickknack-collecting psycho.

The girl. If I called her that one more time, even in my own mind, I was going to lose it.

My laptop was on the kitchen counter, which overlooked the living room. I opened it up and typed Rapid Confession into the Google search bar. A bunch of photos and articles came up, many of them as recent as yesterday. The band was about to "explode on the music scene like a Molotov-cocktail" (according to *Spin*) and "was the best thing to happen to rock and roll since the Foo Fighters" (so speaketh *Rolling Stone*). I scrolled until I found cheeky promotional photos naming each band member.

"Kacey Dawson," I muttered. "Hallelujah."

I stared at the promotional pic. Even flipping the bird with an "I don't give a fuck" expression on her face, Kacey Dawson was breathtaking.

"Get a grip, Fletcher."

I snapped the laptop shut and headed for the bedroom. On the kitchen wall, the phone's answering machine was blinking insistently. I hit the playback button.

"You have three new messages."

I should've just gone to bed.

"Hey, Jonah, it's me, Mike Spence. From Carnegie? Look…I know you're going through some heavy shit now, but…let's hang out, man. Let's grab a beer for old time's sake. Or at the very least, call me back and—"

I jabbed delete, and the machine moved to the next.

"Hello, honey, it's Mom. Just calling to see how you are. I really do hate your late hours. I know I sound like a broken record, but…well, call me in the morning. And we'll see you for dinner on Sunday as usual? Your father wants to barbecue. Call me, sweetheart. I love you. Okay. Love you. Bye."

I erased that one too, wishing I could erase the tentative tone in my mother's voice as easily. She sounded like she was always bracing herself for bad news.

The final message played, this one having come in just a few minutes ago, maybe while I was unloading my unconscious cargo from the limo. I knew it would be Theo even before I heard his voice.

"Hey, bro, just checkin' in. Call me back. Later."

Theo sounded casual, but the time of his call and earlier texts gave him away. Irritation flared, but I battled it back. Maybe Theo was working late at Vegas Ink. Sometimes he had clients coming in at all hours. Or maybe he was out late on a date—I couldn't keep track of his women; they came in and out of his life so quickly.

I erased the message just as a text came in on my cell. I grabbed it off the coffee table while Kacey Dawson slept on, oblivious.

Theo: Still at work?

Now I rolled my eyes, as the irritation took root. I jabbed a text.
No, I'm out chain-smoking Marlboro Reds and eating raw steak.

Very funny. Home???

I sighed and contemplated the blank space, my thumb itching to tell him off, to quit hovering over me and leave me alone. I jabbed a few words to that effect, then backspaced the text away with a sigh. I didn't get to be pissed off anymore. Not on the outside, anyway. Not at him or my parents. My whole situation was shitty enough without making them feel worse.

Yes, I'm home now, I texted. Good night, Theo.

C U at shop on Sun.

"I'm sure I will," I muttered.

I silenced the phone and left it on the kitchen counter on the way to the bedroom. There, I changed out of my limo livery and laid it out on the bed that was neatly made and probably slightly dusty. I changed into a white wifebeater and sleep pants from the plain wooden dresser, then headed to the bathroom in the hall to take a piss and brush my teeth.

I brushed and made plans.

Take Kacey back to the Summerlin house first thing in the morning.
Return the limo to A-1, and get my truck.
Go back to my routine.

No problem. One little speed bump, that's all tonight had been.

In the living room, Kacey Dawson looked to be sleeping comfortably—or as comfortable as one could get in leather and vinyl. I remembered from my own college days that being hungover and sweating out last night's booze was a rotten combo. I turned the AC unit at the window on and settled into the reclining chair across from the couch.

I had to laugh at the scene that would greet my guest should she wake up in the middle of the night: a dinky apartment instead of her mega mansion, and a strange dude sleeping in a recliner not five feet away instead of in the bed like a normal person.

"Stephen King should take notes," I muttered, settling into the halfway-lying-down position my doc recommended. "This'll teach you to drink your options away, Kacey Dawson," I muttered as my eyes drifted shut. "Everything in moderation."

Like my sleep.

I woke up at six, my ass numb from sitting in the same position all night. Not being able to change positions sucked, but I never slept much anyway, and I always came awake sharp and alert. It was as if my body knew time was no longer a luxury I could afford to waste.

I steered my thoughts toward something positive. Sunlight— yellow and sharp—slanted in from the front window. The glass bottles and paperweights caught it, captured it, and sprayed it out on the coffee table in mottled reds, blues, and purples.

"Beautiful," I murmured. And I had the entire Saturday at the hot shop before me to create more.

The figure on the couch moaned and sighed in her sleep, reminding me with a small jolt I had some unfinished business to take care of first. I threw off the light blanket and moved to the couch. Crouching beside Kacey Dawson, I studied her sleeping face a moment.

"Hey."

She didn't stir. Her mouth was slightly open. Dead to the world.

"I'm going to go take a shower," I told her. "Don't steal anything."

I pondered writing her a note to tell her she wasn't kidnapped, but then this probably wasn't the first time Kacey Dawson woke up after a hard night of partying not knowing where she was. I left it to chance and took my shower.

She was still out cold when I reemerged, dressed in jeans and a plain T-shirt. My hot shop uniform. At precisely 7:00 a.m., I took my meds, choking down one pill after another. Fifteen in all. My stomach complained instantly, and I got to work making the equally stomach-churning protein shake I drank every morning.

"Sorry, Kacey, this is going to hurt," I muttered and hit the button on my blender, filling my small apartment with a god-awful buzzing.

The massively hungover Kacey Dawson stirred, groaned, and finally sat up, pushing her tousled hair out of her eyes. She looked around blearily, not seeing me in the kitchen behind her, watching her.

I didn't know it then—I couldn't have—but in that moment, the rest of my life, or what was left of it, began.

Chapter 5

KACEY

SOMEONE WAS CUTTING DOWN A TREE. FUCK THAT, A WHOLE FOREST.

What kind of sick bastard...?

I lifted my head, blinking hard. The whirring sound stopped, and my hazy gaze was drawn to the coffee table and its array of colorful glass paperweights. They were pretty—beautiful even—but my appreciation was lost as they refracted the sunlight straight into my eyeballs.

Shifting my gaze, I saw a glass filled with water, two aspirin tablets beside it. I sat up ever so slowly, and a hideous orange-and-green knitted afghan fell off my shoulders. I glanced down at myself. Still one hundred percent dressed. Even my boots.

Dignity intact. Score one for me.

But the thought didn't bring me any comfort. Here I was again, waking up in strange surroundings after a night of drinking I didn't remember. On a couch this time, but it could've been a trash-strewn alley. Or the proverbial ditch mothers were always warning their kids they'd turn up in if they weren't careful. I wasn't careful. I was never careful.

It hurt too much to move or look around. It hurt to blink. I focused my attention on swallowing the aspirin down, chasing them with water. My mouth felt as dry and dusty as the Nevada desert. I would have chugged the whole glass if I thought my stomach could handle it, but I had my doubts. I took a few deep breaths and waited until the churning feeling in my gut subsided, then glanced around at my immediate surroundings.

A small apartment, sparsely decorated with plain, mismatched furniture. On the other side of the coffee table and its glass knick-knacks was an old La-Z-Boy chair facing a flat-screen TV. The walls were bare but for two framed degrees from universities I couldn't read from the couch, and a half-dozen photos. The front windows showed a view of a busy Vegas street. Nothing about the place made any kind of impression on me. Nor was it familiar.

"Well, I'm not chained up and the door is three feet away," I muttered to myself and raised the water glass for another drink.

"True, on both counts."

I coughed the water all over my chest and looked around. "The hell...?"

A guy stood in the tiny kitchen behind me. His dark hair was wet, fresh from a shower, and his sharp brown eyes regarded me with dry bemusement. He was tall, super cute, and totally not my type. I liked the thick, loose curls of his hair, but he was too clean-cut for me. My men were tatted and pierced, and came with an exit strategy in their back pocket after I slept with them. The guy in the kitchen looked like he made breakfast for any woman who stayed over, and instead of kicking them out, told them to make themselves at home.

Nice Guy, with caps.

But God, he had a sweet face. A face I could have sworn I'd seen before. I searched the boozy depths of my memory for when and where...

"I'm your limo driver," he said. "I took you and your band to the Pony Club last night?"

"Oh, right," I said. "That's it."

The guy came around to the front of the kitchen counter and leaned against it facing the living room, arms crossed. "Jonah Fletcher."

"What?" My brain thudded behind my eyes in time to my pulse.

"My name," he said slowly, "is Jonah Fletcher. In case you were wondering on whose couch you were sitting."

"Oh, sorry," I replied, my cheeks burning. "I was just…listening to my headache. I'm Kacey Dawson. Though you probably already knew that."

Jonah's eyes widened slightly into bemusement, and I shook my head—a movement I regretted instantly. "I don't mean because I'm famous or anything, I mean because of your job. My name's probably on some paperwork… Eh, forget it."

I held my aching head in my hands and tried to recall something from last night. A vague sense of Something Not Very Good happening added to the misery of my hangover.

I peered up at Jonah Fletcher. "So, uh…last night. Did we…?"

He arched one eyebrow at me, perfectly. The other didn't even move. "Did we…*what*?"

I huffed. "Do I have to spell it out?"

The stiff, sharp expression on his face softened slightly. "We didn't. You were passed out." He cocked his head. "You don't remember anything?"

"Not much."

"Happens a lot?"

I snorted. "I can't see how that's your business."

"And yet, last night it became my business." He shrugged. "Seems like a dangerous habit, is all. Not all guys are as nice as me."

"That's yet to be determined," I muttered and glanced around. "This is your place? Why not take me back to the Summerlin house?"

"Oh, believe me, I tried. Bringing you here isn't exactly work protocol. I could lose my job."

"What happened?" I asked, mostly because I should, not because I wanted to know.

This guy, Jonah, rubbed his chin thoughtfully and came to sit across from me in a beat-up reclining chair. The chair's upholstery might've been brown leather, but I'd guess it was more likely vinyl—cracked in places and well-worn. Jonah sat in it and hung his arms off his jean-clad knees. A heavy silver bracelet ringed his right wrist. His T-shirt fit tight around his shoulders and biceps. Nice muscles. Lean but defined.

My eyes drifted to the collar of his shirt to take in some of his chest. A quarter inch of a fleshy red line peeked above the seam. Some kind of gnarly scar.

I quickly averted my eyes.

"I tried to take you back to the house," Jonah was saying. "Tried to get in touch with your manager too. No luck. It was either bring you here or back to the Pony Club, but your bodyguard seemed pretty insistent I get you away from that scene."

A lump of dread joined the churning in my guts. "What scene exactly?"

"Not sure. It sounded like there was some sort of riot going on."

"A riot."

Whatever blood was left in my face drained out. A vague memory, blurry and soaked in booze, swam up. Me, urging a bunch of fans to the green room. I couldn't remember the actual moment, but the sound of so many cheering voices thundered in my head and made it ache harder.

"Did, um…did Hugo—the bodyguard—did he say what happened? How it started?"

Jonah shook his head. "You don't recall anything?"

"Pretty sure I don't want to," I said, my voice hardly a whisper.

I fished around in the top part of my boots for my pack of smokes. I shook a cigarette out and was fumbling with the little matchbook when Jonah cleared his throat.

"This is a no-smoking zone, if you don't mind."

"Have mercy," I said with a wan smile. "Besides, everyone smokes in Vegas."

"I don't." The hard tone in Jonah's voice froze my hand. He offered a small smile. "Sorry. House rules."

I set my pack down longingly on the table. "You picked a tough city to live in if you don't like cigarette smoke."

"And yet somehow I manage." He rubbed his hands on his thighs, impatiently. "You don't need to call your people? They might want to know you're okay. In fact, I would prefer they know that you're okay. I'm sort of half expecting a SWAT team to bust down my door any minute now for kidnapping you."

"I guess…" The very last thing I wanted to do was call "my people," but Jonah was watching me.

Just get it over with.

"Can I use your phone?"

Jonah handed over his cell, and I started to punch in Jimmy's number. I was ninety-nine percent sure whatever catastrophe had happened at the Pony Club was my fault, and one hundred percent sure I didn't want to know how bad the scene really was. I chickened out and called Lola instead.

She answered on the third ring. "Yeah?" she said, her voice full of sleep.

"Lola? It's me."

"Kacey?" She yawned. "Where are you? Are you calling from in the house?"

"Um, no," I said. "I'm not…there."

"Well, that narrows it down," Lola said, sighing. "Jesus, Kace. Do I need to send a search party? On second thought, you'd better lie low where Jimmy can't find you. He was *pissed* last night. Jeannie too. Then again, she's always pissed."

I closed my eyes at the accusation and braced myself. "Why is he pissed?"

"You don't remember, do you? You fucking drank yourself into a

Jägermeister coma right after inviting half the audience into the green room. But instead of sticking around to deal with your mess, Hugo saved you. He put you in the limo, right? Yeah, we had to cab it home. Jimmy was not happy about that."

I twisted a lock of hair around my finger. "That's why he was pissed? Because he had to take a cab?"

"Kace, you think he was worried about you? Hon, he figured you were fucking the limo driver." A pause. I could hear the unspoken words. *We all did.*

Another ugly flush of red colored my neck. I steadfastly refused to look at Jonah.

"Well, I didn't. I was in a Jägermeister coma, remember? You can tell him that."

"Whatever. Does it matter? Jimmy called the company and gave them an earful for not picking us up. That limo driver is going to be up to his ass in hot water. Hugo too."

"No, no, he didn't do anything wrong," I shifted on the couch away from Jonah and lowered my voice. My headache ratcheted up ten notches. "Neither of them did. Tell Jimmy it wasn't Hugo's fault. I'm all right."

I heard Lola light a cigarette. I found my fingers inching toward my own pack and had to sit on my hand.

"You realize you totally trashed the place, right?" Lola asked on an exhale of smoke. "According to Jimmy, the Pony Club is talking potential lawsuit to pay the damages."

I nearly dropped Jonah's phone. "Did anyone get hurt?" I asked in a small voice.

"No," she said, the anger deflating from her voice. "But the green room is trashed. Beyond trashed. It looked like a war zone when we left."

"So…what's happening now? Is tonight's show canceled?"

Lola snorted. "Hell no. Not with sixty grand worth of ticket sales on the line."

"Oh."

"I'll tell Jimmy you're okay, but maybe… I don't know, Kace. You might want to lie low for a couple of hours. At least until Jimmy gets over his own hangover. I mean, to be fair, everyone was pretty wasted last night." Now I could hear a small smile on my friend's lips. "It was an epic show. *Epic*."

"Was it?"

"Oh girl, you don't even know. We're on the verge of mega stardom, and you're missing it. No, you're almost *wrecking* it."

"But I didn't, right?"

"Nope. The show must go on." Lola sighed again. "Get some rest. Sober up for tonight's show. You're still good to go, right?" she asked, and I could hear the warning tone in her voice. This wasn't just my big break but hers too.

"Sure," I said weakly. "Thanks, Lola. And tell Jimmy—"

"That you're sorry? Yeah, yeah. Time for some new material, Kace. Talk to you later."

I handed the phone back to Jonah. "Thanks."

"Are the cops going to be busting in the door any minute now?" he asked darkly. "Or am I going to lose my job? Or both?"

"No. Well…maybe."

Jonah's eyes widened. "Maybe *which*?"

Shame and humiliation flushed my skin red. "The second one. Listen, I'll talk to your boss at the limo place…" I started as Jonah bolted out of his chair with a curse.

He ignored me and began jabbing at his phone.

"Harry? It's me, Jonah. I—" He shot me a glare as he listened to whatever was being said on the other end.

I held my aching head in my hands as Jonah tried to explain the situation. Finally, a cell phone appeared in my line of sight.

"Would you mind telling my boss why I couldn't finish the job last night?" Jonah asked tightly.

"Yeah, sure." I took the phone. "Um…hi. Harry, is it? I'm Kacey.

From Rapid Confession. I had…a bad night and Jonah was nice enough to let me crash on his couch. *Nothing happened,*" I added, prompting a strange look from Jonah. "He wanted to go back to pick up the rest of my band, but I wasn't doing so hot. He took care of me. Okay?"

Harry promised not to fire Jonah and barked that he wanted the limo back, ASAP. Then he hung up.

Jonah glared at me. "Well?"

"You're not fired. But Harry wants the limo back. Like, now."

He nodded. "Okay, fine. Let's go. I'll take you back to your band's house on the way."

"Um…" I plucked at a stray thread on the afghan.

"What?" Jonah snapped. "You heard my boss. I gotta return the damn car." He cocked his head at me. "Don't you need to get back?"

No, I thought. *I really don't.* I just wasn't up to facing it. None of it. Not yet.

I offered Jonah a weak smile. "The aspirin hasn't made a dent in this headache. Would it be okay with you if I took a nap while you take the limo back? I'll call a cab later and be out of your hair, I promise."

Jonah's dark eyes widened. "You want me to leave you alone in my home while I return the limo—a limo you puked in, by the way—so you can take a nap?"

"I promise I'll just nap and go," I said, then felt my stomach drop. "Wait. I puked in your limo?"

Jonah looked like he had a smart-ass retort ready to go, but he must've felt sorry for me because he said in a gentler tone, "Don't you have a show tonight?"

"I have some time before I have to be back."

Jonah rubbed his chin, looking torn. "After I return the limo, I was planning on going to work. My *other* work," he added. "I have a tight schedule, a really tight schedule, and I need to keep to it."

"I'm sorry. I don't want to interfere." I looked up at him and offered a smile. "What do you do for your other work?"

43

Jonah waved a hand at the glass on the coffee table.

"You're a collector?"

"No, I make these."

My eyes widened as I looked at the glass art with new eyes. There were two sphere-shaped paperweights, one that looked like it was filled with sea life from a coral reef, and the other holding an incredibly intricate swirl of color. Beside the paperweights was a bottle striped with gold dust soaked in ribbons of red.

I picked up the paperweight with the sea life in it: anemones with white and yellow tentacles, ruffled ribbons of color, and—somehow— the speckled colorations of tropical fish.

"A piece of the ocean in my hand," I murmured. I glanced up at him. "You *made* this?"

"Yeah. It's what I do. I'm not a limo driver. That's my night job. By day I'm an industrial artist. Lighting, metal, glass. Mostly glass."

"You're really good," I said. "More than good. This is astonishing."

"Yeah, thanks." He rubbed the back of his neck, watching me hold the glass.

He probably thinks I'm going to break it. I carefully set the paper- weight back down.

"So I gotta get to the hot shop," Jonah said. "That's where I make them, the glass. I'll be there until about two this afternoon." He pressed his lips together, thinking. Finally, he said, "I guess...well, I guess you're welcome to stay here until then."

"Really? You don't mind?"

"I don't know if I'd go that far," Jonah said with dry smile. "There's some food here in the fridge, if or when you're up to eating. Help yourself to the bottled water too. If you really need to smoke, there's a little courtyard in the middle of the complex. You'll see the sidewalk just to the right as you go out. It has benches and an ashtray."

"Okay, sure. Got it," I said, relief flooding me that I had a few hours before I had to face the music. So to speak.

At the kitchen counter, Jonah scribbled something on a piece of paper and brought it back to me. "This is my cell number. If you need anything, just call. Phone's in the kitchen."

I took the paper and met his gaze. Up close, his eyes were warmer. A deep, rich brown.

"Thanks a ton for letting me crash," I said. "I really appreciate it. Not many people would let a total stranger hang out in their place unsupervised."

Jonah smiled tightly. "Tell me about it."

He pocketed his keys and went out, locking the door behind him. He left me alone in his place. Me. The girl who wrecked the Pony Club just hours before, puked in his car, invaded his space, and almost cost him his job. He was being so cool about it. More than cool.

He trusts me. Sort of.

Not that I deserved trust. I winced at the thought of what the green room was going to look like tonight. Having to go and do another show filled me with a strange kind of dread.

What is wrong with me?

I figured I could get into less trouble if I slept, and I wasn't lying to Jonah about needing a nap anyway. My headache thundered, and I wanted to sleep for a million years. I lay down against the couch cushion and pulled the old afghan over my shoulders. It wasn't as ugly as I'd thought at first. Its weight was comforting. Like a good hug.

My heavy gaze fell over the beautiful array of blown glass on the coffee table. Gorgeous swirls of color and design, trapped and floating in the center of the paperweights, wrapped like ribbons along the body of the bottle.

"Beautiful," I murmured. My scattering thoughts imagined it would be peaceful and quiet inside one of those paperweights. I could float weightless in a glass ocean, suspended in beauty, surrounded by color and stillness. No noise. No pounding drums or tearing riffs or screaming fans. Just...silence.

And safety.

I was asleep within moments.

Chapter 6

KACEY

I WOKE UP, UNABLE TO REMEMBER WHERE I WAS UNTIL MY GAZE FOUND the glass paperweights. My limo driver's apartment. Jonah Fletcher. Fletch, like the Chevy Chase movie. I smiled to myself and stretched.

The light streaming in from the window was sharp and white, the kind that arrived with high noon. The DVR clock said it was one. I'd slept for six straight hours. My stomach was no longer queasy but clamoring for food.

I wanted a cigarette more. I took my pack and headed outside, toward the courtyard Jonah told me about.

The heat smacked me upside the head, and my headache threatened to return. I didn't know how anyone could get used to desert heat. Born and raised in San Diego, where it was almost always seventy-four degrees and breezy, I couldn't tolerate this kind of stark, dry heat for longer than a day or two. It was like living in an oven. Though I sort of loathed the idea of rejoining the band, I was glad we were leaving Nevada on Tuesday.

I sat on one of the wrought-iron benches in the dinky courtyard, shaded by one-half of the L-shaped apartment complex. The court-yard was dirt and crushed limestone, lined with cactus and some other desert brush I didn't recognize. Nothing here was real green, only pale green, as if coated in desert sand.

I puffed my cigarette and mentally examined my thought about rejoining my band. Did I really *loathe* the idea? We were on the verge of stardom. Buckets of money and loads of fame lay ahead.

So why did I feel like I wanted to walk away?

Because you don't want to end up dead, came a helpful thought.

I shivered despite the insane heat and took a long drag on my smoke. An apartment door facing the courtyard opened, and an older lady in a peach-colored housedress, slippers, and curlers in her short hair started out. She stopped when she saw me.

I waved. "Hot enough for ya?"

The woman snorted and flapped both hands at me, then retreated behind her door with a slam.

I glanced down at my boobs, which were pushing out of the bustier, and had to laugh. I was still encased in the latex and vinyl of my show outfit and sweating like mad. The old lady probably thought I was a prostitute. Sweat trickled down my back, and I could feel it along my sides where the corset-like top squeezed me. Going outside in the heat had been a bad idea.

I crushed my cigarette under my boot and headed back to Jonah's apartment, praying I hadn't locked myself out. Not only had I not locked myself out, I'd left the door slightly ajar.

Nice, I thought. *He lets you crash and you leave his door open.*

The apartment complex didn't exactly scream *Wealth and riches lie within*, but Jonah had his beautiful blown glass. It looked valuable to me.

Back inside the merciful air-conditioning, I sat back on the couch and pulled off my boots. My fishnets were torn in a dozen places. I took them off too, closed my eyes in relief, and stretched my legs. The cigarette had done nothing for my hangover. My tongue felt too big, and my teeth tasted like I hadn't brushed them in a week. Maybe Jonah had some mouthwash. Or I could finger-brush my teeth with his toothpaste.

After taking a short pee in the one bathroom in the place, I went to wash my hands in the sink. I expected to find all kinds of scary "guy living alone" nastiness—shaving residue or phlegm wads. During the short time I lived with Chett, he was always leaving disgusting messes in the sink or toilet.

Jonah was not Chett.

Like the rest of his place, the sink area was clean and uncluttered. I started to rinse my hands, but the reflection in the mirror stopped me cold.

What was left of my eye makeup was smeared down my cheeks, as if I'd been crying. My lipstick had left a pale red stain under my lower lip, like some kind of rash. My hair was a tangled mess, and my pale skin appeared sallow under the fluorescent lights. Mortification that I had been sitting around talking to Jonah like this all morning punched me in the gut.

"God, Kacey…"

I cleaned up the smeared eyeliner and lipstick with toilet paper, then opened the medicine cabinet in search of toothpaste. I froze at what I saw.

The Crest and the Listerine were there, but they were crowded out by row after row of medication. Orange pill bottles with white caps as far as the eye could see.

"Holy drugstore, Batman."

I turned some of the bottles my way to read the names. None were remotely familiar.

Prednisone. Rapamune. Gengraf. Cyclosporine. Norvasc.

"What the fuck?" I turned more labels to face me. Some had names I thought I recognized from TV ads: pain meds, a few for high blood pressure, two for lowering cholesterol, and one bottle of antibiotics.

Why would a young guy need meds for cholesterol and blood pressure?

The pink seam of the scar on Jonah's chest reared its head in my memory. Some kind of heart condition? That would explain the anti-smoking and the small pharmacy he had going on in this medicine cabinet.

I closed the cabinet door quickly, toothpaste forgotten, feeling like I'd just walked in on someone naked or had read a highly private diary entry. I left the bathroom and went into the kitchen in search of more water. I needed to wash out the bad taste in my mouth from having snooped into Jonah's life.

In the fridge, I found the bottled water Jonah mentioned and not much else. Some wilting vegetables, packaged salads, and at least three trays of various casseroles covered in tin foil. I took a peek in the freezer, taking a moment to appreciate the cold air, and saw more packaged food: Lean Cuisine and "heart-healthy" brands, as if Jonah were on a diet.

This was not the fridge of a typical Las Vegas bachelor.

And the medicine cabinet is?

My stomach twisted with nerves instead of hunger. I'd never been good around sick people. I never knew the right thing to say, could never find the right balance between sympathy and pity. I clammed up during any kind of health discussion, and hospitals gave me the absolute heebie-jeebies.

You're being stupid. You need to eat. You haven't eaten since…

I couldn't remember the last time I'd eaten. Apparently, I was on a diet too. A liquid diet.

A bowl of cereal might be safe. I opened a few cabinets, looking for a plain old box of Cheerios. Instead, I found a shit-ton of vitamins, supplements, and protein powders.

I closed that cabinet in a hurry.

"Dammit."

Jonah had said I could help myself, but now my appetite was gone completely. He wasn't just a total stranger; he was a total stranger who had a serious medical condition. It felt really intrusive to know all this so soon. I was getting a crash course on his extremely personal shit, and he knew next to nothing about me. I wish I'd been brave enough to just let him take me back to the Summerlin house.

I wandered back into the living area, not entirely sure what to do. The TV might have a news report about what happened at the Pony Club last night, so I left it off and tried to let the quiet of Jonah's place settle me.

I couldn't sit still. As a kid, my mother had been quick to diagnose me as ADHD, using it to excuse my exuberant behavior to my dad, who got irritated at the slightest noise or sign of rambunctiousness. I was always restless in my own skin. As I got older, I felt like two people trapped in the same body, an introvert who shied away at her dad's angry lectures, and an extrovert who practiced her electric guitar in the garage as loudly as possible to piss him off. At constant war with myself.

Right now, the introvert in me whispered to enjoy the quiet.

The extrovert wanted a drink.

Bookshelves lined one wall of Jonah's living room: industrial arts, art history, biographies of artists—some I'd heard of, most I hadn't. I liked romances, horror, and a fun mystery now and then. Jonah was all nonfiction. Boring.

I kept moving.

On the opposite wall hung a bunch of framed pictures. Most showed Jonah smiling with what looked like his mom and dad, and a good-looking, broody guy. A brother, maybe? The guy had the same basic facial structure as Jonah, the same dark hair, but he was shorter and bulkier. His features were more chiseled. His eyes were a lighter brown and harder. Dark tattoos snaked around his well-built arms.

He looked exactly like the kind of guy I loved to take home for the night, losing myself in everything that was masculine and strong and powerful about him. A guy who would bail at the first rays of sunlight the next morning, no strings attached, just how I liked it.

Jonah looked like the kind of guy you wanted to meet on the side of the road at night if your car had a flat.

Or if you got blackout drunk and wrecked a Vegas club.

"That too," I muttered absently and kept perusing.

The same hot brother and two other friends—a handsome guy with dark skin and a wide smile, and a pretty girl with long hair—showed up in a lot of pictures: at a club, at a party, surrounded by tall green trees on a camping trip, or on a desert plain with the sun rising or setting behind them.

In almost every picture, Jonah wore a bright, open smile that made his whole face light up. Such a contrast to the stiff, serious expression he wore around me. I couldn't help but smile back at him.

I noticed that one girl—a beautiful brunette with delicate features—was beside Jonah in a lot of pics. Jonah usually had his arm slung around her, that same happy smile on his face, while the woman looked pinched and posed, as if she had turned her "best side" to the camera.

Above the photos were the two framed degrees I'd noticed this morning. One was a diploma from the University of Nevada, Las Vegas, and the other from Carnegie Mellon.

Carnegie Mellon...that was a big-time university. Maybe even Ivy League. Jonah was talented *and* smart. He looked young, only a few years older than me. Shouldn't he still be at Carnegie Mellon? Or did whatever medical condition he had force him to quit?

I touched a photo of a laughing, smiling Jonah. "What happened to you?"

He's fine. He's making glass stuff at a hot shop, whatever that is. You, on the other hand, started a riot and then blacked out. The better question is, what happened to you?

"I'm fine," I told no one, even though I'd have given anything for a Bloody Mary just then.

All at once, that damn bustier felt like it was ten sizes too small instead of only two. I couldn't breathe and started to sweat all over again. The AC unit was churning quietly at the window overlooking the busy street. Rather than give the neighbors a thrill, I went back into the kitchen, pulling at the laces that held the bustier together on the sides. I peeled it off and let it hit the floor, leaving me in a black strapless bra as I threw open the freezer.

I was too short. The icy air hit my face but not where I needed it. I spied a step stool near the cabinets, dragged it in front of the freezer, and climbed up. I lifted my hair off my neck and held it bunched to my head, letting the air hit me under the arms and chest, cooling my burning skin and dampening my urge for a stiff drink.

"Um…hello?"

Jonah. I hadn't heard him come in over the whir of the freezer. I nearly toppled off the stool.

"Oh my God, seriously?" I snatched my bustier off the ground and held it over my chest like a shield. "Scare a gal to death, why don't you?"

He looked like he was biting back a smile. "Sorry. I was just trying to figure out what you were doing."

"Fishing out one of your Lean Cuisines with my boobs," I retorted. "What do you think I was doing? I'm cooling off."

"I'm pretty sure that's what the air conditioner is for," he said, jerking his thumb behind him.

"Yeah, but it's by the window, smart guy. I didn't want to flash the entire street."

Jonah held up his hands. "Point taken."

A short silence descended where it was obvious neither of us knew what to do or say next.

I huffed a sigh. "Look, are you going to stand there staring at me all day, or can you maybe help me out? Your neighbor already thinks I'm a call girl. This is a stage outfit, not leisure wear."

Now it was totally obvious he was trying not to smile. "Hold on a sec." He went into the bedroom and came back with a plain black T-shirt. "This work?"

I turned my back to him and pulled the shirt over my head. It was too big and a V-neck, which was totally not my style, and it smelled like him.

Once more, the feeling of being too personal too soon with this guy came over me. Now I was standing barefoot in his kitchen, wearing his shirt.

"Thanks," I said, turning back to face him. Another short silence, during which Jonah stared at me. Not in a creepy way, more like he was trying to figure out what to make of me.

I got that a lot.

I shifted from foot to foot. "How was your glassmaking?"

"Blowing."

"Pardon?"

"It's glassblowing," Jonah said. "I don't make the glass; I make things out of super-heated glass by blowing air through a pipe..." He waved a hand. "Never mind. It's a long process. I don't want to bore you with the details, and we'd best get you back—"

"It doesn't sound boring," I said quickly. "I can't even imagine how you make that stuff. So intricate. The paperweight with the sea creatures? I mean...how do you do it?"

God, I was babbling like an idiot, trying to stay above the surface, because the thought of going back to Summerlin was like a lead weight dragging me down. Jonah frowned, clearly trying to decide if I really cared or if I was just stalling.

Both.

"I could explain," he said, "but that would take all day, and I have a tight schedule to adhere to, and..."

"Me being here is a huge pain in your ass," I finished, trying not to sag. "I get it. It's cool."

"You're not a pain in the ass," Jonah said.

I cocked my head at him.

"Okay, maybe a little," he said with a small smile.

I took that smile as a good sign. "Hey, you know what? I'm fucking starving. How about we get some food somewhere? I still have about an hour before I need to get back and get ready for the show. Whaddya say? You up for something? My treat."

53

Jonah's face stiffened and the muscles in his shoulders tensed up. "I have to drive tonight, at six, and I'm on a really tight schedule…"

"You keep saying that." I chucked him in the shoulder like we were old pals. "Don't you ever break your routine?"

"No. I do not."

"Oh." I bit my lip. I was nothing if not tenacious. "One greasy post-hangover diner lunch won't take that long, will it? Half hour, forty-five minutes, tops."

Jonah's shrewd dark eyes met mine, and I could feel him studying me. He was observant, this guy, and I felt like my insecurities were written all over me.

Or maybe it's because you look like the poster girl for the walk of shame.

"I said you were welcome to eat anything here," Jonah said finally.

"And it was kind of you to offer, but you don't have much in the way of…actual food."

"I have lots of dietary restrictions," he said.

"Sure." I coughed. "But why exactly?"

Jonah looked to be waging an internal struggle, whether or not to tell me what I already suspected.

"I have a heart condition," he said slowly.

"Oh?" As if I hadn't already snooped through his medicine cabinet. My eyes itched to glance at the scar that began in the hollow of his throat. I kept my gaze plastered to his face. I must've looked like a crazy person, staring so intently, because Jonah took a step backward.

"Anyway. That's another long story and…yeah, I guess we could grab some food if you're really hungry."

"Starved!"

I rushed back to the couch to put my thigh-high boots back on, which looked strange with my leather skirt and men's T-shirt, but I was out of the bustier, thank God.

"I'm ready."

"Okay," Jonah said hesitantly. "A quick lunch, and then I get you back to Summerlin."

"Sounds great."

He probably only agreed to food so we would change the subject, but no matter the reason, I was happy for a stay of execution. It wasn't much, but I took it.

Chapter 7

JONAH

I LED KACEY OUT THROUGH THE PARKING LOT TO MY TRUCK, A SMALL pickup in blue, its flatbed filled with cardboard boxes. I held the passenger door open for her, which seemed to surprise her. This whole lunch outing surprised me, not in the schedule by any stretch. But obviously Kacey was in no hurry to rejoin her band. After whatever catastrophe she'd caused at the Pony Club, staying with me was an act of self-preservation.

I climbed behind the wheel, and my eyes strayed to Kacey's thighs—smooth skin between her boots and the almost nonexistent miniskirt. Part of a colorful tattoo was partially visible on her left thigh, and the urge to see the rest of it was ridiculously strong. Kacey was easy on the eyes. Actually, she was more than that. But so what? She was more Theo's type, with her bleached hair, leather, and tattoos.

But I couldn't keep my eyes off her bare skin. How long had it been since I'd touched a woman?

One year, four months, thirteen days, and eighteen hours.

I scoffed at my inner mathematician, though the number probably wasn't far off. I hadn't been with a woman since my ex-girlfriend, Audrey. Before I got sick.

"What's with the boxes in the back?" Kacey asked, jolting me from my thoughts. "Are you moving?"

"No, they're full of glass," I said, grateful for the distraction. "Old bottles and jars that I melt down to make my pieces. I'm going to take them to the hot shop tomorrow."

"So the hot shop is where you *blow* the glass?" Kacey snickered.

I arched a brow at her.

"I know, I know. I'm twenty-two, but I have the sense of humor of a fourteen-year-old boy." She turned in her seat toward me. "And how do you do that?"

"Do what?"

"Raise only one eyebrow. I've always wanted to."

I shrugged. "I don't know. I just can."

"Do it again."

"Why?"

"Because it's cool."

I arched my brow at her. "Is it?"

She laughed and sat back in her seat, satisfied. The broad smile remained on her lips as she watched Las Vegas passing outside her window. Even only half turned to me, she had a stunning smile.

"So what are you working on?" she asked after a moment. "At the hot shop."

"Well...I'm working on an exhibit for a local gallery. It opens in October. The exhibit, not the gallery."

Smooth, Fletcher. But it had been months since I'd spoken to a stranger about the exhibit. I'd whittled my circle down to exactly three friends, my family, and the curator of the gallery. Until Kacey, I hadn't fully grasped just how small a circle that was.

"Will you sell your glass at this exhibit?" Kacey asked. "Like those beautiful paperweights?"

"Yes, I'll have small pieces like that for sale, but the main focus will be a large-scale installation."

She started to ask another question as I pulled the truck into the parking lot of Mulligan's, a mom-and-pop diner. It was nearly three in the afternoon; the lunch rush was over, plenty of parking to be had. I pulled into a spot near the door.

"This is right up the street from you," she said. "We could've walked."

"In this heat?" I said and shut off the engine.

"Good point. The heat is god-awful. I don't know how you desert dwellers cope."

I held the diner door open for her, surprising her again. She beamed at me, and I almost lost my train of thought.

"I was born and raised in the desert," I said. "I'm used to it, but some people can't hack it. Wimps and pansies, every one."

Kacey snorted and elbowed me lightly in the side as she breezed past me into the restaurant. She sighed with relief as we entered the air-conditioning, then caught me giving her a knowing look.

"Oh, fine. I'm a wimp," she laughed. "Get us a table, smart-ass, while I use the restroom."

I chuckled on my way to the hostess station. It was easy to be around this girl. And it seemed like she found it easy to be around me, like we'd known each other for years instead of hours.

A waitress greeted me. "How many, hon?"

"Two," I said and felt an immediate twinge in my chest.

I'd heard you could cut off a limb but still feel the pain of its absence. I didn't miss Audrey. She'd cut *me* off, right after my transplant surgery. We'd planned a certain life together, but when the virus wrecked my heart and nearly killed me, it wrecked our plans and killed our relationship.

Theo would never forgive her for leaving, but I got over her quickly—even after being together for three years. It hurt that she left, and the timing sure as shit could've been better, but I forgave her for leaving to find someone else, someone healthy with whom she could fall madly in love and build a real life.

I didn't miss her. Yet in answering a waitress's innocuous question, I realized I missed "the two of us." Being part of a couple, holding a door for someone, requesting a table for two, joking, teasing, being someone's smart-ass... My tiny circle of loved ones didn't include a girlfriend and wouldn't ever again. I thought I'd made peace with it, but some part of me, buried down deep, said otherwise.

I sank into the booth and took up a menu to distract myself from thoughts I didn't want. Mulligan's had typical country diner fare—breakfast served all day, and a variety of burgers and sandwiches for lunch. Unfortunately, more than half the items were strictly forbidden to me.

Kacey flounced into the seat across from me, looking scrubbed and vibrant. I tried not to think about the fact that she was wearing my T-shirt, like girlfriends sometimes did with their boyfriend's clothes.

The waitress set two waters on the table. "Coffee?"

"Yes, please," Kacey said. "Desperately."

"Decaf for me," I said.

The waitress moved on, and Kacey shot me a funny look. "Decaf?"

"I can't have caffeine."

"What a tragedy." She leaned over the table. "You know what they say: there's a time and a place for decaf, *never* and *in the trash.*"

I laughed with her. "I'll have to remember that one."

Kacey studied the menu. "I'm so hungry, I might have one of everything. What about you? What are you going to get? Wait..." She let the menu drop to the table. "What *can* you get?"

"Not sure yet. My options are kind of limited."

"Because of your dietary restrictions."

"Yeah."

"Well, shit, Jonah, why did you bring me here?" She flapped her hand at the menu. "This is all grease and fat."

I laughed and held up my hands at her sudden outburst. "Whoa, it's cool. I'll find something."

She bit her lip. "Yeah, but…"

"I brought you here for you," I said. "This is perfect hangover food. I used to come here with friends when I was at UNLV." I tapped the corner of her menu. "Get whatever you want. It's fine, I swear."

She still looked dubious as the waitress came back with our coffees, putting an orange decaf doily under my mug.

"You ready to order, hon?"

Kacey gnawed her lip.

"Order," I told her. "Unless you'd rather we go back to my place and fire up some Lean Cuisines."

"When you put it that way…" Kacey turned to the waitress and said in a deep voice, "*Yes, very well, I'll have a Bloody Mary and a steak sandwich and a steak sandwich.*"

The waitress gave her a look, and I frowned at the Bloody Mary.

Kacey flashed her eyes, looking between us. "It's from *Fletch*? The movie?" She jabbed a finger across the table. "You, Jonah *Fletcher*, can't tell me you haven't seen the greatest Chevy Chase movie of all time?"

"Sorry, I missed it," I said.

"It's a classic," Kacey said. "I have a thing for eighties movies."

The waitress cleared her throat. "So do I, honey, but I don't have steak sandwiches or Bloody Marys."

Kacey ordered a cheeseburger and fries, and I ordered a Cobb salad, hold the bacon, and a side of wheat toast, no butter.

When the waitress moved on, Kacey shook her head. "No bacon? The only good thing about a Cobb salad is you get to put bacon on it."

I shrugged. "Not on the list."

"That sucks. What else can't you eat?"

"No red meat, no chocolate, no salt on anything…"

Kacey nearly choked on her coffee. "Whoa, whoa, whoa. No *chocolate?*"

"I miss salt more," I said. "And butter. Nothing fatty, nothing delicious." I laughed dryly. "In summation, I'm not allowed to eat anything delicious."

Kacey shook her head. "I don't know how you do it."

"Not like I have a choice. And there are worse things."

"I'm trying to imagine something worse than not being able to eat chocolate." She froze, then set her coffee mug down, her smile vanishing. "Oh my God, that's a terrible thing to say to someone with a heart condition. I'm sorry. I do that a lot—just blurt out whatever pops into my head."

"Hey, it's cool. I can't do cocaine anymore either, but that turned out to be a blessing in disguise for all the money I'm saving."

Her embarrassment fell away with a smile. "Yeah, you look like the cocaine type to me."

"Total cokehead. Reformed."

Kacey relaxed and sat back in her seat. "So you went to UNLV? That's where you studied industrial arts?"

"Yes, my brother and I both studied art there."

"And then Carnegie Mellon?"

I sipped my coffee. "You sure ask a lot of questions."

"You have a lot of photos and diplomas on your wall. Before I decided to cool off my boobs in your freezer, I had some time to kill."

I set my cup down before I spilled it. "That's not something you hear every day."

"It is in my world," Kacey said with a rueful smile, as if it was an old joke she'd gotten tired of hearing. But she waved it off.

"Carnegie Mellon is...where?" she asked.

"Pennsylvania. Talk about a weather shock. The first winter I was there, I wanted to hibernate."

"Wimp," she said over the rim of her coffee. "But from one pansy to another, the East Coast has too much weather for me too. I was born and raised in San Diego, where if it drizzles, people lose their shit."

The waitress arrived with our food. I never let anyone alter their diet around me, but the scent wafting from Kacey's plate curled around my nose, rich and meaty and grilled. I glanced down at my salad, which smelled like nothing, and took a bite, mostly for Kacey's sake.

"So you have a gallery opening in October?" Kacey asked, dabbing her mouth with a napkin. "It's too bad I won't be around to see it. I'll be on tour for the next bazillion years."

"A bazillion years…that's a long tour. I hope you like to travel."

She shrugged. "Eh. It's not all it's cracked up to be."

"No?"

"It sounds ungrateful. Most musicians would give their right tit to be signed by a label and go on a multicity tour, right?"

"As I have no tit to give, right or left, I couldn't say for sure," I said with a grin. "But from my professional observation—as your chauffeur—it doesn't look like you're having the time of your life."

Her eyes flicked up to the ceiling. "What gave it away? The trashed concert venue or blacking out and puking in your limo?"

"Tie."

She smiled. "I miss the honest music without all the theatrics, you know? I used to love just sitting with my guitar and picking out a song. Finding a riff or a melody, falling into the zone of writing lyrics."

"Did you go to school in San Diego for music?"

"No, I didn't go to college at all," she said. "But…I've been playing since I was a kid. My grandmother gave me a guitar when I was ten. I liked to play, but mostly I liked writing songs. The guitar was a way to put a tune behind my words. It could have been anything—a piano, drums… I just wanted to write and sing."

"You sing too?"

"Only backup nowadays," she said, not quite meeting my eyes. "And I don't write my own stuff anymore. Just songs for the band."

"Why?"

She traced the line of one dark eyebrow absently with her finger. Her hair was blond, but her eyebrows were darker. And perfect.

"We're a team now. I write for us," Kacey was saying. "But in a way it's better for me. I need the band." She glanced up at me through lowered lashes. "I don't do so well on my own."

I nodded, struggling for something constructive to say. To stay focused on her words and not the little details of her face.

"I feel like everything's moving so fast," Kacey continued, "and I don't have time to sit and sort things out. Like what do I want to do? Is this what I want to do? Be a rock star? Half of me says, *Hell yeah!* The other half of me is scared."

"Scared of what?"

"The lifestyle. The partying. I feel like I do that so I don't have to make any real decisions. I just follow the band, play really loud music, and drink a lot because…"

"Because…?" I asked gently

Her shrug was casual, even if her words weren't. "Because I have nowhere else to go."

An image of the bodyguard carrying her out of the club last night flashed through my mind, juxtaposed with the promo shot of her giving the world the finger. Vulnerable and tough at the same time.

She seems lost…

Kacey sat back and waved a hand, as if her words were cigarette smoke to dispel. "Anyway, that's my angsty hangover story."

I knew that wasn't all of it. I had the impression she had a ton more stories and a ton more songs in her.

Silence fell between us as I sipped my decaf, which was growing cold. A half dozen times I started a sentence, wanting to share something with her. Something deeply personal, as if there were some cosmic scoreboard that needed to be evened up.

But my most personal thing was too much. Too dark. Kacey Dawson was luminous, and I couldn't stand the idea of watching my deepest truth settle over her like a shroud, dimming her light with its awful finality.

I toyed with my MedicAlert bracelet under the table. I could at least tell her why I had to eat a fucking salad instead of a burger.

I started to; then the waitress appeared with her coffee carafe. She refilled Kacey's mug, then started to fill mine.

Kacey's hand shot out and covered my mug. "Wait! Is that regular? He can only have decaf!"

The waitress jerked the pot back with a small cry. "Damn, honey, I nearly scalded you."

"I'm sorry," Kacey said. "I just… It's important." She glanced at me.

"It's not worth you getting burned," I said. But the gesture touched me.

"I'll get the other pot," the waitress said and retreated in a huff.

Kacey's hand was back in her lap, and her cheeks were pink. "Sorry. I got a little overexcited."

"You go all the way up to eleven," I said, figuring an eighties movie reference would smooth things over.

Her head shot up, a smile breaking across her face like the dawn. "*This Is Spinal Tap*," she said. "A classic."

I held on to her eyes, felt the moment between us, warm and thick. "Thanks for guarding my coffee," I said. "It's important."

Her eyes softened. "Will you tell me why?"

"I, uh…I had a heart transplant," I said.

"Oh," she said, sitting back in her booth seat. Her eyes stared far off a moment, then she gave her head a brusque shake. "A heart transplant. But…you're so young. Twenty-five?"

"Twenty-six. The virus that wrecked my heart didn't give a shit how old I was." I smiled ruefully. "Viruses are assholes like that."

Kacey didn't smile. She pointed toward my wrist and the MedicAlert bracelet. "Can I see?"

I slid my arm toward her on the table. She flipped the rectangular tag over, from the red enameled cross to the words inscribed on the other side.

"*Heart transplant patient. See wallet card.*" Kacey looked up at me. "What's on the wallet card?"

"My emergency contact info, my blood type, yadda yadda."

Her gaze pressed me. "'Yadda yadda'?"

"What to do in case I get in trouble."

She nodded. Next, she'd ask what kind of trouble I could get into, and I'd make up something about medication side effects, which was a hell of a lot easier to hear than total heart failure.

Instead, she asked, "Was it recent?"

"Almost a year and a half ago."

Her eyes widened. "That's really recent." She let go of the tag, and the heel of her hand settled on mine. A frozen, soundless moment, then her hand slid backward, palm to palm. Her fingers curled around mine and held still. I stared as my thumb came down on top of her knuckles and slowly moved back and forth.

The waitress came back with the orange-lipped decaf pot. The look on her face was sour until she saw our hands. She smiled as she topped up my cup.

"I'm sorry to hear all this," Kacey said, when the waitress had moved on. She gave my fingers a final squeeze and let go.

I put my empty, destitute hand in my lap. "So am I."

Kacey toyed with her spoon. "Is it hard to talk about?"

"Yeah," I admitted. "Only the people closest to me know."

"And I'm the newcomer busting into your personal space and asking all kinds of questions."

"Yes," I said. "You are goddamn nosy."

She squawked and chucked a french fry at me. I laughed and plucked it off my lap.

"Wait, shit! You can't have that!" Kacey reached across the table to snatch it back. "I did not just almost scald myself over your damn coffee so you could eat a fry instead."

"Your sacrifice is duly noted." I crammed the whole thing in my mouth and nearly groaned in ecstasy. I'd forgotten how good a fried potato could be. Salty, greasy perfection. "Holy God, that tastes good."

Kacey moved her plate out of my reach. "That's all you get, buddy. I'm not going to be responsible for breaking your diet. I've already broken the routine you keep talking about, right? I'm a bad influence on you..."

My laughter died and my smile froze. She was right. In the space of one lunch, Kacey had not only broken my diet, but she'd put a dent in my carefully crafted routine. It wasn't just taking up my time that could've been spent in the hot shop. It was *this*. Lunch. Easy laughter and sharing. Trusting one another with secrets. Fingers curled softly together...

This was a forbidden item on the menu.

This was bad for my heart.

I wiped my mouth with a napkin and set it on the table.

"Yeah, speaking of my schedule," I said. "I only have a few hours before I start my shift at A-1, and you have a show tonight. We should get you back to Summerlin."

Kacey's smile faded away, and her chin tilted at my obvious change in demeanor. "Oh. Sure." Her luminous light dimmed. "Ready whenever you are."

Chapter 8

JONAH

I DROVE US BACK TO MY APARTMENT SO KACEY COULD RETRIEVE HER bustier and the remnants of her fishnet stockings. But when I pulled into the parking lot, she didn't get out of the truck, only sat there, unmoving.

"Throw the stupid bustier away," she said finally.

"You sure?"

"Let's just keep going," she said, but it sounded more like, *Let's get it over with.*

I drove Kacey back to the Summerlin house in silence. I stopped the truck in the grand circular driveway. Kacey climbed out of the truck and stood facing the house.

"I fucking hate Las Vegas," she muttered so low I almost didn't hear her. She turned to me, leaned into the passenger window. "Thanks for taking care of me last night."

"No problem," I said. *Say something else. Say something better.* But the words stuck in my throat.

"And thanks for paying for lunch. It was supposed to be my treat, but I had no money on me. Naturally." She shook her head. "If you wait a sec, I'll run up and get some cash."

"Forget it," I said. "I ate a french fry for the first time in a year. It was worth twenty bucks."

She raised her eyes to mine. "Thanks for that too."

"What? Eating a fry?"

"For cheering me up. Every time I felt a little down, you made a joke to lift me up."

I nodded like a mute idiot, not sure what would fall out of my mouth, a joke or the truth: making her laugh was like hitting a mini jackpot.

She shuffled her feet. "Okay, well. I should get back."

"Break a leg tonight," I finally managed.

"I'll be lucky if that's all I break," she said with a weak laugh. She started to close the door, then stopped. "Thanks for being a good guy, Jonah. There's a shortage in the world."

She shut the door and walked away, her pale hair glinting like spun glass in the sun. I watched her walk to the entrance—to make sure she got in okay, I told myself—waiting until she entered the dark confines of the house. It swallowed her up, and the door shut behind her.

———

Without Kacey, my apartment felt airless and sealed. And silent. Had it always been this quiet? I went to the couch to fold up the afghan. Remnants of Kacey's perfume wafted up, and I nearly put the damn thing to my nose to inhale.

You do not have the time for this.

I had to rebuild my fortifications, reforge the armor I needed to make it to October. I had to erase last night and this afternoon, bury it along with the memory of Kacey's eyes when she smiled or how her bare thigh in her short skirt nearly woke a physical desire I had been denying still existed…

With a silent apology to my departed grandmother, I wadded up the blanket and tossed it in the closet. Then my desire and I took a very cold shower.

After, I stood in my silent kitchen, drinking the dregs of a disgusting protein shake that was no match for the french fry Kacey had pelted me with...

For fuck's sake, get over it.

Dwelling on this woman or any woman was a waste of time. I wasn't a one-night-stand kind of guy. I'd never been wired that way, and starting a relationship now was out of the question. Not with Kacey Dawson, not with anyone.

No more taking beautiful women home with you, or even to lunch. Not anymore.

I checked my phone. It was five o'clock on Saturday night, and I was dressed for work. I had two texts from Theo and a voice message from my father, as usual. Tomorrow I would spend all day at the hot shop, then have dinner with my family. Everything as it should be. My routine had been shaken a little but remained intact.

On my way out the door, I scooped up Kacey's bustier and torn fishnets, then chucked them in the dumpster in the parking lot.

"We now return to our regularly scheduled program."

My boss, Harry Kelton, had been out when I returned the car from last night, but he was in this night. I suspected he wanted to reiterate—in person—that taking drunk girls home was not in my contract.

"Fletcher," he said by way of greeting and pulled my paperwork for the night from the mess on his desk. He tossed me a set of car keys. I caught them one-handed as I studied the night's assignment under the flickering fluorescents and gaped at what I read.

"Rapid Confession? Again?"

Kacey...

Harry laced his hands behind his head, round circles of sweat darkening his button-down under his arms. "Their manager specifically asked for you."

"After last night?"

"I guess he forgave you," Harry said. "Lucky thing too. It's a good charter."

I shook my head in frustration. "It's not lucky if he's pissed off and trying to screw me out of another tip."

"You ditched them last night," Harry said, leaning forward and jabbing a fat finger on the mess on his desk. "*I'm* lucky he hired—and paid for—another charter. It would've well been within his rights to cancel last night's payment, never mind your tip." He leaned back in his chair, making it creak. "Win-win for both of us, Fletcher. I keep his business, and you get a second chance."

"Boss…"

Harry turned that jabbing finger in my direction. "You're my best driver, Jonah, but I'm none too happy about last night. Finish the job if you want to keep yours."

I left Harry's office in a daze, his words echoing in my head.

A second chance…

"Goddammit," I muttered. I almost turned around to storm back into the office and tell Harry to forget it, someone else could take the charter. Except Harry was on the verge of firing me, and I couldn't afford to lose my job.

I strode through the garage, past rows of black and white limousines, town cars, and sedans, bolstering myself.

I can be professional. I'll do my job and get through this night.

"Hey, Fletcher…"

I turned to see Kyle Porter, another driver, headed to his car.

"I heard you got the Rapid Confession gig. *Twice,* you lucky bastard. The guitar chick is fucking hot."

I climbed behind the wheel of my black stretch and slammed the door. "Tell me about it."

By seven o'clock, I was back at the Summerlin residence, parked in the circular drive, waiting for the band to emerge. The sun had only begun to set, streaking the sky orange and purple on the western horizon. Normally, I'd have studied the play of light, thinking how I could recapture those colors in swirls of melted glass. But I was too distracted. What was I going to say to her? Make a joke? Make her smile and laugh? Or just play it cool? Keep to the routine…

"It's you!"

I jerked out of my thoughts to see the band and their manager, bags in hand, nearly at the car. And Kacey…

She bounded up to me in leggings, ankle boots, and an oversize black T-shirt with Ziggy Stardust on the front. She'd piled her hair on top of her head in a messy knot, and her face was scrubbed free of makeup—lit up with a combination of joy and relief that sent my borrowed heart into a fit of rapid beats.

She planted her hands on her hips, giving me a playful, arch look. "Are you stalking me?"

Before I could reply, Jimmy Ray sidled up to Kacey and slung his arm around her. "So this is the heroic limo driver who took care of my girl last night. I hired him again, kitten, as a personal thank-you." He winked at me. "She's a little handful, isn't she?"

I'd seen pricks like this guy a million times during my six months as a limo driver in Vegas. I always treated them with detached courtesy. But Jimmy's hand hovered over Kacey's right breast, and an urge to punch his smug face came over me like a tidal wave.

"Go on, get," Jimmy said to Kacey. He unslung his arm and smacked her lightly on the ass to hustle her into the limo.

An embarrassed smile flickered over Kacey's lips, and she didn't look at me as she climbed in.

Jimmy Ray extended his hand to me, and I took it out of professional habit.

"All is forgiven, buddy." He pulled me close. "I hope you had a good time with my girl last night, but we're not going to make a habit out of it, yeah? Don't wear out the goods."

His hand oozed out of mine, leaving a hundred-dollar bill in my palm.

I crumpled the money into my fist as he climbed in the back. Only the threat of losing my job kept me from chucking it at his feet. I shut the limo door hard—a hair away from slamming it—and loaded the band's bags into the trunk.

Once behind the wheel, my eyes itched to find Kacey in the rearview mirror, but the partition went up, muffling the sounds of loud talk and laughter. I pulled out of Summerlin and drove to the Strip, already glittering in the falling twilight.

Just east of the Flamingo, near the convention center, I veered off the boulevard and maneuvered my stretch to the rear parking lot of the Pony Club, just as I had the night before. I opened doors and unloaded the bags one by one. But now I was acutely conscious of Kacey behind me, waiting her turn. She came last, and I turned to hand off her bag. Her eyes were cerulean blue and made electric by the dingy amber light of the streetlamp that flickered on above us.

"So Jimmy requested you personally," she said quietly, as the others filed in the back door.

"He did."

"I hope he wasn't a dick to you. He can be…"

"Dickish?"

"Yeah. But he's a good manager."

I shut the trunk. "That's all that matters."

One of the band members, a girl with blue and black hair, poked her head out of the back door. "Kace?"

"Coming," Kacey called over her shoulder. "That's Lola, my best friend. She got me into this band. If it weren't for her, I'd probably be on the streets. I can't let her down, you know?"

She sounded like she was trying to work herself up to do something frightening. My instinct was to comfort her or protect her, but from what? How?

"Can I help?" I blurted.

"Will you be here after the show?" she asked, her face open and hopeful, a sad smile at its center.

"Yeah, Kacey. I'll be here," I said gently. "I'll drive you home."

"I'm so glad," she said. She shuffled her feet, not quite meeting my eyes. "There's talk of a party after at Summerlin. A ton of people are coming…the guys from our opening act. You should come. I mean, if you want. If you're allowed."

I wasn't. We weren't permitted to socialize with our fares, but the desire to protect her was fierce, and neither company policy nor my stringent rules about the routine could change that.

Her friend Lola emerged from the back door again. "*Kacey.* You can't make us late again, sweetie. I'm serious."

"I gotta go." Kacey reached out and squeezed my hand. "I'll see you after?"

She hurried to join her band, and I tried to imagine this girl playing electric guitar onstage in front of a screaming audience. She seemed ready to crack in two, and aside from her friend with the two-tone hair, it seemed like she had not one fucking person in the world to help hold her together.

I wiped my hand on my uniform pants pocket as if I could wipe away her touch and the feelings that came with it, but I could still feel her soft skin against mine.

I slid behind the wheel to wait out the show. The line of limos behind mine grew, and I'd bet Trevor was among them, still not having learned to take off his damn jacket while waiting in the heat.

Unlike last night's monotony, I spent this night with my nerves jangling, hoping Kacey was okay and being pissed at myself for caring. Every muffled swell of the crowd made me flinch, and I half expected Hugo to bust out of the back door with her in his arms again.

After two hours, my nervousness settled into a dull pang in the pit of my stomach. A homeless man shuffled up to me, asking me for some spare change. I handed him the crumpled one-hundred-dollar bill Jimmy Ray had given me. The homeless man's eyes were wreathed in a bone-deep weariness. They widened as he offered me a gap-toothed smile of profound relief before slinking back into the night.

Best hundred bucks I ever spent.

It was close to eleven when the show ended. Through the alley that led to the street, I saw a stream of concertgoers file out. I put my jacket back on and waited at the limo door for the band to emerge.

An hour later, I was still waiting, sweating in my jacket like Trevor.

Finally, the door burst open, and out staggered Rapid Confession and the guys from their opening act. All of them drunk and loud and laughing with a post-show high. I searched for Kacey. She was in her concert outfit now: skintight black leather pants and a low-cut black halter top that revealed a valley of smooth skin between the soft curve of her breasts. Tattoos on her arms were stark against her pale skin. Her hair was still piled messily on her head, tendrils falling loose to frame her face.

Kacey looked worn out from the show—sweaty and disheveled and drunk. The drummer from the opener had an arm slung around her neck. They both staggered and weaved. As Kacey climbed none too gracefully into the limo, her eyes met mine, glazed with liquor. She flashed me a watery smile before disappearing inside.

Jimmy and the other band's manager crammed in last, without a glance my way. I shut the door behind them, bottling up the cacophony of conversation.

On the drive to Summerlin, my eyes kept straying to the rearview mirror, and twice I barely avoided rear-ending the car in front of me. But as long as the partition was down, I kept trying to catch a glimpse of Kacey, to make sure she was all right.

Why do you care? She's a rock star. This is what they do.

But I did care. She'd drunk herself into oblivion last night and gotten almost as wasted again tonight. She told me at lunch today she was scared, but of what? The party scene? Or something more? And why, in the space of twenty-four hours, had her fears become so important to me?

I screeched into the circular drive of the pink palace in Summerlin. This time lights were blazing in every window. When I opened the passenger door, a great tangle of staggering bodies and laughter spilled out. I hazarded a guess the limo mini bar was raided down to the ice cubes.

The drummer from the opening act was all over Kacey, and as the group moved toward the house, I watched her try to shove him away.

"Get off," she said and staggered back.

The guy laughed and said something I couldn't hear. He went at her again, an arm snaking around her waist to yank her to him.

"No," she said, her voice muffled against the guy's chest as he pinned her close. His head bent, mouth on her neck, and his other hand slid down to her breast. "Ryan…stop…"

"Hey!" Kacey's friend Lola pulled away from her guy and started wobbling toward Kacey to help.

I was faster.

I grabbed the drummer by his shoulder and shoved him off Kacey so hard, he tripped on his heels and landed on his ass.

"She said *stop*, asshole," I said. The drummer scrambled to his feet, his expression morphing from confusion to shock to anger. I stared him down, and when Kacey fell into me, her face buried against my jacket, my arm went around her.

"Who the fuck are you?" The drummer's lip curled in a sneer. "The *driver*…"

"Okay, okay," Jimmy Ray said, moving between us. "Let's all calm down. We're all friends here…"

"The hell we are," I said, not taking my eyes from Ryan. My one arm held Kacey tight; the other hand balled into a fist at my side. Adrenaline coursed through my veins, and it felt fucking good…and reckless. I wasn't a violent guy, but if this bastard wanted a fight, I'd give it to him.

The band members, with some prompting from Jimmy, moved toward the house. Ryan was too drunk to fight, and I think he knew it. He flipped me the bird and let himself be pulled away by his bandmates. Lola remained behind.

"We're all good?" Jimmy asked. "You okay, kitten?"

Kacey moved away from my arm but stayed close, holding on to the cuff of my jacket. She gave a stiff smile. "Sure, Jimmy. I'm great."

"Screw that," Lola said, glaring at her manager. "If Ryan touches her again, I'll chop his dick off. Get rid of them, Jimmy. Find another opening act."

I liked this Lola.

Kacey waved a hand. "No, no, it's not a big deal. It's okay…"

"No, it's not okay," I said.

Jimmy rubbed his chin. "This has to be a big thing? Right now? I got a hundred people coming to this party…"

Even as he spoke, other cars were arriving, cabs and limos—a steady stream of people. If I didn't move the limo soon, it was going to get boxed in.

I looked down at Kacey. She was drunk, and if I let her go inside that house, she'd only get drunker. Or pass out. Ryan might decide to take what he wanted anyway, and in a house that size, with a party raging, who would know?

Keep to the routine, I thought, even as my hands moved on their own. I took Kacey's face and tilted it gently, making her look at me. Her broad mouth trembled under red lipstick. Dark makeup pulled her eyes into long blue sapphires, pale blue with a darker ring around the iris. I hadn't noticed that before. Beautiful. She didn't belong here.

"You want to leave?" I asked.

Her eyes held mine, liquor dimming the shine I'd seen in them during our lunch. But her voice was steady when she answered, "Yeah, I do."

I smiled at her, strangely proud. "Done."

Her glassy eyes widened in surprise, then with a gust of

whiskey-soaked breath, she wilted against me. "It's all good, Jimmy," she murmured. "Jonah...he's so good to me."

I walked her to the front seat of the limo and helped her in. Her head lolled against the headrest, her eyes closed, and I buckled the seat belt around her to keep her safe.

"Pack her a bag?" I said to Lola, shutting the door.

She narrowed her eyes at me, sizing me up, then nodded and went into the house.

Jimmy looked after her, then swung around back to me. "Pack a *bag*?"

"She's staying with me a few days," I said.

He blew air out of his cheeks wetly. "We're outta here on Tuesday." He was drunk as hell too, but trying to hold on to some authority. "I got twenty-five more cities lined up, and she's under contract. Just so you know the score."

"I know it," I said, my voice stony. I pulled up all of my six feet, towering over him. "She's taking a break from this scene."

And then what? the voice of caution asked me. I ignored it.

"A break. Yeah, okay." Jimmy lit a smoke and jabbed the two fingers that held it at me. "I know where you work. You want to keep your job, you take care of her."

"Better than you have," I said.

"You think you're special to her? Her hero?" He snorted a laugh. "Take a number, buddy."

He retreated into the house, which was rapidly filling up. Lola came back with a duffel bag and a small leather backpack. I took them and walked to the trunk.

"What's the deal here?" Lola asked. "Are you two...?"

"No." I tossed the bags in the trunk. "She needs some time away. Obviously."

"So she stays a few days on your couch and then rejoins us before we leave Vegas?"

"That's the plan." I slammed the trunk lid. "If you're worried whether or not she's safe with me, she is. I swear on my life I would never hurt her, okay?"

Lola nodded slowly. "Okay, fine. This could be good. It wouldn't kill Kacey to stay sober for forty-eight consecutive hours. I love her to pieces, but she's a fucking flake. This is our big break. It's *my* big break, and if she can keep her shit together long enough, she'd see that it's her big break too."

I doubt it. I moved to the driver's side.

"I'm going to call her," Lola told me, following. "To make sure she's all right."

"I would hope so," I replied and slammed the door.

You can't peel out in a limousine, but I came close, and the pink palace faded out of my rearview.

I drove back to A-1 to return the limo, hustling Kacey through the garage into my truck. By some miracle no one saw us. Back at my apartment, it was last night all over again, except that Kacey didn't smell of puke and smoke. The scent of her perfume, her sweat, and a tinge of whiskey permeated the air as I helped her out of the truck.

This time, she wasn't out cold, but swimming in inebriation— sometimes deep under and hardly able to keep her feet, sometimes coming up for air to walk with me. Twice she threw her arms around my neck and murmured in my ear how grateful she was I'd saved her. My skin broke out in gooseflesh and my groin tightened as I went to lay her down in my bed.

"Jonah," she sighed, still clinging to me, trying to pull me down on the bed with her. "You're so good to me. The last good man on earth."

"Kacey, wait…"

I tried to gently pry her arms from my neck, but she was tenacious. Her lips brushed my skin above my uniform collar. Warm, wet kisses under my ear, working up until her teeth grazed my earlobe, and I had to clench my teeth. She licked and teased, her mouth a gravitational pull, and I was being sucked in, ready to collapse over her, into her. My hands wanted the softness of her skin and hair, the full curve of her breasts under my palm...

"Kacey," I said. "We can't..."

"We can," she whispered against my cheek. Her mouth moved along my jaw, her lips blazing a trail across skin that hadn't felt a woman's touch in more than a year. Her hands tangled in my hair, little breathy noises of want issuing from her throat. Her mouth had almost found mine when a pungent waft of whiskey filled my nose, bringing me around like a slap.

What the hell are you doing?

I pulled away before her lips found mine, and disentangled myself from her embrace.

"You're no fun," she murmured and then stretched her arms over her head, her fingers splayed on the wooden bedframe. Her breasts pushed against the flimsy glittery material of her black halter top. "Don't be like that. Come to bed, baby."

Reality doused me like a bucket of ice water.

I could be anyone right now.

"You need to sleep it off," I snapped. I unzipped the duffel that Lola had packed for her and dug around until I found a T-shirt and pair of soft shorts. I laid them out on the bed and started for the door.

No sooner had I shut off the light than her voice carried to me, small and fragile in the dark.

"Wait. Jonah...?"

I stopped but didn't turn, my shoulders sagging. "Yeah?"

"Stay. The ceiling...it's spinning..."

Don't do it.

I did. Drawn in.

I turned and moved slowly back to the bed. The only light came from the street outside, a white light casting a silvery glow over the bed and through her hair, which had fallen from its knot. She held out her hand. I took it and sat beside her.

Kacey sidled up close to me, pressed her cheek against my thigh, and wrapped her arm around my knees. "Where am I?" Her voice was slurred a little, growing weak as sleep took her. "Where am I, Jonah?"

"You're safe, Kacey," I murmured. I held her for a little while, then helped her change into her comfortable clothes—taking care to keep my eyes averted as much as possible from her body, pale and smooth and stretched out before me.

I pulled up the covers. And because I thought she wouldn't remember this in the morning, I stroked her hair until she fell asleep. Then I went out, closing the door softly behind me.

Chapter 9

KACEY

SOMEONE WAS RUNNING THAT DAMNED CHAIN SAW AGAIN.

I jerked awake, blinking at the early-morning light streaming in from a small window. It illuminated a bedroom: bed, dresser, nightstand, all plain in a bachelor-pad kind of way. On the floor next to the bed were my duffel and the small leather backpack that served as my purse. Outside the door, the whirring continued.

Jonah and his god-awful blender.

It took me a blurry minute to put the puzzle pieces together from last night. Memories came to me like scattered photographs: the drummer from Until Tomorrow, our opening act, pawing at me before Jonah knocked him on his ass.

You want to leave?

And I had felt so safe…

I sat up slowly and pushed back the covers to find I was in a T-shirt and sleep shorts. A vague memory swam up: Jonah helping me peel off my leather jeans, helping me change clothes…

I kissed him. Just his neck and ear…but he smelled so good. I tried to pull him to bed and…

"Oh my God." Mortification ran scarlet over my skin, and I held my aching head in my hands. "No, no, no... Not Jonah. Not him."

It wasn't the alcohol. Not entirely. It was the goddamn insatiable need for connection, driving me to find comfort anywhere and any way I could. Jonah took care of me, protected me, and I'd reduced him to the same level as the nameless roadies I took to my bed.

I glanced at the nightstand. A glass of water, two aspirin.

Tears sprang to my eyes.

The clock radio read 7:04. Jonah would be leaving for the hot shop any minute. I got up, opened the bedroom door, and padded into the narrow hallway. The blender went quiet, and I heard men's voices talking. Someone else was here. I shifted on the balls of my feet, frozen. Part of me begged to slip back to the bedroom and hide, pretend none of this happened. The other half, sick of hiding behind Jägermeister and whiskey, pushed me toward the kitchen.

Jonah looked cleanly handsome in jeans and a pale-blue T-shirt. He took a pill from the Sunday compartment in one of those day-of-the-week medication containers. The rest of the compartments were crammed full, their lids bulging into domes. He washed the pill down with what looked like a tall glass of mud and ground-up grass. The grimace that twisted his lips told me the drink didn't taste any better than it looked.

A gruff cough jolted me from my thoughts. The hot guy from the photos on the living room wall leaned against the counter, clad in a black T-shirt and jeans. His muscled arms, inked with tribal tattoos, were crossed against a broad chest. His dark hair was cut short, and a thin growth of stubble grew along his jaw. He was a bulkier, more rugged version of Jonah. It had to be his brother. But where Jonah's face was handsome in its open, friendly demeanor, his brother's was closed down, tense and dark. His angry gaze darted between Jonah's medication and me, as if he couldn't believe the two things could exist in the same space.

The feeling of being a trespasser again twisted my already unsteady stomach, then Jonah turned to me. The smile that broke over his face when he saw me warmed me like a summer sun.

"Um, hi," I said. "Good morning."

"Hey." Jonah caught sight of his brother's astounded expression and shifted his own quickly back to neutral. "Kacey, this is my brother, Theo. Theo, this is Kacey Dawson. She's going to be crashing here for a few days."

"Nice to meet you, Theo."

Despite his Death Glare from Hell, my instinct was to hug Theo; I was big on hugs. And because he was Jonah's brother, I immediately felt a sense of affinity for him. But his cold stare pinned me to my spot.

Theo's eyes raked me up and down, taking in my messy hair, my long T-shirt, which covered my shorts and made it look like I wasn't wearing anything underneath. It was pretty obvious what Theo assumed was happening between his brother and me, and he didn't like it.

"When did this happen?" he demanded of Jonah, not even bothering to hide the accusatory tone in his voice.

This? I'm a this? *I don't think so, pal.*

Before Jonah could reply, I said, "*This* happened last night. We got married at one of those drive-through chapels, didn't we…Johnny? Jordan?" I snapped my fingers, my face scrunched up in confusion. "Wait, don't tell me… It's definitely a *J* name."

Jonah smothered a laugh.

Theo glowered but ignored me. "She's staying here? For how long? When were you going to tell me?"

"Yes, until Tuesday, and I was just about to, but Kacey beat me to it," Jonah said. "And Jesus, you're being rude as hell. Even for you."

The mother of all awkward silences descended on me as the brothers stared each other down and held a private conversation; I could practically hear the thoughts passing between them.

Finally, I cleared my throat and pointed toward a grocery bag on the counter surrounded by creamers and sugars. "What's all this?"

Jonah's eyes slowly left Theo's. "I went out and got a few things."

"That's thoughtful of you this early in the morning." I sniffed at the air. "Decaf never smelled so good…"

"That's because it's regular." Jonah pulled a UNLV mug from a cupboard, filled it, and handed it over.

"Thank you." I moved carefully past Theo. His dislike of me was still emanating off him like heat from a furnace. I took a stool on the other side of the counter, tucking my shirt up a little to prove that I was wearing shorts.

I saw Theo's gaze land on the sugar skull tattooed on my left thigh. For a brief moment, his expression loosened, grew curious. I started to strike up a conversation about his tattoos, when the Death Glare returned like a door slamming in my face.

He pushed himself off the counter. "You ready, bro?" he said. "Let's hit it."

Jonah finished off his protein shake and tossed the cup in the sink. "I'll be back in a few hours," he said to me. "So you're not left stranded for lunch."

Theo's eyes widened. "You're not going to work through lunch?"

"First time for everything," Jonah replied.

"No, I don't want to throw off your schedule," I said. "You have a lot of work to do. I'll be fine here, really." I glanced at Theo. "Really."

"Really," Theo said, deadpan.

"*Really*, I'll be back for lunch," Jonah said. "If you need anything else, there's a convenience store up the street, about a ten-minute walk. Give me your cell number, and I'll call if I'm running late."

Theo watched darkly as Jonah and I exchanged cell numbers. "You're still coming to dinner tonight, right?" he said. He looked at me, his lighter-brown eyes stony and hard. "We do it every Sunday. Family only."

Jonah scrubbed his hands over his face. "Jesus Christ, Theo."

For half a second, Theo looked contrite, then turned to stone again. "I'll be waiting in the truck." He strode to the apartment door and shut it hard behind him.

"Nice meeting you," I said to my coffee cup.

"I'm so sorry. He really has become a pain in the ass since…" Jonah laughed shortly. "Since *birth*, actually."

"Does he work with glass too? Is that why he's going to the shop?"

"No, he's a tattoo artist."

"Really? I was thinking about getting another tattoo. Too bad he hates my guts."

"He doesn't hate you. He's just…protective. He helps me out at the shop sometimes. I have an assistant too. Tania. But she's off on Sundays."

"So he drove here to pick you up?"

Jonah raked his hand through his hair. "Yeah, we're…we're close. And he likes to hang out."

"So under all that glowering and barking, he's a softie."

Outside, a car horn blared, loud and long.

I burst out laughing.

Jonah laughed too, and then a short silence fell. I figured it was now or never if I was going to apologize for last night.

"That was nice of you to let me crash in your bed last night. I was…pretty drunk. Didn't mean to evict you. Or—"

"You didn't," Jonah said. "I don't sleep in the bed. I haven't in about four months."

I blinked. "Um, okay, I'll bite. Where do you sleep?"

He nodded his head toward the living room area behind me. "In the recliner. My doctor wants me to sleep semi-inclined. For better breathing. It's not a big deal," he added quickly.

I frowned. It sounded like a big fucking deal. What would happen if he slept lying down? He'd stop breathing? I couldn't ask that, so instead I said, "Is that…comfortable?"

"It's just another adjustment."

"Why don't you buy one of those fancy beds? Where you can raise the head?"

"Not in the budget," Jonah said, and a sour look contorted his face. He bent forward, hands on the counter, his head hanging between his arms.

My heart jump-started. "Jonah?" Every muscle in my body tensed. "Are you okay?"

"Fine," he said to the floor, sucking in gulp of air. "Just nauseated."

"Do you want some water?" I was already off the stool and rummaging his cabinet for a glass. I filled it halfway from the faucet and pressed it into his hand.

He unbent himself and drank a little. "Thanks," he said. "It's passed."

I could smell his aftershave—clean and masculine. The memory of his skin under my mouth made my knees tremble. I slipped back to my stool, cheeks burning.

Jonah took a last deep breath and set the water aside. "Thanks again."

"Does that happen a lot?" I asked. "When you take those pills?"

He nodded. "They're immunosuppressants. They prevent my body from rejecting the heart, but their side effects aren't fun."

I tried to think up something better to say, something comforting or something funny to make him laugh, but all I could think of was that I was sorry he had to suffer this at all.

From outside, the car horn blared again.

"My brother, the epitome of patience," Jonah said. "See you in few."

He was at the door, turning the knob. In another few seconds he'd be gone, and I still had unfinished business. I mustered my courage. "Jonah?"

He stopped, turned. "Yeah?"

"I'm sorry about last night."

He stiffened. "It's fine. No big deal."

I wet my lips, which had gone dry, and slipped off the stool, moving to stand behind the couch, a barricade.

"No, it is a big deal. To me. I'm really sorry that I tried to… It's not a sex thing." I plucked at a piece of nonexistent lint on the upholstery. "Okay, it's a little bit of a sex thing. Who doesn't like sex, right?" I laughed weakly, then coughed. "But mostly it's just the comfort. The afterward. Being held by a man while I sleep. I'm sure that sounds pathetic, but it's what I like, and I'm sorry I tried to do that to you. You're more than that."

Jonah shook his head, his expression pained. "I can't be more than that, Kacey."

"No, I meant, you're a friend. Or maybe we could be friends. If you want. And that's all I want. Honest, I can't be with anyone right now even if I wanted to. In case you haven't noticed, I'm a mess."

"You're no more a mess than anyone else," he said in a low voice.

My chest tightened, pushing tears to my eyes. "Thank you for saying that, even though it doesn't feel true."

He smiled, and while it wasn't the megawatt smile that lit up his whole face and thrilled me, it was warm and kind. And comforting.

"I really gotta go," he said. "I'm late."

"Thanks," I said as he opened the front door. "For the coffee and letting me stay here. Thanks for all of it. I mean it."

"You're welcome," he said. "I mean it too."

Chapter 10

JONAH

THEO'S BLACK CHEVY SILVERADO WAS IDLING ON THE CURB. "ABOUT damn time," my brother said, scowling as I got in. "That chick is already throwing you off."

"It wasn't her," I said. "It was the damn Gengraf."

"Nausea?" Theo said, his tone instantly morphing from anger to concern. "You okay?"

I shot him a look. "*That chick* got me some water, and I felt better."

Theo snorted. His eyes gave me a final once-over, then he maneuvered his truck through the light Sunday morning traffic toward the glass studio. I watched North Las Vegas go by my window—strip malls and gas stations, apartment complexes smaller and older than mine—but my thoughts were on Kacey's apology.

I can't be with anyone right now...

Perfect. Neither could I.

So why did my chest ache like an old bruise?

"You thinking about her?" Theo said.

"Kacey?"

"No, Mother Theresa. Yeah, Kacey. Who the hell is she?"

"Why are you so hostile? She's just a girl crashing on my couch."

Theo watched the road, his shoulders jerking up in a shrug. "I don't want to see another fucked-up situation like you had with Audrey."

"I was with Audrey for three years. I've known Kacey for all of twenty-four hours. You can chill out."

"How much did you tell her about your situation?"

More than I should have. I shifted in my seat. "She knows I had the operation."

Theo gaped at me so long, I thought he'd crash his truck. He turned his eyes back to the road, his expression grim. "Okay, spill it. What's the deal with her?" he said. "For real."

I rested my elbow on the door, rubbing my chin. "Her deal is she's got a few days off until her band leaves town on tour. She's taking a break. That's it. For real."

"Why doesn't she just stay in a hotel? And since when do you tell total strangers about the operation?"

"She doesn't do well on her own." I glanced at him. "It's not a big deal. I'm giving her a break, and she's good company. She's got a good sense of humor. We get along well."

We just…clicked.

"You met her *yesterday*." Theo's voice was low, but I could hear his temper rumbling within it, like a distant thunderstorm. He kept his gaze steadfastly on the road. "Are you fucking her?"

"Jesus, Theo." Yet the image of Kacey splayed out on my bed reached for me. I'd wanted her last night, wanted to give in to her, have a woman's arms and legs wrapped around me one more time. I wanted to feel a woman's soft body beneath mine, to be on top of her and inside of her and…

"Dude. *Are* you fucking her?"

I forgot Theo could read my face like the front page of a newspaper. "No," I said. "Not that it's your business. She's crashing until Tuesday, then she's going back on tour with her band. She'll be traveling all over for months."

"And you're cool with that?"

"Of course, I'm cool with it. What could possibly happen between us? Or between me and anyone, for that matter?"

Theo's jaw clenched. "Don't start with that doomsday shit. You don't know for sure if..." He shook his head, unwilling to voice the possibility. "The meds might be working. They probably *are* working."

"Then why were you such a dick to Kacey?"

He jerked his shoulders in a shrug. "I give a shit. The doctor said you had to be careful."

"He said I had to not overexert myself. He didn't say I had to become a monk. I miss being with a woman. Being intimate with her."

"You're the one who doesn't do one-night stands..." Theo said. "Something I'll never get." He ran a hand through his hair. "Look, if you want to get laid, get laid. I just don't want another Audrey situation. I don't want some chick to bail on you when you need her to fucking stick around."

"Neither do I," I said. "What Audrey did...it hurt, but I wasn't in love with her."

We'd come to a red light. Theo turned in his seat. "*What?*"

"I loved Audrey, but I wasn't in love with her." I listened to my own words, waiting for some pain to follow. But the only pain wasn't for what I had with Audrey and lost, but for something I never had at all. "I've never been in love."

Theo's eyes widened. "You weren't in love with Audrey? Really? Because you sure spent a shitload of time with her."

"I loved her, but she didn't...consume me. I didn't lose my train of thought when she walked into a room, or feel that feeling you get..." I shook my head, searching for the words. "We were a good match." *Like a pair of shoes*, I thought. "But I didn't have that *feeling*."

"What feeling?" Theo asked dubiously.

"That feeling you're supposed to have when you're with the woman you're in love with. I can't describe that feeling because I've never felt it. Have you?"

Theo gave me an arch look. "I'm saving myself for marriage."

I snorted a laugh. "I think you've got that backward."

Theo's eyes hardened again. "So you weren't in love with Audrey. And you're having this revelation now? Because of Kacey?"

I turned my eyes to my window. "I just met her, for chrissakes. No, I just meant...since we're on the subject. It's something I missed out on. Being in love."

"You haven't *missed* it," Theo said. "You might not be missing anything. If you'd go back to Morrison and get another biopsy..."

I sighed, exhausted from having this same conversation for the millionth time.

"What would happen if I did? I would find a miracle waiting for me? The atherosclerosis isn't going to reverse itself."

"No, but it might've slowed the fuck down or stopped altogether. Maybe you have longer than you think. A lot longer. If you weren't so goddamn pessimistic..."

He held on to a hope that wasn't there, but I knew the truth. I felt it in the marrow of my bones, in the weakening pulse of my heart, its walls and passageways hardening slowly like cooling glass.

"If I get another biopsy," I said, "I'd lose at least one full day at the shop."

Theo said nothing, and anger flamed red-hot in me.

"I'll go back after the gallery opening, okay? Dammit, Theo, I'm just trying to talk about something *real* for a goddamn change. I miss having someone in my life. I'm not selfish; I know it's too late now. But it sucks, okay?"

"Yeah, man," Theo said, retreating to a quieter tone. "That's cool. We've just never talked about it before. About what you want."

"You mean what I want before I die? You can say it, Theo. I wish you would."

91

"What for?" he snapped. "What fucking good does that do anyone?"

"Me. It does me good. So I don't feel like…"

"What?"

So goddamn alone.

We pulled into the parking lot of the hot shop, and Theo killed the engine. He sat straight, eyes forward as he spoke.

"Look, if you want or need anything…just tell me, okay? You're always saying, 'Don't bucket-list me.' But if there's something you want, and I can give it to you, tell me, okay? Anything at all."

Dying, I learned, is a not a team sport. It's a solitary endeavor. Everyone I loved was standing on dry land, while I was alone on a boat as it slowly pulled away from the shore, and there's nothing anyone could do about it but watch it happen.

I immediately felt shitty for letting my anger out on Theo or telling him what I missed or wanted or could never have. What were they but just another burden for him to carry? One more thing he could do nothing about. The pain of it was written in every line of his face.

"Okay, thanks, Theo. Thanks for looking out for me." I mustered a smile and smacked his shoulder. "Come on. Let's get to work."

Chapter 11

JONAH

THEO COULD'VE BEEN A GLASS ARTIST IF HE'D WANTED TO. HE WAS talented and utterly fearless. He loved the fire but hated the fragility of the glass afterward. Theo liked permanence. He worked with thick black ink that punched the skin, made it bleed, then remained embedded forever. Our father thought he was wasting his incredible ability to draw and sketch by working with tattoos, but it was just right for my brother.

We worked in near silence; but for the roar-hiss of the furnace, the hot shop was quiet, and my thoughts drifted to our conversation, to Theo, who had been with me through my illness, through Audrey's betrayal. She hadn't broken up with me; she'd told Theo and then skipped town, leaving him to break the news.

I rolled the pipe in my hand, watched as the flames enveloped it, made it glow hot and white...

I sat on a chair in Dr. Morrison's office. Not the white exam room where he usually saw me, with its long white-papered table and the little tray of instruments, latex gloves, and individually wrapped syringes. That room was for patients who were receiving treatment. Patients still in the fight.

Today, I was in the private office of Dr. Conrad Morrison—cardiovascular surgeon and cardiac transplantation specialist. Rather than a battlefield, this was where victory champagne was popped...or where white flags of surrender were thrown.

Theo sat next to me, slouched down, gnawing on his thumbnail, his leg jouncing. I could feel my younger brother's energy radiating out. He took the yellow glow of his fear and burned it until it was red-hot and ready to combust.

I expected to be racked with dread. I felt nothing. No dread. Not even fear. I was beyond fear. Numb.

We waited for five minutes in that office—I watched the clock circle off each one. Five minutes that felt like years and also no time at all. The door opened, and Dr. Morrison walked in, a file folder tucked under his arm and a grim look on his face. My borrowed heart slammed against my rib cage, shattering the numbness. I immediately wanted it back. Feeling nothing was better than this bone-deep terror.

Dr. Morrison had the appearance of an eighth-grade social studies teacher—late fifties, receding hairline, tall and somewhat lanky. His eyes were sharp. Surgeon's eyes, with a vast wealth of medical knowledge and expertise behind them.

He offered me a thin smile and extended his hand to shake. "Jonah. Good to see you. Sorry to have kept you."

I half rose to my feet on watery legs and shook his hand. "No trouble," I said, eyeing the file folder tucked under his arm.

That file that told a far-fetched story of a perfectly healthy young man—who'd never been sick in his life but for a bout of tonsillitis in the fifth grade—struck down by a virus that destroyed his heart. It was thick now, filled with tissue-type analyses, diagnostics, blood work, lab work, an urgent surgery, a mile-long list of immunosuppressant medications, and *finally, biopsy results. Seventeen of them. Number eighteen was from the day before. Its results would be on top.*

"Theo," Dr. Morrison said with a nod. He didn't offer his hand, and Theo didn't rise from his seat, only nodded in return. His leg jounced faster.

Dr. Morrison moved behind the large mahogany desk to sit in the leather chair. He set the folder on his desk but didn't open it. He folded his long-fingered hands. Those hands had removed my diseased heart from my body fifteen months ago, and then cradled a new one. They'd gently lowered it into the empty space, reattached all that needed reattaching, put my rib cage back in its rightful place, and sewn me back up.

Instead of welcoming the new heart, and despite the various cocktails of immunosuppressant drugs I'd been taking religiously for the last thirteen months, my body attacked. A slow but relentless attack, hacking away at this foreign intruder piece by piece, leaving behind wounds that became scars. Ultimately it was the scars that were killing the new heart. And killing me.

Dr. Morrison inhaled. "The results of your latest biopsy are not what we were hoping for..."

He spoke and I heard the words, a string of medical jargon that I had become infinitely familiar with over the last year so that I didn't require a layman's translation. Words like atherosclerosis, stenosis, cardiac allograft vasculopathy, *and* myocardial ischemia. *A bunch of Latin spliced with English, sewn together with science and authority, and distilled into the most final of bottom lines.*

"I'm sorry, Jonah," said Dr. Morrison, his voice heavy and low. "I wish I had better news."

I nodded mutely. I'll have to tell my mother.

The thought burrowed deep into my guts like a boiling poison, burning the last numbness away. I nearly puked in my lap. Somehow, I spoke instead.

"How long?"

Dr. Morrison steepled his fingers on his desk. "Given the rapid progression of the CAV, six months would be a generous estimate."

95

I nodded, mentally doing the math.

Six months.

My art installation was due to be finished for the gallery exhibit in October, five months from now.

That's cutting it close...

Theo bolted from his chair, bringing me back to the present. He paced behind me like a panther, his dark eyes fixed on Dr. Morrison. The anguish in his voice struck me with every syllable.

"Six months? What happens in six months? Nothing. Screw your six months. He goes back on the list, right? The donor list? If this heart is failing, then you give him another."

Dr. Morrison pursed his lips. "There are some ethical implications—"

"Fuck the implications," Theo said. "If he's on the list, he's on the list. A new heart comes up, he gets it. Right?" He turned to me with blazing eyes. "Right?"

I couldn't take another heart from someone else on the list who could live a long and happy life with it. I had a rare tissue type. The rarest. Finding a donor who was a close match was almost impossible. Thirteen months ago, in a rush to save my life, they'd given me the best heart they could, the closest match, and my immune system was wrecking it. It would only do the same to another.

I wasn't a martyr by any stretch, and I didn't need to be. Medical ethics and procedures would take the decision out of my hands. Dr. Morrison's next words confirmed it.

"Yes, Jonah is back on the donor list." He turned to me. "But your rare tissue type will again be a factor, and the chronic rejection manifested here, as well as the way your kidneys are handling the immunosuppressant medications. I can't say I'm optimistic the board will approve a replantation..."

I could feel Theo's rage like a hot wind at my back. "What do you mean they won't approve it? They'll just...they'll let him..."

He was on the edge, I could hear it, and I couldn't take it anymore. I had to protect my little brother, just as I always had. Keep him safe.

I rose to my feet, my legs strong now. "Thank you, Dr. M." I offered my hand. "We'll be in touch."

Dr. Morrison stood up as well but didn't shake my hand. Instead, he patted my cheek in a grandfatherly manner. "You'll be in my prayers, Jonah. Tonight and every night."

"Prayers." Theo spit the word in the parking lot. "What the fuck good will prayers do? He's a scientist. He needs to get his ass in the lab or something and figure out how to stop that goddamn rejection."

Then it hit me. All of it. Like a lightning bolt striking the top of my head and tearing straight down, nearly cleaving me in two.

I gripped Theo's arm, and he stopped with a jolt.

"What is it? Jonah? Talk to me…"

I pulled him close, the blood flooding my brain and my words coming out on shallow puffs of air. My head swelled. I could feel time racing past me, second by second, and I couldn't be done yet. I wasn't done yet.

"Help me, Theo."

"What is it?"

"You have to help me."

"Are you…? Do you need a doctor…?" His head whipped around the rows of parked cars, ready to call for help.

"No doctors. Not anymore. Theo, listen to me. I need your help."

"Tell me," he said. "What do you need? Anything, Jonah. Anything."

"Help me finish it," I said, my eyes boring into his. "I have to finish it, Theo. The installation. No matter what. I have to leave something behind."

"Don't talk like that," he said. "You're not going anywhere…"

I had to make him see. I held on to my brother, clutched him tight. He held me back. He was solid and real, while I was already dissipating into the air, particle by particle. "Don't let me vanish, Theo. Please. Help me…"

Theo's eyes flared at my words, and his grip on my arms became painful. "I'll help you," he said through gritted teeth. "I'll help you. Anything you want or need…I'm here. And so are you. You're not going to vanish, Jonah. Goddammit, you're not."

I nodded and sucked in several gulps of air.

"Okay. Okay, thanks. I'm sorry. I panicked, but I'm good now. Sorry. Let's go. We can go now."

I started walking, and Theo had no choice but to follow. I could feel him watching me like a hawk. The solidity of him calmed me more. Not his anger—that was a shield between himself and the world—but what lay beneath. His devotion to those he loved. Unwavering and unbreakable. Permanent.

The blood drained from my head and my borrowed heart settled down. Still, it ticked away the time with each beat. I had a finite number of pulses that could be counted and measured.

Six months.

I can do this, *I thought as we climbed into Theo's pickup truck. If I made a schedule and kept to it. If I worked as much as I could, no stops, I'd make it. I'd leave something behind. I wouldn't vanish into thin air, I'd use my air to infuse and shape the molten glass, capture my breath within it, and when it hardened, a part of me would remain locked inside forever.*

Forever, *I thought, feeling a little of the heavy weight lift, a lessening of the dark shadow trailing me, even in the bright sunshine of the desert. A little bit of hope to carry me through. A purpose.*

It was time to get to work.

The gather of glass on my pipe dripped back into the furnace, jerking me from my thoughts. Like the glass, my life had been molten and malleable and full of potential. Now it was solidified—fired and hardened. No refiring. No starting over with someone new because there was no time for someone new to become someone significant. I had my installation. Something that endured, that wouldn't wither and die. Something that lasted. The memory was more than a year old, but nothing had changed. It was time to get to work.

"Let's grab some lunch and keep going," I told Theo.

His eyebrows rose. "Yeah? I thought you were going to—"

"I'll text Kacey and tell her I have to work through. She can order a pizza or something," I said, ignoring the ugly feeling in my gut, the guilt that hung heavy in my heart for ditching her.

Theo rubbed his jaw, looking like someone who'd fought to get his way and now felt bad about it. "If you're sure…"

"I'm sure," I said, pulling out my phone. "I have to stay on schedule."

And that was the truth.

End of story.

Chapter 12

KACEY

I took a shower to wash last night off me. All of it: the show, the booze, and how I'd thrown myself at Jonah. After, I wrapped myself in one towel, made a turban over my hair with another, and stepped out of the steam. I swiped the foggy mirror over the sink to see my reflection. My hand lingered on the warm glass. On the other side were Jonah's medications.

He trusted me with them, and that made me feel good about myself in a way I hadn't felt in a long time. But thinking about Jonah's actual heart transplant made my guts twist, like I'd just tossed back something super strong on an empty stomach. Terrible medical catastrophes struck innocent young people every day, but this one seemed like some cosmic screwup. A terrible mistake. I couldn't work out why the situation felt so wrong.

I moved my hand to the bare skin above my towel. I tried to imagine what it would be like to have someone else's heart beating in my chest. Did it feel like his own? Could he feel it wasn't? Once, when I was a kid, I accidentally swallowed an ice cube. I felt the cold, hard rock of it in my chest as it went down. I wondered if Jonah felt that way—not the cold, but the presence of something hard and heavy and foreign in his chest.

You're being stupid, I told myself. *I'm sure it doesn't feel any different. Or it feels better. His old heart was sick. The new one has given him life.*

The thought bolstered me a bit, though the suspicion of something being not quite right didn't leave me.

I put on cutoff shorts and a tank top, and exited the bathroom. But for the AC churning on the window, the apartment was silent. Peaceful. I sat on the couch to admire Jonah's beautiful glass on the coffee table. I picked up the nautical paperweight, the sea life forever suspended in a quiet ocean.

Worlds away.

Twenty-four hours ago, my residence had been one of five bedrooms in the Summerlin house, the halls echoing with dozens of voices, loud music, and drunken laughter at all hours. I wasn't the only partier in our group—just the most dedicated. My room in that house was trashed, clothes strewn all over, makeup messes in the bathroom. The only glass around wasn't delicate art but overflowing ashtrays or empty bottles littering the floors.

The peaceful quiet of Jonah's apartment seeped into me. I absorbed it, tried to bank it, sock it away for later, when I had to hit the road again.

My chest tightened at the thought of saying goodbye to Jonah. I'd only known him for a handful of hours, but it felt like longer. I was different around him than I was with other men. Instead of engaging in a fumbling, grasping union of bodies in a drunken haze, we talked. It felt like laying the foundation of something more lasting. Jonah had some magic quality about him that let me feel like myself. I liked being around him, and I think he liked hanging out with me. Given time, who knew what might come of it?

Only we didn't have time. Anything we started was just going to be torn up again when I left on Tuesday.

"We can stay in touch," I murmured to myself. The crazy, relentless tour schedule loomed in front of me like an endless road, but a text or call from Jonah might make it more bearable. Just thinking about it made leaving a little less daunting.

The ring of my cell phone broke the silence. I jogged to the bedroom and fished the phone out of my bag to see Lola's number.

"Hey."

"Hey, girl," she said, sounding tired on the other end. "You still alive?"

"Yeah, but you sound rough," I said. "How was the party?"

"Oh God, I can't even…"

I heard the flick of a cigarette lighter, and it occurred to me I hadn't smoked since last night's show. Or wanted to.

"It was epic," she said, exhaling. "Booze was consumed. Police were called. Sex was had by many, including yours truly."

"Oh yeah?" I sat on the edge of Jonah's bed. "Who?"

"Jason Hughes. The bassist from our soon-to-be former opening act. It's too bad, really. He's hot. You should appreciate the sacrifices I make for you."

"For me?" Then I remembered Ryan Perry, the drummer, getting grabby with me last night. Jonah had stepped in, and Lola demanded Jimmy fire Until Tomorrow.

"Yeah, for you," Lola said.

"Maybe we could—"

"We have twenty-five more cities and six months' worth of touring left with those guys. You really want to take your chances?"

I glanced down at my hands in my lap. "I'm sure Ryan was just drunk and being stupid."

"Yes, to both. Neither excuses him." Lola exhaled, her voice revved up to lecture mode. "You get drunk and stupid too, Kace, and it would only be a matter of time before he took advantage of the situation. Hell, I'm surprised it hasn't happened yet."

"Wow, thanks," I said, my cheeks burning. I almost told her I could take care of myself, but I had zero evidence to back that up. Lola had watched over me since I was seventeen years old, when the band's success swept me up in a whirlwind of recording and nonstop touring. I'd never stood on my own two feet and hadn't ever been sober long enough to try.

But I could try. If I had the guts...

"Sorry I'm grouchy, hon," Lola said. "I don't want anything to happen to you. I don't want anything to wreck this, Kace."

"I know," I said. "But getting a new opening act is a hassle."

It might be easier for Rapid Confession to get a new guitarist.

The words rose suddenly on my tongue, shocking me. But I couldn't spit them out.

"I don't see an alternative," Lola teased, "unless we assign Hugo to you twenty-four seven."

To babysit me.

I suddenly didn't want to talk to Lola anymore. I had tonight and all of tomorrow before I had to be back on RC time, and I didn't want to waste a second of it.

"I gotta run," I told my best friend. "Talk later?"

"Sure, I'll shoot you a text. Oh hey, how's it going with the limo driver? He's adorable. And hot. Not many guys can pull off that combination. Are you two getting along?"

I could practically see her knowing grin, and my irritation flared. She wouldn't understand if I tried to tell her we were building a potential friendship, and she definitely wouldn't believe I hadn't slept with him. Hell, if Jonah hadn't been the gentleman he was last night, I would've slept with him.

A sudden pleasant shiver raced down my spine at the thought, and I crossed my legs.

No. This is different. Jonah is different. He's not a guy I fuck at random. He's...

"He's wonderful," I said. "Goodbye, Lola."

I hung up, and jammed the phone into my bag, all the way to the bottom.

Not an instant later, I heard a text come in. I dug it out and my heart rose to see Jonah's number. It sank when I read the words:

Have to bail on you for the day. Too much work, then family dinner. Maybe order pizza? Sorry.

"Shit," I said. My hand let the phone drop back into my purse. Disappointment bit deep, not just from him canceling, but the terse, dry text itself.

I typed, No prob. CU later, and looked it over, satisfied it was casual and unconcerned. As it should be, I reminded myself. He had a schedule to keep, and he was keeping it.

I hit Send.

———————

The hours passed slowly. I didn't know how you could miss someone you'd only known a day and a half.

Around noon, I did what Jonah suggested and ordered a pizza— vegetarian, in case he wanted some later—and a six-pack of Diet Coke from a local place that delivered. I channel surfed while curled up on Jonah's couch. When I got cold, I went looking for the green-and-orange afghan, finally finding it balled up in the hall closet.

I had seconds on pizza for dinner and found *When Harry Met Sally* on a cable channel. One of my all-time favorites, but I found myself drifting to sleep around nine o'clock. My own sleep patterns were a mystery, since I usually stayed up until whatever party was over, and then crashed out after. But nine seemed early as hell. I guessed I had a lot of catching up to do.

I nodded off sometime after the "stupid wagon wheel coffee table" scene and woke up at the end of the movie, when Sally and Harry were at the New Year's Eve party. Sally was in the midst of declaring how she hated Harry, with the echo of the word *love* resounding behind every *hate*. I teared up like I always did. It took a long time for those two to find their way to each other, even though they were right there all along.

My fantasy was the opposite. I'd always dreamed my true love would swoop into my life, sweep me off my feet in one heroic gesture.

I'd know him at once—a flame would burn between us immediately. No doubts or games. Love—and lust—at first sight. He'd rescue me from all the hurt and loneliness, and I'd never doubt I was loved.

I'd thought Chett was that guy. I was the proverbial moth to his flame, drawn to his light, only to be burned to a husk when it proved to all be a fucking lie. And then I had nothing. No job. No money. Not even a high school diploma. God knew what would have happened to me had I not met Lola.

I went from hanging on Chett's coattails to hers, and even now I was taking shelter under Jonah's roof. It had never bothered me before, but it did now.

It bothered me a lot.

I shut off the TV. Now the only light came from one little lamp. I thought about going to bed, but my eyes grew heavy, and I was too tired to...

"Kacey?"

A gentle hand on my shoulder.

"Hmm?" I blinked awake. Jonah stood over me, and then crouched beside the couch. "You're back," I said.

"I'm back." His expression was pained, his rich brown eyes heavy. "I'm sorry I left you alone all day. It was a shitty thing to do."

"No..." I sat up, more awake now. "You have work and your family."

"It was shitty. You're only here for a little while, and I should've come back for lunch."

A warmth spread in my chest, and I became so aware that only about a foot separated us. "I survived. I ate pizza. A lot of pizza."

He smiled a little. "I was thinking maybe you'd like to go get dessert. Ice cream or something. I know it's late..."

"I'd love to," I said, and that warmth deepened to a flush that colored my cheeks. "Can you have dessert?"

Jonah's bright smile returned, a slow tilt of his lips to a full-blown grin that made his eyes light up. "I'll figure something out."

Chapter 13

JONAH

I drove us to Sprinkle Cupcakes and parked along a back street. Harrah's Casino rose up on our right and the Strip was a straight walk west from the little cupcake shop. It was closed at this hour, and Kacey's face fell until I showed her the ATM.

"This is a *cupcake* ATM?" she said, staring at the bright-pink square built into the wall of the closed shop. "Oh my God, that's the best thing ever."

"I thought you might like it." I slipped my actual ATM card into the payment slot and the menu screen lit up. "Go ahead."

She punched her order into the screen. A machine inside the ATM hummed and a little door slid up to reveal her cupcake: a red velvet with cream cheese frosting.

"That is so cool."

I ordered a plain vanilla cupcake. I turned from the ATM, juggling my wallet and dessert, just as Kacey broke off a frosted piece of red velvet and offered it to me.

"Want to try?"

"Hold on…" I tried to stuff my wallet in the back pocket of my jeans, but the damn thing wouldn't go. Kacey stood on her tiptoes and held the little piece of cake to my mouth. I had no choice but to eat it off her fingers.

Her head cocked, her eyes bright and electric underneath the amber streetlights. "Good, right?"

I nodded, though I wasn't tasting any cake.

"You have a little frosting…" She reached again, and her fingertips brushed the corner of my mouth. A whisper touch that crackled like a little current of electricity, straight down to my groin, where is sat heavy and warm.

I offered her mine. "Taste?"

That's all I could manage. *Taste.* I scoffed inwardly. *Me Tarzan, you Jane.*

Kacey took a small bite of my cupcake, and I watched as she licked her lips, staring at her mouth.

"How is it?" I said, a split second before my stare would need an explanation.

"Good." Kacey stepped back and flashed me a smile. "You have excellent taste, Fletcher."

We headed west, toward the Strip, ambling along a walkway between shops and restaurants, lined with potted plants and trees. It was after eleven on a Sunday, but Vegas was wide-awake. Couples, groups of laughing friends, and tourists speaking other languages walked past us or parted around us. We strolled and ate our desserts, heading across the boulevard toward Caesars Palace. Then I turned us south.

I wanted to show her the Bellagio Hotel.

"Let's stop here," I suggested. We leaned our arms on the white cement wall that buffered the pond in front of the Bellagio. Across the water, the hotel was lit up in gold and pink, curving toward the smaller structures of the casino below it like an open book.

"It's beautiful," Kacey said. She turned around to face the Strip. The small-scale Eiffel Tower glowed in front of the Paris Hotel and Casino across the street. "Italy on one side, France on the other," she said.

"You've really never been inside a casino?"

She shook her head. "Our tour schedule is so crazy; we haven't had any free time until after the show last night. That's why we're here until Tuesday—so Jimmy can hit the strip clubs and do some gambling. The last time I was here, I was too young to be allowed anywhere fun."

"Did you come here with your parents?"

"No," Kacey said, turning her gaze to the still, dark water in front of us. "I don't see them much anymore."

"Too busy with the band? Will your tour take you through San Diego?"

I took a bite out of the cake, and when I looked up, Kacey's entire demeanor had changed. She hugged herself, though the night was warm with a soft breeze, and the light in her eyes had dimmed as she cast her gaze over the dark water.

"No, it's not on my schedule," she said. "I haven't seen my parents in over four years. My dad kicked me out of the house when I was seventeen."

I nearly dropped my dessert, and the bite in my mouth was like a jagged rock. I swallowed with difficulty. "He kicked you out of your house? At seventeen?"

My tone was far too loud and hard. I was demanding an answer from her bastard of a father, not her. But Kacey didn't flinch or retreat. I think she understood my outrage, maybe even felt a little boosted for it.

"I snuck my twenty-two-year-old boyfriend home through my bedroom window one night. My parents caught us…in a compromising position, and that was it. My dad had never approved of anything I did; he hated my playing electric guitar, but that was the last straw. He let me pack a bag and locked the door behind me. I hadn't even finished high school."

I chucked what was left of my cupcake in a nearby trash can, appetite lost. "What kind of asshole turns his daughter out on the street? And what about your mom? She didn't help you?"

Kacey's shoulders jerked up in a shrug as she picked at her cake. "She didn't say a word. She never has. She's quiet and meek. My dad isn't abusive to her, not physically. But he can turn off like a faucet. Cold, bone-dry silence for days if he's really pissed, and my mom can't handle that."

"So she let you go?"

Maybe I shouldn't have asked, but I couldn't help it. I didn't understand how people could turn on their own children. That kind of parental failure—no, *violation*—was completely alien to me. My childhood had been ridiculously free of troubles. Sure, Dad was hard on Theo, and Mom was a compulsive worrier, but that was the extent of my complaints. My parents were good people.

They should've been your people, I thought, looking at Kacey. In a weird twist of fate, we each ended up with the wrong set of parents. Mine would've loved her and doted on her. They would've nurtured her music and been proud of her accomplishments. They'd give firm, appropriate discipline instead of throwing her out of the house.

A terminally ill child was something her parents deserved. My plight, given to that cruel father and spineless mother, would make more sense. If Kacey and I switched families, I'd no longer be afraid of the emotional burden I was leaving behind, and she'd be cherished forever.

"My mom didn't fight for me," Kacey was saying. She chucked her cupcake away too. "She lost her voice when she married my dad. I don't know if I can ever forgive her for that. But even so, I still call her sometimes. She doesn't say much, but I think she likes when I call. To know I'm still alive anyway."

"How did you survive on the streets?"

"I wasn't on the streets. I followed Chett, the boyfriend my parents caught me with. He told me he wanted to marry me, so I tagged along as he followed one get-rich-quick scheme after another. I followed him here. He was running out of money, so he had this great idea I could be a model." She made air quotes around the word. "I shut that shit down immediately."

"Good." My hands closed into fists, and I jammed them into my pockets.

"But once I told Chett I wasn't going to cooperate, it was all downhill. I was underage. I couldn't drink, gamble, or even get into an eighteen-and-up club. He got tired of me real quick. Dropped me on my ass when he met someone else. Some showgirl."

"What did you do?"

"I hitched back to California, thinking I'd try again with my parents. Go back to school. I did really well in school, actually."

"I believe it," I said.

Kacey smiled gratefully. "I made it as far as Los Angeles. I was staying at the YMCA and met Lola. She was nineteen, and in the same sinking boat as me. She'd just scraped enough money together waiting tables to get a cheap studio apartment and let me crash with her. When I turned eighteen, I got a job at the same restaurant, and we spent off days busking in parks. I sang and played my guitar while Lola played drums. A few months later, we found a want ad from a gal who wanted to put a band together, and the rest is history." She held up her hands. "And that is why, to this day, I've never stepped foot in a casino."

I nodded absently, my emotions roiled into a frothy rage at the men in Kacey's life who had failed her so fucking badly. "What happened to Chett?"

"Don't know. Don't care." She said it calmly enough, but I'd learned by now that everything Kacey felt was revealed in her large luminous eyes. She cared about everything, passionately.

She goes all the way up to eleven.

That thought helped to quell the anger that was chewing at my gut.

"Feel that?" Kacey asked. "That's the night dying a slow and painful death thanks to my sob story."

"I'm sorry I pried."

She waved my apology away. "I don't mind. I like talking to you. I don't normally talk about my life. Ever. Then it gets bottled up and I do something stupid like call my parents. I get rejected, rejection makes me drink myself into a stupor, I start a riot in a green room, and next thing I know, I'm waking up on my limo driver's couch."

"A vicious cycle."

"Oh, I don't know," Kacey said. "The couch part wasn't so bad."

A short silence descended. Despite every admonishment to keep to my schedule and not get close to this girl who was leaving in two days, I felt myself leaning in, wanting to hold the pain she'd trusted me with. Wanting to give her something in return.

"Do you want to come to the glass studio tomorrow?" I asked. "You could see how it all works, or maybe watch me make something..."

I felt the back of my neck redden. I sounded completely arrogant and totally boring at the same time. As if I'd asked her to watch me polish my coin collection.

But then Kacey clapped her hands together. "Are you kidding? I'd love to."

"Really?"

She used her index finger to lift one of her dark brows in an arch. "Really."

I leaned back, laughing harder than I had in months. Rusty gears inside me creaked from lack of use, and my embarrassment faded to nothing.

"I've been dying to see how you make that beautiful glass," Kacey said. "I was beginning to think it was for show, Fletcher. You ordered them from Etsy and passed them off as yours to impress the chicks."

"I'm legit, I swear."

Her laugh echoed across the pond, and within it, I heard traces of a beautiful singing voice. She started to say something else when music filled the plaza in front of the Bellagio, the haunting flute introduction of "My Heart Will Go On."

Kacey grabbed my arm. "Is that the *Titanic* song? Oh my God, it is. Why are they...?" Her words trailed away as Celine Dion's voice rose up and the Bellagio fountains began their show.

Jets of water arced up from the pond, swaying in time. They moved gently at first, almost shyly, like couples on a first date, touching and then collapsing over the expanse of water. Blue light illuminated them from below. As the song gathered momentum, more jets rose higher and crashed harder, creating clouds of mist. The colors changed to red, pale purple, and then silvery white. The song hit its crescendo, and Kacey's grip on my arm tightened. Her eyes grew soft, and she watched the water dance, but I could look nowhere but at her. The show was at my periphery, a backdrop to her.

The song mellowed to its final notes, and the tall jets of water were graceful arcs again, crossing each other in pairs, like dancers or lovers, then slipping beneath the surface as the song ended.

Kacey sniffed and wiped her eyes. "I wasn't expecting that." She looked up at me. "It was beautiful."

"Yes," I said softly. "Beautiful."

At my apartment, I unlocked the door and held it open for Kacey. She smiled almost shyly at me as she went in.

Holy shit, this is a date, I thought, locking up. *I just took Kacey out on a date and now...this is the end of the date.*

"Thanks for the cupcake," she said from the living room. "And the water show. Did you plan that?"

"I know this city. Aside from my time at grad school, I've lived here all my life. And it's part of my job to know where all the best shows are."

"You're good at your job," Kacey said. "You go above and beyond, actually." She moved close to me, rested her hands on my forearms, and craned up to kiss my cheek. "Good night."

I waited until she stepped back to speak, not trusting myself to open my mouth while hers was so close to mine.

"Good night," I said. I stared as she went into my bedroom. In a few minutes, she'd be in my bed, her hair spilling across my pillow...

This is bad. Very, very bad.

I changed to the sleep pants and T-shirt I'd stashed in the hall closet and leaned back in the recliner. I laid my hand over my ailing heart, which ached for reasons that had nothing to do with my chart or diagnosis, or any terrible biopsy. It ached because I could still feel Kacey's soft lips on my cheek, and I missed her.

She was fifteen feet away and hadn't yet left Vegas with her band, but I missed her just the same.

Chapter 14

KACEY

J ONAH WORKED ALL THE NEXT MORNING AT THE HOT SHOP. H E CAME back for me around noon, and we grabbed some lunch at a Chinese place, talking and laughing about everything and nothing. After two lunches and a cupcake, I felt a little bit like I'd become part of Jonah's routine. It wasn't true, but it made me happy to think so.

He drove us out to an industrial part of town on the outskirts of Vegas. The scenery outside my window was filled with more desert than civilization. Lots of warehouses and ramshackle buildings with aluminum siding. He parked the truck in front of what looked like a small airline hangar with three chimneys. The heavy metal door creaked as he slid it open sideways, and he ushered me inside the space.

Jonah laughed to see my expression. "I know it's not much to look at."

I couldn't argue with him there. The hot shop was about a thousand square feet of cement and steel, hotter than the midsummer Nevada heat outside and smelling of burned wood. An air-conditioning unit was waging a losing battle against two furnaces—one large and one small—that lined a single wall. In front of one raging furnace was a bench that had rails on either side, like high armrests made out of stainless steel. Next to the bench was a table upon which sat a thick, charred dictionary and tools soaking in a bucket of water: tongs and cups and strange-looking ladles.

"You leave the furnaces on?" I asked, fanning myself as the heat wrapped around me and squeezed.

"I turn them down at night," Jonah said, "and fire them back up for the day. It takes too long to get them hot enough otherwise. Alarm system over there"—he nodded his head at a wall unit with blinking lights—"alerts my phone if there's a problem."

I meandered past a rack of stainless-steel pipes on the near wall, each about three feet long. Beside that was a small metal table with nothing on it.

"So this is where the magic happens," I said.

"On a good day."

"What makes a bad day? You break something?" My feet crunched shards of glass on the cement floor as I walked between the furnaces and the metal table.

"Breaking a finished piece would definitely suck, yes." Jonah rapped his knuckles on the wooden table with the strange-looking tools. "Mostly a bad day is one where I haven't gotten enough done."

"The gallery has you on a pretty tight deadline?"

Jonah wore a strange expression on his face, a thin smile that didn't touch his warm brown eyes. "You could say that." He glanced at his watch. "Tania's on her lunch break. She'll be back soon, and you can meet her."

"Does it always take two people to make a piece?"

"Not always," Jonah said. "I make most of the individual pieces myself—those that are going to be for sale at the gallery. But for the larger sections of the installation, I need help."

I glanced around. "Where's your installation?"

"Through that door." Jonah indicated a door on the far wall. "That's where I keep all the finished pieces."

"So…" I rocked back on my heels. "Can I get a sneak peek? Seeing as how I won't be here in October for the gallery opening, it's only fair."

"I'll show you, but it's not going to look very impressive."

He led me to the back room. Dim light streamed in from the windows, illuminating dozens and dozens of cardboard boxes, some open and overflowing with packaging bubbles or the little curls of Styrofoam my grandmother called "ghost poop." Other boxes were sealed up tight and stacked, no more than three feet high, with *FRAGILE* stamped all over. Other flattened cardboard boxes were stacked in piles or leaned against the cement walls, waiting to be filled. On one long worktable—easily twenty feet long—were pieces of Jonah's installation.

I moved slowly toward the table, paranoid I would break something even without touching it.

Long curls of yellow and orange glass were laid out next to ribbons of blue and green, infused with gold flecks and dark-purple swirls. Frothy white glass took up another section of the table, pearly with incandescence. The last section held glass sculptures that took my breath away: delicate seahorses and sea dragons, glowing white jellyfish suspended in black spheres, and even an octopus, its tentacles curling a good foot and a half long and its skin rippling with ribbons of color.

Carefully, I let my fingers trace the blunt edge of a piece of glass that looked like a large ice cube with coral fronds. Within swam a sea turtle—perfectly rendered.

I looked at Jonah, so many questions trying to pour out of my open mouth that none did.

He jammed his hands down the front pockets of his jeans. "Not much to look at right now. Most of it is already packed away."

I shook my head. "These are amazing. I've never seen anything like this in my life."

"Thanks."

"The rest is in the boxes? To send to the gallery?"

He nodded. "I won't be able to wire them together until I'm in the gallery space itself."

"But how do you know what to work on if you can't see the whole thing? That's like…writing a song but never playing it through until showtime."

Jonah shrugged and tapped his temple. "I have it up here."

I think he mistook my shocked expression because he waved his hand like he was getting rid of a bad smell. "God, that sounds pretentious as hell."

"No, I think I get it." I gestured to the table. "This looks like an archaeological dig of Atlantis. Like you're finding the pieces one at a time and can't put them all together yet."

"Yeah, I like to think so." His eyes roved over the scattered pieces of his art. "I think part of working with glass is that you don't know exactly how it will turn out. The shape and flow of it… The fire dictates so much of what the glass does, how it changes the color and form. With some pieces, like the sea life, I design it from top to bottom, obviously. But for the installation as a whole, I try to follow it, instead of forcing it to be what it doesn't want to be."

A short silence fell. He glanced down at me, and the eyebrow went up. Laughter burst out of me, and I elbowed his side. I loved hearing him talk about his art. Art I knew nothing about, but was so incredibly beautiful, even strewn all over a table in pieces.

"Okay, show me," I said. "I'm dying to see how you do this. You can work and entertain me at the same time."

He looked thoughtful for a minute, then nodded, as if answering a private thought.

We went back to the main floor of the hot shop. Jonah grabbed one of the stainless-steel pipes from a rack on the wall, and I took a seat on the bench with the two rails.

"I'm going to need that," he told me. He pulled a chair from the opposite wall and set it up for me near the bench.

117

"Are you going to make something for the installation?"

"No," he said. "A small piece. To sell at the gallery. I think a perfume bottle."

"I love pretty perfume bottles."

"Do you?" he asked, his face turned away as he put one end of the pipe into the larger of the two furnaces, spinning it in his hands, back and forth, all the while. When he pulled the pipe from the furnace, a small molten sphere clung to the end, about the size of a tennis ball. He went to the stainless-steel table and rolled the glass over it, back and forth until it resembled a thick arrowhead, then put it into the smaller furnace, like he was roasting a marshmallow over a campfire. The fire inside this smaller furnace glowed ten times as hot as the larger one that held all the melted glass.

Jonah rolled the pipe in his palms over and over. Sweat had broken out over his neck and biceps, and I watched those muscles move as he worked.

"Kacey?"

I tore my eyes from his arms. "I'm sorry, what?"

"Color?" He carried the pipe with its glowing arrow of glass to a shelf full of trays. I kept a safe distance from the torch in his hands and saw that each tray was filled with crushed bits of glass in various colors.

"Go ahead," he said.

"Purple," I said solemnly. "For Prince."

"Good choice."

Jonah pressed one narrow side of the glowing arrowhead shape into the tray of violet-colored crushed glass. Deftly, he turned the pipe and pressed the heated glass down on the other side. It looked spongy as it picked up the glass bits. With two streaks of purple crumbles now clinging to the melted glass, Jonah took the pipe to the small furnace, always rolling the pipe in his hands. When he pulled it back out, the crushed glass was melted down.

"Why do you roll the pipe back and forth?" I asked.

"If I don't keep it moving at all times, the glass explodes into a searing-hot mess of liquid pain that scorches all it touches within a twenty-foot radius."

I crossed my arms and gave him a dirty look.

"It keeps the gather centered."

"Anyone ever tell you you're a smart-ass?"

He grinned. "A few people. Once or twice."

I had to agree with Lola—he was pretty damn adorable.

I took my seat in the chair, and Jonah put the far end of the pipe to his mouth and blew a short breath into it.

"That glass is blown," I said, laughing.

"If you think that's funny, the small furnace is called a glory hole."

"For real?"

"For real." He sat on the bench with the metal rails. "Get your mind out of the gutter, Dawson."

"Can't. It likes it there."

Jonah smirked at me, his eyes warm. He sat facing forward on the bench, like he was sitting on a horse, and set the blowpipe along the rails so the glowing ball of glass was in front of him. He used the rail to roll the pipe with one hand and took up a wooden ladle from the bucket of water. The glass hissed and sent up steam as he cradled it in the wooden ladle, rolling them together so the arrowhead shape became a small sphere.

"When did you know this was what you wanted to do?" I picked up a pair of tongs that looked like they were made of two knife blades. "How does one fall into glassblowing?"

"By drinking my weight in beer and whiskey shots and almost getting arrested for drunk and disorderly," he said. "Which, in Vegas, is no small feat, I might add."

"Okay, this I gotta hear."

"On my twenty-first birthday, a bunch of friends and I got drunk and went casino-hopping. We gambled and drank and then drank some more, until I was pretty wasted."

"I'm trying to imagine you drunk and can't do it," I said. "Which really isn't fair, all things considered."

"You're a much prettier drunk," he replied, his eyes meeting mine. "All things considered."

I felt the blush climb up my cheeks, and Jonah cleared his throat. "Anyway," he said. "My best friend, Oscar, was the ringleader of the whole expedition. He had five casinos on the itinerary, followed by a strip club."

"A strip club? For shame."

"It wasn't my thing, to be honest," Jonah said. "But I never made it there anyway. We staggered into the Bellagio, and I lay down on the floor in the middle of the lobby and refused to get up."

"The *floor?*" I clapped my hands together. "This makes me feel *so* much better about puking in your limo. Please continue."

He laughed. "I don't remember much except the ceiling was spinning. But holy shit, what a ceiling. Seventy feet of blown-glass art. A riot of colors that was somehow harmonized. Planned chaos, if that makes sense."

I rested my chin in my hand. "It does."

"I honestly thought I was hallucinating," he said. "I'd learned from my classes at UNLV about Dale Chihuly, a master glassblower, and that his work was here in Las Vegas. But I'd never been into glass. Or even into the Bellagio. But that night, even drunk off my ass, the installation stayed with me. I wanted to know how it was possible to make glass do that. Make it look like a flower garden had erupted out of the ceiling.

"I came back to the Bellagio the next day. Hungover as hell, to see if that ceiling was as impressive as I'd remembered, or if I'd just been a drunken idiot, mesmerized by pretty colors."

"You weren't a drunken idiot."

"The jury's still out on that," Jonah said with a grin, rising to refire the piece. "But I wasn't mesmerized; I was obsessed. I read everything I could about Dale Chihuly. He became my idol, and still is. I changed my focus from lights to glass that week, and the first time I held a blowpipe and watched a piece come to life, I knew it was what

I would do for the rest..." He coughed and wiped his sweaty chin on his shoulder. "For the rest of my studies."

"I love hearing how someone finds their passion," I said. "Or how it finds them." I glanced around the space. "But this isn't like painting where you can just pick up a brush and a canvas. Can I be nosy?"

"You want to know how one affords this space, the tools, an assistant, and all the glass a guy could want on a limo driver's salary?"

"Something like that."

"I don't pay for any of it. I won a grant from Carnegie Mellon." He returned to the bench and took up the damp burned dictionary to roll the glass in, as if he were polishing it. The smell of burned paper filled the space, and even though molten-hot glass was mere inches from his bare hand, it didn't seem to bother him in the slightest. He rolled and shaped with the practiced ease of someone who had done it thousands of times.

He's a professional, I thought. *A master.* I felt strangely proud watching him. "It doesn't surprise me that you won a grant."

"It was kind of a consolation prize, actually," Jonah said. "I got sick in my third year at Carnegie and couldn't graduate. I was in the hospital about five months, and when I got out...I didn't go back. My parents wanted me to stay here. My mother especially."

"I can imagine," I said quietly, just above the constant hiss-roar of the fire.

"But I had a full scholarship at CM, and when I told them I couldn't stay to earn my degree, they gave me a grant to do this installation. Sort of like a thesis project."

"You must be something special, Fletcher, for them to throw so much money at you." I tucked a stray lock of hair behind my ear. "But it's too bad you had to leave Carnegie. Can I ask...?"

"How I got sick?" He went to the furnace for another refire.

I nodded. "I don't understand how a twenty-five-year-old guy winds up needing a heart transplant."

Jonah nodded, and when he spoke his voice was flat. "A bunch of us took a trip to South America last summer. Peru, Colombia, Venezuela. I caught a virus while camping outside Caracas. They think it was from swimming in a river, though my friends and girlfriend at the time all swam too. I later learned I had a genetic disposition that made me susceptible to the virus."

He returned to the bench, rolling and polishing.

"I also learned I have a rare tissue type, which made finding a donor heart a little tricky. I was in a pretty bad way when we got the call that one was found, as close a match as they could get. I had the transplant, and...all's well that ends well, right?"

"I'm glad it ended well," I said softly.

He said nothing but hung the blowpipe upside down from a hook on the ceiling above him. It looked as though it had a glowing light bulb on the end. He took a second pipe to the big furnace that held the glass and came back with a small gather.

"What's that going to be?" I asked, glad to be able to ask something harmless for a change.

"The neck of the bottle." He sat on the bench, rolling the pipe, and took up a pair of what looked like oversized tweezers. He pressed one tong into the small piece of glass, hollowing it out, and then began to pull the glass, forming a lip.

"It's like taffy," I said.

"Pretty much."

He worked for a bit, stretching the neck out, then cutting off the end to make a perfectly round opening.

"Awful quiet in here," Jonah said, and his smile was warm again. "I'm sitting with a soon-to-be world-famous guitarist in front of me, but I don't hear music. Makes no sense."

I swung my legs out in front of me to examine my boots. "My acoustic is in a truck with the other band equipment. I think."

"If I turn on the radio, will I hear one of your songs?"

"Probably," I said. "'Talk Me Down' is kind of big right now."

"I've heard it. I'm not a fan of the music, to be honest, but the lyrics were pretty good."

"I wrote it."

Jonah stopped and looked at me sharply. "You did?"

"Surprised?"

He thought about it for a second. "Nope."

My cheeks heated, and I had to look away. "Shucks."

Jonah took the first blowpipe from the ceiling hook, then sat back on the bench. "Can I ask you a question?"

I grinned. "No."

He glanced at me, then back to his work. "You don't seem too keen on being a rock star, so why don't you do your own thing? Write what you want and sing it yourself?"

"I do sing a little. Backup. Rapid Confession already has a lead singer, and Jeannie will never let you forget it." I smiled ruefully. "She doesn't mind if I write hit songs so long as she gets to sing them. It's her band. And I've been in *her* band practically since my dad kicked me out. It's all I know how to do."

Jonah married the bottleneck to the round ball of glass, then broke off the whole piece from the first blowpipe. He took it to the big furnace, explaining he was adding another layer of clear glass over it. He returned to the bench for more rolling and shaping.

"I'm starting to see a little bottle," I said. "It's already beautiful. You're so talented."

"So are you," he said, not looking up from his work. "But all the pieces of your talent—singing, guitar, songwriting... They're scattered all over, like my installation. Or a *constellation*. Put them together..." Now he looked up, his smile gentle. "The whole might be pretty spectacular."

A hundred different emotions boiled up in me. Jonah's words were fragments of my own thoughts. Insights I'd never had the guts to string together on my own. I nearly snapped at him to mind his own business, and in the next heartbeat I wanted to throw my arms around his neck and thank him for...

123

For what?

I had no idea.

And I desperately wanted a drink.

"It's done," Jonah said, rising. He'd broken off the entire piece from the blowpipe, cradling it in an oversize glove, like a catcher's mitt, and took it to yet a third oven. "This is the kiln. It has to cool slowly. It'll be finished tomorrow."

He shut the door and turned to regard me where I sat, not having moved from my chair.

"I'm sorry if I got too personal." He rubbed his hand over the back of his neck, sweat beading his brow. "It's really easy to forget I only met you two days ago."

"I know what you mean," I said. My turbulent thoughts settled, along with the thirst for a shot of something strong. I moved to stand beside him at the kiln. "You're easy to talk to, Fletcher." I shot him a look. "Maybe a little *too* easy."

"Likewise, Dawson."

I peered into the screened window. "I can't see it." I turned so we were face-to-face, only a foot of space between us. "I want to see it before I leave Vegas."

"I'll make sure of that," he said quietly.

Our eyes met, as if our gazes were reaching for each other. I couldn't move. I didn't want to. I wanted to stay in his space, feeling his gaze soft on me, breathing the scent of his skin and clothes. His presence glided all up and down my body. The passing seconds seemed to expand and crystallize. If I moved, I'd break them.

I don't want to go.

I almost said it. The words were in my mouth.

Then don't, he answered in my mind, and I felt a tangible relief as if he'd spoken aloud. As if I had a different life than the one waiting for me in two days.

"We should get back," he said, his voice heavy and, to my ears, hung with regret.

I nodded. "Okay…"

The front door rattled open, and a woman's voice called out. "Hello? Sorry I'm late. You would not believe… Oh. Hi."

A young woman with caramel skin and dark eyes approached us. She wore jeans and an athletic runner's tank top. Her hair was a burst of dark ringlets held at bay by a colorful headband. She was gorgeous.

"Tania King," Jonah said, "this is Kacey Dawson. She's a…friend."

"So nice to meet you, Kacey," Tania said, offering both her hand and an easy, friendly smile. "And where do you know each other from?" she asked, her eyebrows arched almost to her headband with curiosity.

"Kacey's in town for a few days with her band," Jonah said. "She's staying with me until Tuesday."

Now Tania's eyes looked ready to burst from her skull. "Really? That's *wonderful*. And unexpected…"

"I was just giving Kacey a tour of the hot shop," Jonah put in.

I bobbed my head. "It's amazing. Jonah made a piece for the gallery opening to show me how it's done. He's incredibly talented."

"I agree," Tania said. "And I love to tell him how talented he is because he can't take it. At all. Look at him."

Jonah was rolling his eyes and shaking his head as the blush crawled up his neck. His modesty was genuine and therefore sexy as hell.

Shit, now I'm blushing…

"So which piece did you make?" Tania asked him. "I'll scratch it off the list."

Jonah scrubbed his hand through his hair. "Um, it's…"

"A perfume bottle," I said. "It's beautiful."

Tania wrinkled her brow. "A perfume bottle. I don't recall that—"

"I have to drive Kacey back to my place," Jonah said quickly. "I'll come back to finish out the day."

"Sure, sure," Tania said. She held Jonah's eyes a moment, then turned to me. "Will I see you again before you leave?"

"No," I said. "We fly out tomorrow."

Again, Tania's eyes met Jonah's. A silent conversation seemed to pass between them, reminding me of the one between Jonah and Theo in the kitchen yesterday.

"Well that sucks balls," she finally said.

"Tania doesn't express herself very well," Jonah said dryly.

"And aren't you lucky I don't?" she said. "It was a pleasure to meet you, Kacey."

She offered her hand again, but I hugged her instead. "You too, Tania. Maybe I'll visit sometime soon."

"Yes," she said. "I think that would be a very, very good idea."

———————

"Tania's awesome," I said as we drove back. "Has she been your assistant long?"

"Since I began the installation," Jonah said. "About two months ago. She's a senior at UNLV. Industrial arts and all kinds of talented. I'm lucky to have her."

"She seemed so happy to see me. That felt nice."

Jonah shifted in his seat. "She's like that. Friendly." He glanced at me, then back to the road. "The truth is…I've sort of walled myself off to a lot of people since I began my installation." He spoke slowly, as if inspecting each word before he let it out. "I have Tania, Theo, my parents, and my best friends, Oscar and Dena. They're all I have time for. I think Tania was happy that I brought someone new to the hot shop."

"Oscar and Dena are the friends I saw in your photos? The cute guy with a wide smile? Pretty girl who looks Middle Eastern?"

"That's them. Dena's parents are from Iran. She and Oscar have been together for ages. I'm actually supposed to hang out with them tonight. We get together every week. It's part of my routine, like dinner with my folks."

"Oh." I twisted my hands in my lap. "That's cool. I think I'll—"

"But I was thinking that since it's your last night here, maybe I'd cancel."

"No, no," I said, even as happiness bloomed in my chest. "I don't want to interfere..."

"I feel like vegging out with a movie." We came to a red light, and Jonah turned to me, a grin tilting his lips. "Is there an eighties classic on the agenda?"

"There could be."

The light turned green, and he turned his eyes back to the road. "Sounds good."

"Yeah," I said, resting my chin in my hand to conceal the idiotic smile on my face. "Sounds perfect."

Chapter 15

JONAH

WHEN MY CELL PHONE RANG AROUND EIGHT O'CLOCK, I KNEW IT would be Theo. I'd already gotten an earful from Tania when I'd returned to the hot shop that afternoon: question after question about Kacey. I stuck to the story; she was leaving the next day.

"And the perfume bottle?" Tania asked, her lips curled up in a knowing smirk. "I don't recall it being on the gallery manifest."

"I added it."

"Whatever you say, boss," she'd said and let the matter drop.

Theo, on the other hand...

"Oscar texted me," he said now. "You're *canceling* tonight?"

"It's Kacey's last night—"

"So, it's about that girl."

"*Kacey.* Yes. I—"

"Are you going to sleep with her?"

"Jesus, Theo."

"Are you?"

I sat on one of the two stools at the kitchen that served as my dining table, turning away from the hallway bathroom where Kacey was washing her face.

"I'm being polite to my houseguest. I don't want to invite her out—she's trying not to drink—and I don't want to leave her alone to be bored all night. And by the way, news flash"—I lowered my voice and made sure the water was still running in the sink—"it's none of your business who I sleep with."

"You know what Dr. Morrison told you," Theo said. "You have to be careful. Don't overdo it."

"Theo…"

"And you have to use a condom, no exceptions."

"I'm hanging up now."

But of course, I didn't hang up. Because he was my brother, and beneath his tough talk, he was scared shitless for me. "I told Oscar and Dena we'd hang out on Wednesday to make up for it. You free?"

"I'm at the shop late Wednesday," Theo said. "She's leaving tomorrow?"

"Tomorrow."

There was a silence on the other end.

"Hello?" I said. "Want me to tell her you said goodbye? Safe travels? How about an autograph?"

"I'll talk to you later," Theo said, his voice suddenly stony. The phone went quiet.

Kacey emerged from the bathroom, wearing a T-shirt that came to mid-thigh and nothing else. I stared at her long, bare legs and the bottom edge of a tattoo peeking out from beneath the hem.

"Don't look so scandalized, Fletcher," Kacey said, hauling up her shirt. "I'm wearing shorts."

I blinked. Yes, indeed, she was wearing shorts. Short shorts.

"Your tattoo," I said. "What's that called? A sugar skull?"

"A voodoo sugar skull. See the top hat? I love voodoo mythology and magic. Marie Laveau. Veve." She held up her leg for inspection, and I pretended to study her skull, which was done in vibrant colors with two large blue flowers in the eye sockets.

"It's nice." I coughed. "So…movie?"

Kacey clapped her hands together. "The original *Nightmare on Elm Street*. 1984. I've seen it twice. Johnny Depp is a *baby* in this sucker."

I watched her move into my kitchen and begin bustling around with pots, opening cabinets, and turning on a burner on the stove as if she'd done it a hundred times.

"You're cooking too?"

She dangled a bag of popcorn kernels. "Homemade. No fats or preservatives or—"

"Flavor?" I finished and then laughed at her huffy expression. "Did I have popcorn stashed somewhere?"

"No, I bought it today," Kacey said as she added kernels to the pot. "Can't watch a horror flick without popcorn. But I'm using coconut oil. Low cholesterol, heart healthy. And I got you this…"

She handed me a canister from the counter. The label read *Milton's Salt Substitute*.

"Sodium free," Kacey said, shaking the covered pot on the stove. "Fake salt. I'm going to use it on my popcorn too, out of solidarity. Oh, and drinks."

Kacey rummaged in the fridge, and I was afforded a generous glimpse of the smooth, flawless skin on the backs of her legs before she turned around and handed me a bottle of green tea with lemon and honey.

"Green tea is the healthiest thing ever, apparently. Personally, I never drink iced tea unless it's of the Long Island variety, but I thought we'd give it a shot."

I set my bottle on the counter and watched her shake the pot that was now bursting as the kernels popped. "When did you go grocery shopping?"

"While you were at the hot shop this afternoon. I love Tania, by the way. She's a quality human."

"Yes, she is," I said.

"Popcorn's ready," Kacey said. She dumped it all into a larger bowl, eyeing me up and down. "What's with you tonight, anyway?"

"What do you mean?"

"You're kind of scattered. Something on your mind?"

"I'm just shocked you did all this."

"That I went to the grocery store? Or that I braved the heat? I guess I have a lot of work left to do in the responsibility arena if buying popcorn and drinks comes as a shock."

"*Shocked* was the wrong choice of words. I meant, I'm touched you did all this. For me."

"It's the least I could do since you let me crash here."

She smiled at me and I smiled back, until the moment grew too long for friends to be smiling at one another. I tried some of the popcorn.

"How's the fake salt?" she asked.

"Not bad."

We moved our food and drinks to the couch. I sat at one end, figuring Kacey would sit at the other. Instead, she set the popcorn bowl in her lap and curled up right next to me, tucking her legs under her. She was flush against me, shoulder to shoulder, her left breast soft against my arm.

"Is this okay?" she asked, taking up the TV remote. "It's a horror movie, for one thing. And I'm kind of touchy-feely."

"I noticed." I could feel every place where we touched. "Why?"

"Ready for some pop psychology? My dad was a big believer in withholding physical affection. He hardly ever touched or hugged me. And he was always badgering my mom not to go overboard and coddle me. It would only make me weak and soft."

"Are you serious?" My imagination conjured a sweet little girl, running up to her dad with a scraped knee or with an A on a spelling test and being coldly rebuffed. "Your dad *never* hugged you?"

She shook her head. "But his little plan backfired. Instead of making me tough, I went the other way. I want to touch everyone. To make contact, you know?"

"Is that why you hug people when you meet them? Like Tania, today?"

"I don't hug *everyone*. Only good people. I have a sixth sense about it."

"You didn't hug Theo yesterday," I said. "He's a good guy."

"Can you blame me? He looked like he wanted to bite my head off." The glow of the TV turned Kacey's eyes electric blue. "But he's a good guy. I *wanted* to hug him, but I don't think he would've liked that. I don't think he likes *me*."

"He doesn't trust easily," I said. "I'm sure he likes you fine."

Kacey turned to look at me, and because she was practically sitting in my lap, her face was inches from mine. Her face was open, her features even more striking this close, free of the elaborate makeup she usually wore.

"Why would he need to trust me?" she asked.

Shit. Good question. "He doesn't trust anyone new around me," I said, infusing my words with as much nonchalance as possible. "Since my surgery, he's become ridiculously overprotective."

"Why? I mean, aside from the obvious reasons."

"My regimen is pretty severe, and he worries I'll become distracted."

"He's worried I'll corrupt you? Take you out for steak and booze?"

I glanced at this girl who wasn't used to being trusted and heard myself say, "He doesn't trust women around me. Because of Audrey. My last girlfriend."

Now Kacey sat up and turned her full attention toward me. "Audrey. Is she the girl…?" She pointed at a framed shot of Audrey and me at Carnegie that hung on the wall next to the AC unit.

"That's her," I said. "We were together for three years. We traveled a lot and planned to keep traveling after graduation. To see the great cities of the world and be inspired by their art."

"She worked in glass too?"

"No, a painter. We had a life planned out, and then it fell apart, and she didn't know how to cope with the chaos. She was with me in South America when I got sick and flew home with me while I waited for a donor heart. But being around illness or hanging around hospitals wasn't her thing."

Kacey leaned back, a shadow crossing her face. "What happened?"

"She stuck it out until I got the call that a heart had come available."

Kacey's eyes widened. "She *left*? When you were about to have a heart transplant?"

"More or less," I said. "But the upshot is, she told Theo she was leaving, and it turned him into a paranoid guard dog…"

"What about you?" Kacey cut in.

I tensed. "What about me?"

"She left. Is that why you stick so religiously to your schedule? To protect yourself?"

Words stuck in my throat, and I could only nod.

"I'm sorry if that's personal," she said. "I was thinking about how we've both been hurt by people who were supposed to love us. I protect myself too. By drinking, partying, making loud music." She turned back to face the television. "I hate that people leave when they're supposed to stay."

I nodded, at a loss for words. We watched the movie and ate our popcorn while the minutes ticked closer to tomorrow.

On-screen, a young woman thrashed in her bed. Her boyfriend screamed as the girl died a bloody death, her body dragged up the wall and cut to ribbons by unseen hands.

Kacey buried her face in my shoulder. "Tell me when it's over," she said, her voice muffled.

"What, this scene?"

She nodded against me, clutching my arm. Her hair was soft against my cheek.

On the TV, the boyfriend's screaming stopped. "Okay, she's a goner," I said.

Kacey turned her head to peek at the screen with one eye, then both. "Sorry. I'm a total wimp about horror movies."

"It was your idea."

"It's a great movie."

"But you're scared to even watch it."

"So?" Her challenging eyes were bright and vibrant, as if backlit with a cerulean light. "What's your point?"

"No, nothing." I laughed, shaking my head. "Makes total sense."

Kacey elbowed my side, then curled into it again.

She felt so soft and warm against me, while I was a brick wall with my hands tucked under my crossed arms to keep from seeking her. I wanted to fill my hands with Kacey, hold hers, or lay my palm on the bare skin of her thigh, which was pressed against mine. Or put my arm around her because—*my God*—wasn't this the last time I'd ever sit on a couch with a girl and watch a movie again? Have her hide her head in my shoulder during the scary parts, or share a bowl of popcorn? This was my life, what was left of it, and I was missing it.

I tried to lose myself in the movie. Minutes ticked by. On-screen, a young feathered-haired Johnny Depp failed to stay awake despite certain death. "You had *one* job, Johnny," I intoned.

Kacey buried her face in my shoulder, her fingers clenched around my arm, as Johnny was sucked into his bed and a geyser of blood erupted to spray the room.

"Tell me when it's over."

"How would I know if it's over?" I said, laughing. "You've already *seen* this."

"Twice."

"All right, the screaming's stopped, you can come out."

Kacey lifted her head, and Jesus, she was so beautiful—exhilarated, with her eyes full of laughter, as if she'd just gotten off a roller coaster.

Her beauty sucked my breath away. If I kept sitting here with her, I was going to do something stupid. Something unfair to the both of us.

I got up, muttering about needing the bathroom. I felt all along the right side of my body an unpleasant coolness where she had been touching me and now she was not. In the bathroom, I stared at my reflection in the mirror.

"Keep to the routine, Fletcher. The fucking routine."

That mantra was a frail, rickety bridge between what I wanted and what I would never have. It would fall to pieces in a stiff wind, but it was the only bridge I had. Without it, I would free fall to nothing.

"Keep. To. The. Routine."

When I returned to the living room, Kacey sat up, yawning and stretching. She smiled when she saw me. A surprised smile. As if we hadn't spent all evening hanging out together. As if I'd been years away in Africa and not two minutes in the john.

But I felt it too. I missed her. Every time I closed my fucking eyes, I missed her.

I stood apart from her, staring, while in my mind I closed the distance between us, took her down to the couch cushions again, but this time, I lay over her. Kissing her luscious mouth, tasting her tongue as it slid over mine. Her thighs parted for me, revealing panties that were damp when I touched her...

Jesus Christ...

I took shelter behind the kitchen counter so Kacey wouldn't see the raging hard-on tenting the front of my flannel pants.

"I'm getting some more ice for my tea," I muttered. "Need some?"

"Sure."

I opened the freezer and stayed there, inhaling the cold air until my blood had cooled and it was safe to turn around.

Or maybe I could slam my dick in the door...

"How's that drink doing ya?" I asked, cringing as the words left my mouth. Clearly, the blood had yet to return to my brain. "I mean, how is it without something harder to drink than iced tea?"

"Not bad," she said. "Actually, it's been pretty easy to lay off the booze these last few days. I thought I'd be jonesing, but here I feel like I can chill. I don't need the buffer."

"Buffer?"

"The booze buffer. The one that goes up between yourself and real life when you're drunk. Everything is so much easier to take. Easier to not give a shit. You can put yourself at a safe distance."

"Safe distance from what?"

She shrugged and glanced at the couch cushions beneath her. "Life. The life I've found myself living. A life that happened to me, instead of one I made." She became intent on a stray thread, winding it over her finger. "Vegas is different from what I thought it would be. After all that shit that went down with Chett, I thought it would be haunted. But it's not so bad. Better than being on the road with the band. I can see that now. So I was thinking I might"—the thread on her finger went round and round—"stay."

The blood drained from my face so fast I had to grip the counter.

Stay.

The word hung in the air. A crystal bubble of perfection.

She's going to stay. I can see her every day; I can talk to her; I can touch her...

My thoughts ran rampant, carried on the rapid tide of my pulse, which was buzzing in my ears. It was so loud, I could hardly hear Kacey's next words. But I felt them. I felt each word, little bullets that struck me, each with a new emotion: fear and joy and guilt and something damn close to happiness.

"I think I want to quit the band," she said, still concentrating on her loose thread. "I'm under contract, and I have no idea if it's even possible to get out of it without being sued. But I think I might try. I think I might do what you said. Try to put all the pieces together. Write my own songs and sing them myself. Of course, I'd have to get a regular job in the meantime, but that would be good for me too."

Her face...she wore a look of conviction I'd never seen before; her voice was clear and strong as she built a life for herself here.

A life with me?

"I'd get my own place and take care of myself," she was saying.

"Instead of letting Lola handle all the responsibility. Pay my own bills, go back for my GED. Stand on my own two feet for a change…"

Her words trailed off, and she looked over at me. She saw my stricken expression, and all her hope vanished. It slipped from her features like a mask, and the light burning in her eyes dimmed.

"Anyway," she said, and cleared her throat. "Like I said, I don't know if it's possible. I'm probably locked into my contract."

Still, I said nothing, a thousand thoughts warring, a thousand words locked in my mouth.

Kacey swallowed hard and lifted her chin up against my silence. "Never mind, it's a stupid idea." She threw the pillow aside and flew off the couch, toward the bedroom. "And I'm not feeling well. I'm going to hit the sack. Good night."

The door slamming shut jump-started my synapses. "Kace, wait."

In my room, she had her duffel bag on the bed and was grabbing clothes out of the drawers.

"Wait," I said. "Stop. I'm sorry. We need to talk about this."

"You don't have to say anything," she said. "I fucking get it. I read it all over your face. Only you're wrong. Dead wrong."

"Wrong?"

"You've got that 'scared shitless' look guys get when the girl starts talking marriage and babies on the first date." She threw her clothes in the bag, piece by piece. "But let me tell you something: me wanting to move here is *not* a marriage proposal. I don't want your babies. We're not even *dating*. And I don't *want* to date you. At this moment, the last fucking thing I want to do on this earth is date you."

The words stung, but I hardly felt them. The possibility of her moving here both scared me to my bones and lit up the shadowy places in my heart.

It's my heart, dude, and you're wasting it.

God, the chaotic hope and dread of the situation was making me dizzy, and now I was hallucinating my donor's voice. I shook my head to clear it out.

137

"What…? Would you really quit the band?"

"Yes, Jonah, I really would." She planted her hands on her hips. "Are you that shocked? I told you things I haven't told anyone. I told you *everything*. How I was unhappy…and scared…"

"You did. And I hoped you'd quit. But I didn't think you'd move *here*."

She flinched at that, and her jaw clenched against the tears in her eyes.

"Dammit." I scrubbed my hands over my face. "I didn't mean it like that."

"No? What did you mean?"

We faced off, her waiting for an answer and me trying to quell the chaos that raged in me. The push and pull of wanting her to stay and what lay ahead if she did.

"You hate the desert," I said finally. "And the heat. And this city."

"I never said that."

"I believe your exact words were, '*I fucking hate Las Vegas*.'"

She stared at me, pain etched into every contour of her face. My arguments were stupid and empty, and we both knew it. We'd known each other only a few days, but we had a connection.

"Look, let me explain," I said. "I didn't mean—"

"Don't worry about it," she said. "It doesn't matter what I said, or what you said. None of what we ever said to each other means anything. So you're safe, okay? I won't distract your work or disrupt your precious schedule anymore."

"Kace…"

"I didn't think about moving back here for you," she said, her voice cracking now. "Let's just get that clear. I had this *crazy* idea I'd actually face all the horrible heartache Chett caused me, in the city where he ditched me. Or write about my dad and exorcise that particular fucking demon with a song. Or ten. Or a hundred. However many it takes until I get it *out*. I thought I'd try being on my own for the first time in my life. I thought I'd get serious about my music.

And I thought, maybe, I'd have a friend I could call and hang out with sometime." She zipped her bag shut. "But I was wrong."

"You weren't wrong," I said, rubbing my tired eyes.

"No? You have a funny way of showing it." She took up her duffel and shouldered her purse, still wearing her sleep shorts and a T-shirt. Bare feet at one in the morning, and tears threatening to break.

"Kace," I said softly. "Where are you going?"

"I'm not staying here," she said. "I'll get a cab back to Summerlin. Back…"

The tears spilled over, and her shoulders crumpled at the weight of her life, which fit entirely in one small duffel.

I moved close to her, took the duffel from her hand and the bag from her shoulder, and let them drop to the floor. I wrapped my arms around her. She stiffened, then melted against me. I held her as she cried against my chest. A full-blown ugly cry, because she knew it was okay to cry like that. With me.

"I'm so scared," she whispered. "I'm scared of what I want…of going after it and fucking it all up again. Scared of having to call my parents or Lola…crawling back to them for help because I had the opportunity of a lifetime in the palm of my hand, and I threw it away." She held on to me tighter. "I'm scared that I'm so busy being scared that I'll never *be* anything at all."

I stroked her hair. "You will. You'll find it. You can be scared and still find it. I know you can. And I don't want you to think I wouldn't be happy to have you here in Vegas. I would. I want you to stay, but—"

"I don't expect you to take care of me," she said. "I just need a friend to tell me I'm not crazy. And I was hoping that friend was you."

"I can be that friend, but…"

Oh shit, here it is…

My heart pounded and adrenaline raced through my veins. "I have to tell you something."

"What?"

139

My jaw worked and no sound came out. I had nothing planned. No standard speech. I kept people away, so I didn't *have* to tell them. But now here was Kacey…

She looked up at me. Her eyes were beautiful and shining and filled with trust I hadn't earned. I almost told her to forget it. That I was an asshole, and she'd be better off not speaking to me ever again.

But a part of me—the part that leaped for joy that she might stay—wanted something more with this beautiful, energetic, impulsive woman. My world had been fading to gray until she burst in like a bombshell of color and light, and dammit, I wanted it. I wanted to keep her in my life, even if only as a friend. It had to be only as a friend, and even that felt selfish and wrong. But maybe, said this little voice, I could be honest with her and let her decide for herself.

But not here. Not in my plain little apartment. I had to take her somewhere beautiful, to show her what I was holding on to and why.

"Are you up for a field trip?"

She nodded slowly. "Okay."

I breathed a sigh, but it gave me no relief. "Get dressed. I want to show you something."

Chapter 16

KACEY

ON THE DRIVE TO WHEREVER JONAH WAS TAKING ME, MY MIND concocted a hundred possibilities for what he was planning to tell me. Something big. Something that warranted this excursion. And judging by the haunted look in his eyes, it wasn't something good.

My heart clanged against my chest.

Calm down. It might not be as bad as you think.

Whatever it was, I was going to listen. To be there for him. When I told him I was thinking of staying in Vegas, a future was born between us. Maybe a romantic one or maybe not. Just…being together. A bond. We had an undeniable connection.

Soon the Eiffel Tower loomed on our right. Across Las Vegas Boulevard, the Bellagio Hotel and Casino was illuminated majestically behind its lake. Jonah turned into the casino entrance and parked.

"Another water show?" I asked.

He gave a quick smile. "Not tonight."

The water was still and dark as we walked along it. No colored lights or dancing jets. Shivers ran up my bare arms, despite the heat.

Beside me, Jonah looked handsome in jeans and a black T-shirt. The medical alert bracelet on his right wrist caught the glittering lights of the hotel.

The Bellagio's air-conditioned lobby made me shiver harder. A few people crisscrossed the marble floors or waited at the registration desks. The refined *ding* of an elevator echoed off marble. Beneath my feet, a gorgeous mosaic spread out in all directions, leading to a lush seating area with potted plants. Beyond that was the registration area with elegant arches in pale cream and gold. A coffered ceiling made me feel as if I'd stepped into a Roman palace.

Then my gaze was drawn upward, to the centerpiece of the Bellagio lobby, and undoubtedly, the reason Jonah had brought me here. The ceiling's beams flowed toward a masterpiece of light and glass. Hundreds upon hundreds of what looked like upside-down umbrellas, rippling along the ceiling in riots of color.

"*Fiori di Como*," Jonah said, walking beside me. "*Flowers of Como* by Dale Chihuly."

"Your idol," I murmured, staring at the magnificent bouquet of delicate glass flowers bursting from the ceiling.

"Seventy feet long and thirty feet wide," Jonah said, his voice low and reverential. "Over two thousand pieces."

"It's amazing," I said, then looked to Jonah. "Your installation is better."

He smiled, but it was a smile laden with something beyond sadness. Something so deep and profound, I longed to turn back, to find an exit and run away from whatever it was he was going to tell me.

"Dale Chihuly is a true master," Jonah said. "A virtuoso. I could only hope to create something like he has. Something more than just a beautiful piece of glass."

"Like what?" I asked in a small voice.

"A legacy," Jonah replied. "Let's sit for a minute."

He led me to the plush maroon couches directly under Chihuly's blown glass. The couch was soft and invited me to slouch into its cushions, but I sat ramrod straight, bracing myself.

Jonah leaned forward, resting his forearms on his thighs and turning his MedicAlert bracelet around and around. I could see him measuring words and assembling sentences, working up the courage to tell me something that was going to change everything.

"If you're going to ask me to marry you, the answer is no," I said. "We hardly know each other. I need at least three more cupcakes."

Jonah laughed lightly.

"That's not it?" I said, trying to lighten the moment, but my voice wouldn't play along. "Are you gay?"

Jonah looked at me then, his dark eyes warm and soft. "Strike two," he said.

"Okay," I said, swallowing hard. My next and last question stuck in my throat. Once asked and answered, my life would never be the same. "Are you sick?"

"Yes, Kacey."

"How sick?"

"Terminally sick."

The words dropped into the space between us like a grenade ready to blow. My chest constricted as if I'd inhaled subzero air. I nodded vigorously, spastically, as I tried to both process and reject the news.

"Okay," I said. I raked my hands through my hair and kept them locked behind my neck. "Okay. Is it your heart?"

"Yes," Jonah said. "Chronic transplant rejection."

My brain raced through everything I had ever heard about organ rejection, which wasn't much. "I thought that was something that happened immediately."

"Acute rejection sometimes happens right after surgery. They give you drugs for that to calm the immune system down, and usually they work."

"But you take all those drugs."

He nodded. "I do. But instead of an all-out protest, my immune system has been chipping away at the heart over time, rejecting it slowly, despite the meds."

My arms crept across my middle, clutching handfuls of my shirt and hugging myself tight. "How do you know that's what's happening? You don't look sick."

"Heart transplant recipients have to have a biopsy every month to test for this sort of thing. At my third biopsy, eight months ago, they found evidence of atherosclerosis, and—"

"What's that?" I said, my voice harsh and accusing, as if he were making words up.

"Hardening of the arteries," he said. "The actual diagnosis is cardiac allograft vasculopathy. CAV. The immune system attacks the heart, leaves scar tissue. The scar tissue builds up and starts to wear down the heart until it eventually fails."

I hated the ceiling then. All that brilliant color and joy and beauty. A party raging over the horror and unfairness strangling me. I looked at the plain buff floor, trying to breathe.

"How...?" Again, I had to swallow the hard lump lodged in my throat. "How long?"

"Four months, at this point. Maybe more. Maybe less."

My own heart went into free fall, and my skin went cold, head to toe, as if I'd been doused in ice water. "Four *months*?"

Four months.

Sixteen weeks.

One hundred and twenty days.

Four months was *nothing*.

"Oh my God," I whispered, the words squeezed out of my chest. I felt the tears wet on my face. Felt a drip slide under my jaw and start creeping down my neck. I was crying. I was breathing and pulsing and living.

And Jonah was dying.

He reached a hand out as if he wanted to comfort me, but let it drop. "I'm so sorry," he said.

A bark of laughter escaped me, echoing off the marble arches. "Why? Why are you apologizing to me? And why didn't you tell me before?"

"If you could see your face right now, you'd know why."

The tears were dripping off my chin then. I just stared at him, open-mouthed and tasting salt.

"Fuck," he said, smashing a fist on the arm of the couch. "I fucking *hate* doing this to people. I hate what it does to you and what it does to me. It makes it so goddamn real, when I'm trying to keep my head down and get by. Get through. Make it to October with a finished installation and"—he gestured to the ceiling above—"this. A legacy. I just want to leave a part of me behind that means something."

"Your schedule…" I said, using a bit of my sleeve to wipe my face. "Now I get it. But I don't get why you pushed all your friends away. To spare them? Don't you think they'd rather decide for themselves? Don't you think they'd want to be with you…?"

"I *know* they do," he said. "But I had to tell *my mother* what I just told you. I have to watch my family and friends count down the minutes whenever they're with me. The pain in their eyes, the careful words, the hugs goodbye that last a little too long. I take it from Oscar and Dena and Tania; I take it from Theo and my parents… I take it from them because I have to. Anyone else…I can't stand it. I have my circle, and that's it. I don't want to tell people outside the circle. I don't want them to have to find out. I don't let anyone in…"

"And yet," I said, gulping air, getting a hold of myself. "Here I am."

"Here you are…" Jonah said, his eyes roaming my face. "Believe me, I didn't want to let you in. But it was almost as if…"

"What?" I whispered.

"As if I didn't have a choice," Jonah said. "I tried to keep the circle closed and my walls up, keep to my routine…but you got in anyway." He gently swiped a tear from my chin. "You feel it too, right?"

I nodded. "Yes."

"Kace…" He shook his head, raked his hands through his hair, wrestling with himself. "I don't want to put you through…what's going to happen. That's why I acted like such an asshole earlier tonight. I saw it unfold to the end, and I…I can't do it to you."

We sat in silence. People came and went, passing our couch, oblivious to what was happening.

"How do they know it's four months?" I said. "How can they be that specific?"

"They can tell. Although…"

"Although what?" I said, grasping at the word like a drowning woman for a hunk of life raft.

"I'm supposed to have a biopsy every month. So they can be even *more* specific. But I stopped going."

"Why?"

"Because it's a fucking awful procedure, and it lays me up for forty-eight hours. I have too much work to do at the shop to lose that kind of time. Second, I don't need a biopsy to know. The symptoms will kick in."

"What symptoms?" I asked.

"Fatigue and shortness of breath, mostly." Jonah toyed with the MedicAlert bracelet. "I have those now, a little. I can't run anymore or hit the gym like I used to. But when I start to get tired doing little things or find it hard to catch my breath for no reason, I'll know. I don't need to count down the days in the meantime."

A sliver of hope, a tiny flame in gale-force wind, came to life in my heart. "So…you don't *actually* know. You have no idea how bad—or not bad—the cardio…the CAV thing is. Maybe it's stopped. Maybe the drugs you take are working."

"Don't…" he said.

I barreled on. "You're like Schrödinger's cat. So long as you never get another biopsy, the lid on the box is closed. You could live a long time. *Years,* even. Happily in the dark."

He smiled a little. "Ignorance is bliss, right? But I don't have false hope, and I don't want you to either. I'm not in denial, but I'm not inviting in the cold, hard light of day to torture myself. Can you see the difference?"

I nodded, and he took my hand then. His fingers curled around mine and held on tight. *His hand…strong and solid. A burn scar on the pad of his thumb, a few nicks…but otherwise healthy. He has to be healthy…*

"I've tried to convince myself the doctors are wrong," Jonah said. "But you can't talk yourself out of the truth. I'm not without hope, but I'm realistic. They might be wrong. They probably aren't. That's my bottom line."

"But what if they are wrong? What if—"

He shook his head. "All I can do is live day to day… I take extra medications to try to slow the CAV down. I made my strict diet even stricter, and I sleep in a recliner instead of a bed. Anything and everything to squeeze out a little more time to do my work and see that gallery opening."

I fought for another argument, but I had nothing left. I exhaled roughly. "Can the record just show I got through this conversation without a drink *or* a cigarette?"

He busted out laughing, and our eyes met, a moment, a heartbeat, and then we were in each other's arms, holding on tight.

"Jonah…" I whispered against his neck.

"I know."

"I don't… I can't…"

He rocked me gently. "I know."

We stayed there a long time, until Jonah gave me a final squeeze and held me by the shoulders. "Let's get back. It's late. We'll get some sleep, and in the morning…"

"Jimmy comes to take me to the airport," I said. "What do I do then?"

"You go with him. Talk to Lola. Decide to either stay with the band or work out how to quit if that's what you need to do. You'll find a way."

"And what about you?"

"Don't worry about me."

I looked up at him sharply. "A little late for that, pal."

His smile was gentle and quiet, and his voice quavered as he spoke. "Either you'll keep in touch with me or you won't. If you do, I'll be here for you. And if you don't, I'll understand. I promise you I'll understand. Okay?"

I didn't say okay. Not one bit of this was okay. My mind hadn't wrapped around everything yet; I had more tears to cry, but now my eyes felt drained and numb. We walked out of the Bellagio hand in hand, out from under the glass flowers, a garden that would never wilt or die.

We went back to his place. Without discussion, I piled the pillows high on the bed so he could lie inclined; then I curled up next to him.

I understood why he didn't tell everyone his situation. Pain like this went beyond the realm of private or personal. It lived down deep, beneath everything superficial, and drew everyone who knew it down deep with it. It closed distances.

We lay curled up in each other, and I laid my head against his chest.

"Does this hurt?" I whispered.

The rumble of his voice in my ear was drowsy. "No. I'm all right."

"Does anything hurt right now?"

"No, Kacey." Jonah stroked my hair, held me tighter. "Right now, nothing hurts."

He rose and fell with easy breathing. Beneath my ear, his heart beat strong and steady.

A flicker of hope in me flared, determined to burn all night long.

Chapter 17

KACEY

I LOOKED OUT THE WINDOW TO SEE A BLACK SEDAN ROLL INTO THE parking lot of Jonah's complex. Jimmy Ray got out, leaned against the fender, and lit a cigarette.

I turned to face Jonah at the kitchen counter. "He's here," I said.

"Okay."

"I have to go," I said, trying to muster strength for the decision that lay ahead. I'd gone to sleep last night floating on hopeful peace and woke up feeling seasick. The impact of Jonah's revelation descended like a storm howling through my head. Last night I thought I knew what to do. This morning, I didn't know where I was and didn't trust myself to be strong enough for anyone. The band, Jonah, or even myself.

My only certainty was if I didn't continue the tour while I tried to figure things out, the legal hammer would fall for breaking my contract, and I'd be left with no options at all.

I turned from the window. "Let's go."

Jonah touched my shoulder gently. "I'll walk you out."

He carried my bags for me to the parking lot, where Jimmy

waited impatiently, the heat cloying and making him even more anxious than usual.

I leaned close to Jonah. "I don't want to say goodbye with him watching."

"Neither do I."

"Need one more minute, Jimmy," I called, my voice scratchy with the echo of tears.

Jimmy checked his watch and mumbled something as Jonah set down my bags at the edge of the parking lot. We walked over to the small courtyard, and I noticed he wore a light jacket even though the temperature must have been pushing one hundred degrees. He pulled a softball-sized box from the pocket and held it out to me.

"A going-away present," he said, a tremor at the edge of his voice.

I took the box and opened it. The sun glinted off glass, and tears blurred my eyes. It was the perfume bottle, finished and perfect. Elegant ribbons of violet and indigo swirled around its small, squat body. The neck opened in a flat circle, and the stopper was a beautiful clear marble. I held it up, letting the sun shine through the empty interior.

Not empty, I thought. *It holds Jonah's breath.*

Afraid I would drop it, I put the bottle back in its box and held it tightly to me. I looked up at him. "I'm afraid," I whispered. "I'm afraid if I go, I'm failing myself. If I stay, I fail the band. And you. You said hanging around hospitals wasn't your ex-girlfriend's thing. It's not mine either. I'm so scared I'll fail you if I stay."

His smile was so sweet and warm, but sad too. Yellow tinged with blue. "You can't fail me. I don't expect anything from you, Kacey. Only friendship, as much or as little as you want to give."

"I don't know what to do."

"You will," Jonah said. "Go to your room in your next house or hotel, away from the band. Shut the door and lock it, and in the quiet, ask yourself what you really want to do. You, Kacey Dawson. What do you want for yourself? Don't think about me or Lola or Jimmy or anyone else. Just you."

What I wanted. I thought I knew, but could I come back here for it? Could I find the strength to stand on my own? And if I did, how fast would the four months go? Could I watch Jonah…?

I shuddered, unwilling to even finish the thought, and the coward in me whispered I didn't have the backbone for what I wanted.

"Contracts are almost impossible to break," I said. "I might be stuck no matter what."

"You might. But the right thing will always find a way." He took a step closer. "Be safe, okay? Above all else, be safe."

I nodded and leaned against him. His arms went around me, and I turned my face into his chest, inhaling deeply. I wanted to take some of Jonah with me, the part that kept me settled and calm and quiet.

We walked back out to the parking lot, where Jimmy was pacing in front of the sedan and tugging at the collar of his dress shirt in the heat.

"Jesus, kitten, I'm dying out here. Let's go already. We got to be at the airport in two hours."

He and Jonah eyed each other hard while the sedan driver took my bags and stowed them in the trunk. The driver held the door open for me, and Jimmy motioned for me to get in.

Jonah leveled a finger at Jimmy. "You take care of her."

"Of course. We got a brand-new opening act, as promised." Jimmy's smile was bright and fake. "I take care of my girls. They're like daughters to me."

Jonah raised an eyebrow, and his stare hardened to ice.

Jimmy coughed. "Never mind," he said, climbing into the car. "We got a schedule to keep."

I turned back to Jonah. He looked down at me, and our eyes locked. In the next heartbeat, I was standing on my tiptoes and pressing my lips to his. He made a sound in his chest, as if in pain, and I felt the answering ache in mine. I pulled away before the soft kiss became a hard promise I couldn't keep.

I turned and climbed into the car and didn't look back. Not even to wave.

I wasn't ready to say goodbye.

Chapter 18

KACEY

THE SUMMERLIN HOUSE WAS TRASHED. I STOOD IN THE CENTER OF MY room, staring at the mess. The cigarette burns in the carpet, the makeup residue in the sink, unidentifiable stains on the carpet.

"I packed for you," Lola said from the door.

I jumped, my heart pounding. "You scared me." My nerves were shot. I sat on the unmade bed and smoothed out the comforter, as if it helped. "This place is a disaster."

Lola shrugged. "That's what security deposits are for." She crossed her arms. "So…are you with us?"

"I'm here, aren't I?"

"You're with us, but are you *with* us? They don't call it a band for nothing, you know. We need to play as a whole. Are you ready to do that now?"

I shrugged, not looking at her. "Sure."

I heard Lola sigh and shift on her heels. "Is it the guy? The limo driver?"

"What about him?"

"Is he another Chett? Another guy who's going to fuck you up for God knows how many years? Because honestly, Kacey—"

"He's dying."

Lola's arms dropped to her side. "What do you mean he's dying?"

I stared at her, shaking my head.

Her chin tilted. "You mean like, *dying* dying?"

I nodded.

"Cancer?"

"Heart failure. Slow heart failure."

Slow failure that's going to take him so fucking fast…

"Shit." Lola sat next to me on the bed. "Oh, honey, I'm so sorry." She put her arms around me, though I hardly felt it. "Well. You met him on Friday night, right? Or Saturday morning? Whenever you regained consciousness on his couch?"

"Yeah," I said. "So what?"

"So…it sucks he's sick, but you've known him all of four days. If that."

I blinked at her. "And?"

"I'm just saying, you found out before you got in too deep. The last thing you'd want is to get involved with someone who can't give you a future."

"No." I shot off the bed, shaking my head vigorously now. "No, you are not going to do this."

"Do what? Give you a reality check?"

"Talk about him. You don't know—" I waved my hands. "Never mind. I'm not talking to you about him. Or these four days. They're mine. So let's…fucking go already. We have a plane to catch."

"Glad to hear it," said a voice at the door. Jeannie leaned against the jamb, arms crossed over her midriff-baring black shirt. She tossed a lock of dark hair out of her eyes. "You're ready to rejoin us?"

"We're cool, Jeannie," Lola said, staring at me, her eyes soft with compassion but hard with *Don't fuck this up*. "She's ready. Right? She needed a little break. Some time to chill. Nothing wrong with that."

"Yeah, I rested up," I said. "Now I'm ready."

"Good," Jeannie replied. As I pushed past her, she threw out the empty threat she'd been using on me since I joined the band: "Because there are a hundred guitarists who would *kill* to have your job."

I muttered under my breath, "Promise?"

Friday was the first concert in Denver, and I did the show sober.

To say it was a disaster was being kind.

I fucked up my solo on "Talk Me Down," I came in late on three different songs, and I riffed the opening chords for "Taste This" at the end of the set, forgetting we'd played it already. Jeannie had to stop the show and make a joke about an early encore while shooting me a death glare.

"What the actual fuck, Kacey?" She screeched at me in the green room. "You go and take a leave of absence for four days, supposedly to get your shit together, and then come back more flaky than before. Are you *trying* to ruin us?"

Violet and even Lola were waiting for an answer.

"I'm sorry," I said. "I was out of it tonight. I'll be fine tomorrow, I promise."

But I wasn't. Not on the inside, anyway. I managed to get through the next night's concert without fucking up, but the second it was over, I hit the green room liquor stash hard.

The first burning taste of whiskey nearly made me puke. The second was better. By the fifth, the ache in my heart wasn't entirely gone, but it was bearable.

We partied back at our hotel, with the band—and fifty of our closest friends—crowded into the suites Jimmy rented. I'd never been claustrophobic, but I felt it that night. Too many bodies, talking too loudly and drinking too much. Smoke—from pot and cigarettes—hung in the air like a gray haze, and the music was so loud I could hardly hear the guy hanging off my shoulder. He was tall, handsome in a slick kind of way. Like a mobster. His stubble grazed my cheek as he leaned in. Not a roadie or part of the crew. A friend of the record execs, maybe. Or not. I didn't know who he was, and I was too drunk to find out. Did it matter?

He could be anyone, and I could be anyone to him.

"Anyone plus anyone equals no one," I slurred.

"You're wasted," he laughed. He leaned in, his breath wet with vodka on my ear. "You want to get out of here?"

"Yeah," I said. "I really do. I really fucking want to get out of here."

He smiled with hooded eyes and started to walk me out. I resisted and stepped away from him, staggering a little.

"Let me powder my nose," I said.

That perked him up even more. "You got some blow?"

"I have to *take a piss*," I said loudly.

I passed Jimmy and Violet and Lola, all talking and laughing. I ducked and weaved to avoid being spotted. Bypassing the bathroom, I hurried out of the suite, down the hall to my own room. The swirling pattern on the carpet made me dizzy. I expected the mobster guy to appear any moment behind me, as if this were a bad horror movie I'd already seen and I knew what was going to happen.

I fumbled the key card into the lock and practically fell inside. I slammed the door, locked it, and threw the dead bolt. The strength ebbed from me, and I slid down the door, tears streaming down my cheeks. I swiped my eyes, and my mascara left streaks on the back of my hands.

Even two rooms away, I could still hear the party. I covered my ears, staring down at the purse in my lap, my cell phone sliding out. I picked it up, went to my contacts, and found Jonah's number. My thumb hovered over the call button but wouldn't touch it. I couldn't call him drunk and hysterical. It would worry him to the core, and what could he do about it anyway?

It was too fucking humiliating. We'd been separated as many days as we'd been together, and I'd already fallen apart. He'd probably finished eight more pieces of his installation. His legacy. I was drunk on a hotel room floor.

I kicked off my black stilettos and struggled to my feet, my sights on the mini bar. I threw it open, grabbed a tiny bottle of something brown, and started to twist the top, ready to turn the night into oblivion.

Then my bleary gaze landed on the perfume bottle. The beautiful, perfect vessel with its delicate ribbons of purple spiraling around the middle. I stared. It was no accident my sober self had set it on top of the little cabinet above the mini bar, instead of leaving it in the bathroom with the rest of my perfume.

I set the booze down but didn't pick up the perfume bottle. Jonah made it for me. If I broke it, I'd have nothing left of him.

I sucked in a deep breath, took a bottle of water from the cabinet, and shut the door tight.

Then I went to bed.

Behind my closed eyelids, my thoughts swam together in a blurry infusion: dancing water and lights, fire and glass, and an ugly green-and-orange afghan around my shoulders. I wrapped myself in the colors and finally slept.

Chapter 19

JONAH

"Hey. Jonah."

I lifted my gaze from the bubbles fluttering to the surface of my nonalcoholic beer. Oscar peered at me.

"You still with us?" he asked.

"Sorry?"

"You okay, man?"

"Sure. Great." I took a sip and pretended to be interested in the people moving and talking around us. Theo had had to work late at Vegas Ink, so it was just Oscar and Dena sitting across from me at a tall table in the Lift Bar at the Aria hotel, one of the few that didn't allow smoking anywhere on premises.

The Lift was a far cry from the unfussy restaurants we usually hung out in, or the little house Oscar and Dena rented in Belvedere. The Lift had huge thick pillars of what looked like gold tree bark, rising up from a carpet of swirling shades of violet. Guests drank twelve-dollar cocktails at purple tables and chairs, and a solid gold wall backed the bar. It was elegantly gaudy to my mind, but I needed the distraction.

Or so I told myself. I'd never been dissatisfied with our usual hangouts before, but Kacey Dawson had splashed color and light into my life, and now what had been usual for me now seemed plain and drab. The Lift was anything but plain and drab, but the purple made me think of Kacey. Rubbed her absence in my face.

Who am I kidding? Everything makes me think of Kacey.

"Tell me about the girl," Oscar said. "I heard from Theo you had a rock star crashing with you. Rapid Confession is on the radio twenty-four seven at work. They're the big time, man, and you had their guitarist on your couch?"

"Not a big deal. She needed a break from the party scene, and now she's back with her band."

"But she was with you for *four days*." Oscar wagged his eyebrows. "Anything interesting happen during that time frame you'd like to report?"

I expected Dena to scold her boyfriend for being crass, but her dark-eyed gaze was intent on mine. "Was she good company? Did you enjoy having her there? Tell us *everything.*"

I knew Dena's interest was slightly more refined; she studied classical literature and Middle Eastern poetry and was a true romantic. Still, it was an anomaly I'd let someone else into my circle, and the curiosity flowed off them in waves, battering me from all sides. I took a sip of my fake beer to help quell my irritation. They meant well, but I felt like a kid coming home to report a first crush.

"There's not much to tell," I said. "She mostly rested up while I worked at the hot shop or A-1. I went to dinner with the family on Sunday, and she hung alone with a pizza."

"You canceled with *us* though, to stay in with *her*," Oscar said. He smiled knowingly over his beer. "And Theo said she's hot."

"He did?" I took a sip of beer. "That's…interesting."

"He did." Oscar leaned back in his chair. "So you had a beautiful rock star in your apartment for four days. Please tell me you did not let a situation like that end with a hug or a handshake."

Dena swatted Oscar's arm. "Will you see her again?"

"I don't know. I don't think so. She wants to get out of her band contract, but it's not easy to do. If it's truly something she wants to do…"

"Would you *like* to see her again?"

With everything I am…

"I don't have much say in it. She's going to be on tour for months."

"There are magical devices called phones." Dena rested the heel of her hand on her chin, eyebrows raised. "You can call her, can you not? Text? Skype?"

"She needs space to figure out what she wants without interference from me," I said. Oscar started to reply, but I cut him off. "Look, I don't know what's going to happen next, okay? What I *do* know is I have a lot of work to do before the gallery opening. So it's better to not have distractions."

A short, tense silence fell, followed by the guilt that always assailed me on the rare instances I snapped at anyone. I started to apologize for being shitty company, but Oscar and Dena weren't my best friends for nothing. Their concern for me was palpable in that noisy, ostentatious bar. Oscar leaned toward me, his expression serious for a change, while Dena slipped her hand across the table into mine.

"Tell us."

I set my beer glass down, turned it round and round on the purple table. "She had to go," I said quietly. "They'd ruin her if she broke her contract. She needs to decide what's best for her, and I couldn't ask her to stay anyway."

"Why not?"

I gave them a look. "You know why not. You know why I don't get involved. I have nothing to offer her but friendship, and even that has an expiration date." I scrubbed my hands through my hair. "It was stupid. The whole thing. Reckless and stupid."

"What about what you want, Jonah?" Dena asked. "What do *you* want?"

I looked at my friends, who'd been in love with each other for as

159

long as I'd known them. Dena's search for deeper meanings was the perfect counterbalance to Oscar, who skimmed along life's surface like a Jet Ski. She grounded him; he made her laugh. My gaze strayed to their locked hands, his dark skin against her pale skin, fingers entwined. I remembered Kacey's hand in mine at the diner.

It wasn't enough. I want more…

But I couldn't have more.

I mustered a smile. "I want to finish my installation, and I want another eight-dollar nonalcoholic beer."

Oscar burst out laughing and seemed content to let the matter drop. Dena's smile fell soft on me the rest of the evening, and I knew she wouldn't let me off so easily.

———————

Being the perpetual designated driver, I dropped off Oscar and Dena at their house, northwest of the Strip.

"Don't forget," Oscar said, clasping my hand and pulling me in for a half hug before he climbed out. "Great Basin camping trip in three weeks. Make sure you take the time off from work."

"Already been scheduled," I said.

The cheer in my voice was forced; I worried about the loss of work in the hot shop and the loss of tip money from my job, but Oscar and Dena had planned this trip for months. They wanted the time with me, and I couldn't say no. They were my oldest friends, the only friends I couldn't push away when my last biopsy results were made known. They were ingrained in the fabric of my life, no matter how long a life it turned out to be.

Dena came around to the driver side, wearing the maternal look that meant I had a lecture coming, usually prefaced with a quote from her favorite poet, Rumi.

"*That which is false troubles the heart, but truth brings joyous tranquility,*" she said.

"And what does that mean, love?"

"It means you miss this girl. Don't pretend you don't. You'll feel better for being true to your feelings." She rested her hands on the open window. "I don't like to talk about your schedule, you know that."

I nodded. *My schedule* had become a euphemism for the time I had left. The *gallery opening* was the finish line I needed to cross.

"And I know you want to leave a beautiful piece of art in your wake. Your focus is solely on the destination, not the journey." Dena placed her palm on my cheek. "Shouldn't you also try to do the most important thing along the way?"

I covered her hand with mine. "What's that?"

"Be happy."

Chapter 20

KACEY

DAY NINE WITHOUT JONAH. DAY FIVE WITHOUT BOOZE.

I watched the bubbles dance in my champagne flute, but I didn't drink it. Not a drop since that last drunken night in the Denver hotel room. Every nerve ending in my body screamed for a sip, but I only turned the delicate glass around and around. Did they give sobriety chips for making it five days? I doubted it, but they should. Every fucking *hour* where I didn't give in to the need was a battle.

I sat in a huge half-moon booth with nine other people in the VIP section of some club. The music was loud and relentless; I could feel the bass thudding in my chest. Bodies writhed on the dance floor one level below. In our booth, talk and laughter zigzagged around me. The girls from RC were flirting with the guys from our new opening act. Everyone was happy our latest set of shows had gone well, but all I could think was I was in the wrong place, doing the wrong thing with the wrong people.

I sat wedged between Jimmy Ray and Phil Miller, the owner of this club and, no coincidence, the Pony Club in Las Vegas. He turned to me now, shifting his bulk toward me with a gust of sweat and too much cologne.

"So you're my little troublemaker, are you?" he said.

He smoked a cigar that smelled vaguely like licorice. I hated licorice. My shoulders flinched up and stayed there. I had four people on my right, five on my left. I was stuck tight in the middle of the booth.

"You know, it's gonna cost me a small fortune to fix up my green room."

"Sorry about that," I muttered.

Jimmy turned our way. "Come on, Phil. Let's not jump right into business without a little pleasure first, right?" He slung his arm around me, his hand grazing my bare arm. I was wearing a silk tank top layered over another, tighter tank top, both low-cut. Phil's gaze seemed permanently glued to my cleavage. "Kacey likes to have fun, is all. Sometimes a little too much fun."

The Pony Club's owner chewed on the wet foot of his cigar. "Hell, I can't blame you, sweetheart. I like to have fun too." His right hand landed on my thigh over my leather pants. I brushed it off, humiliation and anger heating my face.

Phil and Jimmy exchanged a look I didn't like, and then Jimmy whispered in my ear. "A lawsuit would be really bad right now, kitten. Our label doesn't have the deep pockets of Sony or Interscope." He gave my shoulder a squeeze. "You'd be doing us all a big favor if you put Phil Miller in a really good mood."

My head turned toward him slowly. "And how, exactly, would you like me to do that, Jimmy?"

He leaned back a little, laughing. "What's with the blue steel glare? Just...have a few drinks with him. Maybe a dance or two. See what happens."

"See what happens."

Suddenly, sitting in that booth, surrounded by people in a crowded club, I felt utterly alone. *If Jonah were here, he'd break Jimmy's nose and Phil's grabby fingers. That's what would happen.*

But he wasn't here. I had to stand up for myself.

I didn't punch Jimmy in the nose—I didn't want to hurt my own hand, which I needed to play guitar and write songs. Instead, I grabbed Jimmy's gin and tonic and tossed it in his face. The others at the table ceased their shouty conversations and went silent under the pulsing music, staring at us or—in the case of the guys from the opening act—laughing.

Jimmy pulled out a handkerchief. Small ice cubes and gin glittered on the lapels of his coat. "That was a little hasty, kitten…"

"It was overdue," I said and shouldered my small purse. I climbed onto my chair, my bootheels digging sharp furrows in the upholstery, and then onto the table. Glasses toppled and spilled as I picked my way across.

"What the hell are you doing?"

"I'm quitting; what's it look like I'm doing?" I hopped off the table, landed without breaking an ankle—which would have put a serious damper on my exit—and strode out of the club. Voices shouted after me, Lola the loudest, but I kept going without looking back.

I left the club and hailed a taxi. The ride to the hotel felt like ages, minutes ticking by, more time spent out of touch with Jonah. Not a word in nine days, or even a text. My muted phone lit up with texts galore from Lola, from Jimmy, and then phone calls from both. I ignored all of them.

In my suite, with the door shut and locked, I sat on the bed, my heart pounding. Phone in hand, I looked to the purple glass bottle on my nightstand. It now held a few ounces of my favorite perfume.

I inhaled as my finger picked out Jonah's number, but my finger hovered over the call button. It was two in the morning on a Friday.

He might still be at work. He might not be able to talk. I could text instead.

What if he was doing better now? Maybe he'd moved on, gotten back to his schedule, focused and on track without me to distract him.

Maybe he meant what he said about it being better if I didn't contact him again?

My gaze returned to the perfume bottle—a tiny little blob of glass, but it had been my talisman of strength and willpower these last nine days. I had to tell Jonah I quit the band, but I'd give him an out: a text was easy to ignore, and if he did, I wouldn't send another.

I quit the band. I hope you are well. <3 Kacey

I hit Send before I could rethink the heart emoticon. I watched as the text's status read Delivered then Read. No little rolling dots of an answering text came in.

"Okay. That's fine," I said, my voice shaking, and then I let out a startled cry as my phone lit up with Jonah's number.

"Hi," I said, blinking through the strange and sudden tears in my eyes.

"Are you okay?" His deep voice full of concern and—I was sure of it—happiness.

"I am. I'm really good. I did it. I quit the band. Just now. Tonight. Jimmy tried to pimp me out to the Pony Club guy—"

"He *what?*"

"—but I threw a drink in his face. For real. It felt amazing."

"Good for you," Jonah said, but I could hear the anger coloring his words.

"So now I might be ruined for life, or I might've gotten out by the skin of my teeth. I don't know yet, but I know it was the right thing. I can feel it. And I wouldn't have had the strength to do it if not for you."

"No," he said. "You would've gotten there. I knew you had it in you."

A teary laugh burst out of me. "I didn't."

"I'm really happy for you, Kacey," Jonah said quietly, and I thought I could imagine him standing outside his limo, waiting for a fare, his back turned on the world so he could talk to me. And he was smiling.

"Me too," I said. "But now I'm a homeless vagrant bag lady." I drew in a breath as tears filled my eyes again, pushed up on a tide of emotion I could hardly contain. "Got any hot real estate tips?"

Jonah said nothing for a moment, and when he spoke, his voice was thick and gruff. "I hear Las Vegas is nice this time of year."

My hand flew to my heart, and I needed a second before I could manage a whispery reply. "I was hoping you'd say that."

"I was hoping you'd ask."

"I'm still scared I'm going to fail you like Audrey did."

"You won't fail me," he said. "You're *nothing* like Audrey."

The intensity in his words struck me right in the heart and sent a tingle skimming over me. I wiped my tears, bolstered by his belief in me.

"There's no failing anyway," Jonah said. "You'll be my friend, and I'll be yours, and we'll take it day by day. Okay?"

I nodded against the phone. "Day by day. Moment by moment. Okay," I said and heaved a breath. "I can do that."

"Me too," he said. "My fare's coming out. I have to go…"

I felt as if a heavy burden had been lifted from my shoulders, and whatever doubts I had about quitting the band were blown to ash.

"I'll see you soon, Jonah. Good night."

"Good night, Kacey."

Part II

"We do not remember days;
we remember moments."

—Cesare Pavese

Chapter 21

KACEY

I was home: 212 Banks St., Apt. 2C, Las Vegas, Nevada.

From my living room window, I had a view of Flamingo Avenue, and a few blocks beyond was the Strip. I could just see the red of Harrah's enormous sign. I had one bedroom, one bath, a tiny kitchen, and a postage-stamp balcony. It was all mine.

And three blocks from Jonah's place.

I'd left the Rapid Confession tour four days earlier, with two suitcases of clothes, my acoustic guitar, and a thirty-thousand-dollar settlement.

Jimmy—with the inadvertent help of a very pissed-off Jeannie—had been able to get me out of my contract. An executive at our label had a niece who could play guitar, and they booked her on a flight before the words *I quit* had left my mouth. The powers that be crunched some numbers and came up with thirty thousand dollars. It was what was left after my advance was paid back, plus fees, damage costs to the Pony Club, and projected royalties on tour sales so far were added.

Jimmy said I was lucky to get anything, but I had a feeling I'd been robbed six ways from Tuesday, broken contract or not. Lola confirmed it. She called while I was hanging around my new place, waiting for my last piece of furniture—a couch—to arrive.

"You got fucking ripped off," she told me from Vancouver. "Thirty grand? Are you shitting me? Jimmy says we're going to pull down at least a million each after this tour. *Each.*" I heard her exhale a drag from her cigarette. "I don't know, Kace…"

I felt a little pang at the "million each." I was human, after all. But mostly I just felt happy. "It's all good, Lola. I got a new place and started a new job."

"You told me. Slinging cocktails at Caesars Palace? You honestly think being around free booze all night is going to be better for you than the band?"

"Yeah, I do. I didn't drink booze because it was there," I said. "I drank because it made it easier to pretend."

"Pretend what?"

I shrugged and ran my fingers along the cheap tile. But it was *my* cheap tile on *my* kitchen counter. "Pretend that I was doing what I wanted to do. Being on my own like this is better for me."

Lola hissed a sigh. "No one put a gun to your head to join the band."

"Lola," I said firmly. "I love you. You're my best friend. You saved my ass, and I'll never be able to repay you for that. If I'd kept going like I was, I would've wound up dead or in an extremely bad place. You know this."

Another sigh, this one softer. "Yeah, I know. So how about the simple fact that this sucks because I miss you?"

I smiled. "I miss you too. How's the new chick?"

"She's okay. Jeannie doesn't hate her. Yet."

"Give her time."

"How's your new place? You didn't go overboard with your huge fortune, did you? Thirty grand sounds like a lot, but it's going to go fast. Especially on a cocktail waitress's salary."

"No kidding. I had to buy a car—used—and furnish my little place. They just opened an IKEA here last month. My apartment looks like a live advertisement."

I didn't have the guts to tell her I also spent five thousand dollars on a top-of-the-line bed, currently en route—or possibly already delivered—to Jonah's place. It could be adjusted to raise the head or foot so a person could sleep in any position they wanted. I couldn't stand the idea of Jonah spending one more night in that goddamned recliner just to keep his chest elevated, and I knew he'd never buy a bed like this on his own.

"So what happens next?" Lola asked. "You're going to write your own songs again? Become a YouTube star? I'm not being facetious— you're really talented, hon. This could be the start of something big."

"Thanks, Lo," I said, my eye turning to the perfume bottle on the windowsill. I smiled. "I'm going to take it slow. See what happens."

A pause. "And how's your friend? The guy with the heart condition?"

"He's fine. He and his brother have been coming over whenever they can to help me assemble the furniture."

The thought made my smile broaden. Jonah had taken his personal time between the hot shop and A-1 to help me, dragging Theo with him whenever his brother wasn't working at Vegas Ink.

Lola's next words killed my smile. "Your friend, Jonah…can he lift heavy stuff like furniture?"

God, everyone's a doctor.

"Of course," I said. "He's totally fine."

"Totally fine? A week ago, you told me he was dying."

I clenched my teeth. I could control the words when they stayed in my head. Hearing someone else say them made emotion surge up in my gut.

"I was in a bad place when I said that," I said. "Poor choice of words."

"Kacey…"

"He's fine. He's strong—"

"Fucking hell…"

"I mean it, Lola. I have to go."

"Where?" Lola demanded. "Back to burying your head in the sand? This isn't like a bill you can't pay, so you chuck it in the garbage and pretend you never got it. And the next thing you know, they shut off the lights and you're left in the dark. I know it's what you do, Kacey. You just brush shit aside and pretend everything's okay until it isn't."

"It's not like that," I whispered.

"No? Sure sounds like it."

"He's fine. He really is."

My thoughts went back to when Jonah picked me up at the airport ten days ago. He held up a big sign with my name on it and joked that it was the last time he'd be my limo driver. I threw my arms around him and hugged him tight, and I felt his heartbeat against my chest, strong and steady…

"So he's been cured?"

"Shut up, Lola. He's fine right now. I'm not going to spend whatever time we have dwelling on maybes and what-ifs. And it's fucking awful of you to try to ruin my happiness."

"I'm not trying to ruin anything for you, Kacey. I'm trying to protect you."

"Well, I'm done needing your protection. I know what I'm doing."

"Do you? Because it sounds like you've taken yourself out of one shitty situation and plopped yourself smack in the middle of another." A pause. "Are you two…together? Please tell me you're not crazy enough to get involved with a guy who's…really sick."

"We're just friends. Good friends. One of the best I've had in a while. He makes me feel like I can be myself." I sounded petulant, but I had made a plan to live moment by moment. I wasn't ready to look ahead four months. Not yet.

Maybe never. Maybe his meds are working…

"Well, I'm happy for you, Kacey," Lola said, pulling me out of my thoughts. "And I want the best for you. But I don't want you to become lost."

"Lost?"

"When the lights finally go out."

I bit my lip, trying to find something to say, some retort. My doorbell rang. "I have to go, Lola. The IKEA people are here."

"Okay, hon. Take care."

"Love you. Bye." I hung up and set the phone on the counter. Then turned it to silent. Then face down.

I answered the front door, not to IKEA deliverymen, but to Jonah. My face broke out in a huge smile, as if I hadn't just seen him two days before, and the blood rushed to my cheeks.

Jeez, get a grip.

He looked handsome as hell in simple jeans and a dark-green T-shirt. He stood with his hands jammed in the front pockets of his jeans, a bemused look on his face.

"You're not my couch," I said, feigning confusion.

"Not since last I checked. But speaking of bulky household furnishings, I got a very interesting delivery yesterday," he said, rocking back on his heels.

"Did you?"

"I did. You wouldn't know anything about an expensive-as-hell, adjustable, state-of-the-art, remote-controlled Sleep Number mega-*bed* I found on my doorstep, would you?"

I pretended to be alarmed. "On your *doorstep*? God, I hope not. That bed sounds *awesome*. I would've thought it'd come with actual people to set it up."

"Oh, it did. A whole team of technicians who were 'under orders' to not take no for an answer." He sighed and shook his head, his expression turning grave. "Kace, it's too much. Too expensive. You didn't need to do that."

"Yes, I did," I said. "I wouldn't have quit the band if you hadn't given me a place to crash and get my head on straight. This is my thank-you." I planted one hand on my hip. "Are you going to stand in the door all afternoon? You're letting in all that god-awful heat."

Jonah stared at me a moment longer, eyes narrowed.

I stared back. "What?"

"I'm debating whether it'll do any good to argue with you."

"It won't," I said. "In or out? You're like a goddamn cat."

He relented with a small laugh and a shake of his head and bent to pick up something from the ground next to him. "So, this is your housewarming present, of which I was quite proud until you sent me the mega-bed." He arched a brow. "I should've made you a damn chandelier."

I ignored his sarcasm, too busy staring at the beautiful lamp in his hands. It was two lamps, actually, made from antique square-shaped amber whiskey bottles. The bottom had been cut out of each, and oblong Edison light bulbs were attached to the neck inside. The cords came out the bottlenecks and were woven through small links of a wrought-iron chain that connected the two lamps as a pair.

"Oh my God." I stared at the lights, then at him. "They're beautiful. You made these? What am I saying? Of course, you did."

"Want to test them out?"

I bit my lip, glancing around. "I don't know where... Oh, the balcony."

We went to the sliding glass door that led to my tiny balcony overlooking the street. "I plan to have a sitting area out here. Potted plants and a little chair and table to have coffee in the morning."

Jonah gave me a look. "You? In this heat?"

"I need to get used to it. No one likes someone who bitches about the weather every other minute."

"You got that right," he muttered.

I gave him a little shove toward the balcony door. "Out. Lights. Hang."

He strung up the whiskey-bottle lamps on two plant hooks—one slightly lower than the other—and plugged them into a covered outdoor socket. Lit from within, the amber glass glowed as if still filled with whiskey.

"They're gorgeous," I said. "I can't wait to see them at night." I glanced up at him beside me. "Now I have *two* Jonah Fletcher originals. I won't have to work at Caesars after all. eBay, here I come."

His eyes rolled. "I wouldn't put in your two-week notice just yet."

"I'd never part with them anyway. But I think it's only a matter of time before the world learns how talented you are."

He looked down at me. "I could say the same about you."

The air thickened between us, and his brown eyes were soft. When his eyes held mine like this, I felt like he was looking down deep, to a place I rarely examined myself but where I might have a good song lurking if I did.

The seconds ticked. I was supposed to look away, but I didn't look away, and neither did he, until a passing car screeched at a red light, the sound tearing the moment. Jonah jammed his hands in his pocket, and my eyes roved for something to look at besides him.

"So the whiskey bottles," I said, nodding at the lights. "Are you repurposing my bad habits?"

He smiled. "No, just a friendly reminder."

"Of what?"

"That you can find beauty everywhere, even in the things that scare you the most."

A warmth spread in my chest, and I almost teased him for being deep, but my phone call with Lola came back to me, and how she'd voiced what actually scared me the most: being lost in the dark.

I turned my eyes to my new lamps, then to the man who made them. *Lola's wrong. Somehow, some way, his lights will stay on, and I'll never be lost in the dark.*

Chapter 22

JONAH

WHEN KACEY'S COUCH ARRIVED, IT TOOK HER, THEO, AND ME HALF the evening to put it together. When it was done, and the empty box and pages of instructions were thrown out, her apartment was complete.

"Well," she said, surveying the finished product. "It's definitely like one of those model rooms in the IKEA store. They should pay me for the free advertising."

Theo mustered his version of a smile. He'd warmed up to Kacey—slightly—over the last ten days. His eyes didn't automatically roll when she talked to him, and he actually engaged with a couple of her teasing remarks.

Now, as we readied to leave, she threw her arms around his neck. "Thanks, Teddy," she said and kissed his cheek. "Is it okay to call you that?"

It was definitely *not* okay. I braced myself for Theo's harsh rebuke against being called Teddy, but he only muttered something about waiting for me in the truck and slipped out.

Wide-eyed, I watched him go, then swung my gaze back to Kacey. "He *hates* Teddy. Nobody calls him Teddy."

She grinned, shrugged. "Didn't seem to mind it coming from me. Besides, it fits him. He's got a soft side."

"Yeah, he does," I said. A short silence curled up between us. It happened often since she'd come back. The jokes and teasing fell away, and it was just Kacey and me in each other's space, waiting for something to happen next. A word or a touch that might change everything…

But it can't. I can't take her down that road with me because eventually we'll come to the place where I have to go on, and she can't follow.

"Okay," I said. "I'm going to head out before Theo throws a fit."

Kacey put her arms around my neck and gave me a kiss on the cheek, just as she had Theo. I felt her body all along mine, and my breath caught. My own arms were stiff and careful, as if I might break her.

Or break me.

"Thanks for helping me out tonight and all the other nights," she said, her hands gliding down my shoulders before falling away.

"You're welcome," I said. "Have a good night, Kace."

"You too. Oh, hey, I was thinking about stopping by the hot shop sometime this week. Can I bring you guys some lunch?"

"Again? That'll be the fifth time in two weeks. You don't have to feed us."

"I know," she said. "But I want to. Leave it to me, Fletcher. I'll take care of you."

It's too much. Say no. Keep to the routine…

Fat chance. Kacey was here now, and part of my routine. I'd told her to come back to Vegas because I missed her and wanted her in my life, but I had no idea how hard it would be to keep her at a safe distance. I was a starving man at a banquet, hungry every day for what was right in front of me.

"Sounds great then," I said and got the hell out of there before I did something stupid.

Theo sat behind the wheel of his idling truck. But instead of a scowl or a gripe about making him wait, he only watched me get in, studied my face as if he was looking for something.

"What is it now?"

Theo turned back facing forward. "Nothing."

He drove us along mostly empty side streets in residential Vegas—apartment complexes and small homes on either side. The Strip wasn't visible, but I could see its glow above the rooftops.

We hit a red light, and Theo said, "She's into you."

I stared at my brother, my mouth going dry. "You think?"

"It's not obvious?"

"Enlighten me."

He shrugged. "The way she looks at you."

My heart jumped in my chest. I did my best to sound casual as hell and not like a kid in junior high. "How was she looking at me?"

Theo glanced at me sideways. "Like she can't stop. And you're just as bad. I'm amazed we got the couch built."

I faced forward, my thoughts running rampant at this revelation. Of course, my eyes were drawn to Kacey anytime she was in the room. I couldn't help it. She was radiant. But to hear she'd been doing the same to me...

A junior-high warmth spread through me, a soft glow of hope that I'd been keeping tamped down.

"She's afraid she'll fail me," I said slowly. "Pull an Audrey."

"So you've talked about it?" Theo asked. "Being together? Is that why she moved back?"

"No, we're just friends. It's all we can be." I rubbed the place on my cheek where Kacey had kissed me. "It's hard enough."

"But you have feelings for her," Theo said. It was not a question, and his voice was curiously quiet.

"I… Maybe. I don't know," I said. "Sometimes I think I shouldn't have told her to come back here."

"But you did," Theo said in that same low tone, "because you *do* have feelings for her."

I sighed, partially in surprise that I could talk about this with Theo when I expected another lecture. It felt good to talk about this with my brother instead of being walled off by his worry.

She looks at you...like she can't stop...

We'd arrived at my apartment complex. Theo threw the truck in Park and turned to face me. "What do you want to do?"

"What can I do? I don't have time, and she knows it. I told her about the last biopsy."

"Well, there you go," he said, waving his hand. "You told her."

"Yeah? And?"

"And she's still here."

Chapter 23

JONAH

FRIDAY NIGHT. I WAS LYING IN MY BED, READING. OR TRYING TO. My focus kept wandering. Three a.m. is the stillest, quietest part of night, even in a city like Vegas, and the silence amplified the thoughts rattling in my head and heart. They filled the room, demanding to be acknowledged, begging to be answered.

Kacey…

"Knock it off," I said under my breath.

What is she doing right now?

She would've gotten off her shift an hour ago. Been home twenty minutes later if she wasn't delayed.

"She's sleeping," I said. "It's what you should be doing."

I tossed the book aside, clicked off the lamp, and settled into my bed.

She bought me a bed.

"I'm aware," I said.

The bed was infinitely more comfortable than the chair, but I still couldn't sleep. I lay on the right side. The left seemed to stretch for miles, like snowy tundra. Cold and barren.

I miss her.

"Shut it, Fletcher. Go to sleep."

I closed my eyes, knowing it was futile. Then my cell phone on the nightstand buzzed a text.

"Dammit, Theo."

But it wasn't Theo. I sat up, the heart in my chest thudding.

Kacey: Are u awake?

I managed to wait a whole ten seconds before replying. Always. What's up?

I called my dad.

"Holy shit," I whispered, knowing what it meant for her. I waited to see if she'd say more. No blinking little dots indicating she was typing. I hesitated, a thousand replies at the ready. Replies that could comfort from a safe distance. *How did it go? Are you all right? Tell me about it?*

I texted back:

I can come over

No punctuation. Neither a question nor a statement. Vague enough she could tell me no.

The rolling dots, and then her reply:

Okay.

———————

I could've walked to Kacey's apartment, but I shaved three minutes off by driving. Outside her door, I hesitated.

What are you doing?

"Being a friend." The stifling night air chewed up the word *friend* and spit it back out at me. "A friend who makes house calls."

I knocked on the door and heard a muffled, "Come in."

Kacey's plant-filled apartment smelled of her perfume and the scented candles she loved. I inhaled deeply, both to catch my breath from the flight of stairs and to fill myself with her.

She sat curled up on her couch, her legs tucked under her. The coffee table in front of her was littered with crumpled tissues. Only the lamp beside the couch was on, glowing yellow over her hunched shoulders. Her gaze flicked to me as I sat in the chair opposite. Even with red-rimmed eyes and a face swollen from crying, she looked incredibly beautiful.

"You want anything?" she asked. "Something to drink or…?"

I shook my head. "I'm fine."

I cleared my throat, my nerves perched on the edge of their seats, staring. Both the smooth skin of her legs and the way they were folded small into a corner of the couch woke some primal male urge in me. I wanted to protect her. To hold her and shield her from whatever hurt her. To put my body between her and the world, and while I was at it, wrap those legs around me and slide inside her…

"I'm sorry, it's so late," she said.

"I was awake anyway." I leaned forward. "Tell me what happened."

"Would you…? Never mind."

"What? What can I do?" *Anything. I'd do anything for you.*

Her eyes met mine, and her voice was tiny as she asked, "Would you mind sitting next to me? I promise I won't try to jump your bones or anything."

"Sure," I said. I moved from the chair to the couch, leaving a few inches between us, but she closed the distance at once, scooting next to me. Automatically, my arm went around her shoulders.

Because that's what friends do when a friend is upset.

Except my friend smelled amazing. And I was hyperaware of my friend's skin touching mine and the way I could feel the soft roundness of her breasts against my chest. I expected her to cry. I welcomed a weepfest—it would help bolster my insistence that I was only being a kind, supportive friend. But she snuggled up close and wrapped her arm around my waist, and when she spoke, her voice was watery but calm.

"I didn't plan on calling my dad," she said. "I wasn't even thinking about him today. They accidentally double-booked my shift with another girl, so I got off work early. Around eight. I came home and turned on the TV, surfed around for a while, and landed on *Say Yes to the Dress*." She tilted her head up to look at me. "Have you ever seen it?"

"Never heard of it," I said.

"It's this stupid, silly, fabulous reality show where they follow different brides-to-be as they go shopping for their wedding dresses. They bring along a best friend to help them choose. Or a bunch of bitchy friends. Or their overbearing mother. But the episode tonight…" Kacey sniffed. "One bride brought along some friends. And her father."

She inhaled, and I felt the fluttery shudder of her breath huff against my chest. I held her tighter.

"So she's trying on dresses, and they're all pretty, but none of them are quite *it*. Until finally she tries on The One. And her whole group knows it's The One because they all start crying. The bride cried, and then her dad cried, and then *I* cried because I wanted what she had so badly."

"The dress?"

Kacey elbowed me in the side. "Smart-ass. The dress was awful, actually. Mermaid-style. She looked like she was wrapped in bandages. The *point is*, I wanted what she had with her dad." Her body wilted, leaning harder on mine.

"Tell me more," I said.

"This dad…he'd been a Marine, retired now, and super tough-looking. But a total softie when it came to his daughter. He didn't bother to hide his feelings. He told the camera she would always

183

be his little girl. He said how much he loved her and was proud of her." Kacey's voice cracked, then broke. "This girl has this beautiful relationship with her dad that I'll never have with mine. It hurts. I hate how it hurts. I want not to care, but I can't stop caring. I can't. He's my dad. I love him. Isn't he supposed to feel the same?"

"He is," I said. Still holding her, I reached for the tissue box on the table and plucked one.

"Thanks," she said, dabbing her eyes.

"So you called him?"

"Like a dummy. I thought, *I may not have what that girl and her father have, but I can start somewhere. I can try.* I didn't let myself overthink it, just grabbed my phone and called him. And *he* answered, not my mom, and I thought, *That's a sign.*" She reached for another tissue. "Yeah, it was a sign all right. That I'm a fucking idiot."

"You're not an idiot," I said. "What did he say?"

"He was quiet, as usual. But I was nervous, so I started babbling like a moron. I told him I'd quit a successful rock band and threw away millions of dollars and fame and fortune. So I could sling cocktails at Caesars because I knew it was healthier for me. I was better for it. I told him I was living on my own, paying my own rent, and writing my own music. I said I was happy, even if my songs weren't seeing the light of day outside my notebook yet." She sniffled and burrowed her face closer to my chest.

I slid my hand into her hair. "What did he say?"

"He said, 'Okay then.'"

I waited for more, but nothing came.

"'Okay then' what?" I said.

"That was it. '*Okay then.*' And he hung up. He just…hung up on me."

My mouth hung half-open and useless as she sobbed against my chest, her tears wetting my shirt. I put my other arm around her as well and held her close. "I'm sorry," I said. "I'm so sorry."

She pulled free and fired the balled-up tissues across the room. "I'm tired of feeling like this. I feel so pathetic wanting my own father to need me in his life." She stared down at her empty hands. "He doesn't need me."

"I need you." It was the truth, and sometimes truth refuses to be contained. It bursts out, usually when it's least convenient, but also when it's needed most.

She smiled wanly, laid her hand over my chest where her tears had dampened my shirt. "You're sweet. I had no one, and you gave me friendship and a place to live."

"I need you," I said again.

Her eyes settled on mine. "You do?"

I nodded. God, she was so close to me, I could smell her skin. Sweet, like caramel. "Friends serve different purposes, right? Some things you can only say to certain people; some things you can say to others."

Kacey's gaze was unwavering. "Tell me something you can't tell your other friends," she said softly. "Something you can only tell me."

For a few seconds I was lost in the blue pools of her eyes, struck mute by the thousands of things I wanted to tell her. "I'm scared," I said.

Her hand crept into mine. "Okay."

"But who wouldn't be?"

She didn't say anything. I felt her acceptance and trust pouring into me from her eyes. I could spill my guts to her, and she'd listen, or I could keep it to myself and she'd understand.

"Everyone is watching me, all the time. I feel like…I can't do or say anything without weighing it carefully. Because everything I do means something, even when it doesn't. I can't raise my voice or get angry or irritated because I can't leave that kind of memory. I have only a finite number of words left to say. I have to choose them carefully."

She nodded and let me continue. Which I did, telling her more than I meant to, telling her what I couldn't tell anyone else. The words poured out of me and into Kacey's lap.

"My actions too. I'm being constantly watched, studied, examined.

Am I tired from a long day at the shop, or is it something worse? They treat me like I'm breakable. Like the whole world is a potential threat. Someone might say the wrong thing and upset me, and God forbid I should ever be upset. But I am upset."

Kacey nodded.

"I get scared or pissed off that this happened to me," I said. "I took care of myself, you know? I exercised like a bastard, I ate right, and I still got really fucking sick. Like being hit by a truck even though I looked both ways and the street was empty."

I rubbed my hand hard on my knee so I wouldn't clench it into a fist. The other held Kacey's tight. I worried I was bruising her fingers, but I couldn't let go.

"So yeah…I'm scared," I said. "And that's something I can't tell my other friends."

She let go my hand and then she was in my arms, hugging me around the neck. "Thank you for telling me."

I froze, my senses infused with her. The softness of her hair on my cheek, the caramel scent of her warm skin. My arms went around her, stiffly at first, but she was so soft. She melted into me, *wanting* to be held. And like telling her what I couldn't tell anyone else, I wanted to hold her like I held no one else. Stroke her hair, inhale her sweetness. Kiss her and never stop…

Her head lifted off my shoulder, but her arms still ringed my neck. She looked at me, her lips parted expectantly, her eyes warm and soft. In the silence, she raised her hand and laid her palm on my chest. My heart pounded under her touch, and a soft smile came to her lips.

"It feels so strong," she murmured.

The top of my scar was just visible at the hem of my collar. Kacey hooked her index finger on the edge of my shirt and drew it down, revealing another inch of angry red. Head cocked, she studied it, ran her thumb over the shiny ridge.

I fought not to pull back…or lean forward into her touch.

Halfway between panic and desire, I froze but for my heart, which was galloping.

"You're the first woman…the first person to touch my scar."

"That's not right," she murmured and leaned forward to press a gentle kiss on that ugly seam. Then she curled against my chest, exhausted and spent, safe between me and the couch cushions.

I lay back, taking her with me. I held her, relishing the feel of her body along mine, memorizing the softness of her hair falling through my fingers. I closed my eyes, letting all my other senses absorb the warmth and comfort of having a woman in my arms. This woman.

I was tempted to stay all night. To kiss her good morning and fuck the consequences. But when the first light of dawn sliced through the window, it glinted off my watch. I had forty minutes to get home and take my immune suppressants. If I delayed, those consequences would fuck with *me*.

I slipped off the couch, covered Kacey with a throw blanket, and quietly left.

Chapter 24

JONAH

DENA AND OSCAR WERE ECSTATIC ABOUT KACEY COMING BACK IN town and insisted on doing something special to welcome her to Vegas. I smelled an ulterior motive, but I was touched they wanted to bring her into our regular Monday hangouts.

"Kacey's coming out with us tonight," I told Theo on the phone. "A welcome dinner. You should bring Sally."

"Holly," Theo corrected.

Holly Daniels was his on-again, off-again girlfriend. Or the closest thing he'd had to a girlfriend in his life. A petite woman with a loud laugh and short dark hair, she'd been one of Theo's customers at Vegas Ink. I teased him that Holly had only wanted one tiny tattoo but had kept coming back until she'd won Theo over. Every time I saw her two full sleeves of tattoos along her arms, I had to bury a laugh.

"So it's a couples thing?" Theo said.

"No. Well…" My hand wandered up to my collar and the top of my scar, where I could still feel Kacey's kiss. One little brush of her lips branded on my skin and in my mind. I kept coming back to it.

"Hello?"

I snapped to. "No, it's not a couples thing. It's a friend thing. Bring Holly, bring someone else, or bring no one. It's up to you."

"Where we going?"

"Kacey wants to go to dinner and a casino. I thought the MGM Grand would be good to—"

"You can't go to a casino and be around all that smoke. Doesn't she know that?"

"She does," I said, "but it was my idea. She's never been to a casino, and the MGM has excellent ventilation. I researched it."

He grumbled something incoherent.

"Come on, bro. Oscar and Dena are down. It'll be fun. Something different."

"Different," Theo said. "Christ, you have it bad."

"I'm being optimistic," I said with a grin. "Come on, Teddy."

A pause. "Where we eating?"

"Your favorite, the New Orleans Fish House," I said. "All the spicy-as-hell crawdads you can eat. Eight o'clock."

That won him over. Or maybe he wanted to watch over me like a damn mother hen all night, but he agreed to go.

I told Kacey I'd pick her up at 7:45 p.m. She opened her door wearing an oversize off-the-shoulder blouse in some kind of shimmery material. It slipped over her skin like molten silver, leaving one shoulder bare, and hung to her thighs where a short black skirt peeked out. But it was the black stockings she wore just above her knee that drained the blood from my brain.

She'd piled her hair onto her head and secured it with some kind of clip or band with a large black silk rose over her right ear. Her striking features were done up in dark cat's-eye makeup and bright-red lips. A cloud of her perfume—her favorite and the one she kept in the bottle I had made for her—wafted over me.

I was so busy staring at her that I hadn't noticed she was staring at me.

"Wow, Fletcher," she said. "You…you clean up nice."

I'd put on a dark-gray suit with a bright-blue tie that may or may not have been the same color as Kacey's eyes.

"You look…" I trailed off, staring, because no words existed.

She smiled and moved in to straighten my tie. "Thank you."

When we arrived at Emeril's New Orleans Fish House, the hostess led us through the amber-colored elegance of the restaurant to the table where Dena, Oscar, Theo, and Holly were seated. Kacey, of course, hugged Dena and Oscar off the bat, and they hugged her back, telling her how much they'd heard about her, and that time there was no mistaking her blush. She glowed with happiness under the light of Dena and Oscar's warm welcome, and I thought I never loved my friends more.

"Don't you look handsome," she said to Theo, smoothing the collar of his dress shirt. "Hi, I'm Kacey," she said to Holly, whose full sleeves of tattoos were on display in a sleeveless blouse. I buried a smile while Kacey held Holly's hands to admire the ink.

"Wow, amazing." She turned to Theo. "Yours?"

He nodded, shrugged.

By the time we finished our appetizers, any qualms I'd had about Kacey fitting in were gone. She and Holly talked tattoos, and even got Theo to roll up a sleeve to compare ink, before Kacey fell into a conversation with Dena about poetry and songwriting.

Oscar leaned in from my left. "Are you going to eat or stare at Kacey all night?"

No point in denying it. I didn't even try. "I'm going to stare at her all night."

Oscar grinned and chucked me on the arm. "You do that."

At dessert, Oscar steered the conversation toward camping in a hairpin turn of a topic change, and asked Kacey if she'd ever been.

"Never," she said. "I'm not much of a nature person, except for the beach. Where are you camping?"

"Great Basin National Park."

"It's quite stunning," Dena said. "It's a little bit of everything—desert, forest, lake. You'd love it."

"You should come with," Oscar said.

"You should," Dena said. She turned to Holly. "You too. Then there'd be six of us."

"I'm in," Holly said, while from behind her shoulder, Theo stared daggers at Dena.

"It sounds great," Kacey said, then turned to me. "What do you think? Would you...like the company?"

Maybe I was supposed to be guarded or wary, but I was just happy. *Tonight, I'm trying it Dena's way. Be happy. Be normal. A part of the circle, not alone in the center.*

"I would love the company."

Kacey's cheeks reddened prettily, and she turned back to Oscar. "Thanks for inviting me."

"Don't thank me until you've crapped in the woods and heard mountain lions outside your tent. This is your initiation, kid."

"Bring it," Kacey laughed.

And her smile was the most beautiful thing I'd ever seen.

Chapter 25

KACEY

"So who's up for a little bit of gambling?" I said as we left the restaurant. "I've got forty bucks burning a hole in my pocket."

Dena exchanged a look with Oscar, then yawned. "I overdid it on the crème brûlée," she said. "My pillow is calling."

"Yeah, me too," Oscar said, glancing at Jonah. "Why don't you guys go ahead without us? We'll do it again some other time."

"You sure?" I said.

"Next time," Dena said, hugging me.

"I'll gamble," Holly said. "I haven't in ages." She tugged on Theo's arm. "You want to?"

Now Theo ricocheted a glance between Oscar and Jonah, and shook his head. "Don't feel like it. Calling it a night."

Holly pouted before hugging me goodbye. Theo slid stiff arms around me and bent his mouth to my ear. "Try to keep it under an hour in the casino. He shouldn't be around the smoke."

"Got it," I said.

Theo seemed to hesitate, his eyes flicking toward Jonah, then back to me. "Have a good time," he said. He turned abruptly, leaving Jonah and me alone.

I watched Holly jog to catch up to him.

"Have he and Holly been together long?" I asked.

"By his standards, yes."

"Oscar and Dena are wonderful people."

Jonah made a face. "They're like a bad vaudeville act."

I laughed. "Come on. I promised Theo we'd only stay an hour in the casino."

"Jesus, he's ridiculous."

I slid a hand into the crook of his elbow. "He's his brother's keeper."

The casino was a short walk from the restaurant. We stepped inside the slightly dim space where most of the illumination came from slot machines, row upon row of them. A legion of glowing, flashing lights. Cones of bright light blared down on the blackjack tables, reflecting off the dealers' white shirts and the white cards on green felt.

"What's your poison?" Jonah said. "Blackjack? Roulette? Poker?"

"Blackjack," I said.

The casino was crowded, and we had to amble far down the line before finding a table with one open seat, immediately to the dealer's right.

"It's a five-dollar ante," Jonah said. "Go for it."

"There's no room for you."

"I'll watch and coach from afar."

"I don't need coaching."

The eyebrow went up. "The seat to the dealer's right is the most important seat at the table. You up for that kind of serious responsibility?"

I narrowed my eyes at him. "I was born ready." I made to sit down, then paused. "Wait. The face cards are worth ten, right?"

Jonah laughed, and I took the vacant seat. He stood behind to watch the hand in progress play out.

To the dealer's left sat two young guys who looked serious about their five-dollar antes. Beside them, two older ladies chatted nonstop and played almost as an afterthought—counting their cards' totals and hitting or staying automatically. Beside them and to my right sat an older gentleman in a ten-gallon cowboy hat and a denim button-down shirt. He pulled a packet of Marlboro Reds from the front pocket.

"Sir," I said. "I'm going to win one hand and then go. Would you mind not smoking until then? Please?"

He eyed me through grizzled skin scrunched up around his eyes and laughed. "You're in the hot seat, girlie. You know how to play to win?"

"Watch me," I said. As the cowboy put his smokes away, I leaned back into Jonah. "How do you play to win?"

"You need chips. Lay your money on the table."

I put a twenty-dollar bill on the green felt. "I'll take one chip," I told the dealer, and he gave me one blue-and-white striped chip with a *20* embossed in gold on the front.

"It's only a five-dollar ante," Jonah said.

"Go big or go home, right?"

"You got that right, girlie." Cowboy pulled a black fifty-dollar chip from one of several small towers of chips and set it as his ante. "Do right by me now, hot seat. I'm countin' on ya."

Jonah snickered from behind me.

I leaned back. "Double down on eleven, right?"

"Oh, *now* you want coaching?" He clucked his tongue.

The dealer—an expressionless man in his late twenties—deftly slid cards out of a chute to each one of us, face up. He dealt himself one down, one up—a three of clubs.

The rest of the players got lucky: nothing lower than seventeen, and Cowboy split his eights, laying another fifty-dollar chip beside his first. He was rewarded with two eighteens and crowed at his luck.

I was dealt a three of diamonds and a two of hearts.

"Are you fucking kidding me," I muttered.

Cowboy made a face at my cards. "Not good, girlie."

"You're telling me. Hit."

A two of spades.

"Hit," I said again.

The five of clubs.

"Shit."

The rest of the table began to grumble.

Jonah leaned over me. "You have twelve. Dealer is showing thirteen—probably."

"How do you know? Are you the Rain Man?"

Jonah's grin colored his words. "No, but I'm an excellent driver."

"Ha ha. *Help.*"

Jonah crouched down so that his chin hovered just above my bare shoulder. His breath was warm on my neck, sending pleasant little shivers skimming down my spine.

"It's a safe strategy to always assume the dealer's down card is worth ten. More of those in the deck."

"Okay…"

"So he's got thirteen, we assume. You have twelve, and your next card's going to be a face card—"

"How…how do you know?" I tried to keep focus, but God, Jonah smelled good. And his hand rested on my back, his thumb rubbing a soft circle. I didn't think he even knew he was doing it. I squeezed my legs together.

"Probability," he answered. "You've taken a lot of small cards. Good chance the next one is worth ten. Let the dealer bust with it. Don't hit."

The sentiment was vehemently echoed by the other players. "Don't hit."

"It's *probable,* not definite." I looked around the table. "Sorry, guys, but I can't sit on this pathetic twelve."

Loud protests as I brushed my fingertips along the green felt. "Hit me."

The dealer laid down the eight of diamonds.

"Twenty." I clutched Jonah's arm and shook it. "I got twenty."

He shook his head, laughing. "Yes, you did."

"You got damn lucky, is what you got," Cowboy said with a chuckle. "Now stay, girlie."

"*Stay,*" the other players echoed.

I waved my hands over my cards. "Stay."

The table went quiet as the dealer flipped over his down card. A queen to give him thirteen.

"Dealers have to hit up to seventeen," Jonah murmured in my ear.

My heart pounded fast as I watched the dealer hit and bust with the jack of diamonds. The table erupted in cheers.

Jonah gripped my shoulder. "Holy shit."

"I won," I said, as the dealer laid a second blue-and-white-striped twenty-dollar chip beside my first.

"Not only did you win," Jonah said, "if you'd sat on your twelve, the dealer would have taken your eight to his thirteen."

"And had twenty-one," I said.

"The whole table would have lost."

"He's right, girlie," Cowboy said. "You're a ringer, ain't you?"

"Could be." I took my winnings and vacated my seat. "Good luck, everyone! It's been real." I tapped the brim of Cowboy's cowboy hat as we left the table. "You can smoke now, sir."

"You just won me two hundred dollars, Lady Luck," he said, wheezing a laugh after us. "Maybe I'll quit while I'm ahead."

"Now what?" I said to Jonah, taking his hand. "Where to? I swear I've never had so much fun sober in my life." I stopped at the long lines of slot machines, buzzing and clunking and glowing. "Slots. Oh my God, do you want to? Just a few, then we'll leave, I swear."

Jonah laughed. "How could I say no?"

I went to the change window and came back with four rolls of nickels.

"You want to play *nickel* slots?" Jonah asked.

"I want to play *some* kind of slots, but plunking quarter after quarter into a machine feels wasteful. This way, I get the experience without feeling like I'm throwing a ton of money away."

Jonah narrowed his eyes and stroked his chin thoughtfully. "Very wise."

"Smart-ass." I took his hand again. "Let's go play with the high rollers."

We found the casino's sole bank of nickel slots and set up shop. Jonah took off his suit jacket and tie and slung them over a vacant machine. Then he handed me a plastic bucket from a stack between the slots.

"For your winnings," he said.

"Better get me two," I said, tearing into my rolls of nickels. "I'm feeling lucky...*punk*."

The slot machines had buttons to push in addition to the levers to send the pictures of cherries, diamonds, and bars spinning. Jonah hit the button, but I insisted on pulling the lever.

"To get the full effect," I said.

"You've really never gambled before? Not even at Caesars?"

"I'm too busy hustling free drinks, and when my shift is over, I just want to get the heck out of there and change my clothes. Holy shit, you should see the getup they have us wearing. Togas, gold sandals, and leafy headbands."

The metallic plunk of a small handful of nickels hit Jonah's tray. A small win. I had the same, just enough to keep playing.

"It's funny we have the same work schedule," he said. "Wednesday through Saturday nights, six to two a.m.? Exactly the same schedule."

"I requested those days." I turned my face to the machine, pulled the lever. "Because they're the best shifts."

Out of the corner of my eye I saw Jonah smile. "They are the best."

I slipped my last nickel into the machine and came up with nothing.

"I'm out," I said with a sigh. "I think the system is rigged."

Jonah laughed. "I guarantee it is. I'm almost out too…"

He dropped a nickel, hit the button, and the pics on the machine went round and round. One cartoon diamond solitaire with *jackpot* written across the middle jerked to a stop. Then two. Then three, all lined up in a perfect row. The entire machine lit up with flashing lights and music, and a torrent of nickels cascaded into the tray below.

I jumped out of my seat, my hands flying to my mouth. "Oh my God, you won. You *won*!"

Jonah stared, a half smile of shock appearing at the edges of his open mouth. "Holy *shit*, look at that."

The nickels kept pouring out, overflowing the tray and falling onto the carpet in a jingling avalanche.

I clutched his shoulder. "Oh my God, how much did you win?" I scanned the top of the machine for the payouts. "It says three diamonds is…five thousand nickels. Wait… That's…"

"Two hundred and fifty bucks," Jonah said, standing up, his hands on his head.

"You hit the jackpot," I said, throwing my arms around his neck.

He looked down at me, his hands slowly coming down. The slot machine lights reflected red, blue, and green in his eyes. The chime of falling coins dwindled away in my ears. The entire casino faded into the background.

"I did," he whispered. His hands took my face, and he kissed me.

I froze as his lips covered mine, then I melted against him. His warm, soft mouth stole the strength from my legs, and I staggered back. He followed, pressing me up against the bank of slots, nickels sliding under our feet. A small moan escaped me, an unconscious sound of want rising from deep inside. I hadn't known how badly I desired this until it was happening.

Jonah brushed his lips over mine and then moved in closer, pressed harder. My lips parted for his, and I moaned again at the first taste of his tongue sliding against mine—sweetness and a tinge of spicy heat from our dinner. I wanted more, but he retreated to kiss my lips, sucking lightly, exploring everywhere, before coming back to plunge deeper.

My hands found their way into his soft, thick hair. I pulled lightly, pulled him closer to me, opened my mouth wider to take all of his kiss. His body pressed all up and down mine, and I wanted him on my skin and in my veins.

This. This... All along it's been this.

Jonah groaned softly, his hands roaming over every inch of skin available to him: my neck, my shoulder, my face. God, the way he held my face, cupped my chin in his hands... He kissed me as if I were something delicate and precious, something he cherished and held with reverence.

My first kiss. This is my first real kiss.

The clatter of nickels trickled to a stop. Jonah's lips brushed mine once more before he pulled away. He opened his eyes.

And my heart broke.

"Kace," he whispered, his face full of pain. "Oh damn, I shouldn't have done that."

Every good and beautiful feeling from our kiss was wrenched out of me. "Jonah..."

"I can't do this to you. Or myself."

I clung to him, pulling on his hands, still out of breath. "What are you talking—"

"Is this your machine?" came a screeching voice from behind him.

Jonah dropped my hands and turned around. An old lady in polyester and a perm peered at the yellow light flashing on the top of our machine.

"They'll come by to fill it back up," she said. "You going to take your money or not?"

"We got it, thanks."

Jonah busied himself with scooping nickels into the plastic pails. I helped, and every time our hands touched, desire crackled up my arms. I wanted him. Wanted his hands on me, his mouth on mine, to feel him inside me. But Jonah wouldn't look at me, and his mouth was pressed in a thin line, as if he were trying not to breathe.

My feelings churned in me like a maelstrom of hurt and humiliation and confusion. I had just begun to taste something good and perfect, and then it was torn away.

We changed the five thousand nickels for two hundred and fifty dollars. Jonah tried to press some of the bills into my hand. "Take it. Or at least half. They were your nickels to start."

"It was your jackpot."

I was your jackpot.

He shook his head, mute and struggling. The misery exuding from him was like a thousand little arrows to my heart.

"Let's get out of here," I said, tugging his arm. "Out of the smoke."

"Yeah," he said with a bitter smile. "It's not good for my heart. Everything I do is for the good of my stupid fucking heart."

We left the casino and walked in silence, back along the Strip's busy sidewalks to his parked truck. The drive to my apartment was silent. In the parking lot, he left the engine idling and clenched his truck's steering wheel so tightly, his knuckles had gone white.

"I'm such an asshole," he said finally. He turned to look at me for the first time since we left the MGM Grand, and his eyes were heavy and exhausted. "Kace, I'm sorry."

"For *what?*"

"I shouldn't have kissed you. It was wrong and stupid, and I'm sorry. We're friends. We have to stay friends. I just got caught up in the moment, and you looked...so beautiful."

"Jonah..." I reached for him, but he flinched away.

"Please don't. I've fucked up enough for one night. My willpower is hanging by a goddamn thread."

A short silence descended in which I heard only my own heartbeat, thudding hard against my chest. I reached again and pried his hand from the wheel. His MedicAlert bracelet glinted in the streetlight.

"You don't have to be sorry. Don't apologize. That kiss was beautiful. Didn't you feel it? It felt *right* and perfect, and it means something. Jonah…"

"God, Kace," he whispered, his voice breaking. "You should go. Please. Just go."

"I don't want to," I said, my own voice cracking. "I don't want to waste another minute. I was away from you for twelve days when I quit the band. *Twelve* days I'll never get back." Tears streamed down my cheeks freely now. "Listen to me. I'm more afraid of not being with you than I am of being with you. Or of what might happen four months from now."

Jonah's hand gripped mine tight, and his own eyes shone.

"Four months," he said, shaking his head. "Do you know why I keep my damn schedule? Why I keep my head down and work every day to get the installation ready for the opening? It's not just to finish the work. It's because when I do only that, I keep time as an abstract idea. Instead of a linear stretch of days it's…a sphere. A glass sphere in which I work, visit my family, have drinks with friends, over and over, round and round. Each week no different from the next. That's how I hold time still."

Tears splattered my skirt. "And now I've messed it all up?"

He shook his head, his eyes brimming, his voice hoarse and tremulous at the edges. "No. You've been a brilliant light in my drab, dark world. But if you let me kiss you again…if we start something right now, time won't stand still. The end, *my* end, won't be some nebulous thing off in the distance. It'll race toward me, because…"

His voice choked off, and I held his hand tighter, our tears falling together.

"Because why?" I whispered.

"Because, Kace, the days will count down until there's only one left," he said through gritted teeth. "The one where I have to say goodbye to you."

The words pummeled my heart, cracked and broke it.

It's real. Like Lola said. I can't pretend this away.

Jonah heaved a breath and turned away, wiping his cheek on the sleeve of his shirt. "It'll be hard enough as friends," he said, his voice full of gravel. "It'll be so much worse if we try to have more. If we make love. If we fall…" He shook his head, frustration coloring his agonized expression now.

"Jonah…"

"It's late. I have a lot of work to do tomorrow."

I couldn't take the cold finality in his tone. I nodded mutely and reached for the door. "All right. Thanks for dinner and my first time in a casino…"

And my first kiss.

Jonah reached across the seat to take my hand again. He held it tightly, pressed my fingers to his lips, and then let me go.

Chapter 26

JONAH

IN THE EARLY-MORNING HOURS ON THE FRIDAY OF OSCAR'S CAMPING trip, my phone chirped with a text from Kacey.

> Yesterday @ lunch, Tania told me she found a $250 bonus in her paycheck.

> Who said nickel slots don't pay? I typed back.

> Wasn't me. Smart-ass. :P

I eased a sigh of relief. Things hadn't been tense between Kacey and me that last week, but they weren't one hundred percent back to normal either. She was as sweet as ever, still bringing Tania and me lunch at the hot shop or sending me random funny texts like this one. She was doing what I'd asked her to do: she was being my friend. Upholding her end of the bargain, while I had been the selfish bastard who kissed her and nearly fucked everything up between us.

None of us—Oscar, Theo, or me—had a car or truck big enough to hold six passengers and our camping gear, so we each drove up in pairs. The drive to Great Basin National Park was four and a half hours. I thought for sure Kacey and I would spend the entire time in an awkward silence, the kiss and everything after hanging between us.

But long silences and Kacey Dawson didn't mix. She was all smiles when I picked her up at her complex and chatted nonstop about various topics and camping itself.

"I never spent a night outdoors," she said. "Will we see stars?"

"You'll see so many stars, it'll look unreal," I told her.

"I've never seen a sky packed with them. City lights always drown them out."

"I know. The first time we went, I couldn't believe the canopy. You'll love it."

"I know I will," Kacey said, settling into her seat, kicking her boots up on the dash. "But I still don't know if bringing my guitar was a good idea. I'll be *that* gal who breaks into song at the party."

"You've been depriving us of your talent long enough. You owe us at least one song. Consider it the price of admission."

She peppered me with dozens of other questions about the trip, none of which concerned the sleeping arrangements. Not that I even knew anything. Oscar assured me he had it "taken care of" and muttered something about Holly and Kacey sharing a tent.

When we arrived at the campsite, Theo's black truck and Oscar's silver SUV were already parked side by side, facing a flat clearing of dirt at Upper Lehman Creek. Trees—fir, pine, and oak—rose up amid tall pale-green grasses carpeting the forest floor. I could just see the creek from our site. It meandered all through the campgrounds, rushing softly over smooth stone. A metal fire ring was at the center of the site, and Theo was already setting up his orange tent on the east side.

Kacey jumped out to hug everyone, and Oscar pulled me aside.

"Holly changed plans on us, bro," he said. "She can't be parted from Theo. Looks like you and Kacey are going to be tentmates."

I crossed my arms over my chest and raised an eyebrow. "You're so full of shit."

Oscar laughed. "You and Kacey. One tent. That's the God's honest."

"I know, but... Never mind."

"Wow, this is amazing," Kacey said, joining us, her gaze sweeping over the view. She was adorable in her slouchy oversize jeans rolled up to mid-shin, black combat boots, a tight white tee, and a green plaid shirt about ten sizes too big. I put the day's temp at eighty-six. Kacey wore a knitted beanie on her head anyway, as if it were fifty-six.

"Oscar, this place is so beautiful."

"Isn't it?" His smile was nostalgic. "I used to come here with my parents every year when I was a kid. They eventually got burned out on it, but I never stopped coming. I force my closest friends and my best gal to come up with me at least four times a year."

"At least," Dena said, wrapping her arms around Oscar from behind, her chin against his shoulder. "But I love it here. I find it inspirational." She turned her dark eyes to Kacey. "I hope you find it the same. I hear you brought your guitar?"

"Yeah." Kacey glanced down, kicked an acorn. "Maybe I'll play something. I do a mean 'Kumbaya.'"

Oscar jerked his chin at me. "J, why don't you show her around our site, get her familiar with the area. We'll get Theo to put up your tent for you."

"The hell I will," Theo grunted from behind, on his knees in a shallow pond of orange nylon, directing Holly on how to help him.

I turned to Kacey. Her blue eyes were seemingly more stunning in the overcast haze of the Basin, instead of the relentless white heat of Vegas.

"You want to see the creek?" I asked.

"I want to see everything."

———

I took her around the site, through the woods, and along the creek. It was only a few feet wide but with a solid current of clear, cold water. Kacey put her hands in it and jumped back with a yelp. She shook her hands dry and wrapped them in her shirt.

"Please tell me we don't have to bathe in this," she said, laughing.

"Not at all. The town of Baker has pay showers."

"Thank God."

"Just a short, four-hour hike down the mountain."

Her smile dissolved. "For real?"

"Oscar likes to go all or nothing. We're roughin' it, city girl, for two whole days."

Kacey blew out her lips. "There'd better be some serious stars tonight."

"I guarantee it."

We walked on through the trees, the creek's whispering and babbling the only sound.

"Do you know where you're going, Fletcher?" she asked, stepping carefully over a fallen tree.

I stopped walking. "I thought you had the map?"

"Very funny. If we get lost, I'm not eating bugs or moss or… lichen. I'll tell you that right now."

"You won't have to. Sasquatch will probably get to us first."

Kacey stopped cold. "Please don't kid around. Bigfoot? For real? Are there Bigfoots? Big…feet up here?"

"Bigfeet?" My laugh started as a low rumble, picked up steam, and then I was laughing so hard tears stung my eyes.

"Shut up!" Kacey said, giving me a playful shove while trying to conceal her own laughter. "They scare me. And they're real, you know," she insisted, jabbing a finger at me. "You can't tell me they're not. I once saw a documentary…didn't sleep for a week."

"Come on," I said, wiping my eyes. "I'll show you why we're here. Sasquatch-free territory, I promise."

We walked on until the trees thinned and then gave way to a

clearing of that long hairlike grass, at the edge of the world. The mountains rose up on all sides, dressed in the pale, dusty green of summer trees, no longer the vibrant green of spring and not yet the golds and reds of fall. Below us, the Basin spread out for miles, a silvery-blue lake tucked among more green. There were no boaters out yet to disturb the surface; it was as still as glass.

"It's so beautiful," Kacey murmured, her gaze sweeping all around and then up to the overcast sky. "If the clouds pass, we should see stars tonight."

I nodded. "If it's clear enough, you can see the edge of the Milky Way."

"Really? That would be amazing."

I watched her gaze follow a hawk as it soared across the Basin. Seeing the stars reflected in her eyes…that would be amazing. A chance of a lifetime.

———

Twilight descended, and the six of us sat in foldout chairs around the fire pit, roasting hot dogs and marshmallows. Talk and laughter crisscrossed the circle, stories ending and others picking up in their wake. I watched the firelight cast a glow over the faces of the people I loved best. I captured the moments in mental snapshots.

Oscar's laughing face, firelight catching Dena's earring, Holly's squeak of alarm when her marshmallow caught fire, Theo holding a hot dog straight up and turning his head sideways to bite it. And Kacey leaning her chin on the heel of her hand, glancing sideways at me, leaning toward me…

I committed these moments to memory with the hope I might take them with me wherever I went next.

Soon, the only light left was from our low fire. The trees bent over us to form a canopy, and while it looked as if the clouds had passed, only a smattering of stars was visible beyond.

Food eaten and trash cleaned up, Dena opened the artistic half of the evening by reciting a few poems: a little Walt Whitman, a few lines from Thoreau. She closed as she usually did with Rumi, and while most poetry didn't move me, Dena recited a line that jumped out at me: "*You are not a drop in the ocean. You are the entire ocean in a drop.*"

I looked at Kacey sitting beside me. *She is not merely an ocean. She is an entire universe.*

Oscar called on Kacey to play for us.

"Rock star in the house," he said to Holly.

"Really?" she said from her chair beside Theo's, their hands linked.

"Former rock star," Kacey said. "And I don't think you can call yourself a star if you quit the band eight nanoseconds before they get famous."

She was right. I heard on the radio at the hot shop her old band was tearing up the charts and had added four more shows to their sold-out concert series.

"Which band?" Holly asked.

"Rapid Confession," I said as Kacey was digging her guitar out of the tent.

Holly nearly spit out the beer from her longneck. "Are you kidding? I fucking love that band."

Theo shot her an irritated look. Kacey just smiled as she shouldered her guitar strap.

"Why did you quit?" Holly asked.

"Not my scene." Kacey sat on the ground in front of her chair, near my legs. The firelight made her face glow. "So," she said, tuning her guitar. "Any requests?"

"Um, *yeah,* how about 'Talk Me Down'?"

Kacey smiled thinly but kept her eyes on her guitar. "I don't play that one anymore."

I was nervous as hell for some reason. Aside from some loud—but intricate—electric guitar riffs on the radio, I'd never heard Kacey play. Or sing. My stupid heart pounded like I was the one in the spotlight, and my palms were so sweaty I had to wipe them on the front of my jeans.

"How about old school?" Dena said. "Tom Petty?"

Kacey nodded as she strummed a few notes. Then her fingers hit the five opening chords of "Free Fallin'."

"Nice," Dena murmured.

The chords repeated, then Kacey began to sing.

After two lines, I closed my eyes, blocking out everything except her voice. Pure and sweet, but a little gravelly too. Tough as hell tinged with vulnerable. She sang about a good girl who loved her mama, and a bad boy who broke her heart. Kacey's hand strummed the strings harder as the verse ended, and she hit that chorus high note clear and hard, with a tapered edge at the end.

Before the next verse, Kacey smiled at Dena, murmuring, "Don't leave me hanging…" Dena joined in, then we all did. Through the rest of "Free Fallin'" and into "I'm Yours" by Jason Mraz, "Brass in Pocket" by the Pretenders, and "Wonderwall" by Oasis.

Last, Kacey sang Snow Patrol's "Chasing Cars" alone, her voice filling up the night. I leaned back in my chair, only the side of her face visible to me, lit up gold with firelight as her sweet, scratchy voice asked someone to lie with her and just forget the world.

The ache in my heart rose to my throat, and I felt something change in me. A shift. A reckless, selfish hope that maybe, if Kacey were still willing, I could lie with her this night and every night thereafter, for however many I had left to me.

The song ended. Followed by silence.

Holly sniffed and wiped her eyes. "You have a beautiful voice."

Kacey smiled as the others murmured agreement. With a snap of his head, Theo came out of his reverie like a man who'd been under hypnosis. All of his walls shot back up. His face hardened, his brow furrowed, and he took a long pull from his beer bottle.

Kacey's eyes found mine, soft and serene in the firelight.

"All right, kiddies," Oscar said, taking up a pitcher of water to douse the fire. "Time for bed."

Good nights were said, and we retreated into our tents. Kacey and I took turns waiting outside while the other changed into sleeping clothes. She put on an old blue men's button-down. The temperature had dropped to sixty degrees or so, and she shivered as she snuggled down into her sleeping bag.

I changed into flannel pants and a T-shirt and slid into my bag. We lay in silence, staring at the tent roof, a shard of silver starlight our only illumination.

"Holly was right," I said. "Your voice is beautiful. You could have a solo career if you wanted it."

She rolled on her side toward me. "If I wanted it..."

"Do you?"

"I don't know. Just this morning I tried to finish a song I started several years ago. About Chett. I'd written it on the road. All the pain of his ditching me. I squeezed the words from my heart and onto the page. God, the pain had felt so real back then. But when I read them today...they felt empty. Silly, even." She heaved a sigh. "I guess Chett's not worth even a song. Ironic, since that's why I came back to Vegas. To write about him." She shifted in her bag. "I guess it's time to find some new material."

I nodded, struggled for something more to say.

Kacey flopped onto her back. "This tent is the worst."

"Sorry?"

"This is the worst tent ever," she said, pointing at the angled nylon roof over our heads. "Look at it. What the hell is the point of sleeping out in nature if you can't see it?"

"To protect you from the elements," I said. "Only a thin strip of nylon separates you from rain, wind...*Sasquatches.*"

"Shut up."

"The worst Mother Nature has to offer."

"And the best," she said. "I mean, there's not even a window to see the stars. Don't tents usually have a screen or something?"

"Some do," I said. "This one doesn't."

Kacey climbed out of her bag and rolled it up into a sloppy bundle she tucked under her arm.

"Where are you going?"

"I want the stars." She stopped at the tent flap and looked over her shoulder at me, a question in her eyes.

Are you coming?

She didn't wait for an answer but stepped out. To where I had no idea, but if I didn't follow her, she might get lost in the dark of the forest. At least, that's what I told myself as I gathered up my own bag and followed her out.

Chapter 27

JONAH

THE GROUND WAS COLD AND HARD UNDER MY BARE FEET AS I FOLLOWED the beacon of Kacey's pale hair through the woods, away from the clearing of dark tents where my friends slept. She followed the creek, and I thought I knew where she was going. The only place she knew to go: the clearing near the edge of the valley, about a hundred yards away from the campsite.

Only a few trees edged the clearing, towering columns in the dark. Below, the valley spread out in rolling hills of deep green that looked almost black in the night, and a canopy of stars wheeled overhead like diamonds. The moon was huge and full, and cast silvery light over everything.

She dropped her sleeping bag on the smoothest flat of ground, cushioned by dried pine needles and long, soft grass. She stood a moment, her back to me, slender and luminous in the moonlight. Her head turned, taking in the view of the valley before her, and then tilted up to the stars above. Her shoulders rose and fell with a deep inhale. The breath filled my own lungs, along with a desperate urge to move behind her, hold her body to mine, fist my hand in her hair, and kiss the soft skin of her neck.

Kacey shook out her sleeping bag and climbed inside. I laid mine out beside hers, and together we lay on our backs, looking up at the stars.

"So incredibly beautiful," she said. "Amazing all of this is here, in every night sky, but we rarely see it." She rolled over in her bag to look at me. "You're awfully quiet tonight. What are you thinking about?"

You. My thoughts are filled with you. Always.

"Can I tell you what I'm thinking about?" she said before I could answer. "I'm thinking right now, we're lying here with less than a foot between us, but in separate sleeping bags. Because we're friends. You're there, and I'm here, and we're pretending friendship keeps us at a safe distance."

My heart began to pound. "I know. I shouldn't have told you to come back to Vegas. And I shouldn't have kissed you."

"I had to come back," she said. "I never should've left. If I'd moved to some other city, I would've been alone and miserable and missing you. We lost twelve days when I left. I want that time back, and I don't want to lose any more."

"Kacey…"

"I can't keep going on like this, Jonah," she said, turning to look at me. "As friends. I know I should try, but I can't. I can't…not touch you. I want to be able to kiss you if I feel like it, and I think you want that too. Like our first kiss at the casino. It was everything to me. Everything."

"It was for me too," I said. "I want to kiss you again. I want to kiss you so bad I can't breathe. I want to be with you every second of my life, but… God, Kacey, how much time is that? How do I put you through that?"

"And what about you? You continue on, alone?" She shook her head. "You can trust me. Trust me when I say I can take it. You and me. I can take it. Whatever happens."

"I do trust you. My pushing you away was never about mistrusting you. It was me not wanting to hurt you. That's all I've ever wanted, since the first moment I saw you. To protect you. To keep you safe."

She smiled then, her eyes filled with happiness. And God, somehow, even with all the crazy stuff going on in my life, it all boiled down to whether or not Kacey was happy. I wanted to make her happy any way that I could, because that's what she did for me. Little by little, day by day, like sunlight seeping through the cracks of a boarded-up abandoned house, Kacey was invading me. Tearing down the shutters, ripping out the boards, and letting the light in.

"Come here," I said.

She wriggled in her sleeping bag for a moment before climbing out of it. My heart stuttered at bare legs, a flash of pink underwear, and the outline of her breasts under her button-down shirt. I held my bag open, and she slid in, her body curving perfectly into mine, as right and perfect as our kiss.

She sighed, her breath fluttering as she put her hands on my face. "I'm sorry I left."

"I told you to go."

"I should've stayed. I never should've left at all. And I promise you, Jonah, I'll never leave you again. Never again."

"I'm going to leave you," I said, my voice hardly more than a whisper. The words hung between us, the crux of all our pain and tears and hesitation.

But Kacey smiled—*smiled*—with brave tears sliding down her cheeks. "Not yet. Not tonight. We might not have months or years, but we have moments. Thousands upon thousands of them. Let's take each moment, seize it, and wring it dry. Okay?"

I gazed down at her. "Okay."

"This is a good moment," she whispered.

"One of the best…" I let my head sink down toward hers. Our lips brushed, and hers parted for me immediately. Our tongues met, and I shuddered as a current raced through me, burning through me like a fuse.

"God," I whispered against her mouth.

"This," she breathed back. "This moment."

She pulled me into her kiss, and this one went on and on. She felt perfect beneath me, fit perfectly against me, and our mouths moved in perfect tandem, our tongues sliding and touching so softly. The need that had been growing and simmering between us sparked and caught fire. My hands became greedy. She moaned and pressed herself into my touch, while her own hands roamed—in my hair, down my back, around my waist. She found me hard and stroked me through my flannel pants.

"Jonah…" She pushed toward me, drawing me close with her leg. "I want to. So much. Can you?"

"Oh, I can," I said. "And I'm *going* to."

She let out a little sound of want into my mouth as I kissed her hard, while my hands sought her breasts under her shirt. The feel of them, the weight of them, and her soft skin against my rough palms. All of her, her breath, the scent of her, the way she kissed me… I'd never wanted a woman like this. Ever.

"Don't stop kissing me," she whispered against my mouth when I came up for air. "I'll die if you do…"

My mouth took hers again, while our bodies rocked together, her hips rising to meet mine. I pulled her in tight, grinding down hard, as if we were already naked and I was inside her.

Her fingers struggled with the buttons on her shirt. "Take it off," she whispered.

I tore it open instead, a button flying off, and she gave a little cry that was half surprise, half want as her breasts came free. The cold air hardened her nipples immediately, and I put my mouth on one, sucking and swirling my tongue. Desire coiled up from my groin to my head. Dizzy with want and need, I moved to the other breast as she arched her back into my mouth.

"Oh God, *yes*…" Her voice drew out in a hiss, and her hand slid under the waistband of my pants. Her fingers closed around my aching erection, stroking me.

"If you keep doing that," I said, my mouth on her neck, sucking and nipping, "this won't be a very fun night for you."

"No," she said. "You're going to come with me. We're going to come together."

"You're an optimist."

"And you're not naked enough," she replied. She hauled my T-shirt off and flung it away. Skin to skin, her breasts pressed against my chest. My hands tangled in her hair, holding her head as I kissed the sweet caramel lusciousness of her mouth.

"I want this…you…" I wanted to feel all her exquisite softness and heat everywhere.

I stripped off my pants and boxers. She wiggled out of her panties and pulled me back to her. Her mouth took mine again, and her legs were parting, and I was so damn hard…

"Shit, I don't have anything…"

"My shirt pocket," she whispered at my neck.

I could've wept with relief, but that would've taken too long. I fished a condom out of the front pocket of the torn shirt she was still partially wearing and tore off the wrapper. Within seconds, I was ready.

"Jonah," Kacey whispered, spreading her thighs and taking me in her hand to guide me. "I want you so badly…" The words fell apart as she arched her back and I slid inside her.

I had no words. No thoughts. Only the pure, perfect sensation of her warm, wet tightness taking me in, holding, squeezing, and enveloping me until I was buried as deep as I could go. Then her fingernails dug into my shoulder blades, she tilted her hips, and I was deeper.

"Jesus, Kace," I groaned. I gripped her hip with one hand, lifting her body to meet mine. Pushing down into her, pressing her into my thrusts, keeping it slow. In the moonlight, her face contorted with pleasure, her eyes shut, mouth open, her throat and back arched to take me all the way every time.

"Jonah," she breathed. "More…please…"

Her hips rose and fell faster now, and I matched her pace, keeping in tandem without thought. Her legs came up to wrap around my waist, pushing the sleeping bag off us. I felt no cold. Only her skin on mine, the sweet heat of her body, and the sounds of her growing pleasure stifled against my shoulder.

"You feel so good," I told her, moving faster now. "How can you feel this good?"

"It's you. God…" Her eyes widened over my shoulder. "You need to see the stars."

I wrapped my arms around her and rolled to my back, pulling her on top of me. She rose up against the skies, riding me. And holy God, the stars…millions of them wheeling in a brilliant backdrop to Kacey's beauty. They were nothing to her. Nothing.

She shrugged out of her torn shirt and flung it away. Her naked skin glowed pale and radiant, the dark ink of her tattoos lacing over her arms like vines. Her breasts, full and beautiful as they rose and fell, her back arched, her hair like white silk spilling down her back.

I fought not to come, clutched at the world to wait for her, to make it as impossibly good for her as I could. Her gasps turned to cries, my whispered name growing louder in her mouth. She leaned back and put her hands on my thighs behind her, her body arched and open to me. It did me in. I couldn't take it anymore. I half sat up, gripped her hips hard, and drove her down as I came up into her, again and again.

"Come, Kace," I growled through gritted teeth. "Let me see you come."

She cried out, and her body shuddered and clenched tight around me. The sight of her face as she came, the unbelievable beauty of it, the fact that I was making her look like that, bringing her this pleasure, put me over.

I rose up a final time and came harder than I ever had in my life. On and on I came, exploding into Kacey, who was whimpering now, her voice cut to shreds, and then finally to silence broken only by our labored breathing.

Kacey stared down at me, a bewildered smile on her face. Slowly, she sank down onto me, her breasts pressed to my heaving chest. She tucked her head under my chin, and the softness of her hair fell over my neck. With effort, I lifted my trembling arms and held her, the silken skin of her naked back under my hands. I stared at the canopy of stars overhead, sort of lost myself.

And sort of found.

"You all right?" she whispered.

"Oh yeah."

"Your heart is beating so fast."

I slipped my hand between our chests. "So is yours."

I felt her laugh sigh across my bare skin. "That was unreal," she whispered. "I've never... I mean, I *have*, but not like that. Never like that."

A star shot across the deep blue-black of the sky, streaking through the diamond-strewn canopy. "Yeah," I whispered. "Never like this."

"Do you think the others heard us?"

"I'm pretty sure the entire tristate area heard us." My hands trailed lazily over her back. "A park ranger is going to come over that hill any minute now to investigate who's been torturing a mountain lion."

"And who is the mountain lion in this little scenario?"

"You are, of course. I have the claw marks to prove it."

Kacey snuggled closer against me. "I don't care who heard," she murmured after a moment. "They want this for you anyway. Oscar and Dena."

"They all want me to get laid?"

"They all want you to be with someone."

I nodded. "Yeah. I guess they do."

Kacey lifted her head. "And now you're with me." Her eyes glanced down for a second and then back up to meet mine. Hesitant.

I smiled gently at her, this beautiful woman lying naked with me, her skin flush with the hard ridge of my scar, and she was unafraid.

"I'm with you, Kacey. I can't not be with you."

"No going back, okay? No second-guessing. If we do, we just waste time. I don't want to waste a single moment with you. Not one." She pushed herself up onto her elbows. "Do you promise me? No going back?"

I took hold of her shoulders and pulled her up over me, then moved my hands into her hair. Her eyes were wide and intent, and I knew that she was still asking me to trust her, when no one else had.

"No going back," I said and sealed the vow with a kiss that was soft and gentle, but deep with intention. My best intentions, despite my worst fears.

Little moments, day by day. This is what I have to give.

I kissed her deeper, and the need to have her rose up again. She moaned softly into my mouth, and I felt her body begin to move against mine.

"I don't suppose you have a second condom in that magic pocket of yours?" I asked between kisses. "Please say yes."

Kacey laughed against my lips. "See for yourself."

My right hand snaked out and took hold of her discarded shirt. I felt a crackle in the pocket, and my head fell back in relief.

"Did you know we were going to sleep together tonight?"

"I hoped we would."

I raised an eyebrow as I tore open the packet. "*Twice?*"

Her voice and eyes and smile all softened. "I hoped so bad…"

She took me inside her, and as my body was racked with pleasure, I felt the most bittersweet of emotions, soaring and plummeting at the same time: joy that I had this woman in my life, and a profound ache that I had met her too late.

I would love you forever, Kacey, if I only had the chance.

Chapter 28

KACEY

THE SUN WAS WELL OVER THE HORIZON WHEN JONAH AND I TRUDGED back to the campsite hand in hand. Now that I could touch him, I didn't want to stop. My body still hummed like a live wire, and instead of feeling satiated by two mind-blowing orgasms, I just wanted more.

We approached the ring of tents to find everyone else up and sitting around a low fire, sipping coffee. They all stopped to stare at our approach. Oscar started a slow clap until Dena elbowed him in the side, hiding a smile behind her hand as she watched us with warm eyes. Holly buried an embarrassed giggle in her shoulder, though she looked tired, as if she hadn't slept much the night before. Theo only gaped, his expression unreadable. I met his eye with a small smile he didn't return, and he quickly looked away.

Jonah stopped, took in all the stares. "Did you guys hear that last night? Mountain lion. Loud one too."

Everyone burst out laughing. Except Theo.

I swatted Jonah's arm and took my seat around the fire. Theo's dark stare followed me, prickling on my skin. Dena handed me a thermos of hot black coffee. Our eyes met, hers full of warmth and something like gratitude.

I sat on the ground between Jonah's feet, leaning back with my elbows on his knees. A perfect fit.

All of this, I thought, sipping my coffee. *So perfect.*

We all took a hike through the woods that morning, following a rough path that cut downward toward a small body of water called Stella Lake. The guys skipped rocks across the surface, insulting the hell out of each other in an affectionate but cutthroat competition. Holly, Dena, and I walked around the perimeter under a leaden sky that threatened rain.

Holly had been quiet all morning. She stuck close to us on the walk but said little, her hands jammed in the front of her sweatshirt.

"I cheated on the 'no cell phones' rule and checked for weather updates," she finally said. "A huge thunderstorm is going to roll through here."

Dena and I looked up at the same time. The sky was flat and gray, and in the distance, darker, heavier clouds gathered.

"So I was wondering if we were going to leave early," Holly said. "Like, today. And if we do, could I get a ride with one of you guys?"

Dena's expression warmed with concern. "Why? What happened?"

"Theo and I broke up," Holly said.

"When?" I asked.

"Last night." She tugged at her eyebrow piercing. "Right after everyone went to bed."

Dena glanced at me, then back to Holly. "I'm so sorry, Holly. Can I ask why?"

"He's an asshole, that's why," she said with sudden fire. "He told me he was tired of trying to make something work when it obviously wasn't. He's always been kind of...hot and cold with me. But this time it felt...final." Her eyes filled with tears that she quickly brushed away. "Anyway. I don't want to spend that long drive back with just him in the truck."

"No, of course not," Dena said, putting her arm around her. "You can ride with us. I'll find out from Oscar what he thinks about this potential storm, and we'll figure it out, okay?"

Holly nodded. "Thanks a lot. I appreciate it. I'm going to go back up. I'm sick of camping." She looked to me, her voice hardening into petulance. "You got the good brother."

Dena and I watched her turn and storm back up the trail, then exchanged wide-eyed glances.

"Well, on the one hand," Dena said as we continued around the path, "it was shitty of Theo to break up with her while she's stranded hundreds of miles from home. On the other, I don't know why he brought her at all. She's the closest he's gotten to having a girlfriend, but she never sticks."

I shrugged. "She's not the one."

"Definitely not. He isn't looking for the one. And he shouldn't."

"No?"

"*Lovers don't finally meet somewhere. They are in each other all along,*" she recited.

I smiled, a warmth expanding down low in my stomach, along with a sense memory of Jonah sliding into me. "I like that," I said.

"I do too," Dena said in her gentle voice, the kind of quiet tone that made you feel like she was telling you something only meant for you to hear. "Rumi, again. Never ceases to amaze me how his words still feel so true and potent, hundreds of years after he lived."

We stopped and watched the guys skip rocks. Even fifty yards away, I could see laughter in Jonah and Oscar's stance, and glowering sullenness in Theo's.

"Jonah is one of the best men I've ever known," Dena said. "It's been hard seeing him shut down the part of him that longs for love and wants to care for someone. When he had that last biopsy...he made a decision not to get involved with anyone again. He used Audrey's breakup as the cover. But now he's with you. He *un*made the decision. Now he has a chance."

"A chance of what?"

"Of being happy. He is happy with you." Dena's dark eyes met mine intently. "He won't jump out of planes or visit far-flung places of the earth. He has no bucket list. He only wants to finish his installation. And I worried—we all did—it wasn't enough. I have no doubt he'll finish. But I wanted him to *share* his beautiful art with someone. And now he is."

She put her hand in mine, gave it a squeeze. "You don't have to tell me. I'm sure he fought to protect you. To keep you—"

"At a safe distance," I said.

She sighed, nodded. "He's pushed so many friends away for the same reason. But he couldn't keep you away, could he?"

I shook my head, a smile spreading my lips. "No, he couldn't."

"Of course not," Dena said with a laugh and turned her gaze on Jonah. "You were in each other all along."

Chapter 29

JONAH

OSCAR CONFIRMED A HEAVY RAINSTORM WAS SET TO DRENCH THE Basin. By the look of the dark clouds rolling in, he guessed an hour tops.

"I saw the weather before we left," Oscar said, "but I hoped it would miss us, so I took a chance. Sorry, guys."

"This sucks," Kacey said to me. "Turns out I like camping. It's peaceful here. Away from the city and cars and other people. And I wanted more time here with you." She looked up at me and traced the line of my jaw; then her eyes flicked toward the others packing up. "Can we stay? I want to see the rain."

I wrapped my arms around her waist. "Thunderstorms out here are pretty gnarly," I said. "You sure you want to?"

She nodded. "I'm from San Diego, remember, where a drizzle that lasts more than five minutes is a downpour." She pressed her body closer to mine, brushed her lips over my mouth. "I want to dance in the real rain."

I stared, all the blood in my brain draining due south. "Stay it is."

"Just watch out for mountain lions," Oscar said. His eyebrows flicked up twice. "You can always tell they're coming by how loud their roar is."

She socked his shoulder. "I'm never going to live that down, am I?"

"Never."

Theo strode over, pulled us aside. "I don't suppose I can talk you out of this?"

"She wants to feel the rainfall," I said.

"Real rain," Kacey said. "I've never seen it before. I'm a dork, I know…"

"And I'm a fucking wreck worried Jonah's immune system can't handle cold rain. We all got a job here."

"I swear, Teddy," Kacey said. "I want him healthy as much as you do."

"Jesus, I'm standing right here, guys," I said.

Theo looked at me a long time. "Yes, you are." He gave his head a shake and jabbed a finger at me. "Stay dry."

"Scout's honor," I said, holding up a hand.

Theo snorted and started away. "You were never a scout."

"That's for damn sure," I said. I hauled Kacey to me as soon as the cars vanished down the hill. I held her tight, kissed her hard.

"You have to wait for the rain," she breathed against my lips.

"Don't want to," I said, my hands slipping up her shirt. Now that I could touch her, I couldn't keep my hands off her. Couldn't get enough of her nearness, her body, her kisses…

"You have to stay dry," she said, leading me to the tent. "We promised Teddy."

In the tent, I divested her of everything she wore except the old men's button-down. Just as she melted against me, ready to give in, the sky cracked open. A flash of light lit up the world on the other side of the tent. Kacey sat up and pulled aside the tent flap, watching the slanted sheets of rain outside.

"Oh my God. That's real rain." She slipped out of the tent and gave a little squeal as the cold water hit her, drenching her instantly. "Oh shit, Theo was right. This is cold as hell."

"Come back," I said.

"Not yet," she said, letting the water wash over her, her hips swaying slightly. "I wish you could come dance with me."

"You'll thank me later when you're shivering with cold and I'm dry."

"Will you warm me with your body heat?"

"Damn straight."

She closed her eyes and let the rain fall over her, face to the sky. Her breasts were visible through the wet material of her shirt, her nipples hard, and I could see every contour, every line and curve. The water raced in rivulets down her cheeks like tears, but her smile was quiet and private.

"I might get lonely out here."

"I'm watching you," I said. "I like watching you."

"I like you watching me," she said. She lifted her hair off her shoulders, and her breasts rose too.

I sucked in a breath and fought the urge to go to her. To put my hands on her.

Wait. Just wait... And watch.

Kacey let her hands fall and opened her eyes. Her lips were parted, water dripped off her chin, and she slowly ran her tongue along her bottom lip. Her eyes never leaving mine, her hands rose again, this time to her shirt. She unbuttoned the top four buttons but no more, revealing the perfect valley of smooth skin between her breasts. Her fingertips pulled aside the soaked material and traced over one hard nipple.

"Jesus…" I said, my voice hoarse with want.

Her hand slipped down low, to the edge of the shirt, lifting it. A dull ache settled in my groin, and my mouth went dry as if I were dying of thirst, and there she was, drenched in rainwater.

"Come here," I said.

"If I do, will you touch me?" she asked, her fingers brushing over the bare flesh between her thighs.

"Yes," I said, on my knees.

"Will you put your mouth on me?"

"*Yes.*"

Her fingers moved in a slow circle. "Here?"

"God, yes."

She slowly came toward me, her hands undoing the rest of the buttons. The last one parted as she reached the mouth of the tent, and the shirt dropped from her shoulders to the ground.

"You were right," she said, falling into the towel I held out. "I'm cold."

I wrapped her up and pulled her in, down to her knees, my mouth finding hers immediately. Her skin was cold, but the heat of her tongue sliding against mine…

"Kacey…want you…"

I kissed her, my hands running the towel over her body, drying her skin and leaving it warm and soft.

"You smell like rain," I said, moving my mouth between her breasts. She moaned softly as I took one nipple, warming it with my tongue and then nipping and sucking to keep it hard.

"Jonah… God, what are you doing to me?"

Her fingers twisted in my hair as I moved to the other breast, sucking and grazing it with my teeth while I dried her back and her hips. Then I hooked an arm around her waist and laid her on the floor of the tent. I dragged the towel over her stomach, down, between her thighs, down each leg in turn, and then flung it away. She lay open and spread before me, her lips parted slightly, and her eyes glazed with desire. I wanted to strip naked and plunge into her, satisfy the ache. But there was something electric and powerful about my being fully clothed while she lay naked beneath me.

And yet I was hers completely. She owned me. No other woman had ever made me feel like this: undone, completely unraveled, and yet complete. Kacey made me whole. Healthy. Invincible. And my body was desperate to show her.

I knelt over her, lowered my mouth to hers, and our tongues met in a brazen, raw kiss. She reached for my erection, stroked me through the material of my pants, and I groaned at the touch. I wanted to squeeze her hand around me hard, to have that release…

"I want this to be good for you…" I breathed.

"It's already good," she said, nipping my lower lip.

I shook my head. "I can do better than good." I lowered my mouth to her ear. "I want to make you come so hard the entire fucking valley hears you."

I took her wrists and pinned them above her head. Our eyes met and held, hers mirroring the lust in mine. I kissed her again, hard and rough, and she undulated beneath me, her hips straining up to meet mine, pushing against my hands pinning her.

Releasing her wrists, I dragged my tongue and teeth down the smooth skin of her throat, between her breasts, blazing open-mouthed kisses along her stomach. When I reached her thighs, she was whimpering, and I took a moment to breathe her in, draw out the moment a half second more, before bending my head to her and tasting her.

She cried out, her hips rising, back arching. I swirled my tongue over her most sensitive flesh, forgetting the raging need coursing through my veins like a wildfire. I delved deeper, harder, my mouth exploring her until she screamed my name.

Yes, I thought. *Yes. Louder…* Her body tensed, her back arched. Her hand dropped on my head and pulled me deeper into her while she came on my tongue, her voice filling up the tent. I could've stayed right there, but then she pushed up on her elbows, breathless and spent.

"Jonah," she gasped. "Come here. Please…"

I let my mouth fall from her, leaving her shuddering and wet, then stripped off my shirt and jeans. Her shaking hands helped me roll on a condom—Christ, had I ever been so hard in my *life?*—then I went crawling up her body.

She held me around the neck, pulling me to her and kissing me, kissing the taste of her off my lips, while her thighs spread wide for me.

"I want you hard," I said.

She nodded mutely, her lips pressed together. They flew apart in a cry as I thrust deep inside her.

"*Yes...*" she hissed. "Oh, God, yes..."

Yes, my body agreed. *Yes* to how I fit so perfectly within her heat. *Yes* to how fucking good she felt around me. *Yes* to how sweet her mouth tasted. *Yes* to the push and pull of our bodies toward the edge. And *God, yes* to her, this woman who'd burst into my life like a wrecking ball, smashing through my routine, bringing me back to life when I had already resigned myself to death. *Yes* to her chaos, her raw emotion, her desperate need to be touched and held and loved. And *yes*, more than anything, *fuck, yes* that it was *me* she wanted, that she unleashed herself in all her messy imperfection on *me*.

"Yes," I whispered. To all of it. To us. To *her.* "Yes..."

I felt the slow build in her, heard her cries take on a rhythm, each louder than the last. Her hands clutched my neck, her legs wound around my waist. I thrust deep, hard, and slow, caught up in my own rhythm but holding on for her. She was coming around again, building another orgasm from the first, stoking the fires back up. It took everything I had to wait, but finally she threw her head back and raised her hips to mine like an offering. I gripped her hard and plunged deep, and if we didn't come together, it was damn close.

The rain finally stopped a little after noon, and Kacey and I packed up the tent and our belongings. Our eyes met as we worked. The air was thick between us, full of the love we'd made. And my heart was growing full of her.

We texted Theo to let him know we were alive and dry, then drove back to Las Vegas. I kept my right hand on her thigh, and she twined her left hand through my hair. We talked and laughed as usual, but in between were thick, warm silences that didn't need to be filled with anything at all.

We'd hardly shut the front door of my apartment when she was in my arms again and I had her up against the wall, kissing her, my hands tearing through her clothes. She still smelled like rain and hot coffee from our lunch stop. I wanted to wash the road off me. Off us. We were an *us* now, and it fueled my lust almost as much as Kacey's body.

Somehow, we made it to the bathroom and showered, hardly able to get clean as we couldn't stop touching each other. We kissed between swipes of a soaped-up washcloth. I tried to take her against the wall, but she slipped through my arms and dropped to her knees. My shoulder blades hit the tiles. I stared blankly at the steamy ceiling as her luscious mouth unraveled what was left of my sanity.

Out of the shower, I dried her skin as I had in the tent, then set her on top of the vanity so I could pull her thighs apart and put my mouth on her. I went down until she was knocking things off the sink, her cries making the medicine cabinet rattle. I wanted to go deeper and harder so she would go *louder*. I needed her to fill my mouth and ears, wanted as much as she could give to me. As many moments as I could grab before they slipped out of my fingers. Before *I* slipped through her fingers.

Ravenous, we ordered in from a Japanese place and managed to stay dressed long enough to eat it.

"Now come to bed," she said.

I lay back on the pillows, and she crawled on top of me. She gripped the bed frame above my head, her hair falling toward me like pale rain, her breasts swaying as she rode me, coming down hard as I rose up to meet her. And that time, without a doubt, we came together.

Chapter 30

KACEY

I woke wrapped up in him. My head pillowed on his shoulder, my arm thrown across his chest. I stirred and peered up to see he was already awake. He hardly slept much, my Jonah, but he never seemed tired. Even last night, he'd been short of breath after our lovemaking, but he'd recovered quickly.

My Jonah, I thought. *He's mine now, and I'm his.*

I traced my finger along his scar. In the morning light, bare to me, I could examine it for the first time. It ran the entire length of his sternum, to just above the faint lines of his six-pack, which had been more promi- nent before he got sick. I'd seen a picture of him in South America, shirtless. Possibly at the very same spot where he'd caught the virus. His muscles had been more defined then, but they were still there now.

Because he's strong, I thought fiercely.

Jonah took my hand that touched his scar. "Not too pretty, is it?"

"It's not bad," I said softly.

"*This* is beautiful," he said, turning my hand over to inspect the tattoo that started at my wrist and went up the inside of my arm, almost to the elbow. It was a guitar, all black ink, made out of F clefs and musical notes. "Show me the others. Introduce me."

I sat up to show him the blooming rose on my right shoulder, wrapped in thorny vines and buds that trailed down my arm. "I got this in Seattle. The sugar skull I had done in Portland, and these little stars"—I showed him the smattering of tiny black stars on my middle right finger—"were in San Diego. My second open act of rebellion against my father. The first was playing electric guitar. The second was this impossible-to-hide tattoo, especially when *playing* said electric guitar."

Jonah laughed lightly as I snuggled back down against him.

"What time is it?" I asked.

"Nearly seven." He pressed a soft kiss against my temple. "I have to go get some work done. Then tonight is Sunday dinner at my parents' place."

"Ah yes. I remember the first Sunday when Theo distinctly *un*invited me to the family dinner."

Jonah made a sound that might've been a laugh. "Well, I'm inviting you now. Can you come?"

I raised myself up on one elbow. He was so handsome, his dark hair against the white pillowcase. "You want me to meet your parents?"

He nodded and twisted a lock of my hair in his fingers. "I want them to meet you. Moreover, I don't want to be apart from you any longer than necessary."

"You've really got this pillow talk down, don't you?"

"I've been practicing, can you tell?"

"Very smooth."

He silenced my laughter with kisses. God, even first thing in the morning he tasted so good. So clean. I broke away with a small sigh, rested my chin on his chest. "I'd love to meet your parents. Actually, I take that back—I'm nervous as hell to meet your parents, but I can't go tonight. I had to take another gal's shift at Caesars to cover the weekend. I'll be slinging free booze in a toga from one o'clock until nine."

"Next Sunday?"

"Next Sunday works," I said. "It'll give me a week to prepare myself. And a week for Theo to get used to the idea. Still not sure that he likes me. At all."

Jonah wore a funny smile. "I think he likes you plenty."

"He doesn't show it well. And poor Holly—the way he just dumped her in the middle of the woods?"

"Yeah, that was shitty," Jonah said. "One of the Bigfeets might've grabbed her and taken her for a mate."

"Oh, aren't you hilarious?" I bent to kiss him again, simply because I could. The kiss deepened and started to turn into something more, then Jonah's watch alarm went off from the bedside table.

"Your meds," I said, kissing around his mouth.

"Yeah, my meds."

I threw on a long shirt and underwear; he put on sleep pants and a white undershirt. We went to the kitchen together, and he introduced me to his regimen.

He gave me the quick rundown of how to make his protein shake. He started swallowing one pill after another while I blended the powders and supplements. Soon, he had to grip the counter and breathe through a wave of nausea.

"Not sure what's worse," he said, his head hanging down. "When it comes or that I know it's coming."

I poured him a glass of water and rubbed his back.

This is real. This is what it means to be with him.

A whisper in my mind told me I didn't have the guts to handle anything worse. I swallowed it down, silenced the thought. I *wanted* to be with him. Not just swept up in an emotional moment under a starry sky but breathing side by side with him through the nausea.

"Do you have other side effects?" I asked.

He nodded, taking a long sip of water. "Insatiable horniness."

I snorted a laugh. "I noticed. What else?"

"The steroids cause excessive hair growth. Everywhere. I spend a good two hours a day shaving it all off."

I narrowed my eyes at him.

"In fact, I'm glad you're here," he said. "My back has some real hard-to-reach places."

"Smart-ass." I rolled my eyes and kissed the tip of his nose. "C'mon, I'm being serious. Or trying to."

"I have nausea, sometimes my ankles swell, but it doesn't last." He shrugged. "I don't have too many other side effects. I'm lucky in that respect."

I nodded while he busied himself with making me coffee. I sat on a stool to drink it, right across from Jonah choking down his protein shake. Déjà vu. Minus the burned-out hangover.

Jonah met my eyes. His smile stretched out warm, almost proud. "Look at you here," he said softly. "Just like before, but everything's different."

"Different better," I said, and climbed halfway across the counter to kiss him.

"Wait—" he started to say, but my kiss was faster.

I grimaced and sat back in my seat.

"I tried to warn you," he laughed.

"Mmm, I taste grass and twigs, a hint of powdered milk, and smidge of ass." I wiped my mouth on the back of my hand while Jonah laughed. "I'm going to learn to make you something that tastes better than...whatever the hell that is."

"Figure that out, and you'll be greatly rewarded."

"In bed?"

"In bed. On the counter. The floor, the couch..."

"That's no reward; that's our life now," I said, slipping off my stool to come around and kiss him again. I didn't give a damn about the aftertaste. Whenever the urge to kiss him came over me, I would kiss him. No more living life halfway. We had to go full tilt, just like the card players did. I would hit instead of stay. Always.

We dressed, and Jonah drove me back to my place. I jumped out of his truck and came around the driver's side. "Have a great day; call me later."

"I will," he said.

I kissed him deeply, my hand slipping to the back of his neck while his cupped my cheek.

"I miss you already," I said.

He brushed his thumb along my jaw and said softly, "Talk to you soon, Kace."

I watched him drive off, and it was as if some invisible clock began ticking in my head. Counting down the seconds while at the same time adding them up to form minutes, and eventually the hours until I could see him again.

"Moments," I murmured to myself as the Nevada heat beat down on me. "We have thousands of moments."

At eleven or so, I was watching a movie on TV while toweling my hair from a shower when someone pounded on the door, hard enough to make it rattle. I muted the TV and grabbed my phone, ready to hit the emergency button.

"Who is it?"

"Theo."

Well, shit. I tossed my phone down and twisted open the locks. Theo filled the doorway, his tatted, muscled arms crossed over his broad chest.

I crossed my arms as well. "Next time bring a battering ram. It's more effective."

"Can I come in or not?"

"Be my guest."

He strode past me with purpose but once he was inside, he seemed unsure. He jammed his hands in the front pocket of his jeans.

Just like Jonah does, I thought.

Theo stared at my muted TV where Jon Cryer was dancing like a precious freak in a record store.

"It's *Pretty in Pink*," I told Theo. "Have you seen it?"

He snorted in the negative.

"Classic movie! Everyone gets all pissy that Andie ends up with Blane at the end instead of Duckie. But honestly, if the movie had played out for another year, Blane would've broken her heart. And Duckie would be right there for her, just like he always was. I'm not saying Blane is *bad* for her. Not at all. They make each other happy, but Duckie? Duckie's in it for the long haul."

I watched a few more muted seconds before realizing Theo was staring at me as if I were an alien life form.

"Sorry," I said. "I get carried away with eighties movies. They hold the philosophy of life for me." I shut off the TV. "So. Can I get you something to drink?"

"No."

He had a pretty good glower going on, but it didn't intimidate me. Even now, when his gaze on me hardened into something close to anger.

"Okay then," I said. "You want to tell me the purpose of this visit? I'm sure you didn't come here for *Pretty in Pink* 101."

"You and Jonah," he said. "You're sleeping together."

"I thought we established this back at Grand Basin."

Theo began to pace my tiny living room, his hand scrubbing through his hair. "Listen, there's some shit you need to know if you're going to be...with him. Shit he won't tell you because he's too damn stubborn."

"Like?"

"His immune system is fucked, okay? Because of the drugs he has to take. If he gets a cold or an infection, it's not like you or me getting sick. It could kill him."

"I'm aware," I said. "He seems healthy now—"

"Yeah, *now*. Four months ago, he caught a cold from somewhere, and it turned into pneumonia. He was in the hospital for two days."

I shivered involuntarily. "Oh. Okay."

"So you have to be careful. If you even *think* you're coming down with something, you have to stay away from him. You can't...kiss him or sleep in the same bed. Promise me."

I nodded. "Of course. Jonah's talked to me about it, and I understand. I'll be careful."

"And when you have sex…" Theo's face turned red, and he turned his glance to anywhere in the room but on me. "You have to take it easy on the sex."

"All right, that sort of falls under the category of None of Your Business."

"Not if his goddamn life is at stake," Theo spat. "Everything he does is my business."

"I think he can handle his bedroom matters, bossy," I said, trying to lighten the energy between us. "He'll know what he's up for. No pun intended."

Theo's face went even redder. "He might, or he might not," he said. "Like I said, he's a stubborn bastard."

And you're the epitome of grace and tact, Theodore. I kept the snark to myself though. "It seems to me he's doing a really good job of being careful," I said. "And I will too. I will, Theo, I promise."

He nodded, his hard stare unrelenting. I held still in it, letting him see me. Despite his rough manner, I liked Theo. He was Jonah's family, and I wanted him to like me too, especially now that Jonah and I were together.

"I promise," I said again.

His hands went back in his pockets. "All right."

"Is anything else bothering you?"

"I want to know what your intentions are."

I blinked. "My *intentions*? To make an honest man out of him?" I laughed and went to give him a playful shove, but he stepped aside.

"You're just going to leave."

I froze, my laughter catching in my throat. "No, I'm not," I said softly. "I would never…"

"This is a big fucking deal," Theo said. "This is the rest of his life. Do you get that? *The rest of his life.* If you hurt him…"

I leaned my hip on the back of my couch for support. "Hurting him is the last thing I want."

We stared across the space of my little living room. Slowly the steely glint in Theo's eyes softened. His hands came out, looked for something to do, and then he crossed his arms over his chest. "Okay. And what happens when it gets bad? What are you going to do?"

"I'm not thinking like that," I said, and felt my own anger flare. "What about hope? What about *not* being so goddamn sure he doesn't have a chance?"

"He does have a chance. He does…"

Theo's arms fell to his sides, and his shoulders slumped a little. His face seemed to tear down the middle, revealing the pain beneath. I remembered Jonah telling me Theo had stood beside him every minute of his illness. He was there when Audrey left. He was sitting next to Jonah when the results of the last biopsy were read. He'd had a front-row seat to all the terrible things in Jonah's life. I'd be blind not to see it had made him take responsibility for his brother the only way he knew how.

"You're a good brother to him," I said softly. "You don't need me to tell you, but I will. You are." I moved close to him, rested my hand on his arm. His shoulder went up and down dismissively, but he didn't shy from my touch.

I hesitated. "How are you?"

He made a face. "What?"

"I think…maybe you don't get asked that a lot. Especially lately. So I'm asking. How are you doing?"

He stared down at me, his thick brows furrowed, as if I were speaking a foreign language. Under my hand, his skin raised gooseflesh, the fine hairs on his forearm lifting. We both noticed it at the same time, and he jerked away.

"I'm fine," he said, striding toward the door. "It's him we need to take care of." The door slammed behind him.

"Okay," I said to the empty space. "Good talk."

Chapter 31

KACEY

The following day, a Monday, I arrived at the hot shop promptly at noon, two bags from SkinnyFATS in hand: chicken salads with arugula and capers for myself and Jonah, a breaded buffalo chicken salad for Tania. I had to juggle the bag with a tray of three smoothies as I hauled the hot shop's sliding door open. It screeched and protested, and by some miracle I managed not to spill anything.

Tania and Jonah were working at opposite ends of a blowpipe. Jonah's eyes were narrowed in concentration as he rolled and shaped.

"Air," he said.

Behind him, Tania blew into the pipe. The glass swelled.

"Right there," Jonah said, his eyes on the piece. "Perfect."

When it was safe to interrupt, I approached. "Hey, anyone hungry?"

"Starved!" Tania enveloped me in a hug that smelled like sweat and burned paper. "You're spoiling us with these lunchtime visits. Not that I'm complaining…"

I hugged her back, thinking, *I have five friends here now.* I'd never stayed in one place long enough to have so many.

I glanced over Tania's shoulder at Jonah. He smiled to himself, as if satisfied, and hung the blowpipe from the ceiling. He joined us and kissed me hello.

"SkinnyFATS," Tania said, poking into the bags. "I love this joint." Her head flicked up. "Wait, what just happened?"

"Nothing," Jonah said, giving me a second kiss.

"It just happened again." Tania looked from him to me and back. "When did this *happen*?"

I laughed. "Over the weekend."

"Twice on Sunday," Jonah added.

"Oh my God." I rolled my eyes at him.

"Holy shit!" Tania hugged me again, then gathered Jonah in. "I'm so happy for you guys. This is amazing."

"Nah, it's just lunch," Jonah said, rummaging in the bag and coming up with an orange smoothie. He raised an eyebrow at me. "They were out of mulch?"

"Fresh out, smart-ass," I teased.

His cell rang. He fished it out of his back pocket and looked at the number. "It's Eme," he said. "Hey, this is Jonah…" He walked out of the hot shop with its constant hiss of burning furnaces and churning air-conditioning to take the call.

"Who's Eme?" I asked Tania as we set up lunch on fold-up table and chairs, well away from the fire and trays of loose glass.

"Eme Takamura," Tania said, forking a bite of her salad. "She's the curator of the gallery that's displaying Jonah's installation in the Wynn."

My eyes bulged. "His installation's at the Wynn? Isn't that a big-time hotel?"

"Super big-time," Tania said. "Jonah didn't tell you?" She sniffed when I shook my head. "Figures. He's modest to the point of annoying. Anyway, Eme got wind of him through Carnegie, and after seeing some of his work, she set up to house his project in the Wynn Galleria."

"That's incredible."

"What's incredible is you and Jonah. I'm so happy for you guys, I can't stand it."

"You seem surprised," I said.

"You kidding?" she said around a mouth full of greens. "I'm shocked. I honestly thought..." She trailed off as she wiped her mouth with a napkin.

"You thought what?"

Tania glanced up at me, then around to the door where we could see Jonah pacing and talking. "The Jonah I know has always been so serious. Intent on his work, you know? Since you've been back in town, he's been different. He smiles more. Laughs more. He's always been a smart-ass, but now he's a kinder, gentler smart-ass. He still works his butt off—and mine—but it's as if some kind of weight or shadow has been lifted. And now finding out you two are together..." She shook her head. "It's not every day he lets someone into his life. You're the first since I've known him. It's huge. Maybe now he'll rethink letting everyone else back in."

"At least for his installation," I said. "I want everyone to see it."

"Me too. He's so talented. And a truly good guy. Selfless. Maybe too selfless, trying to protect everyone he cares about, so much that he neglects his own happiness."

The door screeched open, and Jonah returned, his hands fidgety with his cell phone. "Eme wanted a progress report. I told her two more weeks and we can start moving boxes over to the space."

"Two weeks is enough," Tania said.

But studying the display of his phone, Jonah looked pale.

"Something wrong?" I asked.

"Eme said she sent out invites for the installation opening," he said, his voice tight. "Big names, a lot of her connections. She sent one to Chihuly Studio."

Tania's fingers rose to her lips. "And?"

Jonah's glance darted between us. "She got a response saying Dale is really busy in early October, but he'd try his best to attend." Jonah scrubbed his hand through his hair. "Eme sent an invite to the *studio*. I thought maybe they'd send a representative, if they sent anyone."

"But *Dale* might come?" Tania rose to her feet. "Personally?"

"Holy shit," I said.

"Oh my God, holy shit." Tania threw arms around Jonah, who looked dazed over her shoulder. "Holy…" She threw him off, seized her fork, and crammed a few bites in her mouth. "Eat. Hurry up. Let's get back to it. There's a bunch of stuff with the still water I want to finish."

"And the rays of sunlight," Jonah said.

"And holy *shit*, Dale Chihuly. In person." One last bite, and Tania bustled off to the back room, leaving Jonah and I alone. I got up and slipped my arms around his neck, hugging him tight. I left my hands entwined in his hair and locked eyes with him.

"Look at my talented boyfriend."

"Boyfriend, huh?" He wrapped his arms around my waist. "I…" He glanced away with a short laugh. "I was going to make a joke right there, but I like *boyfriend* too much."

"Dale freaking Chihuly," I said.

"I know. It's surreal. But not for sure. He's busy. He might not make it at all…"

"Or he might." I glanced down, ran my hand over Jonah's chest. "What can I do to help? Maybe contact some of your old friends from UNLV or Carnegie?"

Jonah stiffened. "I don't know. We'll see. I have too much work to do right now."

"I'll do it." I pulled him closer. "You're being exhibited at the *Wynn* for God's sake. It's a big deal. Don't you think it would be awesome to have all your old friends there?"

"I haven't talked to them in a year," Jonah said. "The first thing they hear from me is an invite to a gallery show? They'll think I'm a pretentious asshole."

"Not if you let me handle it."

Jonah leaned back, sliding his palms down my arms to take my hands instead. "I can't be distracted with reunions right now, Kace. The fact that Dale Chihuly might come is screwing with my brain enough. I appreciate it, but I just have too much to do. Okay?"

"Okay," I said. "Just promise me you'll think about it."

"I will." He drew me back into him and kissed me long and hard. "Boyfriend," he murmured.

"Do you know what girls do for their boyfriends?"

"Is this a trick question?"

"They take care of them. You've taken care of me since the day we met. Let me have a turn."

He sighed with a little smile. "We'll see."

Chapter 32

KACEY

THE REST OF THE WEEK FLEW BY IN A BLUR. JONAH WORKED HARD AT the hot shop. I slung cocktails at Caesars at night and started a half-dozen songs during the day, none of which sparked me. The Chihuly invitation made Jonah a nervous wreck. The approaching Sunday dinner with his parents did the same to me.

I went shopping at a local thrift store for something plainer than my usual getups. Something that covered my tattoos and wasn't made from leather or vinyl. I combed racks, consumed with wanting to make a good impression. All I found were echoes of my father, telling me what a disappointment I was. All the old demons followed me into dressing rooms as I tried on garment after garment. I felt like a fraud in everything. I came home with nothing.

"Either they like me or they don't," I muttered to myself back at home as I dressed in my own clothes and applied my usual cat's-eye black eyeliner and red lipstick. I sucked on a Diet Coke, wishing it had a slug of rum in it.

I tied my hair in a side braid and slipped on a black sleeveless tank dress. It came to mid-thigh, meeting up with my tall black boots, which came just over my knee.

Jonah arrived at my place wearing jeans and a dark dress shirt rolled at mid-arm, his hair still damp from the shower.

"You look amazing," I said, fastening a long necklace with a Celtic-looking silver pendant. "As usual."

"That's my line," he said, his eyes raking me up and down. "And you…are fucking beautiful."

My cheeks burned as I smoothed down the billowy folds of the dress. "I thought about wearing a normal dress. But it felt wrong. I mean, this is who I am. The tattoos and the hair and the makeup… it's not a rock star act; it's me."

Jonah moved to take me in his arms. His hand ran up my tattooed arm. "I like it," he said. "I like you."

"I just want *them* to like me. I'm afraid I might not be what they're expecting."

"Listen." He held me tighter. "My parents expected *nobody*. The fact I'm even bringing someone to dinner is in your favor. Trust me, my mother is going to flip over you."

I glanced up at him. "And your dad?"

Jonah gently brushed a tendril of hair from my eye. "He's going to love you."

———

The Fletchers lived in a modest two-story house in a cute suburban neighborhood of Belvedere. We drove past row after row of houses, all separated by rock lawns and wrought-iron fences. Theo's truck was already parked along the curb in front of the Fletcher house. I hadn't seen or spoken to him since his unexpected visit last week. Another knot twisted in my gut as I got out of the car.

At six fifteen on a late July evening, the heat had mellowed to a bearable ninety degrees. Las Vegas had been my official home for three weeks, and I was already getting used to the weather.

I clutched Jonah's arm as he led me up the short walk to the front door. "Shit, I didn't bring your mom anything," I said. "Can we go back? I saw a flower shop on the way—"

The front door opened, and a short, plump lady beamed at us from the threshold. She was in her mid-fifties, with chin-length brown hair, dressed in slacks and a short-sleeved blouse.

"I thought I heard voices," she said.

"Hey, Mom," Jonah said.

She hugged him tight and held his face for a moment, her eyes taking him in. "You look wonderful," she said. She turned to me. "Doesn't he look wonderful? And you must be Kacey." She stepped down to embrace me. "I'm so happy to meet you."

Her embrace smelled like warm bread, and it soothed my nerves. "I'm happy to meet you too, Mrs. Fletcher," I said, inexplicable tears filling my eyes. I couldn't remember the last time my own mother had hugged me.

"Please, please, call me Beverly." She started back to the house, waving us in after her. "Theo's already here, and the lasagna is just about done. Do you like lasagna, Kacey?"

"I love it," I said, slipping my hand into Jonah's.

"Did I forget to mention she's a hugger?" he whispered to me.

I nodded. "I love *her*."

Beverly led us through the living room. It was simply furnished, a little cluttered, with Jonah's beautiful glass pieces displayed on side tables, bookshelves, and windowsills. A gallery of photos on one wall showed Theo's artwork—he'd been a talent since he was a toddler—and Theo and Jonah at every stage of life: Little League, school portraits, prom pictures. Mugging side by side from preschool to adolescence, one smiling bright, the other making a face or scowling.

"You've been adorable your whole life," I said, pausing to examine a middle school photo, Jonah's teeth obscured by braces.

"Let's move along; nothing to see here," he said, gently dragging me to the kitchen.

Theo sat at the island, its counter brown-speckled granite that matched the backsplash. The cabinets were a soft, scuffed white. Like the living room, the kitchen was simple and cluttered. The heart of the house, filled with warm, comforting smells and good food. The last of my nervousness fell away, and I went to wrap my arms around Theo from behind and kiss his cheek.

"Good to see you, Teddy." He smelled good—a clean, sharp cologne over the softer smell of his soap.

He tolerated my hug and kiss, and hunched further over his beer bottle.

Beverly shut the oven door and shot me a knowing smile. "Theodore is named after my husband's great-grandfather, who went by Teddy. But Theo refuses to answer to it. Right, honey?"

Theo's jaw clenched. "Not that anyone fucking listens."

"Language," said a voice at the kitchen door. Mr. Fletcher joined us at the island. He was a tall, slender man, with dark hair graying on the sides. He stuck his hand out to me as if I were a potential business partner. "Henry Fletcher," he said, giving a firm shake. "A pleasure, young lady."

Jonah shot me an amused look, but I nodded politely. "Thank you, sir. It's nice to meet you."

"No sirs here. You can call me Henry or Henry." He winked. "Whichever you prefer."

"Something to drink, dear?" Beverly asked, opening the fridge. "I have beer, soda, wine. I picked up O'Doul's for you, Jonah."

"I'll have one of those too," I said.

Beverly handed the green-labeled bottles to us. "The night is so lovely, I thought we'd eat in the backyard. Do you mind, Kacey? We can stay indoors if you prefer." A nervous lilt wove through her words. And her hands never stopped moving. Fussing, arranging, doing.

"Outdoors is perfect," I said.

"Wonderful," she said. "I'll turn on the lanterns Jonah made his first year at Carnegie. You've never seen anything so beautiful in your life."

"They really are something," Henry said.

"I believe it," I said. "Jonah's work is astonishing."

Jonah waved his hand. "Enough."

"Astonishing, yes," Beverly said, her eyes resting on her son.

"And an ample payoff of the tuition investment," Henry added.

"Dad," Jonah said quietly.

Theo's muscled shoulders hunched, and he took a slow, deliberate pull from his beer bottle.

"I'm merely stating a fact," Henry continued. "The arts isn't an easy sector to make a living in. One has to direct one's talents appropriately."

"And not squander them working at a tattoo parlor," Theo said.

Like a stick wedged into a gear, the levity of the room came to a screeching halt. Henry and Theo exchanged long, hard glances.

"Who wants to help me set the table?" Beverly asked, her voice taking on a shrill edge. She reached into a cabinet and lifted down a stack of plates.

"I got it." Theo took them from her hands and shouldered out the door toward the patio.

"I'll help too," I said, taking napkins and silverware and following.

Mrs. Fletcher beamed, and the night was rolling again.

"Wonderful!"

———————

The outdoor dining table sat beneath a pergola, clusters of glass globes hanging down like elegant fruit. Here we ate lasagna, bread, and a green salad. Solid home-cooked food. The kind of meal my mother made when I was a kid. But dinnertime at my house was a sullen, cold event where I was always talking too loudly, even when I wasn't speaking. My father's stony, oppressive presence turned the good food to dust in my mouth.

The Fletchers' table was full of laughter, nonstop talking, and bickering. A bit of silent tension lingered between Theo and Henry, but Beverly defused it with stories of her sons' youth that had me choking on my bread.

"I swear," she said, pouring herself a glass of cabernet. Her third, I noticed. "Lake Tahoe has an enormous beach. *Plenty* of sand for everyone. Millions of grains, and these two fought over one bucketful."

I nudged Jonah on my right. "You fought over *sand* at the *beach*?"

"So speaketh an only child," Jonah said. "Sand appropriation is critical to four- and six-year-olds." He glanced at Theo with a sly smile. "So are imaginary butterflies."

Theo jabbed his fork in Jonah's direction. "Don't even."

Jonah ignored him. "Once, Theo got pissed at me because he caught an imaginary butterfly and I let it get away."

Theo reached across the table to poke his brother with the fork. "Shut. Up."

"I love this story," Beverly sighed.

"That makes one of us," Theo said.

Jonah brushed off the fork and rested his elbows on the table, regarding his brother with affection. "Theo cupped his hands over thin air and told me he'd caught a butterfly. I asked to see it, but he was afraid it would fly off."

"When was this?" I asked.

"Last week," Jonah said.

"Try twenty years ago, asshole," Theo muttered.

"Language, please," Henry said.

Jonah's voice grew low, the teasing ebbing out of it. "Finally, he said I could hold it. He put his hands in mine, all the while describing the butterfly's wings—bright blue, rimmed in black. How it opened and closed them, as if it were breathing. He even told me how its legs looked like black hairs against my skin. Remember, Theo?"

I glanced at the tough, built, tattooed man sitting across from me, glaring daggers at his brother. Yet I could easily see the sweet little boy he'd been, describing this nonexistent but precious butterfly.

"But I wasn't careful enough," Jonah said. "I opened my hands too much, and Theo said the butterfly flew away. He cried and cried."

"Are you fucking done?" Theo said.

"Language," Henry murmured.

All the teasing was gone from Jonah's face now. "I never apologized for letting it go," he said. "I tried to give him another one—a monarch in orange and black, but it was the blue butterfly he wanted. And it was gone forever. I'm sorry about that, bro."

Theo sat back in his chair. "Are you serious?"

Jonah shrugged. "Just clearing the air."

The brothers stared silently. A silence full of love despite Theo's hard tone. Full of that one memory and thousands like it.

"So," Beverly clapped her hands together. "Who has good news?" She turned to me. "I believe everyone has good news from the previous week, even if only a little."

"Jonah has amazing news." I put my hand over his and gave it a squeeze. "Right?"

His mother leaned in. "What's that, dear?"

Jonah toyed with his fork, his gaze flickering to Theo and then down to his plate. "So, Eme Takamura—the gallery curator? She says Dale Chihuly is going to try to attend the opening for my installation."

Beverly's hand flew to her throat. "Really? Honey, that's wonderful news."

"Remarkable," Henry said. "Well done, son."

Jonah sat back in his chair. "Well, hold on, he hasn't said he's *going* to be there. Only that he'd try."

"Still, the fact he'd even consider it," Henry said. "It means he's taken note of your work."

"I guess," Jonah said.

"It's fucking awesome," Theo said. "He'd better show up. Be an idiot not to."

For once his language went unadmonished. Another loaded look passed between the brothers, and I found myself smiling, as if I'd become a translator of their unspoken exchanges.

"Theo has good news," Jonah said. "One of his clients is going to be photographed for *Inked* magazine. He'll be credited on one of the designs."

The barest smile flickered over Theo's lips.

"That's wonderful," Beverly said.

"Body pollution is what it is," Henry said.

Jonah set his empty bottle down hard. "Jesus, Dad."

I leaned back in my chair, fighting the urge to cover the tattoos on my bare arms.

"What?" Henry said. "No one is a bigger fan of my sons' talents. Theo is an exceptional artist, but it boggles my mind to think of spending one's life drawing on other people."

"Because it's art," Theo said. "It's permanent art people carry with them. And when I get my own place, I'll be a legit business owner."

"You'll be taking a risk," Henry replied.

"Can we not do this right now?" Jonah said.

As the Fletcher men glowered at each other, I thought Henry was nowhere near as intimidating as my father, but his disapproval of Theo left the same bad taste in my mouth.

"Not every guy who can draw can be a tattoo artist," I said in the silence. "It's a special skill, being able to take a person's vision and turn it into a reality. And you're absolutely right it's a risk. The artist has to ink it perfect the first time, because there's no second time. Jonah can recycle the glass and start over. Theo gets one shot. No do-overs."

I felt all eyes on me, but I only looked at Theo, who stared back in that way he had, like he couldn't believe I was real.

"Obviously I'm biased," I said, running a hand along my arm. "But I don't see it as body pollution. It's expression. Every one of my tattoos means something. And getting the tattoo is as much a part of it as having one. Because of the trust and collaboration with the artist." The silence deepened. I shrugged and took a sip from my fake beer. "Just my two cents."

Henry shifted in his seat. "I suppose that's one way of looking at it."

Everyone seemed to exhale at once. Jonah's hand found mine under the table, and he gave it a squeeze.

Beverly stood up, gathering plates. "Who wants dessert?"

Chapter 33

KACEY

IT WAS NEARLY ELEVEN WHEN WE SAID OUR GOODBYES. BEVERLY pulled me in for a long hug. "I'm so happy to have met you. Come back next Sunday. Every Sunday. Can you?"

I nodded, melting in her embrace. "I'd like that."

She released me and turned to Jonah. "I'll see you next week, honey?"

"Of course," he said.

He kissed her cheek, and she patted his. She held still then, her gaze unapologetically memorizing every detail of his face.

I looked away, my eyes stinging. I felt a shift in my soul as I was exposed to this moment between a mother and her son. For the whole drive home to my place, I couldn't think of anything to say. Words wouldn't capture it. They might even ruin it...

"What you said to Theo was amazing," Jonah said.

"It was the truth."

"But it was new. Dad is so hard on T, and he's grown deaf to hearing me defend him all the time. He needed a fresh perspective."

"I was worried I'd crossed a line."

"Not at all."

"I heard faint echoes of my dad in your dad. Don't get me wrong, yours is nothing like mine. It's just I know how Theo feels."

"Never good enough."

"To say the least. Does he really want to open his own shop?"

"He does, but unless he gets a big chunk of cash for a down payment, he needs a cosigner on a loan. That's a huge point of contention between him and Dad. My parents had to take out a second mortgage to help cover my hospital bills because my insurance only went so far."

"Oh."

"Theo would never complain about that, of course. It's just our parents have always been one hundred percent supportive of me, and less so with him. The balance is horribly skewed."

Jonah pulled into the lot of my apartment and parked.

"It must be so hard for him," I said.

Jonah brushed his knuckles over my cheek. "I think you won him over a little tonight. And my parents loved you. I knew they would."

"It was a good night," I said. I unbuckled my seat belt and climbed into his lap, straddling him. "Let's end it with a bang."

"Literally or figuratively?" Jonah murmured, his hands sliding up my thighs as our mouths met.

"Both." Our kisses quickly became more heated, even as a passing car lit up the interior of the truck and the steering wheel dug into my lower back.

"This isn't as easy as it looks in the movies," Jonah said, breathing hard. "Change of venue?"

I nodded. "Upstairs," I said, then added in a husky Southern drawl, "*Take me to bed or lose me forever.*"

Jonah's brow furrowed. "*Body Heat?*"

"*Top Gun.*"

"So close."

In my bedroom, Jonah's humor fled, and he caught fire. I'd never felt so wanted by a man in my life. His kisses turned bruising, and his hands stripped me of my clothing. His eyes were dilated, the deep brown of them almost black. I tore off his shirt, fumbled at the zipper on his jeans.

"Leave these," he said, as he fingered the thigh-high tights I wore under my boots. "And the necklace."

A white-hot thrill skimmed through me at his rough-voiced need. His breath came hard as he stared at me, naked but for the black nylon along my legs, and the curved silver horn between my breasts.

"Kacey…"

I let out a little sigh, my legs weakening. We grabbed for each other again, and he backed me up against the bedroom wall, his tongue, teeth, and lips mauling my mouth. I could feel him between my thighs, hard and ready. I fumbled in the nightstand next to me and blindly fished out a condom.

He gripped my hips, barely holding back while I tore the condom wrapper open and rolled it down over him. Then his hands slipped under me, lifted me, and I wrapped my stocking-clad legs around his waist as he groaned into my mouth. My arms went around his neck, my nails digging into his skin and my teeth biting at the slope of muscle between his neck and shoulder. Already, the sensation of him inside me was so intense, so dizzying and hot, I was delirious.

"I've never had it like this. I swear…" I said into his skin, clutching him, clinging to him.

"Me neither," he said finding my mouth again. "All I want is this. You…"

His body moved against mine fast and hard. He filled me up, the heavy pressure stoking a sweet ache of pleasure into something that roared and consumed. I held him to me as tightly as I could, taking his thrusts deep while the glow of need in my belly burned brighter than molten glass.

My shoulder blades ground against the wall at the force of him.

EMMA SCOTT

His name whispered out of my mouth, and then screamed from my throat as he drove into me again and again, until I came to the edge and plummeted over. My body shuddered and clenched around him. He let out his own masculine sounds of climax, deep in his chest, and *God*, if that wasn't the hottest sound I'd ever heard in my life.

Jonah's grinding hips slowed. He released my legs, letting my feet find the floor, but his body still held mine to the wall, his hands closed around my wrists. Within the hard grip, his mouth turned gentle, soothing the burn of his stubble and the bite of his earlier kisses from my skin. Carnal need and tender care. Desired and cherished.

Loved.

Jonah makes love to me, I thought, kissing him back, my fingers soft on his skin where they'd scratched him. *No matter how hard or rough we are, he's still making love to me.*

"You make me feel so good, Jonah," I whispered. "Better than good. Like I can start all over again."

"Kacey." He held my face in his hands, his dark eyes intent on me. "You make me feel alive."

He kissed me again, slow and soft, while I burned with hope, sure there weren't thousands of moments left to us, but millions.

Millions.

Chapter 34

KACEY

"Have you ever been to a beach?" I asked Jonah. "Not a lakeshore, but a real ocean?"

We lay around in bed on a Tuesday night—typically our date night, but we'd opted to stay in and fool around.

"Sure. Why?"

"I miss it. Growing up, the beach was such a part of my daily life. I used to ditch school in the mornings, and my best friend and I would go to one of the coffeehouses along the boardwalk in Pacific Beach, or a breakfast place that had surfboards hanging from the walls. We'd hang out at the beach until after lunch, then go back to school so we wouldn't miss last attendance. Sometimes it got us out of a trip to the assistant principal's office. Most times it didn't, but it was always worth it."

Jonah brushed his hand over my cheek. "You're pretty fair for a beach lover."

"Big hats and SPF one thousand," I said. "And I preferred swimming or bodysurfing in that big ocean. Big and endless. If you think the stars were spectacular at Great Basin, wait until you see a moonrise over the Pacific."

He nuzzled my ear. "Sounds like you're planning a trip."

"I really want to take you to San Diego. Walk on the beach and hang out at all the cool spots I used to love."

"And see your parents?"

I shuddered. "No. God, no. It would just be awkward and uncomfortable…"

"I can handle awkward and uncomfortable. If you want to see them, you should."

"I don't. I want to be with you, in the places I used to love best." I lifted my head to look at him. "Can you? Two days. Flights are pretty cheap, and I still have some Rapid Confession money—"

"You should save it. Don't spend it on me."

"I want to spend it on *us*. But if you can't spare the time from the hot shop, I understand."

"I can."

I caressed his face. "Really?"

"If it's important to you, I can."

I let out a little cry of excitement and kissed him. "Let's go next Monday and Tuesday. So we don't take time from your parents. Of course, Theo will have a cow…"

Jonah laughed. "He might, but how beautifully happy you look right now is more than worth it."

———

Theo's flight safety demonstration lasted half an hour. From what to do if the cabin pressure in the airplane dropped, to making sure we brought all of Jonah's meds and stored them properly so they wouldn't get confiscated by the TSA. And, of course, where the nearest hospital was to our hotel. But I never took Theo's concern for Jonah for granted. I patted his cheek and told him I'd take good care of his brother.

I'd booked us into a place with the most San Diego name ever: the Surfer Beach Hotel on Pacific Beach Drive. Its proximity to the beach made it a little pricey for my budget, but I wanted us to be able to walk along the ocean at night, in the morning, or anytime the urge struck us. The price was worth it.

At the airport rent-a-car, Jonah led me to a black Ford Mustang convertible.

"You didn't think this entire trip was on you, did you?" he asked, holding the door open. "I've got savings. Between the two of us, we can make these two days pretty damn awesome."

We put the top down, cranked the music up, and Jonah gunned the engine with a whoop of laughter. Singing loud, we cruised along a post–morning commute stretch of freeway and arrived at the hotel around ten. We had the entire day ahead of us.

"What do you want to do first?" I asked, tying on the top of my black bikini.

"What do you want to do second?" he replied, throwing me down on the bed.

"Yes," I whispered, as he trailed kisses down my neck, his hands working the knot on the back of my bathing suit. "This first."

It was after eleven when we made it out to the beach.

We set up near the shore, and I kicked off my flip-flops to bury my feet in the hot, soft sand.

"You smell that?" I asked, inhaling deeply.

"Seaweed?" Jonah asked, eyeing a clump that had washed ashore and was buzzing with sand flies.

"The *ocean*," I said.

His arms slid around me from behind. "I want to smell it in your hair after we swim," he murmured. "And on the bedsheets later…"

I turned and kissed him, my hands sliding over his chest and arms. His skin was hot, slippery with sunscreen. I tugged him to the water.

The cold of the ocean bit down hard, taking my breath before it relaxed into a soft coolness. I dove under the foam of a wave, just as I used to do when I was a kid. The cold water on my face and the pull of the ocean were just as I'd remembered, and the nostalgia was so strong, I had to get my bearings for a minute. But there was Jonah. My here and now, and the moment felt as big as the ocean.

Jonah flopped backward into a cresting wave and disappeared beneath the surface. He came up out of the water, the sun glistening in the beads of water along his chest. Water arced off his head as he whipped the hair out of his eyes. I bit my lip as a shiver went up my thighs.

Jonah swam up and kissed me. God, he tasted so good. Like himself—clean and warm—but with the tang of saltwater mixing in. He groaned into my mouth, then broke away with a gasp.

"Holy shit," he said. I could feel his erection straining against his swim shorts. "You taste like salted caramel." He kissed me again and pressed my hips to his. "We're going to have to live here."

"Oh yeah?" I said, ringing my arms around his neck.

"Literally right here in the water. I'll be arrested if I come out."

I laughed and walked backward, deeper into the ocean, shielding the front of his body with mine. I fell back, taking him with me, and we kissed above the surface and below it, before coming to rest in the water, neither of us speaking.

Jonah held me as I floated on my back, my head in the curve of his shoulder, and I had the fleeting wish that we *could* live here. Not in San Diego but in this day, these moments, over and over again, forever.

———

We had dinner at the Chart House, a beachfront restaurant that was a splurge, but life was short and money was for spending today. Afterward, we walked along the surf, hand in hand, carrying our shoes. The full moon hovered over the horizon. Its light spilled over the black ocean in a cone of molten silver.

"This was a good idea," Jonah said. He stopped walking and cast his gaze out over the waves. "Every decision I've made since I met you has been good. Taking you home that first night, eating at that diner, letting you stay for a few days, asking you to come back when you left."

"I was a little persistent on some counts," I said.

"Thank God you were." He turned to look at me, and his moon-filled eyes were fierce. "My family and friends ask me what I want. What I want to do or see besides make glass. And I've only told them what I *don't* want. I don't want to travel to some far-flung place, just so I can say I went. I don't want to climb a mountain or jump out of an airplane. A little bit of exhilaration and then back on the ground again—those manufactured moments aren't what I want."

He brushed his hand over my hair, pulling me close.

"*This* is what I want. You and me, in a place like this. Outside of time. Going for a walk along the beach, eating or swimming or making love when we feel like it." I heard his breath catch and his next words were gruff. "This is living, Kace. This is exactly what I wanted, but I didn't know who to ask."

I felt tears sting my eyes, and I let out a breathy little laugh. "It was me."

"It was you." He held my face in his hands, brushed his lips over mine. "Always and only you."

We packed a lot into the next day, starting with an early-morning stroll on the beach and breakfast at the Pannikin coffee shop.

"This is where me and my best friend, Laura, used to come when we ditched class," I said. "This building was once a train station."

Jonah plucked the corner of his napkin, shredding it into careful strips. "Your parents' house must be close by then."

"A mile and half east," I said. "But we're not here for that. The things I like about San Diego are far away from my house."

Jonah smiled gently. "Show me all of them."

I took him to my favorite fish taco stand for lunch, followed by a doughnut from the best doughnut shop in the world. We strolled the Pacific Beach boardwalk, crowded with pedestrians and skateboarders.

"Do you want to see the place where I had my first kiss?"

"Not especially."

"What? Think you can't top fourteen-year-old Ricky Moreno with his braces and bad breath?"

The twist of Jonah's mouth was smug as he slid a hand around the back of my neck and kissed me. A man's kiss, demanding and deep, leaving me breathless.

"Ricky who?" I murmured.

He arched his brow in that way I loved. "Damn right."

We started walking again, arms crossed over one another's backs.

"The kiss at the MGM Grand really was my first," I said.

"My jackpot kiss?"

"It was the first time a man kissed me because it was the perfect time and place for a kiss. The right moment. Not because he hoped it would lead to something else."

"But I did want it to lead to something else," Jonah said. "This. Us."

I smiled at the warmth that spread through me for those words. "That's a first too."

The day melted away as we wandered San Diego, then wound up back at the hotel. To make love, to sleep a little. We showered and went for dinner at a little crab shack, and after, we climbed into the rented convertible as twilight deepened to night.

"There's still time if you want to see your parents," Jonah said. "Don't not go on my account, Kace. It isn't about me."

I took a breath. "I really don't want to see or talk to them. But maybe…we could go by the house. I wouldn't mind that." It was the truth: I wanted—needed—to know if the house was still my home.

Jonah revved the engine. "Let's do it."

"All right. But…put the top up, okay? So they don't see me."

He smiled and pushed the button. The car's top unfolded and dropped down, clicking into place.

I directed Jonah to the Bridgeview neighborhood, where the houses were smaller than the big behemoths of Mission Hills to the west.

"That one," I said, my heart pounding in my ears. "Stop here."

Jonah pulled to the curb. Across the street and a bit down was the two-story house in pale-blue paint with white trim. My parents' old Subaru was parked on the street.

"They can't use the garage," I said absently. "It's full of old furniture and antiques my dad inherited when my grandmother died." My eyes swept the house, lingered on the yellow squares of light from the front windows. "They're home," I said softly.

Jonah leaned over the console, his head by my shoulder. He took my hand and gave it a squeeze. "Whatever you want to do, Kace."

The house blurred as tears filled my eyes. "I'm so proud you're with me, Jonah. It would fucking suck to watch my dad miss everything wonderful about you because he's ashamed of me."

"Do you want to go in alone?"

"I don't think I can."

"Maybe he's changed," he said. "He's cold on the phone, but maybe if he saw your face, up close. Saw how beautiful you are, and how much you love him. Because it's all right there in your eyes, Kace. He might see it, and things would be different."

"I don't know," I said slowly.

The front door opened, and my parents came out.

I clutched Jonah's hand in a vise grip as they went down the walk toward their car. In the light of the streetlamps, I could see my mother, small and birdlike, wearing a neat blue dress with a black purse. Beside her, my father was tall and lean in a navy suit and yellow tie.

"They're going out," I said.

"You can do it," Jonah said softly.

I mustered my courage, my will, added it to the overwhelming desire to talk to my parents. Seeing them after four years swamped me with nostalgia, even if so little of it with my dad was good.

"Okay," I said, and reached for the door handle.

But then my father stopped at the passenger door of the Subaru. He turned to my mother.

"Wait," I whispered, laying a hand on Jonah to still him.

My father was saying something. We were parked too far away to hear, but I could see my mother tilt her head up. Her brittle, plastic smile bloomed into something spontaneous and joyful. She tossed her head—a carefree, almost girlish gesture I'd never seen before. Her laugh floated across the street, and my father brushed his thumb over her chin—a lover's caress. Romantic.

"Dad." My mouth shaped the word without a sound as he opened the passenger door for my mother. When he moved around to the driver's side, his stride was almost a strut, his angular, stony face soft and amused.

"Kace, they're going," Jonah said.

"Let them go," I whispered.

"Are you sure?"

But the car was moving away from the curb and disappearing down the street. My fingers lifted off the window frame in a small wave.

Jonah's fingers caressed the back of my neck. "Why?"

"They looked so happy," I whispered. "I've never seen them look like… It was such a moment, you know? If I'd gotten out and surprised them, it would have ruined it."

His hand played soft in my hair. "I'm sorry."

"Maybe he's better," I said, "now that I'm gone. I'm not trying to be a martyr. I just mean…maybe *he's* happier. Which makes *them* better together. I wouldn't want to mess that up. God, they looked so in love…" I exhaled and looked back at Jonah with a weak smile. "Let's go back to the hotel. We have an early flight in the morning."

Jonah started up the car, drove ten feet, then jerked it to a stop and threw it into park. He turned to face me, one hand on the steering wheel, the other along the back of my seat.

"When you're ready, you'll come back," he said. "And your father might talk and reconcile, or he might hold on to his stupid anger and turn you away. If he does, then he's a goddamn idiot. You wanting to be loved by him doesn't make you broken, Kace. He's the broken one for letting you go. It's *his* loss. I want to hate him for what he's done to you, but instead I just feel sorry for him."

He kissed me then, fiercely, as if sealing a pact, his hand tight in my hair.

"Needed to get that off your chest, did you?" I asked.

"Yep," he said.

"Feel better?"

"Much." He put the car in drive and pulled away from the curb again.

I turned to the window to watch my old house go past. "Me too."

Chapter 35

KACEY

END OF SEPTEMBER

I SAT ON MY BED, GUITAR IN MY LAP AND NOTEBOOK OPEN BESIDE ME. I tapped a pen on the lower body of the Taylor acoustic, sighing at the blank pages. No lyrical flow today. Wasn't happening. Chett was a dead subject to me, and I didn't want to write about my dad. Basically, I wasn't too happy to go digging in the dark pits of my past.

Which, all things considered, was a good problem to have.

For six weeks now, Jonah and I had been together. A couple. Almost every night after work, he'd come to my place, or I to his. He didn't need much sleep, and I was a night owl with nowhere to be in the morning. We spent the deep hours lost in each other, making love—sometimes hard and rough, sometimes slow and gentle—then talking, eating, and laughing before falling back into bed.

We had our little routines. Sunday nights at the Fletchers' house, outdoor dinners beneath Jonah's glowing lamps. Lots of laughter, good food, and better conversation. Tuesdays were our date nights. ATM cupcakes, a fountain show at the Bellagio, or just staying in to watch a movie.

He left a stash of his medications in my kitchen, and I bought a blender at a yard sale so I could make smoothies for him. And nearly every day, I brought lunch to the hot shop where Jonah and Tania were hard at work finishing the installation pieces. The gallery show at the Wynn was only two weeks away, but Jonah said he felt confident he was going to make it.

He is going to make it, I thought. *And beyond. He's healthy. His body is strong.*

I felt the strength in his body almost every night. My little flame of hope was a torch now, and not even a hurricane could douse it.

My cell phone rang from the nightstand, jarring me from my thoughts.

"Hello?"

"Kacey Dawson?" asked a woman's voice.

"That's me."

"Ms. Dawson, I'm from *Sound Addiction* magazine. I was wondering if you had any comments about the recent shake-ups in your former band, Rapid Confession?"

I frowned. "What recent shake-ups?"

"Word is the tour is in danger of canceling shows due to squabbles between Jeannie Vale and the new guitarist, Elle Michaels. Is this true?"

"I have no idea."

"There's also talk of a messy lawsuit with a club owner. Fans are griping that the live shows aren't as solid as they were when *you* were on stage."

"Well, shit, that's nice to hear."

"Given the fact that your replacement, Ms. Michaels, is now reportedly on the verge of quitting—or being fired, depending on who you talk to—I wonder if you've given any thought to returning?"

I smiled. "Not one second."

"That's interesting, Ms. Dawson. No one's been able to get a comment from you about your own departure from the band. Would you care to comment now?"

"No, but thanks for the call."

I hung up and punched Lola's number. Voicemail.

"Lola, it's me," I said. "What the hell is going on? I just got a call from a mag about the band canceling shows? Call me."

I ended the call and stared at my junky old laptop. I only used it to watch makeup tutorials on YouTube. With a few keystrokes into a Google search bar, I could get answers to my questions, but now I wasn't entirely sure I wanted to know. My days as the lead guitarist for Rapid Confession seemed far away now. And I liked it that way.

A text came in from Lola: Can't talk now. RC is hurting w/out you. Jimmy wants to talk. Just FYI.

Shit, the last thing I wanted was my old life coming to intrude on my new one. Aside from occasional phone calls with Lola, I'd left the band in the rearview. Money was tight, and I wasn't anywhere close to having even one decent song under my belt, but...

I was happy.

I texted back, Tell him to forget it.

No answer. Lola was either busy or getting on a plane, but hopefully she'd pass on my message. I thought about texting Jimmy myself, but that was like taking a ball-peen hammer to my little glass bubble of happiness.

"No chance," I muttered. I checked the time. It was nearing lunch. I put together sandwiches and salads, and took them over to the hot shop.

Jonah came outside as I got out of the car. "How are you?" I called across the small parking lot.

"Done," he said.

"Done?" I said, confused.

Tania had come out as well. She threw her arms wide, echoing, "Done."

"You're *finished*?" I said. "The installation? All of it?"

"Done," Jonah said. "With nine days to spare."

Tania let out a laugh. "I need to hug someone—besides the boss here—or I'll burst."

"Me," I cried, breaking into a run. I hugged the hell out of Tania, then turned to fling my arms around Jonah's neck.

"Holy shit," he said. "It's done."

All at once, I didn't like that word. All at once, the ground disappeared beneath my feet. Swamped with a thousand emotions, I held Jonah close, pulling him tight against me, strangely afraid to let go. Afraid of something I couldn't name yet.

Done.

Finished.

I pulled away far enough to search his eyes. "Are you happy with it?"

"I think I'm still in shock. I've been at it for so long..." He blew out his cheeks and gave a wobbly smile. "Eme says she'll send a truck around for the last pieces and all the stuff that will be for sale."

"I can't believe it." I took his face and kissed him. "I'm so proud of you."

"Thanks," he said, yet his eyes seemed to mirror the foreign emotion clogging up my heart. His bewildered gaze held on to mine as he slowly shook his head. "It's *done*..."

Chapter 36

JONAH

"Jonah," Eme Takamura said, shaking my hand. "I'm so pleased to see you again."

The curator of the Wynn Galleria was crisp and smart in a dark-gray pin-striped suit, impeccably tailored to her petite frame. She was business from head to toe, but for a red silk hibiscus flower tucked behind her ear giving an artistic burst of color.

"This is so exciting," she said as we walked through the lobby. Her voice was warm and slightly accented. "My team is in the space, awaiting your guidance to assemble your masterpiece. Your assistant faxed over the sketches and the diagram, and Wilson—he's our team leader—tells me the specs are right on the money. A perfect fit."

"That's great. Really good news."

"Are you well, Jonah?" she asked, glancing up at me. "You look a little pale."

"I'm nervous as hell," I said with a short laugh. "I want it to not suck."

She laughed, a prim, delicate sound in the back of her throat. "Yes,

I would prefer it 'not suck' as well. But from the pieces I've seen—still in the boxes, mind you—I believe you've avoided that fate."

"Speaking of nerves, heard anything more from Mr. Chihuly?"

"Unfortunately not. But to my mind, it means he's still aiming to see the exhibit on opening night. I count no news as good news."

"So do I."

She led me to the gallery, a small L-shaped space, explaining how my glass would be exhibited. The long wing would hold the individual pieces for sale, and the installation would be in the shorter wing.

Scaffolding had already gone up in the short wing, and a team of two men and a woman were carefully bringing in boxes from an adjoining storage room. Each box was marked with numbers and their general location in the installation.

Eme introduced me to Wilson, the team leader. I guessed he was in his fifties, a huge guy built like a barrel who looked like he'd break more glass than not.

He must've read my thoughts because he bellowed a laugh as he shook my hand, saying, "I'm on loan from a glass studio in Los Angeles. I know I look like a lumberjack, but I won't break nothing."

"I trust you," I said. Not that I had a choice. Nerves were firing off little tingles in my hands and feet, making them numb.

This is it. This is really happening.

"My assistant should be here any minute," I said. "Let me give her a call to see where she's at."

"She's here," Tania cried, rushing in. "I'm so sorry. Accident on the boulevard. Bad one too. Snarled up everything."

She was introduced to the team, and then all eyes turned to me.

"Ready?" Tania said.

I took a huge breath. "Let's do this."

———————

We called it quits around four o'clock. The other workers cleared out, and Tania and I both sank onto a bench, surveying the work so far.

271

"It's going to be brilliant," she said. "Look at that. Not even a third assembled, and it's already breathtaking. You did it."

"*We* did it. This didn't happen without you."

I stared up at my glass, at the yellow coils and blue ribbons that had been wired together and suspended from the ceiling so far. "Do you think Kacey will love it?"

"Honey, Kacey's going to lose her *mind* over it." She laid an arm across my shoulders. "And if you don't mind me saying, I'm so glad she's here to share this with you. That you have her to share it with."

"Me too," I said. All day, through the mental and physical intricacies of setting up the glass, my thoughts had never been far from Kacey. She was with me all the time. A hundred times I stopped work to look over my shoulder, sure she was there watching.

I missed her.

Tania gave my shirt a tug. "Want to head out? Grab an early dinner?"

"I'm not hungry," I said. "I have to get to A-1 soon anyway."

"Shit, you should quit. In a week, you're going to be famous."

I rolled my shoulders. "I don't know about that."

"I *do* know about that. Have you seen Eme's roster of guests?" She whistled low in her teeth. "Even without Chihuly it's going to be a golden crowd, and all here to see you." She rose from the bench and stretched her back. "Maybe you should take the night off. Take Kacey out somewhere and celebrate."

"Good idea. I might do that."

She ruffled my hair. "Or maybe you should take the night off and just get some sleep. You look like you need it."

After she left, I sat for a few moments more, looking around the room. *This is happening.*

I stood up. Or tried to. My breath caught hard in my lungs, then disappeared without me even exhaling. I tried to draw in another and couldn't get it past my throat, as if I had a steel band wrapped around my chest.

Oh shit...

I sat back down, sucking in shallow huffs of air.

Easy. Nice and easy, I told myself, even as my heart clanged in my chest. My gaze darted around for a stray worker or the janitor locking up. I reached for my phone to call 911...

No! It's not that bad. It's not...

Gradually the band around my ribs loosened. Finally, it fell away, and I could inhale to the bottom of my stomach.

Fatigue. I'd been working my ass off. That was all.

I nodded, rose carefully from the bench, and left the gallery. My stride was sure, my breathing deep and regular. But every nerve ending cried out for Kacey. I needed her. Every inhale and exhale marked the seconds that passed without her, and I felt them slipping through my fingers like sand.

I took some of Tania's advice and called in sick to A-1. My first time doing so in the five months I worked there. Harry was pissed it was such short notice, and I wondered why that didn't bother me more, to leave him in a bind.

Because Kacey is more important than driving up and down the Strip all night.

I had an almost desperate need to see her. I rubbed my palms on the thighs of my jeans as if I were a junky jonesing for a fix. I called her, and though she had to work too, she managed to squeeze out of it.

I took my beautiful girlfriend to a fancy restaurant at Mandalay Bay, which overlooked the glittering Strip. She was more radiant than all of the lights beyond the windows, and she teased me for staring more than once.

The food was delicious and what I needed after a long, emotionally and physically draining day. By the time we left the restaurant, my need to be with Kacey had morphed into a fierce desire to have her alone. We'd planned to catch another fountain show at the Bellagio, but while we waited for the check, I slid even closer to her in our booth.

"I want to take you home," I said in her ear, my hands sliding across the smooth material of her dress. She wore elaborate thigh-high boots that laced up the front and a button-down black dress, every button undone but for a few along the middle. The fabric revealed the smooth valley of her cleavage and flared open just above her boots when she walked.

"No water show?" she asked.

"You mind if we skip it?"

Her hand slipped between my legs, over my dress pants. She found my burgeoning erection and gave it a gentle squeeze.

"I want this more," she whispered back.

At my place, I undid the laces on her boots—one at a time—and the buttons on her dress—also one at a time—until she was down to her black lacy bra and panties. Then we celebrated the installation. We celebrated long and hard into the night, until we collapsed on the pillows, exhausted and satiated. My body felt heavy and thrumming with waning climaxes. Kacey was soft and limp, curled up alongside me, her head pillowed on my shoulder. The clock radio read two fifteen in the morning.

"You were intense tonight," she said.

"I didn't hurt you, did I?"

"God, no." She snuggled closer. "I might not be able to walk tomorrow, but it'll be worth it."

I craned down to kiss her hair. "Just doing what you said at Great Basin. Taking each moment and wringing it for all it is worth."

"I was wondering…" She let her fingers trail over my chest, across my scar, and along my shoulder. "If you'd given any more thought to letting me invite some of your old UNLV friends to the installation next week. Carnegie too, though that's going to be short notice. I know you're not—"

"Yes," I said without thinking. "Let's invite a few. The friends I was closest to."

Kacey lifted her head to look at me, her smile radiant. "Really?"

I nodded. "I'll try to dig up some email addresses for you. I'm sure they'll think I'm an ass for waiting until now…"

"I'll make sure they won't. I'll explain you were busy, on deadline, but now your project is done." Kacey propped herself on her elbows, the swell of her breasts pushing against my chest. "I'm so happy you changed your mind. Can I ask why?"

I started to tell her it was to make her happy, or that I really wanted to see my old friends. I told her the truth instead.

"I don't know. It doesn't feel as important as it once did to keep them away."

She traced a shape on my chest with her finger. "Maybe it's because you accomplished what you set out to do. No distractions." She grinned shyly. "Well, except for one."

"One beautiful, amazing distraction." I pulled her mouth to mine, kissing her softly at first, then deeper.

You need to take it easy…

"Hold that thought," I murmured against her lips. "I need water. Want some?"

"Sure."

I got up and padded naked to the bathroom. The light blasted in my eyes when I flipped it on, and they flinched at the harsh glare. I tried for one of the two glasses on the sink and missed because white lights were suddenly dancing across my vision. I grabbed the counter as the floor spun beneath my feet and my breath turned shallow.

The hell…?

The episode, or whatever it was, passed in moments. My vision cleared, and I breathed deeply a few times until my equilibrium was restored. A side effect of the meds, probably. Or more likely I'd just overdone it with Kacey. That was probably it. Even as I was taking her like a madman, I knew it was too much. But tonight, I couldn't get enough of her. I needed to fill my hands with her, touch her every-where, inhale her, absorb her, as if I could carry her with me even when we were apart.

Nice and easy. Chill. The installation is done, and you have every day free to see her.

I filled both water glasses with steady hands and returned to the bedroom.

"Thanks," Kacey said and drank hers as I climbed back into bed. She set her glass on the nightstand and took mine when I was finished. "Now…where were we?"

She kissed me sweetly, then seductively, but I gently pulled back. "The day's finally caught up to me. Either that or you wore me out. Pretty sure it's the latter."

She huffed a dramatic sigh. "Tease."

"I know. Come here."

I wrapped her up in my arms, tucked her head under my chin, and kissed her hair. Even after sweaty, voracious sex, she still smelled like caramel. I filled up my lungs with her, taking her with me into sleep, where I dreamed of a gently rocking boat and a swiftly receding shore.

Chapter 37

KACEY

It was opening night of Jonah's installation at the Wynn Galleria. I hadn't been this nervous and excited since the night before Rapid Confession's first big concert.

Miraculously, I didn't want a drink. I hadn't had a drink since I'd left the band and hadn't smoked a single cigarette either. I had the urge now and then, but I would never smoke around Jonah, and if I smoked in my apartment, it'd be everywhere when he came over.

So I kicked two bad habits. One for me, one for him.

I put on a little black dress that came to mid-thigh in the front, with wide shoulder straps and a skirt that draped to my calves in back.

"It's a reverse mullet," I'd told Jonah over the phone earlier that day. "Party in the front, business in the back. Do you think it'll be appropriate?"

"I don't know," he said. "My main concern is how easily it comes off."

The joke was a relief. Jonah had been distracted, nervous, and stressed this last week of the load-in. I hadn't yet seen the finished product, and anticipation threaded through my stomach as I piled my hair on my head, letting some loose tendrils fall down. I applied my usual makeup with smoky eyes and bright-red lips and then paced my little living room, waiting. One glance out the window revealed a sleek black limousine pulling to the front of my building, just as my phone chimed with an incoming text:

Here, but running late. Meet me downstairs?

I raced down and got to the curb just as the driver opened the passenger door and Jonah climbed out. He froze when he saw me, jaw dropping open for a beat.

"I got this," he said to the driver, who tipped his cap and returned to sit behind the wheel.

"Good evening," I said.

"You look…" He shook his head as he came closer and slid his arms around my waist.

"You don't have to," I said. "I love your silent compliments."

"Every time I see you, I think, *This is it. She cannot possibly look more beautiful than she does right now.* And then I see you the next time."

Tears jumped to my eyes as I ran my hands down the lapels of his dark-gray suit. "You look…so handsome, Jonah. God, what's wrong with me?" I pressed the back of my wrist carefully under one eye, then fanned my face. "I don't know what this is about. It's a special night for you, and I'm so happy and proud…excited to see your beautiful glass. Shit, I should get a box of tissues to carry around. I know I'm going to need it."

Jonah bent and kissed my mouth. "Thank you for being here with me."

I could feel the tension coiled in his muscles. His expression was troubled, like he had a thousand thoughts on his mind and wanted to say more. But the streetlights flickered on above us. Night had begun to fall, and Jonah turned to usher me into the limo.

"Courtesy of A-1?" I asked.

"God, no," Jonah said, sliding beside me. "Eme sent it for me. It's sort of ridiculous, but I couldn't send it away and ruin the driver's night. But I'm glad it's not from A-1, or I would never hear the end of it from the guys."

"I love Eme for doing it," I said. "You deserve it."

"I don't know about that," Jonah said.

The limo pulled away from the curb, and Jonah turned to watch Vegas go by outside the window. His leg jounced, and I slipped my hand in his. He held it tightly the entire ride over, and then gave it an almost painful squeeze when we arrived at the Wynn.

"Holy shit," he muttered.

The front of the hotel was a rotating cavalcade of sedans, limos, and cars, spilling out guests dressed in semiformal attire.

"I didn't think there'd be so many," Jonah said. "Eme must've invited half of Vegas." He turned to me, his handsome face twisted by panic. "What do I do if they hate it?"

I started to tell him they weren't going to hate it, but I knew from my own experience of putting my soul on display, pouring my heart out into a song, and then handing it to someone else, *Of course they won't hate it* wasn't much of a stopgap against that kind of anxiety.

"Do *you* love it?" I asked. "Is the installation everything you envisioned?"

Jonah nodded. "Yeah, it is."

I smiled and shrugged. "There you go."

He barked a short laugh. "Well, that was easy." He stroked my cheek, studying me intently, and opened his mouth to say something more. He kissed me instead, just as the driver opened the door for us and it was time to go in.

The long wing of the L-shaped gallery displayed the individual pieces for sale, each standing on plain oblong stands of varying heights. Bottles and vases ribboned with color in complex yet precise patterns. Spheres and cubes that contained impossible bouquets of flowers. One cluster of purple and yellow wildflowers had bees hovering over it. Another looked as if it were suspended underwater, blurred and fluid in its shape. Other pieces hung from the ceiling in twists of multicolored glass. Some were lamps, their bulbs hidden among the coils.

I had to bite the inside of my cheek as we walked through the formally dressed people taking in Jonah's gorgeous work. They sipped champagne from crystal flutes or ate delicate finger foods off the trays of passing waiters. A current of muttered, awed conversation wove through the shifting crowd. Every direction my head turned, I heard guests exclaim how beautiful the glass was and how much they'd willingly spend to take a piece home with them.

Jonah looked straight ahead, his hand holding mine tightly, as we made our way to the short end of the L, where his installation hung. We rounded the corner and joined the gathered crowd, all of their voices and gasps pointing up toward the ceiling.

A sea...

I stared up too. Ten feet up to a waterfall of glass in every shade of blue. Ribbons and curls of it, some bearded in opalescent foam. It poured from under a sphere set at the center. A sun of orange, red, gold, and yellow. A fireball full of molten lava.

At the bottom of the waterfall, the water transformed into a placid blue made from flares of glass, like square-shaped plates with undulating edges, each a foot long and just as wide. Lily pads in green, topped with clusters of pink crystal flowers, dotted the azure lake spreading along the floor. Hidden lights at strategic locations illuminated the animal life among the water and greenery: glass fish with scales of bronze, cubes of coral and seaweed, and even an octopus, its tentacles fanned out and reaching.

My hand in Jonah's squeezed so hard, my knuckles ached.

"Jonah, it's..." I didn't have a word for what it was. He turned to look down at me, and I could only stare back.

"Thank you," he said.

My eyes slowly picked out Tania, Dena and Oscar, Jonah's parents, and Theo within the crowd. Then Eme Takamura spotted us. Without a word she pointed, waited for the gazes to follow, then she began to clap. The rest of the crowd joined in as they realized the artist was with them. Soon the space was filled with applause, and Jonah took a step back, overwhelmed. I gently nudged him forward.

"It's all for you," I whispered. "Go get it."

The rest of the night was a bit of a blur. Dena, Oscar, and Theo stuck with me as Jonah, Tania, and the Fletchers were ushered around by Eme, meeting various artists, collectors, and critics. My eyes couldn't get enough of Jonah being greeted and congratulated for his beautiful legacy. Then friends from UNLV approached, and Jonah was surrounded and embraced, again and again, by people he hadn't seen in almost two years.

"His work is astonishing," Dena said, admiring a large egg-shaped sculpture filled with geographic shards, like a prism, pastel gemstones floating among them. "We've seen his work at UNLV, but this... He's taken it to a whole new level."

"He's a damn genius," Theo said. He was less dressed up than anyone else; still I thought he looked extremely handsome in a black button-down shirt rolled up to just below his elbows, revealing his inked forearms.

"No date, T?" Oscar asked.

Theo shook his head.

"That's a first."

Theo shrugged and muttered something unintelligible against the mouth of his beer bottle.

"Is Chihuly here?" I asked. If Jonah's idol arrived, the night would be complete.

Dena scanned the crowd up and down the long L. "I don't think so. At least not *yet*."

"He'll show," Oscar said.

"He'd better," Theo said.

No sooner had he said it than the crowds parted, and a man walked through, flanked by an entourage of four. He was short, rotund, and jowly, dressed all in black. His silver hair brushed his shoulders, and a black patch covered his left eye.

"Theo…?" I whispered, grabbing his hand.

"It's him," Theo said.

My hand in his squeezed tighter, and my breath caught as this man, this master of glass, this *legend*, strode up to Jonah and tapped his arm. Jonah turned. His face turned inside out, morphing through awe, shock, and reverence.

"Jesus, look at him," Theo said softly.

I blinked away tears as Dale Chihuly offered Jonah his hand and Jonah shook it. I was standing too far away to hear any words, but Chihuly was animated as he spoke, his arms gesturing, fingers pointing at different pieces. Jonah's head bobbed. His mouth shaped *thank you* over and over. Then he and Chihuly moved around the bend in the L and disappeared from our sight.

"Oh, my God, Theo," I whispered.

I looked up to see him blinking hard, his jaw clenched so that muscles twitched beneath. He glanced down at me, his pupils dilated, now just letting the tears accumulate.

"He came," Theo said. "And he likes Jonah's work. We saw it happen."

I nodded, fighting back tears.

"We saw it," he said. "You know what I mean?"

I knew. Jonah met his idol. His hero praised his work. Theo and I witnessed it. It would forever be one of the most precious moments of our lives.

———

For an hour, Jonah and Dale Chihuly sat on a bench in front of the glass waterfall, deep in conversation as the crowd thinned out around them. Finally, the master stood up, shook hands heartily with Jonah, then with Eme and Tania, and left the gallery with his small entourage.

"Sold out," Eme said, consulting her iPad. "The entire show sold out. Every last piece. Gone."

Jonah ran a hand through his hair, looking around at his work, his face happy, dazed, and a little bit weary.

"Congratulations," I said, embracing him tight. "But I need a better word. A bigger word."

"Even *she* doesn't have words," Oscar said, jerking a thumb toward Dena. "Not even a Rumi quote."

A hand half covering her trembling smile, Dena shook her head. "I'm at a loss."

Oscar gaped. "You hear that, ladies and gents? Jonah reunited with old friends, sold out his entire show, met his idol, and—wonder of all wonders—rendered Dena Bukhari speechless."

Dena shoved him. "Unfortunately for you it was only a momentary loss." She raised her wineglass. "Rumi said, *Let the beauty of what you love be what you do.* I toast to our dear friend Jonah, whose exhibit is the embodiment of those words. You've created so much beauty, my friend, the world cannot help but be grateful to you for it."

In the limo on the ride home, I sat with my temple resting on Jonah's shoulder. "Dena's right, you know," I said. "The art world is going to lose their minds over you. And you deserve every bit of it."

He nodded against my head. "A legacy," he said. "That's all I wanted." His fingers picked my chin up and he regarded me, his brows furrowed in the dimness. "I never thought to ask for more."

A twinge of unease tainted my happiness, like a drop of black ink in a clear bowl. "Are you all right? You seem a little…"

"Tired," Jonah said. "Tonight was…surreal. More than I'd ever imagined. I feel a little punchy."

"Let's go to your place," I said, my hand on his thigh. "To celebrate."

He smiled and took my hand in his. "Have something particular in mind?"

"I can think of a few things."

But back home, after he changed out of his suit and emerged from the bathroom in his sleep pants, it was a different matter.

"I know I'll regret this later," he said, his gaze trailing over me as I sprawled on his bed in my lacy red underwear. "But I'm about done in. Give me a few hours to recharge?"

I took the rain check and kissed him good night. I curled up next to him and closed my eyes, expecting to be awakened in the deepest part of the night by kisses along my neck—his customary line of attack. Instead, my eyes next fluttered open to full daylight. The clock on the nightstand read 6:00 a.m. Jonah was still sleeping, his warm breath wafting over me.

No big deal, I thought. *He'd been working nonstop on his glass for months. No surprise the bottom fell out. He needed—and deserved—a long rest.*

I dozed until his watch alarm went off an hour later, indicating it was time for his meds. He went into the kitchen, and I drifted between awake and asleep, pleasantly anticipating his return, sure we'd make love now. But instead, he slipped back into bed, wrapped his arms around me, and went back to sleep.

Now I lay wide-awake, listening to him breathe. In and out, a whispering metronome, keeping time, counting down minutes.

When he finally stirred awake at quarter to nine, he frowned at the clock as if he couldn't believe what it said. I saw a sliver of fear in his eyes, and felt its twin slide itself into my heart.

"Come here," I whispered. I kissed him hard, and he responded immediately, gratefully. We fell into each other, grasping and rocking until the headboard banged the wall.

Afterward, I told myself it was the intensity of our lovemaking that sent Jonah back into sleep again.

Nothing more.

Chapter 38

KACEY

Two days after the opening. Two mornings of Jonah sleeping late, waking only to take his meds, then going back to bed. Two days of him hanging around, skimming Facebook on his phone, hardly saying a word to me, or watching mindless noise on TV. Two days of increasing tension between us that had no source, but that scared me to my bones.

On the third day, Jonah and I had breakfast at BabyStacks Cafe, a pancake house off the Strip. It had been my habit to order the same types of food Jonah ate, partially out of solidarity, but also because I ultimately felt healthier. Everything I had done since moving to Vegas had been better for my health, mental and physical.

The waitress came to take our order.

"I'll have an egg-white omelet…" I began.

"Jesus, Kace, get pancakes if you want them," Jonah said. "Order whatever you want." His smile came a little too late. "They have killer pancakes."

I stared as he turned to the waitress. "I'll have a short stack, decaf, and a side of house fries."

"House fries are too greasy," I said.

He handed his menu to the waitress, not looking at me. "One order can't hurt."

I ordered the egg-white omelet with a side of fruit and coffee. The waitress took our menus and left. Jonah's eyes were on the table, brows furrowed as he rolled his spoon between his palms, like a mini blowpipe.

"Hey," I said softly.

It took me three tries of saying his name before he looked up.

"Sorry, Kace, what's up?"

"You tell me. You've been running hot and cold lately."

"Have I?"

"Yeah, you have. I feel dizzy trying to keep up."

He wilted a little and reached across the table to take my hand. "I'm sorry. I'm a little distracted lately. I'm not used to so much time off. I don't know what to do with myself. I guess it's making me a little irritable."

Yes, okay. That makes sense.

I squeezed his hand. "Why not go to the hot shop anyway? Make something just for you?"

He shrugged and muttered something that sounded like *maybe*, and took his hand back.

Silence.

"Tania told me three different galleries want your installation," I finally said. "London, Paris, and New York. That's the trifecta of the art world, isn't it?"

"Why, because Vegas isn't good enough?" He waved a hand. "It's glass. How they think they can move it across the ocean is beyond me, but they can try."

I sat back in my chair, feeling as if I were having breakfast with a stranger. Or worse, my father.

Ten more minutes of silence squeezed by before our food arrived. I picked at my omelet; my appetite had disappeared. Jonah stared at his plate of food and finally forked one wedge of potato. I watched from under my eyelashes as he chewed it slowly, as if it were a lump of gray clay. He swallowed hard and washed it down with sip of water. Then he pushed his entire plate away.

"Guess I'm not that hungry."

After what I would forever call the Worst Breakfast Ever, we headed to Vegas Ink. I wanted a new tattoo and had set up time to visit Theo's studio and see his work.

Jonah said almost nothing on the drive over. But just when the silence was beginning to be oppressive, he suddenly found his smile, took my hand and pressed it to his lips.

Vegas Ink was located in a mini mall just off the Strip. Its walls were fire-engine red and covered in framed examples of the tattoo artists' work there. The chairs were overstuffed faux leather, also in red, and three artists were bent over their clients, Theo among them. The buzz of the needles was almost drowned out by heavy metal blasting over the sound system. A receptionist with a shaved head told us she'd let Theo know we were here. We took a seat in the waiting area, which was really nothing more than an upholstered bench near the front door, facing a wall of photographs. Past clients revealed fresh tattoos, their skin still raised red.

Jonah sank heavily onto the bench and picked up an issue of *Inked* magazine.

"Any idea what you're going to get?" he asked. It was the first time he'd voluntarily spoken all morning.

"None," I said. "But I'm eager to see your brother's work."

"He's talented as hell," Jonah said. "My father gives him too much shit for it. You'll see when you check out his portfolio."

I nodded and waited until Theo rounded the short corner, calling, "Hey, guys."

The mere fact he sounded upbeat and animated filled me with

relief, and I all but jumped to my feet. "Hey. Thanks for making the time for me."

Theo jerked his chin at Jonah. "You coming?"

"You guys go ahead," Jonah said. "I need to give Eme a call. See what's happening with the sale pieces."

"You're not going to help me pick something?" I asked, incredulous. I forced my smile to go wider. "Or where on my body it should go?"

Behind me, Theo coughed.

"Surprise me," Jonah said. He pulled out his cell phone, conversation over.

My cheeks burning, I followed Theo to his chair, passing the other artists. One was a huge burly guy with a bald tattooed head who was putting a feminine spray of violet flowers on a woman's arm. The other artist was a young woman in black clothes and heavy makeup. She had large pale-green eyes, almost cartoonish in her petite face. She looked like a gothic fairy. She gave me a nod as she drew the blood dripping from a fang of a hissing cobra on the back of young man's calf.

I plunked myself in Theo's chair and swiped a tissue from the box he used to wipe the blood away. I dabbed my eyes, but I had no tears. My emotions were too tangled for my body to know what to do, so I sat, anxious and jumpy. In front of me, Theo leaned against the small mirrored armoire upon which sat his ink gun, needles, and ink.

"Did you guys have a fight?" he asked in a low voice.

"No," I said. "Or yes. I mean, maybe I've done something to piss him off, but I don't know. He's been acting so strange lately. Since the gallery opening."

Theo's stony expression hardened, but his eyes went the other direction, filling with concern and something that looked close to fear. I realized I was going to scare the crap out of Theo for no good reason and waved my hand quickly.

"You know what? He did say this morning he feels distracted. Without having to be at the hot shop all day, he's not sure what to do with himself. I think he's just decompressing."

Theo nodded slowly. "Makes sense."

"Can I see your work now?"

Theo handed me a thick three-ring binder filled with photos and samples of his art. Jonah was right: Theo's talent was incredible. I'd seen my fair share of tattoos. Each one of my tattoos came from someone different, each was all beautiful and perfect to me.

Theo blew them all away. His book had everything: basic black outline renderings, lettering in any font or script you could want. Biker tats—roses, skulls, and snakes. Lifelike portraits, abstract and complex shapes, dreamscapes, fantastical beasts, pop culture icons. Page after page of visions. Had I been in a better frame of mind, I could've spent hours poring over his work, certain I couldn't possibly narrow an idea or a concept down.

"You're amazing, Teddy," I said. "This is the best I've ever seen. I want something no one else has, but you make it hard to narrow it down."

I want Jonah to smile again.

I shut the binder and handed it back to him. "Let me think about it, okay? I'll call or text you if I have an idea."

"Sure," he said, tossing the binder in the top armoire drawer and shutting it.

"Sorry if I took up your time," I said, slipping off the chair.

"You didn't, Kacey," he said. It was the first time he'd ever said my name.

We headed back to the waiting area. Jonah sat slouched over, swiping his thumb absently over his phone. He looked up when we approached.

"Find something?" he asked.

I plunked down beside him and kissed his cheek. "Not yet. Your brother is so incredibly talented, I have to come up with something worthy of him."

Theo shook his head, thick arms crossed over his black T-shirt.

"You name it, he can do it," Jonah said, finally tucking his phone away.

The brothers exchanged glances, Theo's gaze scrutinizing. "Tonight's hangout with Dena and Oscar," he said. "You still down?"

Jonah smirked sourly, an expression so unlike him, I had to blink twice. "No need to keep to any routine now," he said. "What's the point? I'll shoot you a text and let you know."

Theo's arms dropped to his sides. "Oscar and Dena are expecting to hang out…"

"I didn't say no; I said I'd *let you know*."

The brothers faced each other down, and then Jonah gave himself a shake and a dirty laugh. He got up and walked out the door without so much as a glance at me.

I smiled weakly at Theo. "I'll talk to you soon."

He grabbed my arm hard, then loosened his grip but didn't let go. "If you need me…if he needs me, you call immediately. Okay?"

I started to protest and instead found myself nodding. "Okay," I said in a small voice.

I left Vegas Ink and climbed into Jonah's truck, which he had idling in the parking space.

He didn't look at me when I shut the door, and finally I couldn't take it anymore.

"What the hell is going on?" I demanded. "You just walk out and leave me there?"

"It's fucking hot out," Jonah said. "I came to start the AC."

"It's October," I snapped. "It's *maybe* seventy degrees."

"So you've been here three months, and suddenly you're an expert?"

My eyes widened. He'd never spoken to me like that. Not once. "What happened to you?" I asked. "You've been different since the gallery opening. Did something happen? Did Dale Chihuly say something to upset you?"

Jonah shook his head. "No," he said, his voice softening. "No, nothing like that. He said amazing things about my work… I can't even remember the words, but I can still feel them, if that makes sense."

"Then what's bothering you? You can tell me."

Jonah met my eyes for the first time in what felt like days, and for a split second, they were the warm, rich brown of the man I knew. Then a wall came down, and he gave my hand a squeeze.

"Nothing's bothering me. Because I have nothing to do. No more work. I'm in the mood to veg out today and watch a movie. Got any classic eighties flicks lying around?"

I nodded slowly. "I rented a DVD of *Airplane!*"

"*Surely you can't be serious?*"

"*I am serious,*" I replied half-heartedly. "*And don't call me Shirley.*"

It was a painful, awkward version of our usual humor. A poor imitation of our typical banter.

Maybe he just needs a good laugh, I thought.

Back at my apartment, we headed up the exterior concrete stairs that led to the second floor. My house keys had migrated to the bottom of my purse. Only when I wrestled them free did I realize Jonah was no longer behind me.

I turned around. The little front area was empty. "Jonah?"

I crept back the way I'd come, almost tiptoeing.

He sat halfway up the stairs, his back to me. The way his shoulders rose and fell rapidly made the horror coil in my gut like a poisonous vapor.

He can't breathe.

I moved down the stairs on leaden legs, gripping the rusted metal railing. I sat beside him, ordering myself to be calm and not feed the panic.

"Hey."

His elbows were propped on his knees, his hands and head dangling as he sucked in air. "I tried to take them too fast," he said between breaths. He threw his head back, looking like a runner who'd just done a fifty-yard sprint.

"All right," I said. "I'm here."

My mind raced through the catalog of every other time Jonah had taken stairs, or lifted a heavy blowpipe, or made love to me vigorously. In every instance he'd been winded—from the damage the CAV was doing to his heart. But it had never lingered like this. He'd always recovered quickly.

Always.

"I lied," Jonah said, as if reading my thoughts. He reclaimed his breath slowly, one inhale at a time. "I wasn't going too fast. I was walking up."

He looked to me, breathing in, breathing out, sweat beading his brow, and his eyes… Oh God, the fear I saw in them. A foreboding that terrified me to the core of my soul. He tore his gaze away, and without another word, he pulled himself to stand and begin the climb again. One foot on a step. Then the other. I wanted to touch him, to help him, but I couldn't. I couldn't admit to myself he needed help.

Once in my apartment, Jonah went to the kitchen and poured himself some water. He slumped against the counter, sucking in deep and even breaths.

"Is it the first time this has happened?" I asked, my own breath going no deeper than my throat.

"No," he said. "Off and on. Since right before the opening."

"That was nine days ago," I said. "Did you—"

My words choked off in a cry as Jonah swept the pill-a-day container of his meds off the counter. The pills and capsules scattered in a spray of blue, white, and orange, rolling and clattering over my cheap linoleum tile.

I froze in the living area, unable to speak.

"I thought…" Jonah bit off his words, swallowed, then spat the next ones out in a rush. "I thought it would be enough. But it's just fucking glass. It's heated fucking sand. Who gives a shit?"

"What are you talking about?" I said, finding my voice. "Your work? It's beautiful—"

"It's bullshit. It doesn't mean anything. It's not important."

"Of course it is."

He gave a little laugh of disbelief. "No, Kace. No. *You* are important. You're the most important thing in my life, and I was so fucking *stupid* to think…to hope…"

His words trailed away, and he shook his head, lips pressed together, eyes shining.

"Don't talk like that," I managed after a short silence. "You got tired, so what? You've had a draining week, leading up to a huge event. I felt the same way after my first big concert."

I went to the kitchen and crouched down, picking up pills. They were everywhere; the tears in my eyes blurred them to little blue or white or orange splotches. I pried the container from where it had slid under the fridge and scooped the meds in. All the wrong pills in all the wrong days, but I could fix that. I could fix everything. I knew his regimen. I knew what went where. I could fix this.

"You can't just throw these away," I said, sniffing and wiping my eyes. "You need these. They're important."

Jonah turned around to lean the heel of his hands on the counter behind him, his head hanging down, his words dropping to the floor. "They're not working."

"Yes, they are."

"Kacey—"

"*You don't give up,*" I shrieked, making him flinch. Making *me* flinch at the hysteria that was lurking just below the surface. I stared him down—full of the hostility that had just leached out of him. "You're *tired,* that's all. Go take a nap. Pile the pillows up on my bed, and take a nap. I'll clean this up and order dinner. We'll watch that movie and laugh our asses off, okay?"

He didn't reassure me or tell me I was right. He pushed himself off the counter, and we went to my bedroom. I stacked the pillows up, and he lay down without protest, sinking heavily onto the bed.

Because he's tired and needs a nap, I thought, closing the blinds. *That's all.*

He threw his arm over his eyes, saying nothing. I was at the door when he called my name.

"Yes?" I clung to the doorframe.

"I'm sorry," he said from under his arm. Now he sounded genuinely wiped out. Exhausted to the bone. "So fucking sorry."

"There's nothing to be sorry about. Just rest. You'll feel better after a nap."

I went back into the kitchen. There were still pills strewn all over. I chased them down, scooped them up, and crammed them into the container however I could. The lids bulged. Pills fell out of my shaking hands to roll away again. Run away from me. Everything was getting away from me. I slid down the front of the fridge and hunched in a ball, sobbing into the hands clamped over my mouth.

I cried hard, great heaving sobs that strangled and smothered. I wept until my face ached. I knew it was red and tear-streaked, my eyes swollen. I had to quit before Jonah woke up and saw me like this.

I grabbed the last stray pills and got shakily to my feet. I set the container carefully on the counter, then washed my face in the sink with cold water. Patting it dry with a dish towel, I crept back toward my room.

Jonah slept now, his eyes no longer covered by his arm. His closed lids were smooth, his breathing deep and even. Only the tiniest furrow in his brow, as if whatever unsettled him went with him into sleep.

I went back to the living room and dug my cell phone out of my purse. I'd order a pizza. Vegetarian. That was better for him. Or maybe salads. Too much cheese on a pizza…

I opened up my call screen and hit a name. A deep, gruff voice answered.

"Teddy," I whispered, tears flooding my eyes again. "It's starting."

Part III

"A man who lives fully
is prepared to die at any time."

—Mark Twain

Chapter 39

KACEY

THE NEXT DAY, JONAH CHECKED INTO THE SUNRISE MEDICAL FACILITY for a myocardial biopsy. Someone told me—I didn't remember who—that it was a same-day office procedure, but his doctor, Dr. Morrison, wanted Jonah to stay overnight for more tests. Kidney and liver panels, and an EKG.

"Are you his girlfriend?" Dr. Morrison asked in the hall outside Jonah's room. Theo stood beside me.

"Yes," I said, hugging my arms. "Kacey Dawson."

"It's nice to meet you, Kacey," Dr. Morrison said. He was a lovely man, with a graying beard and sharp, kind eyes. I liked him at once, but all the while we exchanged pleasantries, I screamed at him in my mind...

FIX HIM.

MAKE HIM WELL.

GIVE HIM BACK TO ME.

Dr. Morrison explained what Jonah would need while recovering from a biopsy. "It would be ideal if someone were with him for the twenty-four hours after the procedure. Presuming he's released tomorrow morning as planned."

"Why wouldn't he be released?" I asked.

"No reason at this time. We'll let the test results come, and go from there, all right?"

We were allowed in Jonah's room then. He lay reclined in bed, an IV of clear fluid hung over him and fed into the back of his right hand, the needle taped just above his MedicAlert bracelet. He threw us a glance in greeting. He'd been sullen and silent all morning. Unreachable. As Theo and I took a seat on either side of the bed, he looked at neither of us but absently cycled through channels on the muted wall TV.

"Mom and Dad are on the way," Theo said.

"They don't need to come."

"You're in the hospital," his brother replied, barely keeping the sharp edge out of his voice. "You think Mom will stay away?"

Jonah shrugged and said nothing.

"Oscar texted me," Theo continued. "He's at work and wants to come. He and Dena both. I told them it's not an emergency."

"Good."

I put my hand over Jonah's, mindful of the IV. He didn't react, didn't move to take my hand or look at me. I sucked down the pain roaring within me, *I'm not strong enough for this. I'm not I'm not I'm not…*

Theo's eyes found mine, searchingly. Like Lola, ready and waiting for me to flake out right before a big show, only the stakes were a billion times higher.

You knew this was coming, I told myself. *You* knew *it wasn't going to be long walks on the beach in San Diego and making love all night, every night. This is it. This is real, and now you're going to stay and fucking take it.*

Except that I didn't think we'd actually be here. I'd always held on to a little flame of hope, and now it was guttering out.

A nurse or technician wheeled in a cart, and Theo got up to make room. As Dr. Morrison and the tech bustled around the machines, the heart tracking Jonah's pulse beeped faster, betraying the stoic expression on his face.

"Hey," I whispered.

He nodded, his eyes straight ahead.

"Do you want to hold my hand?"

"I'll crush it." He turned his head on the pillow and looked at me for the first time all morning. Within the cold, flat lines of his face, his eyes were rimmed with terror. Because this was happening. We were at this dreaded place, and it was worse, so much worse, than I could have ever possibly imagined.

I can't I can't I can't...

I let go of his hand. "Maybe Theo then..."

Jonah's chin rose a hair, then fell.

I surrendered my seat to Theo. He took Jonah's hand in his, and I watched them exchange a look. A commiseration. Theo knew what to do, and Jonah trusted him to do it.

The tech gave Jonah a shot of anesthetic in the neck, just above his collarbone, while Dr. Morrison readied a hideous-looking instrument.

"All right, Jonah," Dr. Morrison said, "you're going to feel a slight pinch and then pressure."

"Liar," Jonah said, his entire body tensed and knuckles white in the hand holding Theo's.

"Guilty as charged," Morrison said, his eyes flicking between his hands and the monitor showing the tiny camera now threading down Jonah's jugular. And I could see everything. I could see inside Jonah's body, taking a narrow dark road down to the heart that was failing him.

"Almost there," Dr. Morrison said. "You're doing great. Try to stay relaxed."

"Exhale," Theo murmured. "Don't hold your breath."

Jonah let the held air out through his nose, keeping his teeth gritted. The heart monitor continued beeping at ninety-eight pulses per minute.

"There we are," the doctor said, and Jonah closed his eyes.

Through the catheter, Morrison inserted a bioptome—a device with tiny jaws at the tip. It pinched off a piece of Jonah's heart tissue, then retreated back up the vein.

Jonah made a sound deep in his chest, and I had to clap my hand over my mouth to keep from doing the same.

"Aaaand we're done." Dr. Morrison turned aside to the tray table. His tech bottled and labeled the tiny piece of heart tissue to take to the lab, while a nurse busied herself with the incision site. Morrison snapped off his blue latex gloves and threw them in a waste receptacle.

"You did fantastic," he said, patting Jonah's leg. "Ah, and here are your parents." He smiled warmly at Henry and Beverly in the doorway. "We've just finished. We should have the results sometime tomorrow morning."

"Wonderful," Beverly said through a tight, nervous smile. She nodded at me in greeting, then went to Jonah's side. "How are you doing, sweetheart? You look wonderful."

"I'm tired," Jonah said, staring at nothing. "I'd like to get some rest now."

"Oh." Beverly swallowed. "But we just got here…"

Henry said, "He needs to rest." He took hold of his wife by the shoulders. "Come on, Beverly. Everyone. Let's leave him to sleep. We can visit in a few hours—"

"No," Jonah said. "In the morning. Come back in the morning."

"The morning?" Beverly's hand crept to the neckline of her cardigan.

"Pending the results of several tests, we're going to keep Jonah overnight," Dr. Morrison said. "Purely as a precaution."

No one moved. Glances darted here and there until the doctor cleared his throat and made a firm gesture toward the door. We all shuffled out, and I waited for Jonah to look at me or call me back. He didn't.

In the hallway, the Fletchers asked questions. Theo answered. Dr. Morrison elaborated. I stood in numb silence, listening to the squeak of rubber-soled shoes on linoleum as nurses passed by. Machines beeped alarms, and a voice over an intercom paged a doctor.

"Kacey?"

I jumped. They were all staring at me. Beverly's smile was a frozen grimace while her eyes melted to panic. "You'll stay with Jonah after he's released tomorrow?"

"Of course," I said, conscious of Theo's eyes on me. "In fact, I should go home and pack a few things to stay over…"

Theo's whiskey-colored eyes met mine. In their imploring gaze, I could hear an echo of an earlier conversation.

You're just going to leave…

I shook my head at him, as if he'd spoken aloud. "I'm going to pack a bag," I said. "Then I'm coming back. I am… I…"

Then Beverly laid her hand on my arm. "You know, Kacey, I'd love some coffee. Will you join me?"

I sucked in a breath and nodded. "Yes, sure. Of course."

Her hand still tucked in my elbow, we headed down to the first-floor cafeteria, a space I typically associated with school, filled with laughter, shrieks, and loud cross talk. The hospital cafeteria was sparsely populated and quiet as a library. Only a few people occupied tables, eating in silence. One or two patients in wheelchairs sat with nurses or family members.

Beverly took a small table near the window while I bought two cups of coffee. We sat without drinking for a long, silent time, watching little blackbirds hop around the courtyard outside.

"It is hard for you to be here, isn't it?" Beverly said after a moment. "It's hard for all of us, but unlike you, we've known Jonah all of our lives. Before the virus. Before the transplant. But you met him only months ago. When he was already sick."

I nodded.

"And here you are," she said. "He was sick when you met him, but here you are. That's an extraordinary thing, I think, to begin so close to the end."

"I…I'm scared." I set my coffee cup down before my shaking hands spilled it. "I don't think I'm strong enough."

"May I tell you a story, dear?" Her tone meant, *I am going to tell you a story, and you are going to listen.* But I welcomed it. I needed the distraction. I needed someone else's words to push out the panicky fear that ricocheted around my thoughts like lightning.

"When Jonah was born, I changed. Profoundly. Forever. I think that's the way it is with every new mother. You spend nine months carrying this little being in you, this little stranger, until finally they're born, and you see their face…"

Her gazed fixed beyond the window, beyond the little birds, to a moment twenty-six years ago. "When I saw Jonah's face for the first time, it was like seeing someone again after a long absence. Not a meeting, but a reunion."

She reached over and briefly patted my hand. "I love both my sons equally, of course. But they're so different. Theo and I have spent our entire lives getting to know each other, and it's not always been easy. But with Jonah, it's effortless."

Beverly's brows knitted together, as if she were trying to recall something now forgotten. "I've known Jonah before. I know I have. Call it reincarnation or whatever you'd like. I'm not religious or even particularly spiritual. But I can't help but feel the universe is a vast place, and the soul of a human being is infinite, even if the body is temporary." She nodded to herself, certain now. "I've known Jonah before, and I know I'll see him again. And that gives me comfort. Not a lot, but some."

She turned to me. "And you, Kacey. You give me comfort. Quite a lot more comfort these days than anything else."

I swallowed the jagged lump in my throat but couldn't move

otherwise. Beverly's words wrapped around me and squeezed until all I could hear was her voice and my own heart thudding in my chest.

"I'm sure you know Jonah had a serious girlfriend in college," she said.

"Audrey."

"Yes. Nice girl, but serious. Driven. She was…precise about how she wanted her life to be." Beverly's mouth became a thin line, and her voice hardened. "I was angry with her for leaving Jonah when he needed her most. Furious. But you want to know something strange? The day after she flew out of the country, the *very next day*, we got the call that a donor had been matched. Isn't that something?"

I didn't say anything. No answer was required anyway.

"Jonah was in surgery when she left. I tried to think of ways to break the news and comfort him. I thought surely he'd be devastated. Betrayed. Yet when I thought of their time together, I couldn't recall anything that would qualify as much of a loss. Nothing significant in *three years*. His eyes didn't light up when he looked at her across our dinner table. His voice didn't change when he said her name. He never spoke of her with…awe. Only facts.

"'Audrey and I are thinking of flying to Cabo. Audrey and I are attending the gallery opening. Audrey and I are having dinner with friends…' It was a news report of incidentals." She looked at me, her smile wreathed in a sheepish guilt. "That's petty and unkind, but it's true."

"I understand."

"His heart isn't well now, but he's much healthier in other ways. Ways I'd always hoped for when he was with Audrey, but never observed."

I felt a tightening in my chest, an anticipation of something I needed to hear, something that would save me from my faltering courage.

"Jonah is always insisting we don't talk about bucket lists," Beverly said. "'Don't bucket-list me, Mom.' But mothers…we all have our own list for our children—hopes we have for them. Dreams and aspirations. My list is full, and all the things Jonah might never do or experience weigh heavily on me. So heavy. A wedding, children of his own..."

She looked at me, her lips trembling, her eyes shining. "Falling in love and being loved in return. That's the heaviest one. But you're here now. And the way he talks about you..." Her eyes filled and spilled over. "His eyes light up and his voice changes when he says your name. His smile when you walk into a room is one of the most beautiful things I've ever seen."

A tingling warmth began to spread through me, warming me against the icy chill of fear and grief. Beverly reached out and brushed a tear from my cheek and cupped my chin.

"And even more beautiful than that, Kacey? *Your* eyes light up when my son is near. *Your* voice changes when you say his name. And the smile you wear when you're looking at him and think no one is watching... Those are gifts I'll never be able to thank you for. To know my Jonah is loved. He'll leave this world loved, won't he?"

I nodded, tears streaming from my eyes. "Yes," I whispered. "He's loved, and he'll be loved forever."

Beverly's smile shone through her tears like a ray of sun through rain. "Wonderful." She patted my cheek and let her hand fall. "Cross that off my list then."

Chapter 40

JONAH

Six weeks.

Dr. Morrison laid it out for me. The biopsy results were as I expected: the hardening of the arteries was accelerating, and blood tests showed that the amount of antibodies my immune system had developed against the donor heart was skyrocketing. Heart failure was imminent. I was back on the donor list with emergency status, but to add insult to injury, the immunosuppressant medications had taken a toll on my kidneys, compromising my chances for a second transplant. In the eyes of the board, I wasn't a favorable candidate.

Six weeks. Not months anymore.

Strings of days.

Hardly more than a thousand hours.

But within those hours, thousands upon thousands of moments...

I stared at the dust motes that danced in a shaft of morning sun lancing from the window. Real warm light against the harsh fluorescents above me.

Dr. Morrison reached across the bed to lay his hand over my wrist. "Jonah?"

I inhaled deeply and let it out in a gusty sigh of relief, as if something heavy had been pressing down on my chest and now it was gone.

The doctor's hand on my arm tightened. "*Jonah?*"

"I'm fine," I said, turning toward him. "I'm good, actually. Knowing the brutal truth…it's better. I feel better."

Oddly, I could breathe again. The twisted coil of anxiety and fear and dread were fading away. My emotions had been in free fall for a week, when the first bout of unwarranted fatigue hit me just before the gallery opening. Kacey said I ran hot and cold, but that barely captured the range of emotions. Hot and cold, angry and guilty, scared shitless and scrambling to make peace. I'd been cycling through the five stages of grief, one after the other—each stage lasting less than a minute—then back to the beginning to start again. I'd had to push everyone away last night—even push Kacey away so I could cope with the inevitability.

I looked at Dr. Morrison now, a sense of peace settling over me, and profound relief from the chaotic emotions of the last few days.

"Would you like to talk to someone?" Dr. Morrison asked. "A counselor perhaps? Or the chaplain?"

"I want to lodge a complaint with the medical board," I said. "Worst. Biopsy. Ever."

He chuckled. "You've always been one of my favorite patients, Jonah. Always." His laughter quieted. "I've already taken the liberty of explaining the situation."

"Thank you," I said. "Not the best part of your job, I take it."

"Never. But they knew this was a probability, and they're taking it well. As well as can be expected rather. They're waiting for you outside."

"Dena and Oscar?" I asked.

Dr. Morrison nodded. "Tania too."

I nodded. "And my girlfriend?"

He smiled. "She's here."

"I'm here," echoed a voice at the door. Kacey stood with her hand on the frame. Her face pale, her eyes swollen and bloodshot, her hair a sloppy ponytail falling loose. She looked so damn beautiful I could hardly breathe.

"Get lost, doc," I said.

"With pleasure." He got up, and Kacey raced past him toward me, threw her arms around me as best she could across the bed, and buried her face in my neck.

"I need to tell you something," she said, her voice muffled.

"I need to tell you something too." I pulled her far enough away to look at her, to brush the hair that stuck to the tears on her cheeks, like spun glass. "I've been such an ass to you, Kace. I'm so sorry. I was freaking out. Every minute I was feeling a different emotion, and I—"

"I love you," she said.

I stared at her.

"I love you," she said. "I'm in love with you."

Her words sunk into my heart. Not the failing organ in my chest, but the part of me that beat for her, lived for her. I felt saturated with warmth and a happiness I didn't think was possible to experience. Not at a time like this. Not in a place like this.

Kacey's hand slid against my cheek, her eyes filling. "Your face right now? Never in million years did I imagine a man looking at me like you're looking at me right now. I love you," she said again. "I know you want to protect me, and it's not going to work. I just love you all the more for it. You can't keep me at a safe distance. I told you, there is no safe distance. There never was."

"You're right," I whispered. "There never was. I love you. I love you so much…"

She laid her head down again, right at the tender spot of my incision, but I didn't care. Love and pain, I wanted all of it.

"I love you," I said. "God, I never thought this would happen to me."

"But it did," she whispered. "It happened, and all we can do now is take care of each other. Live in the little moments, right? Just like we promised. The little moments. We have so many. Thousands upon thousands."

"Too many to count," I said. I sniffed hard as my arms went around her and held her close. As close to me as I could, my lips kissing her hair. "And this right here…the best moment of my life."

We held each other for a long time, and I thought about the choices Kacey made to arrive at his moment. To be here with me, knowing it wouldn't last.

"You're so brave," I said. "You're the bravest person I know."

"Not me," she said. "Brave or scared shitless, I don't have a choice but to love you." She raised her head and sniffled. "It's all your fault, really. You're so damn lovable."

I laughed shortly. "I thought I was a stubborn smart-ass."

"That too." She wiped her eyes. "There's a bunch of other people in the hall who want to give you a piece of their minds. Can I go get them?"

I nodded, smiled. "Yes. All of them. I want all of them."

They all came in: my best friends, my parents, my brother. I faced the ring of people I loved best and called to mind this speech I'd rehearsed a hundred times in the last six months. I'd thought I'd give it alone. That I'd have to face the inevitable with an empty hand. But Kacey Dawson was there, her fingers entwined with mine. I wasn't alone, and my hand wasn't empty.

I cleared my aching throat. "Okay, guys, the plan is there is no plan. No trips. No adventures. No bucket lists. This is what I want: to hang out together. Let's have barbecues and breakfasts. A nice dinner at a fancy restaurant, or a breakfast at Mulligan's. Or cupcakes out of an ATM. Let's talk and tell stupid jokes and laugh a lot and…live."

Nods and murmured assents.

"What I *don't* want is anyone asking me how I feel a hundred times a day," I said. "I promise I'll tell you if I need anything, but everything I could ever need or want is right here in this room. You are the loves of my life. I don't want anything but to be together as much we can. That way, when the time comes…"

I swallowed hard, my vision blurring the faces of my people. "You don't have to worry if I was happy. Or if I had regrets. I have none." I looked to Kacey, my beautiful girl, and touched her tearstained cheek. "No regrets."

"Not one," she whispered. She kissed her fingertips and touched them to my lips.

I took a moment to pull myself together, and quickly wiped my eyes.

"So that's my big speech. I love you all, and that's it. Let's get the hell out of here."

My audience laughed softly through sniffles or coughs, and it was as if a horrible tension had been lifted. I didn't want macho stoicism or restraint. I wanted their true selves and nothing more.

I wanted their moments.

Chapter 41

JONAH

Two days later, Theo came by my place in the late afternoon.

"Where's Kacey?" he asked.

I handed him a beer from the fridge and took a green tea for myself. "She's grocery shopping."

Theo nodded, dropping onto the couch. "You're not working tonight?"

"I quit today," I said, sitting at the other end. "Harry asked if I'd been poached by a different limo company."

"What did you tell him?"

"That his was the only limo service I'd ever work for in my entire life."

"Shit, Jonah..."

"What?" I said, grinning. "Come on, it was a little funny."

Theo snorted, turned his beer around in his hand. "Morrison said your kidneys are shot."

"Apparently so," I said.

He glanced at me. "And that's what's keeping you from being higher up on the donor list."

"I know where this is going."

"I'm just saying I could give you a kidney," Theo said. "It would match. Your body won't reject it because we're blood. We're brothers. You're my brother..." His voice cracked open. He sat hunched over, his elbows resting on his knees. I waited until he'd pulled himself together and put my hand on his arm.

"The medication would eventually wreck it, while my body wrecks the second heart thanks to my craptastically rare tissue type." I chucked him on the shoulder. "So keep your damn internal organs to yourself."

He laughed then. A small laugh, but real. "Fine. But say the word and it's yours. Whatever you want or need...if I can give it to you, it's yours. Okay?"

"I might have a favor to ask you."

His head shot up. "Anything. Name it; give me *something...*"

But the doorknob rattled then. I glanced at it, holding up a finger. "Not now..."

Kacey came in the door, her arms laden with grocery bags. "Hey, my two favorite men in the world in one place. Must be my lucky day."

Theo got up to take the bags. She smiled and ruffled his hair. Then they were putting the groceries away, bickering lightly the entire time, while I sat on the couch, my smile turned away where they couldn't see.

We ate dinner at my parents' house that night, as we did nearly every other night now. Oscar and Dena and Tania were always invited. I wanted my people around me as often as possible.

Early on, Kacey was chatting with Tania, and Dena was helping my parents plate the dinner. Oscar glanced surreptitiously toward the kitchen and pulled his chair closer to mine. He rubbed his hands up and down on his jeans as if his palms were sweaty.

"What's up, man?" I asked. "You in the doghouse with Dena?"

A smile flickered over his lips, then was gone again. "No, but I could be if I don't get this right." He puffed his cheeks with air and said, "I'm going to ask her to marry me."

I sat back in my chair, my chest flooding with happiness. But Oscar was nervous enough without me getting emotional on him. I feigned total shock. "But, Oscar, it's only been *six years*. Are you sure? You don't want to rush into this…"

"I know, I know." He laughed and ran his hand over his short-cropped hair. "I never want to be with anyone else, but I didn't think I needed—or wanted—some ceremony or piece of paper to make it official. But seeing you with Kacey these last weeks…" Oscar's smile froze on his face, his eyes unblinking as if he could lock his emotion down before it could be revealed. "If you love someone as much as I love Dena, then you hold on to her, right? As long as you can, as hard as you can."

"Yeah, man," I said softly. "Sounds exactly right."

Oscar nodded, and we took a moment; he sipped his beer, and I waited until he was ready to speak again.

"So when's the big day?" I asked.

"She has to say yes first," Oscar said and cleared his throat. "But that's another thing I wanted to talk to you about. The date. I want you to be there. My best man. Vegas is the capital of quickie weddings." He stopped at my shaking head and waving hands. "What?"

"You can't have a quickie wedding with Dena Bukhari," I said. "Can you picture our girl in a traditional Iranian dress in a gaudy chapel officiated by Elvis? No, no. She needs the works."

Oscar shifted in his seat. "I know it. But her parents are in London, and grandparents in Iran. The visa situation alone is going to take six months."

I leaned forward and clapped my friend on his shoulder. "It's enough that I know it will happen. I'm happy for you, man. For both of you. Give her the wedding you both deserve. I'll be there in spirit." I chucked his arm. "Literally."

Oscar barked a laugh and looked away. "I'm going to miss you, man," he told his beer bottle.

"Thanks for saying that," I said, because I knew how hard it was for him to do so. "I'm going to miss you too. Both of you. And I'm really fucking happy to know you'll take care of each other."

"She'll take care of *me*," Oscar said. "I'm going to spend the rest of my life trying not to screw up."

I laughed and he laughed, and we got over the emotional hump like a wagon wheel finally lurching over a rock. I didn't need Oscar's tears to know he cared about me, or expect a bunch of sentimental words. I just needed to be around him, and that was enough.

After dessert, my father tapped his knife on the side of his wineglass and took a piece of folded paper from his shirt pocket.

"This arrived in the mail this afternoon," he said. "From Carnegie Mellon. I presumed it was junk mail or a form letter. Good thing I opened it." He cleared his throat and began to read. "*Dear sir. This letter is to inform you, Jonah Miles Fletcher, that you have achieved the degree of master of fine arts from Carnegie Mellon University and all honors, benefits, and rights conferred hereto...*"

There was more, but the table erupted in cheers and applause, drowning out my father. Kacey's arms went around my neck, then she pushed her chair back and crawled right into my lap. I held her face, gazed into the blue depths of her eyes. She was so much. I could spend a thousand full lifetimes and never reach the end of her.

She is a universe...

I realized in that moment my glass legacy was woefully incomplete. The evening drew to a close, a slow migration began for the door, with hugs and handshakes and drawing on of coats. I pulled Tania aside.

"Yes, Master of Fine Arts?" she said. "How may I serve you?"

"Knock it off," I said. "I wouldn't have made it if it weren't for you."

She waved a hand. "It was nothing."

"It was everything. I owe you so much, Tania. And I…"

She leaned forward. "Yes…?"

I grinned. "I figured I might as well ask you for one more thing."

Tania snorted a laugh and swatted my arm. "I'm *very* expensive, you know."

I took her hands in mine. "Meet me at the hot shop tomorrow?"

Her face brightened. "A new piece?"

"One last piece," I said. "The most important piece of my life."

Chapter 42

KACEY

I DROVE US BACK TO JONAH'S PLACE WITH BUTTERFLIES IN MY STOMACH.

"What are you smiling about?" he asked.

I glanced at him. "I keep thinking about your degree confirmation." Which was only partially true. I had plans for the evening, and once inside the apartment, I led him to the couch.

"I have a surprise for you," I said.

"Does it involve you being naked?"

"Maybe," I said over my shoulder on the way to the bedroom. "Give me a minute."

I pulled a box I'd stowed under the bed. It held a dozen pillar candles, and I set them up around the room: on his dresser and nightstand, two on the windowsill. Once I flipped the lamp off, the room glowed with orbs of soft yellow light.

Task done, I called for Jonah to join me.

At the door he stopped and took in the candles, then me. He leaned his forearm high on the doorframe, his eyebrow arched. "You're not even remotely naked."

"Not yet," I said, moving to him and running my hands over his T-shirt. "I know we have to take it easy, so I've been doing some research."

"Research," Jonah said, ringing his arms around my waist. "There's an erotic word. What have you been researching?"

"Tantric sex," I whispered. Then a laugh erupted out of me. "Oh my God, it sounds cheesy as hell. But I read up on it, and I think it'll be good for us. Safe."

Dr. Morrison didn't exactly forbid sex, but gone were the days of Jonah taking me up against a wall in a fit of unrestrained passion. We'd only slept together twice since he was released from the hospital, and despite our efforts to take it easy, both times he'd been scarily out of breath. It was as if the CAV had sped up, like a boulder that had slowly tipped over the side of a steep hill and was now rolling and gaining speed with every passing moment.

"Want to give it a go?" I asked.

"As if I'd say no to you." He reached for me, and we kissed, undressing.

"Come sit on the bed," I told him. "Lotus position."

"I don't speak Tantra."

"Cross-legged."

He sat in the middle of the bed as instructed. His candlelit eyes went wide and heavy with desire as I crawled onto him. I sat in his lap, wrapped my legs around his waist, but I didn't take him inside me, which somehow felt more intimate than if I had.

"I like this," he said against my neck. His mouth moved over my chin. "Kiss me."

"Not yet," I said. "We have to go through all the steps first."

"Steps? Is there a manual I could consult?"

"Stop laughing."

"Right. Sorry. Tantric sex is serious business. Step one is…?"

"Step one: hold me comfortably, and look into my eyes. Nowhere else."

Jonah rested his hands on my thighs, and I held his arms, which held me. I stared into the rich-brown velvet of his eyes.

For all of three seconds.

We both broke down laughing, our bodies restless with nerves. We tried again, laughed again, and kept trying. Gradually the giggles retreated. I relaxed and felt myself falling into his gaze. With every blink, my memory flipped up a moment we'd shared—thousands upon thousands—from the first time I woke up on his couch, to now, with the candlelight flickering around our bodies.

"Now what?" he said softly.

"Now we share each other's breath," I said, moving closer so my lips brushed his. "Find the rhythm."

It happened quickly. Within moments, we were breathing for one another, breathing as one. He inhaled what I exhaled. I breathed in what he let go, filling my lungs with him. The world and its needs drifted away. Time ceased to exist. Only now. This moment. And I didn't need anything but what he gave me.

With every breath, my thoughts fell away. As I drifted deeper in the beauty of his eyes, I felt my *self* cease to exist. No me. No him. Only us. Our skin melted together, creating a third presence, sharing the air, sharing our bodies.

His grip on my hips tightened, and he lifted me onto him. A break in our breaths' rhythm as he slid inside me.

Yes. His mouth shaped the word without a sound.

Yes, this…

I pushed forward, my breasts pressed against his scarred chest. My arms wrapped around his back, my legs around his hips, taking him in as deeply as I could.

Jonah slipped one arm around my waist. His other hand slid against my face, his thumb brushing over my lips. Our breathing fell in sync again. We didn't move but to breathe.

"You," he whispered.

"You…" All I knew or felt or saw. *You.* The whole world in my arms. The unfolding depths of his eyes. The hard, heavy warmth of him inside me. A soft, pulsing pleasure that grew with each moment, until it began to move us.

Our lips met in a gentle, deep kiss. *Inhale*, I rolled my hips back. *Exhale*, I pushed them forward. Jonah mirrored, rocking his pelvis against mine. A tide, ebbing and flowing. Ocean waves falling gently on the shore as we kissed and shared breath. Eyes open, never breaking contact, the heavy ache of pleasure took on more weight, grew more intense.

"Kace," he whispered.

I threaded my fingers through his hair, adding new points of contact, new connections. I felt him in every pore, every breath and beat of our hearts. I'd never experienced anything like this in my life. He was a universe. My love for him was just as boundless.

Tears filled our eyes as our bodies rolled and slid, driving toward a bittersweet crescendo of pleasure. Tears for love. For loss. For the weeks he had, and the years he didn't. For the joy and laughter, the heartache and grief. For this lonely man and the lost woman he'd rescued. For us, and the rapidly approaching time in which there would be only me.

I closed my eyes, sank into his kiss, and gave in to the climax. It rose up and rolled through us, gentle slow-motion swells instead of a crashing wave.

"Look at me," he whispered. "Don't stop."

I opened my eyes.

"I love you, Kacey."

"Jonah." My eyes saw only him. My breath was for his lungs; my tears dampened his skin. My hands were made to run through his hair. I was born to feel him all over me forever.

"Jonah… My Jonah…"

Chapter 43

JONAH

I SPUN THE BLOWPIPE BACK AND FORTH. THE GLASS ON THE END WAS the size of a child-size bowling ball but felt a hundred times heavier. My breath was a shallow wheeze in and out of my chest—I couldn't take deep breaths anymore unless I was sitting down.

"Tania..."

She took the pipe from my hand and set it on the rails as I sat heavily on the bench. I resumed rolling and shaping. My arms felt like lead as I took up the jacks and sawed at the neck. Tania was there, her hands covered in the thick mitts, cupped beneath the sphere.

"Stop if you have to," she told me.

I didn't answer. I didn't have the breath, and I wouldn't have stopped anyway. The glass globe cut loose from the pipe, and Tania caught it deftly in her hands. She carried it to the kiln, but it was too big for her to hold while opening the door.

Using the blowpipe as a cane, I pushed myself to stand and moved as fast as I could across the ten feet. I opened the kiln door, and Tania carefully laid the glass inside, while I slumped against the wall, gasping for breath.

She tore off the mitts to set the cooling timer, then took me by the arms.

"Tell me…"

We had a standing agreement, me and my circle. They didn't ask if I needed help so long as I promised to tell them if I did.

"I'm okay," I said, and it was true. My heart jackrabbited in my chest, irregular and fast, but it was calming down. My lungs sucked in more and more air, and finally I was able to push myself off the wall.

Tania hooked her arm under mine and helped. Together, we looked through the kiln's glass door.

"It's done," I said. It had taken two hours per day for four days, but it was done.

"It's the best thing you've ever made," Tania murmured.

"Because loving her is the best thing I've ever done."

We shut everything down, cleaned up the worktable, and headed for the sliding front doors. I stopped and turned, taking in the space that had felt like a second home to me.

"Did you forget something?" she asked.

"No. I'm just…"

Saying goodbye.

"…remembering." I looked over at my assistant. Tears were in her eyes. "You'll take care of the last piece?"

She nodded. "It's been an honor and a privilege working with you."

"Likewise, Tania. I only wish I could stick around to see your brilliant career."

"So do I, dammit," she said fiercely and threw her arms around my neck. "Though I don't know about 'brilliant'…"

I did. She had applied to the Chihuly Studio in Seattle. I knew Dale's rep had received my letter of recommendation, and I knew they were "extremely enthusiastic" about Tania's work. I knew they'd be notifying her shortly to schedule a round of interviews and studio time.

I could've told her what to expect, but some moments—like her opening that letter from the studio—were meant to be lived in as they happened.

I knew that too.

Chapter 44

KACEY

One morning, Jonah was slow to get out of bed and then only made it to the kitchen before stopping to rest his hands on the counter, catching his breath. He spent most of the day in the chair in the living room.

The speed of his decline terrified me. Seconds were slipping by, taking our moments with them. I fought to hold on to them. To make something of them that was more than fear and grief and agony. Losing Jonah was agony, and if I slowed down to think about it, even for a moment, it would drown me.

I had to keep moving. Stay ahead of it, for Jonah's sake and for mine. I made phone calls; I prepped his medications and made our meals. I took his showers with him, helped him wash and shampoo, then helped him out. I made a flirtatious game of it, but aside from a few warm kisses, Jonah's body was shutting down.

I'd quit my job at Caesars weeks ago and was living off the last of the Rapid Confession money. Those funds were dwindling too, but there was zero chance of me leaving Jonah now. If I lost my apartment, so be it. For now, I was living at Jonah's place, and later—the nebulous *later*—I had plenty of friends in Las Vegas I could crash with until I got back on my feet.

As if the universe were testing me, Jimmy Ray called one afternoon and offered me everything I could possibly want: a new contract with RC, an additional solo contract to write and produce my own album, and an advance that would've left me set for years.

"The label is desperate for you," he said. His voice was hearty, but I could practically smell his desperation through the phone. "Elle is a good girl, but she's not you. Have you been reading the press? The fans want you back. *We* want you back."

I wanted to laugh at the ridiculousness. Jimmy schmoozing like a used car dealer or a carny at a fair. What he offered was so shallow and plastic compared to what I had with Jonah. For all the pain that was coming—and God help me, it was going to be an avalanche—it was worth it. Jonah was worth everything.

"No thanks, Jimmy."

I heard a gasp and a stutter. "No *thanks*? You're going to turn it all down for what? The limo driver?"

"Yes."

"Listen, kitten, this is my Hail Mary pass. I don't want to rub salt in a wound, but Lola says he's dying. And you're going to choose him over everything we're offering?"

"No," I said. "I'm not choosing anything. There is no choice. There never was."

Silence never sounded so good.

I hung up.

The next morning, I checked my bank balance on my laptop with one eye squinched shut, mentally preparing to see a bunch of zeros, or red digits with a big fat negative sign in front of them. Instead, my balance read an almost even five thousand dollars. A deposit had been made from a Wynn Galleria holding account.

I found Jonah resting on the couch, watching *When Harry Met*

Sally—I'd fully converted him to the Church of Eighties Cinema. I stood in front of him, planted my hands on my hips, and tried my best to raise one eyebrow without help from my finger.

He squinted at my feeble attempt. "You either have a really bad headache...or you're trying to read something printed a mile away."

"Five thousand dollars mysteriously appeared in my checking account."

Jonah's smile fell. "I'm sorry it's not more."

"*More?*" I sank down on the couch beside him. "What is it? Where'd it come from?"

"It's what's left from the gallery sale after I paid off my parents' mortgage and gave Theo enough for a down payment on his own tattoo shop."

"His own shop. Holy shit, you're a rainmaker."

"I believe in him," Jonah said simply. "I believe in you. The five grand isn't much, but it's so you can keep living here, get a new job, and keep working on your album. Or whatever it is you want to do."

"I don't need it," I said, my throat filling with tears. "I can figure something out..."

"I know you can," he said. "You can stand on your own, but if I can make it easier for you, I'm going to do that."

I shook my head, blinking back the tears. I couldn't cry too much these days. Once I started, I feared I might never stop.

Jonah drew me down, and I lay curled up with him, my back against his chest. On the TV, the ball had dropped on New Year's and Harry rushed to the party, to Sally, to declare his love for her. Because he wanted the rest of his life to start as soon as possible.

"My life started on this couch," I whispered. "The moment I woke up that morning."

He nodded against my head. "Mine too, Kace. Mine too."

———

That night, we lay in bed together, kissing softly. My hands roamed his skin, trying to memorize his every line and contour. Hoping, wanting the low flame of desire to spark and catch fire.

"Honey, I'm so tired," he said.

"That's no trouble," I said, smiling wide, endeavoring to make my shaky voice seductive and playful. I ran my hands down his chest, toward the waistband of his sleep pants. "Perhaps, a little oral stimulation?"

Jonah shook his head against the pillow. "Not tonight, Kace."

It was the tenth *not tonight* in a row, and the smile slipped off my face like the flimsy mask it was.

Not tonight. But behind Jonah's eyes, behind the warmth and sadness and the infinite thoughts behind them, I read what he was really saying.

Not this night.

Not any night.

Not ever again.

"Okay," I said, my breath tight in my chest, which suddenly weighed a thousand pounds. Tears burned my eyes, and I was too slow to turn away and too weak to keep them from spilling over.

"I hate this part the most," he said.

"Shh."

"I'm sorry."

"*No.* Do *not* be sorry, Jonah. Being sorry means you wish we hadn't happened, and I'm not sorry for that. Are you?"

He shook his head, his own eyes full. "These last months have been everything."

"Everything. I have no regrets. But I'm going to cry a little right now, okay? I can't help it. I can't…"

I can't lose you, is what I wanted to say, but I was going to lose him, and so I cried, and he held me until I stopped.

I wiped my eyes, then pulled off my shirt and unclasped my bra.

"What are you doing?" he murmured in the sleepy, measured voice he had to use now to say anything, to have enough air to speak.

"Want to be close to you." I snuggled up tight against him.

Jonah held me close and fell asleep quickly—he was so terrifyingly tired all the time—but I lay awake for long hours, my strong heart beating against his failing one. I willed whatever strength I had into him. I tried to visualize a current of energy, vibrant and gold, emanating from me and seeping into him. Making him better. Making him well.

Don't leave me.

The next morning, he woke up short of breath, hardly able to sit up without help. Our eyes met, and he brushed his fingers along my cheek. "It's time."

I thought I'd collapse against him then, sobbing and wailing—letting the grief pour out of me. God knew I wanted to. But then I'd have to take him to the hospital, and this last moment, here in our bed, would've been wasted in crying.

Instead, I kissed him like a lover—deep and long, and with everything I had. With every ounce of infinite love that dwelled in me.

I kissed Jonah Fletcher with all of my heart, and with every piece of my soul that would love him forever.

Chapter 45

KACEY

They set Jonah up in a private room, steps from the elevator, the chapel, vending machines, and restrooms. The circle of his friends and family—the Seven, I called us—had access to everything we needed, allowing us to camp out in the waiting room.

No one left for longer than a few hours at a time, and we checked back in via text every few minutes:

Is he okay?

Any news on a donor?

What does the doctor say?

The answers stayed the same for the first twenty-four hours: Jonah was resting, no news of a donor heart, and the doctor said he wasn't likely to get one. Jonah's kidneys—ravaged from the medications—were failing, and he was put on dialysis, which made him all but ineligible for a second heart transplant.

"If you'd let me give him one of mine…" Theo said. He looked terrible—dark rings under bloodshot eyes. He hadn't had a decent night's sleep in weeks.

"It won't help," Dr. Morrison said. "His antibody count has always been much too high. The CAV too relentless."

"So they just took him off the list?"

"Not at all," Dr. Morrison said. "Jonah was never removed from the donor list. But if a new heart were available, we would have heard already. I'm so sorry."

He turned to address the Seven. "Right now, the best thing for Jonah is to remain comfortable and spend time with you."

"He's not in pain, is he?" Henry asked.

"No," Dr. Morrison said gently. "And I will do everything in my power to ensure he stays that way. I promise."

———————————

Over the next two days, we crowded into his room, talking and reminiscing. Laughing at his bedside and stepping out to cry in the hallway. By the third day, when Jonah was struggling through the minutes, some instinctive realization took hold of the group.

It was time to say goodbye.

Tania, Oscar, and Dena took turns alone in his room. Then the Seven became Four: the Fletchers and me.

"How are you?" I asked Theo. We slouched on chairs in the waiting area, while Henry and Beverly sat with Jonah.

"My brother's dying, and there's not a goddamn thing I can do about it. That's how I am."

I stared at my hands through a beat of silence.

"How are you?" he asked.

"I can't really sit over here by myself anymore," I said. "Can I… hold your hand?"

Theo moved to sit beside me. His large, strong hand engulfed mine. I studied the tattoos that snaked around his forearms.

"Your designs?"

"Some."

"What drew you to tattooing?" My voice sounded like I'd been screaming for hours—tear-soaked and hoarse.

"Permanence," Theo said. "Tattoo is art that bites deep. Leaves blood. Can never be washed away. It stays." He looked down at me with his whiskey-colored eyes. "You stayed."

I smiled. "I want a tattoo from you."

"Name it."

"Not sure yet. I'll think about it."

He nodded, and we waited, hand in hand. The Fletchers came out then—Beverly looking frail and delicate, Henry ramrod straight, stoic, and stiff—his grief boiling below the surface.

"Theo, dear," Beverly said in a tremulous voice. "He wants you."

Theo went in, and I sat wedged between the Fletchers, holding her hand, resting my head against his shoulder. They weren't my parents, but I loved them. And I felt loved by them in a way I never had from my own. Even Henry's reserved affection was a million times warmer than my father's.

I hadn't thought of him since San Diego. Or my mother. They'd never met Jonah, and now they never would.

Their loss, I thought bitterly, but in the next instant, that bitterness morphed into fierce pride, and even joy. I had known Jonah Fletcher. I had been loved by him, and it was a privilege I would carry with me for the rest of my life.

Theo emerged, looking bewildered. He gave me a strange look I couldn't define, then said, "He's asking for you."

Jonah lay on the hospital bed, reclined as he had in his chair in his apartment. A nasal cannula ran beneath his nose, delivering oxygen, but his breathing was erratic. He took little sips of air, his chest jerking instead of rising and falling. His dark eyes were stark against his pale face, his thick silken hair now thin and brittle. Tubes and wires ran into his right arm, held there with white tape. The dialysis machine churned continuously from beside the bed. Another monitored his heart. I didn't understand the blood pressure numbers, but the jumping electric tick of his pulse monitor sounded fast and agitated in my ears.

"You sent for me?" I said, as I sank into the chair next to the bed. I leaned my elbows on the mattress and took his hand in mine.

"I'm extracting promises," he said between short, shallow breaths. "No one...can refuse a guy...in my position."

I tried to find a clever comeback, but I had none. Only the howling wish he was in any other position than this one.

"Do you want anything?" I asked. "Anything at all."

"No, Kace. Just you. Here with me."

I nodded. "I'm here. I'm not going anywhere."

He smiled with a weak twitch of his lips. "And that promise."

"What is it?"

"Promise me," Jonah said. His voice was weak and soft, but a desperate intensity wreathed his gaze.

"What, baby...?"

"Love again."

I stared a moment, then shook my head.

He fought to get a breath in. "There's more to you than us, Kace. Please...don't hold yourself back. You have too much to give. So much love, Kacey...so much."

My chest tightened. "I can't even think about it right now, Jonah..."

"In time," he said. "Promise me. If you find someone..."

"Never."

His fingers wove with mine. "No. You will. Love him. Love him with everything. Like you loved me. Love him *more*." His eyes closed. "I'm so happy, Kace. Never like this in my life. It's...a gift. You know?"

I ran the backs of my fingers along his face. "I know."

His eyes opened slowly. "Make someone else...feel like I do right now. Okay? Promise."

I wanted to shake my head and tell him I couldn't do it. Could never do it. I would never again feel for anyone what I felt for him.

"I love you, Kace," he said in between shallow little hiccups of air. "I love you so much. Promise…"

"I love you, Jonah. And…okay. Yes. I promise." Tears spilled over my cheeks as I nodded. "I promise."

His eyes closed again. His body settled back into the pillows, and his next inhale seemed smooth, the exhale relieved. The corners of his mouth lifted, then stretched further. He smiled. He was beautiful then. Peaceful. Serene.

"I need to tell you something," I said. "I know you're tired. Just rest and listen."

Still smiling, he nodded. "Still here."

"I love you," I said. "You're the best thing to ever happen to me. I wouldn't give back one second of our time together. Not one."

"Kace…" he breathed. His hand in mine shook, trying to rise. I brought it up for him and pressed my cheek into his palm. His fingertips rubbed slowly in my hair.

"My heart's breaking," I said. "And I'm so happy. You make me so happy. Your love's made me strong. You've made me a better person…" Sobs like little knives in my throat, words trying to dodge around them. "Being loved by you, Jonah…it's the greatest honor of my life."

He gazed at me, the tears spilling down his pale face. "God, you… So beautiful," he whispered. "So beautiful. Don't want to stop looking at you…but…tired."

"Sleep," I said, drawing the edge of the sheet up. "I'll be here when you wake up. I'll be here the whole time."

I bent over him, kissed his lips gently, and held his face in my hands. "I love you."

"I love you, Kace. Love you…" His eyes closed, and within a minute, he slept.

I rested my aching head on the bed beside him, exhausted beyond anything I had ever known. Wrung out and empty of everything. No joy, no pain, no hope, and no regret.

I'd left no word unspoken.

My head by Jonah's hip, I sank into sleep, where I dreamed I was floating in a sea of glass. Suspended and weightless, beauty surrounding me in ribbons of color and swirls of light. Quiet. Peaceful.

Happy.

Chapter 46

JONAH

KACEY…

No regret.

Only love.

Only you.

I could see a receding shore beneath a sky full of stars. Millions upon millions of stars. Millions upon millions of moments. All of them with her name.

I loved her more than I had ever loved anyone and was loved in return. The knowledge was safe in me, locked in my heart, and when I stopped fighting it and let my eyes fall closed…

I couldn't see the shore anymore, but I knew it was there.

A wind whispered, like a breath. My final breath.

I will love you forever.

Chapter 47

KACEY

FOUR DAYS LATER

I SAT ON MY BED, STILL WEARING MY BLACK DRESS THOUGH THE funeral was long over. My hand clutched a balled-up tissue, damp with tears and blackened with mascara.

From the bits and pieces I could remember, it had been a beautiful service. Friends from Carnegie came, along with professors and instructors. A representative from the Chihuly Studio brought an exquisite glass sculpture of white lilies for Jonah's mother and a note of condolence from Dale himself. The world had lost a vibrant new talent too soon, he wrote.

A minister spoke, Dena recited a poem, and everyone took turns speaking about Jonah: telling funny stories, sharing poignant memories. Over and over, I listened to people tell how he made them laugh, how he brought out the best in everyone. How his belief in them made them brave. I think that was me.

Afterward, Beverly came over to where Theo and I stood together, a small brass urn in her hands.

"The desert, at night, under the stars," she said, pressing the urn into Theo's hands. "It's what he wanted. But I can't do it. I can't…"

I can't either, I thought, sitting alone on my bed. *I don't want to be here without you. I need you.*

Only a knock at my front door roused me to move. Tania stood outside, still in her funeral black, her eyes red-rimmed. In her arms was a cardboard box.

"I can't stay," she said. "I leave for Seattle tomorrow and still have a ton of packing." She put the box in my hands. "But this is for you."

"What is it?"

"Jonah made it for you. I helped, but he did the work. God, his artistry… He was a master. He breathed his life into his glass. I'll never work with anyone better."

We hugged goodbye, both of us stiff with grief, both knowing if we lingered here, we'd collapse. We made a hurried plan to see each other when she came back in a week. If she came back.

I took the box to the couch and set it on my coffee table to open it.

Inside was a sphere of glass, about the size of a cantaloupe, heavy and dark. Crystal stars smattered against the dark blues and black. A planet—red, green, and black—hovered in the center, surrounded by swirls and spirals of light in pale blue that seemed to possess their own illumination. A piece of the night sky trapped in an orb.

"The universe," I murmured, cradling the orb on my lap, running my hands over its smooth surface. Its exquisite beauty caught up my breath. Afraid I would break it, I searched in the box for some kind of stand to set it on.

A note lay at the bottom of the box. Carefully, I set the sphere aside and drew out the folded paper with shaking hands. My eyes filled when I saw his handwriting. I touched the words, hearing his voice speaking behind every pen stroke.

Kacey,

If you're reading this, it means I'm (hopefully) at some celestial diner, stuffing my face with bacon and french fries, and drinking real beer. When I'm done, I'll tip the waiter in rolls of nickels. Because anyone can hit a jackpot, right? You just have to play.

And you have to live. You taught me that. My life was stale and shuttered until you. Colorless and drab until you. I kept my broken heart to myself, until you came and took it in your gentle hands and breathed life into it. Into me.

You taught me how to find life within every moment. You healed my heart, Kacey, when nothing else could.

This ball of glass and fire is as close as I'll come to showing what you've been to me. I tried to put everything you are and everything I feel for you all in one place. But capturing the enormity of you is impossible. It's not enough. Nothing will ever be enough.

You are a universe, Kacey.

I kept waiting to find the end of your love and beauty, the end of your generous heart. I never did. I never will. I don't know how or why you chose me to love, and you did choose. You could've walked away and saved yourself. Instead, you chose to stay, and so saved me. That's my legacy: I loved you and was loved by you.

I'm at peace, and I hope to God I gave you the same happiness you gave me. I hope that the love we have outweighs the pain when I'm gone.

Live fully, sing loudly. Share your beauty with this world, and know I'm watching over you from the next.

All my love to you, Kacey. My angel, my heart.

Your Jonah

I held the letter to my heart, protecting it from the tears dripping off the edge of my chin.

That the love we have outweighs the pain...

I felt myself nodding as a smile spread beneath my tears. If I had to do it all again, I would. I wouldn't change one minute, except to tell him sooner I loved him and that being with him was no more a choice than eating or breathing.

"No regrets, Jonah," I told him, my hand skimming over the piece of the universe. "And I will love you forever."

Epilogue

KACEY

THEO DROVE US WEST, INTO THE HEART OF THE DESERT ON COUNTY Road 20555. No headlights passed us. No streetlights or city lights or even the moon dimmed the star-filled sky. Not the diamond-dust canopy of Great Basin, but hundreds of silvery pinpricks in the midnight canvas above us.

We were silent on the drive through the winding terrain, low dark hills rising up around us on all sides.

"This looks good," Theo said as the headlights illuminated a tiny rest stop overlooking the desert. In the starlight, the land was an undulating plateau of indistinct shapes, stretching out for miles.

Theo parked on the dirt shoulder, then came around to open the passenger door for me. I held the urn secure in my arms, its brass weight warm from my skin and heavy. Outside, the wind gusted cold and sharp.

The headlights cast yellow cones of light around us, glinting off the urn as Theo took it gently from my arms. Neither one of us spoke while he removed the lid and let the wind take the ashes. By the light of the truck, I watched them lift into the sky, where they were blown into wisps—like smoke—and then vanished.

I felt untethered, as if the wind would take me too. Lift me up and tear me into a million little pieces and fling them against the sky.

Then his hand closed around mine.

"Stay here," Theo said softly. I felt his pulse beat through his palm, warm and strong against mine, keeping me from blowing away. Keeping me whole.

My fingers tightened around his as we stared toward the edge of the universe where Jonah now lived.

"I will."

READ ON FOR A SNEAK PEEK
AT FULL TILT #2

All In

REELING FROM HER LOSS, KACEY DAWSON IS GRIEVING AND HEART-broken, her addictive demons hauling her back into the alcohol-soaked abyss she worked so hard to crawl out of. She teeters on the edge of oblivion and must fight her way through the pain to build a new life for herself with her music and somehow fulfill the promise she made to Jonah…one she feels is impossible to keep.

Theo Fletcher has a secret burning in his heart, one that he holds close, while he struggles to keep strong for his family, which is falling apart. His mother's health is fragile, and his father's disapproval is breaking him down. Theo is afraid if he follows his heart, he'll fail, and not just himself, but his brother who believed in him when no one else did.

Drawn together by their pain, Theo and Kacey slowly build a friendship, reforge old ties, help each other to heal, and give one another the courage to reach for their dreams. Together, from the depths of grief and guilt, they learn to laugh again, to trust again, and quite possibly find something beautiful and lasting amid the shattered pieces of their broken hearts.

Available now and free through Kindle Unlimited.

ACKNOWLEDGMENTS

I'd like to extend a huge thank-you to the following people for their support, love, and solidarity. Each and every one of you had a hand in bringing this book to life.

L.B. Simmons, Robin Hill, Angela Bonnie Shockley, Maryam, Melissa Panio-Petersen, Nathalie Raven, Elaine Glynn, Jennifer Balogh, Kathleen Ripley, and my husband, Bill, for your incredible support, for taking the kids to give me time to write, and for believing in me.

Huge thank-you to Colin Lenihan, MD, for his medical expertise on the complex intricacies of heart transplants and chronic rejection. Any and all liberties taken with the science are mine to serve the story, though I have striven to follow Dr. Lenihan's advice as closely as possible to present a realistic account.

Much gratitude to Gregory T. Glass, who instructed me on the fine (and breathtaking) art of blown glass. Thank you for making Jonah's skill and artistry come to life.

To my readers, the bloggers, my friends in this wonderful community…I honestly don't know what I would do without you. You make this incredible, nerve-wracking, wonderful journey worth it, and I appreciate everything you do. You lift me up and share my voice, and for that I will be forever grateful.

And lastly to my editor, Suanne Laqueur. You take my messes and clean them up, you show me the hidden moments that are hiding and lure them out, and you give me the mental will to keep going when I'd rather bash my head against the wall of anxiety and frustration. I don't want to do this without you. You are a universe.

ABOUT THE AUTHOR

Emma Scott is a *USA Today* and *Wall St. Journal* bestselling author whose books have been translated in six languages and featured in Buzzfeed, Huffington Post, *New York Daily News,* and *USA Today's* Happy Ever After. She writes emotional, character-driven romances in which art and love intertwine to heal and love always wins. If you enjoy emotionally charged stories that rip your heart out and put it back together again with diverse characters and kindhearted heroes, you will enjoy her novels.

Visit: emmascottwrites.com
Subscribe: Emma's Newsletter http://bit.ly/2nTGLf6
Hang Out: Emma's Entourage Facebook Group
Follow on Instagram: @EmmaScottwrites
Contact: emmascottpromo@gmail.com